WASTELAND
A Wasteland Novel ~ Book 1
Paula Altenburg
Copyright © 2018 by Paula Altenburg
www.paulaaltenburg.com[1]
This book was previously published as THE DEMON'S DAUGHTER. It's been revised with new material added.

1. http://www.paulaaltenburg.com

On the battlefield of the immortals, as hope springs from the ashes of destruction and despair, one man and one woman unite to set the world free.

Hunter is the Demon Slayer, a man without a past—and without mercy. Airie is the love child of two warring immortals. When Hunter is hired to bring a thief to justice, he's forced to question everything he's ever believed. And Airie, born on a world not her own and raised in a temple to be something she's not, has to decide who—and what—she's going to be.

Welcome to Wasteland.

The Wild West comes to life in this dystopian fantasy series.

PROLOGUE

The mountain was on fire.

Only a few days prior, ten priestesses had dwelled in its catacombs. Now, none but Desire remained. Fingers of flame stroked a sky darkened to an ugly shade of green by a thick layer of low-lying smoke. All around her, conifers crackled and hissed before bursting, struck matches sending showers of bright orange sparks upward to be swept away on the wind. Dry lightning ripped the sky. The haven the goddesses had built against demons had proved to be no haven this day. She shivered despite the intense heat, thankful that the demon fire no longer had enough force behind it to scour the entire world. That didn't mean it wasn't devastating still.

She ran a hand over her shaved head—a symbol of her service to the goddesses—and tried to suck a few extra breaths into a chest rigid from exhaustion. Pain shot through her left arm, but she dared not allow it to slow her. It wouldn't be long now before the fire reached the temple.

She dropped her chin and continued her upward climb. She'd chased after the fleeing priestesses as far as she'd dared, but was too late. The amulet—and its thief—were gone. Allia was her priority now.

Thick gray ash stained the white cobbled stones of the temple's entrance. Relief mingling with growing anxiety, Desire gasped out the words to gain her entry. Inside, pale light glowed from the rock ceiling. The air was sweet and clean here, soothing her burning lungs.

A shriek rang out from one of the deeper chambers, splintering the unnatural silence. She threw off her soot-stained cloak and hurried toward the sound. Murmuring a small prayer at the door, she crossed the gleaming marble floor to the shrouded bed where a woman, belly swollen to grotesque proportions, threw back her head and panted through the last of a contraction. Desire, who had suffered three stillbirths of her own in her younger years, could only stand by and watch helplessly now.

The contraction passed. The woman on the bed opened luminous, indigo-blue eyes. Sweat-dampened skin glowed golden in the muted light, the only indication that the woman wasn't what she appeared to be at first glance. In this world, the goddesses assumed mortal form and lived a mortal existence. Here, their lives were as fragile as any other.

And no goddess had ever given birth before.

Desire knelt by her side. "The people are headed for the river, just as you commanded," she whispered.

Allia's eyes again drifted closed. "The water should protect them. I have enough strength remaining to deflect much of the fire from them, and from us." Ragged breaths punctuated the words. "I'm dying."

Desire feared she was right. "Don't say such things. Childbirth is difficult for all women. Once the baby is born, you can rejoin your sisters."

Allia shook her head. "I can never rejoin them now. Not after what I've done."

"Have you done something so terrible?" Desire asked gently. "You fell in love. That hardly seems such a great crime."

Allia grabbed her arm. Her voice dropped, throbbing on an edge of formality. "Hear my confession, Priestess. I have lain with a demon."

"It's not my place to hear your confession." Desire tried to draw back, afraid to listen to secrets not meant for mortal ears, but the goddess refused to release her. "You are above this."

Not only was she above it, she'd been forced into it. Her sisters had demanded this of her, yet had turned their backs and fled when she needed them most. Desire felt the pain and depth of their betrayal as if it had happened to her. In a way, it had. Without the goddesses to protect them, mortals had no defense against demons.

"No one is ever above the laws of the universe. This isn't our world. Death is to be my punishment for what's happened here."

Another contraction clenched her body with such force that Desire feared she might not survive it. The goddess's fingers dug deeper into the flesh of her arm, but she was too afraid to protest. This was an immortal, and as good and kind as she was, anything could happen if she lost herself.

Then, the contraction passed.

Tears choked Allia's thready voice when she regained it. "The child will be punished for my sins as well. It will be a monster. If it somehow survives the birth, you must promise to destroy it."

Desire had seen demon spawn born from demons mating with mortal women. They were indeed monsters, and to be feared. They clawed their way into the world through their mothers' bellies and fed off their mothers' flesh. But this spawn would be born of a goddess, not a mortal.

"You had no way of knowing that falling in love would result in a child," she said. "You shouldn't be punished for that. Not even goddesses can tell their hearts whom to love."

"All of this—the destruction of the goddesses' mountain, and the danger to our people—is because of me. He won't rest until every last trace of me is banished from existence. He believes I betrayed him." Tears of gold coated Allia's lashes. "I may not be able to tell my heart whom to love, but I knew what to do to make him love me. He will never forgive me for it."

There was little else Desire could say. She limped from the room to the fireplace in the center of the greater common area, where the priestesses received supplicants and offerings, and scooped a bowlful of warm water from a reservoir. An artesian well provided plenty of fresh water and the storerooms remained well stocked, so she wouldn't have that to worry about in the days to come.

She carried the bowl back to the goddess and wiped the lovely, gleaming face with a soft cloth. Soon after, a baby's cries replaced its mother's shrieks of pain.

"Look," Desire said in a hushed, awestruck tone, arms trembling from relief. She held the blanket-wrapped bundle up for its reluctant mother to see. "She's beautiful. Not a monster at all."

Allia twisted away. "Destroy it. It's an abomination. It belongs to no world."

Something deep inside Desire twisted. She'd wanted so much to hold a baby of her own in her arms and three times had been denied the opportunity, yet here was a mother with a beautiful, healthy child and she would not so much as take one look?

This small creature had come into the mortal world by natural means and radiated nothing but innocence. This was no abomination. Far from it.

"She's a girl," Desire insisted. "See? And she's beautiful. She's no monster. If anything, she's a goddess." The baby in her arms puckered a tiny, rosebud mouth, then opened dark, astonishing eyes rimmed with thick black lashes. Love shot through her with all the fierceness of a mother wolfcat protecting its newborn cub, and she knew she could never destroy something so wonderful. "Let me keep her."

"No," Allia said, but Desire sensed hesitation. She was, after all, a goddess—and now a mother. Both nurtured life. They didn't destroy it.

Desire pressed her small advantage, hope catching fire in her heart. "No one need ever know. I can raise her as mine. I feel nothing but goodness in her. I can teach her the ways of the goddesses."

Allia bit her lip. Her face had become alarmingly pale. "You forget she has two birthrights, not one."

"She's a female," Desire insisted. "That makes her more goddess than demon. If you'd only touch her, or look at her, you'd see for yourself."

Not waiting for permission, she placed the baby on its mother's chest. Instinctively, the goddess's arms came up to keep the child from falling. She cradled her daughter for long moments while Desire held her breath.

A single golden tear slid down Allia's cheek. "Keep her, then," she said, and Desire reclaimed the precious bundle. "But she remains my responsibility. I won't leave the world unprotected from her." She lifted a finger. "Bring me that coffer."

Desire took the small silver box from the shelf and lifted the lid for Allia. Inside were two amulets. One, round and flat and carved from a red soil hardened with several layers of natural desert varnish, bore the symbol of a lightning bolt. The other, more delicate in structure, was crafted from a common mountain stone that glimmered with all the colors of the rainbow.

Desire recognized the rainbow. It was a favorite stone Allia had once worn often, but now that Desire thought about it, she hadn't seen it on her in recent months.

The other amulet, however, was ugly and unfamiliar to her.

"The rainbow," Allia said, "is for the baby." A second golden tear chased the first. "I'd like for her to have something of mine in case she should ever want it or need it. Let her know she was born of love, not hate. No child should ever have to live with such a burden. Not even a monster. This amulet," she added, indicating the lightning bolt, "has been invoked by the Demon Lord himself to protect its owner against others of his kind. Wear it until you're certain you no longer need protection from her. Then it's to be sealed in a container and dropped in the river so my Chosen may find it. He's to become the world's protector." She ran the tips of her fingers over the amulet's surface. A flash of gold light suffused it as she murmured a few words in a language the priestess didn't know. "There. It's been invoked by a goddess now too, so that only he and you may wear it."

Desire disliked the lightning bolt amulet and the energy pulsing from it. She slipped it into a small leather pouch she carried, not wanting it next to her skin.

Allia looked at the baby with wonder, then up at Desire. "Dagan. Her father's name is Dagan. You can tell her when the time is right, but not before. I hope someday her father can find it in his heart to forgive me for my part in this."

Allia's form on the bed began to fade, becoming a translucent, golden light that surrounded Desire and the child in her arms before vanishing completely.

Tears flooded Desire's heart and soul. She didn't know what happened to immortals after death. They weren't meant to die. Perhaps, in the end, it was better to be mortal and return to the earth, where at least something of substance remained behind.

The rains came soon after, extinguishing the demon fire. The goddesses didn't return. Neither did the other priestesses, as Desire had hoped they might, leaving her to maintain the temple alone.

She named the baby Airie, which meant rainbows and lightning. Names were precious things, chosen with care and intended to reflect who or what a baby became, often changing when a person reached adulthood and their true nature exerted itself or they'd entered a profession at which they excelled. Desire's own name had been gifted to her when she went into service to the goddesses. Airie, however, would have no other. Her dual nature was evident from the moment of her birth.

When Airie turned six months of age, Desire took the lightning bolt amulet, sealed it in a watertight container, and threw it into the mountain river to be lost in one of its many eddies. She had no need for protection from her.

* * *

Many miles away, across the vast expanse of desert, a blond-headed boy in the Borderlands played in one of the local springs fed by an underground river. He dipped his hand into a shallow pool, searching for freshwater mussels, and found a container wedged in the rocks.

From inside the container, he withdrew a crude red amulet marked with the carving of a lightning bolt.

He slipped its gold chain around his neck, immediately liking the feel of the amulet's warmth against his skin. Ignoring the light rain that had begun to fall, he went back to his game.

CHAPTER ONE

Hunter slapped the length of his toe-grazing leather duster, sending showers of fine red silt into the dry air around him. It was a habit learned from his mother a long time ago in another life, and one he'd never seen the need to break—removing the desert dirt before entering an establishment.

Even an establishment in a place like Freetown, where niceties weren't the rule of the day.

Dusk was settling in and the saloon would soon prepare to close. No honest man stayed out after dark. If they weren't afraid of thieves, they were terrified of demons. Hunter wanted this meeting over with so he, too, could be on his way.

With his hat dangling between his shoulder blades by its straps, Hunter pushed open the swinging door. The dim interior of the saloon meant anyone framed in the doorway was backlit by the setting sun and virtually blinded. Sidestepping to the right, he brushed back his duster, keeping his hand close to the six-shooter at his hip. The short sword strapped to his back came in handy for those times when a gunshot might attract too much unwanted attention, but in a saloon, loud weapons made the better deterrents. And faster, cleaner kills.

A sword, however, worked best against demons if a man was willing to fight them up close. And Hunter wasn't known as the Demon Slayer for nothing.

The smells of ale-soaked pine, smoked meats, and stale tobacco thickened the air. He remained with his back to the raw wooden wall while his eyes adjusted to the change in the light. When they did, he nodded to Blade, the tall, stone-faced man behind the bar.

Blade, polishing the glass in his hand with a pristine white cloth, acknowledged Hunter with the slightest drop of his chin. Hunter let his gaze drift around the near-empty room, searching for the one he'd been summoned to meet.

The whores who worked in the saloon would already have retired to the second floor. In total, three called the saloon home. They worked when they wanted, and with whom they pleased. Blade offered them protection and a roof, and in return, they helped with the cooking and cleaning. But he didn't encourage overnight business, and anyone set on it paid a significant price.

A man with a long, ugly red scar down the side of an even uglier face slouched on a stool at the bar. Hunter noted and dismissed him. A few stragglers sat at well-spaced tables, showing signs of imminent departure. Once the front door was locked, it was locked for the night.

A lone woman sat in the single booth in one shadowed corner of the room. Twisted and misshapen, dressed in a man's greatcoat and coarse woolen trousers, she hunched in her seat, unbothered by the other patrons. It wasn't her appearance that kept her from harassment. Being a priestess protected her far better than simple ugliness ever could, for priestesses served as the only law this side of the godseekers' mountains. They were all that stood between the people and the demons, and in their own way, they were far more ruthless than the basest of cutthroats.

This one was the worst of the lot—and the client Hunter had come here to meet. Mamna was her name, and he didn't like her. He didn't like that she'd made a deal with the Demon Lord, one that put her in her current position of power. He didn't like the way laws were being written by a woman who had no use for other women.

And he didn't like being summoned.

The nails in his boot heels echoed on the whitewashed floor as he walked to the priestess's table. A sneer of disgust twisted Scarface's lips as Hunter passed him. Men knew better than to show open contempt for the priestess, but anyone who dealt with her was another matter. Hunter committed Scarface to memory. It was good to have an idea of who might try to plant a knife in his back. Or die trying.

"Hunter!"

He glanced up. A woman called to him from the top of the stairwell. A smile of pleasure lit her features. She was young, blonde, and attractive—although in a hard way—and he knew her well. Too well, it seemed. To acknowledge her would be a mistake. He knew it.

But he didn't have to.

"Get back to your room." Blade didn't raise his voice. The chill in his tone carried well.

The whore's smile faded. She pirouetted in a swirl of skirts and vanished behind one of the doors on the upper landing.

Hunter slid onto the bench across the battered table from the priestess. The amulet around his neck warmed, but he ignored it. It indicated the priestess had been in recent contact with a demon, a fact that didn't surprise him as much as it left him with a bad taste in his mouth.

He knew why Mamna wanted to meet with him in a public place. She wanted everyone in Freetown aware that she was conducting business with the Demon Slayer, and that there were certain laws in the land even the Slayer could be made to respect. That was why Hunter had kept this meeting to a time when as few people as possible were likely to see them. He respected the law, such as it was. It was a necessary evil. But he hated demons and all who associated with them, the priestess included. He wasn't about to help boost her image.

The priestess examined Scarface at the bar with watery, pale blue eyes lodged in an aging face withered and burnt from a hard life in a harsh desert.

"Try not to kill him," she said to Hunter. "But go ahead and hurt him a little if you like."

Already, she was giving him orders as if she had the right. Hunter allowed his own eyes to turn to ice. "I never kill men unless I have to." It was a less than subtle reminder that, while he might be persuaded to take a contract from the priestess, he would do so on his own terms. He rested one palm on the table, keeping his other hand out of her line of vision. "What do you want?"

Scarface continued to watch him, but Blade, Hunter knew, would be watching Scarface on his behalf. It paid to have good friends. The secret was to keep the group small and he counted his on one finger.

"There's a thief at large on Goddess Mountain," Mamna said.

Hunter shrugged. "There are thieves everywhere. It was bound to happen sooner or later. Besides, the goddesses are long gone and their temple is abandoned. What difference will one thief make to anyone?"

Another subtle jab on his part. The priestesses—Mamna in particular—didn't like to be reminded of the goddesses' departure. It represented betrayal on both of their parts.

Mamna rubbed a gnarled hand over her shaven head. "The mountain is forbidden."

"Then this thief does your work for you. If he's successful at his chosen profession, people will learn to leave the mountain alone and he'll have to move on."

"The thief is a woman."

Hunter laughed out loud. At the bar, Scarface tightened his grip on his drink and Hunter lowered his voice. "More power to her. If she thieves on Goddess Mountain, she's more than likely one of your own."

"She's not a priestess."

Mamna sounded definite about that, and Hunter had to admit he was growing intrigued. A woman on the mountain who stole from trespassers? What kind of woman would she be?

A hideous one, no doubt. Probably bitter as the priestesses about it, too. Women judged themselves far harsher than men did, although from what he'd seen, beauty didn't earn them much in this world.

Mamna pulled a small pouch from a pocket in her greatcoat and slid it to him. He lifted the pouch. It was heavier than it looked, meaning it contained mostly, if not all, gold coin.

Which also meant he was being overpaid.

"There's more to this story," Hunter said flatly.

Mamna had the nerve to feign righteousness. "She's ambushing innocents, most likely supplicants to a temple that no longer has any purpose. All you have to do is capture her and bring her here to face justice."

The last thing Hunter wanted was for Mamna to think his reluctance in accepting this task sprang from not wanting to bring a woman to so-called justice. It would give her a weakness to use against him in future negotiations. He tossed the pouch in the palm of his hand. The coins clinked dully.

Gold. Definitely gold.

Hunter intended to have an explanation he believed, or at least one he was willing to accept. "This is a great deal of money for bringing in one woman."

At the bar Blade made a production of putting glasses away. "Closing time," he said to Scarface.

Scarface grunted. "There are two others still here."

"Those two have no need to fear demons." The shutters on the windows rattled to emphasize Blade's point. Everyone knew demons preyed on fear. They hunted at night, when mortal man was at his most vulnerable, and prone to terror. "I require a great deal of cash upfront if you want to spend the entire night here. A great deal. So my next question is, how much do *you* need to fear them?"

Scarface tossed a few coins on the bar, hitched up the back of his dust-crusted trousers, and left through the swinging doors.

Mamna cleared her throat, drawing Hunter's attention back to her. For the first time, she appeared uneasy. "This is no ordinary woman."

Hunter regarded her for a long moment. "Rule number one—no surprises."

"There won't be any," she reassured him, which offered no reassurance at all.

He dropped the pouch on the table. It landed with a heavy thud. He pushed it toward the priestess with his fingertips. "Rule number two—don't lie to me."

Mamna ignored the pouch. She held his eyes. "It's claimed she has demon blood. If that's true, she must be turned over to the Demon Lord to be dealt with."

Only a great deal of discipline kept Hunter from allowing the revulsion that shivered up his spine to show on his face. Men hated demons, and demons hated men, but spawn, who carried the blood of both, were hated by all. They belonged to no world. Let the demons deal with a problem they had created.

But before Hunter would hand anyone over to demons, the claim that the thief was spawn had to be true—and he didn't believe it was. Any spawn he'd ever seen or heard of were male.

"Impossible," he said. "She's a woman."

Mamna's wrinkled face smoothed as her eyebrows lifted. "Is it impossible?" she asked. "Can you know this for certain?"

All he could say for certain was that Mamna hated women more than demons hated spawn, and for whatever reason, she wanted this woman dead. He should walk away from this job.

But if he didn't take it, someone else would. And to think of an innocent woman being handed over to demons was more than his stomach could handle. Was Mamna testing him somehow? Could he afford for her to suspect a weakness about him that she would, in all likelihood, use against him in the future?

He scanned his memory for anything he might have given away in the past. He'd left behind everything of value to him years ago so that he would have no such weaknesses to betray. Only Blade could be considered a true friend, and Hunter had no concerns over his safety.

No, Mamna had no hold on Hunter. He intended to keep it that way.

He reclaimed the money pouch and slipped it into an inside pocket. He rose to his feet, wanting this meeting to be over and done with so he could think. "How much time do I have?"

"As long as necessary." She shrugged. "No longer."

Which meant not much time beyond what she thought it would take him to travel, two or three weeks at most, but Hunter wasn't concerned about that. He'd take whatever time he deemed necessary, then a little more. It never paid to seem too cooperative.

Mamna hopped from her seat without a word of goodbye and shuffled from the saloon, the hem of her ill-fitting greatcoat dragging on the floor.

Blade closed the heavier exterior doors behind her. He then dropped an iron bar into place, barricading them in.

"Thirsty?" he asked Hunter.

"Please."

The wind picked up, and Hunter hoped the townspeople had gotten themselves locked up in time. On nights like this, demons sought pleasure in their manhunting forms, and pleasure, to them, meant killing men and violating women.

While Blade slung a kettle on a hook inside the large fireplace to heat water, Hunter went around the room and latched all the shutters in place.

"Do the women have their windows closed?" he asked Blade.

"Of course."

The kettle hissed as it began to steam.

"One of these days," Blade said, "that ugly little priestess will pay someone to plant a knife in your back."

Hunter grabbed a broom from behind the bar to sweep the floor. "Dying of old age is overrated."

"Perhaps. But you seem to have forgotten that living to an old age is not."

Blade knew a thing or two about death. Hunter had found him in the desert some years ago, fighting a fierce but losing battle against a demon driven wild by the taste of blood. Hunter had killed the demon and saved his life, although not before the demon had taken a large chunk of flesh from Blade's right leg.

While no longer as agile as he'd once been, Blade was still quite capable of taking care of himself against men. Tall and lean, dark-haired and fierce-eyed, he had the ruthless air of a killer about him. The few times he'd been challenged, that impression had proven correct. Word had spread.

He dropped a metal ball filled with fragrant loose tea into the hot water, then lifted the kettle from the fire with a long hook. He carried the kettle to the bar. "What did the evil little troll want from you?"

Hunter told him, and he frowned. "Did she say she'll hand the woman over to the demons, or was it implied?"

"Implied," Hunter admitted. "But what else would she do, particularly if the woman does have demon blood in her?"

"Who knows? She's made it no secret that she no longer serves the goddesses. She has no reason to do demon work either. Neither do you. She's lying to you for some purpose of her own. You shouldn't take her work."

Hunter leaned on the broom and faced his friend. "If I don't take it someone else will, and they might not care whether or not this woman truly is spawn. What would you have me do—abandon those who are still innocent in this goddess-forsaken world?"

Blade produced two sturdy mugs and set them on the bar. "I wouldn't have you abandon anyone. But you don't need to make something your business that's not. And how do you determine who lives or dies? That kind of choice does something to your soul." He took a cloth and wiped a spill on the varnished surface. "Sometimes I wonder if you've forgotten what true justice really is."

Hunter often wondered the same thing himself. He'd grown hard over the years, to the point where he didn't always recognize the man who looked back at him from the shaving mirror.

Speaking of shaving...

He scratched at the scruff on his jaw.

"People are asking questions about you," Blade continued, interrupting Hunter's thoughts.

"That's nothing new." He was the Demon Slayer. The title inspired curiosity. And there was always someone interested in testing his qualifications.

"These questions are. They have to do with your family."

Hunter tried to think if he had ever let anything slip and couldn't come up with a single instance. He had never visited his sisters, nor spoken of them. Not in all the years since he'd fled from the Borderlands. Not even to Blade. "They won't find any answers."

"No? Everyone comes from somewhere."

Hunter finished sweeping the floor. He put the broom away and took a seat near his friend at the bar. Blade passed him a steaming mug of fragrant tea brewed from desert lavender. Hunter blew on it, watching the ripples crease its mud-brown surface, then took a slow sip to savor the taste. Neither he nor Blade touched alcohol. In their businesses, men who drank didn't live long.

"I have something for you," Hunter said.

He reached in his pocket and withdrew a thick chunk of plastic. The artifact predated the demons to a time when the world was filled with large cities and millions of people. While the wind had buried most of the ruins in sand over time, it also often turned up little things such as this—and these items were worth far more than gold to the right traders. Whenever Hunter found any in the desert he brought them to Blade, who in turn, sold the pieces of the world's past and split the profits between Hunter, himself, and the women.

Blade took the artifact from him, rolled it around in his long fingers, then dropped it into a box hidden behind the counter. He continued to stand, taking a sip from his own mug of tea, his dark eyes brooding as he returned to the original topic of conversation. "I'll try and get to the bottom of whoever's asking questions about you."

Hunter relaxed. If there was anything for him to worry about, Blade would find out.

"Anything new since the last time I was in town?" he asked, ready for a change in subject.

"A few murders. Some shifts in fortune. More migrants from the border regions, seeking their fortunes on this side of the mountains. Overall, no."

Weariness crept over Hunter. Not much ever changed in Freetown in that respect. The rich got richer and the poor served the rich. Migrants came to Freetown seeking quick fortunes and often found servitude instead—assuming they survived the trek across the desert. One would have thought the priestesses, who'd once served the goddesses, would have a greater sense of philanthropy, or even basic kindness. Yet any gold they parted with came at a rate of exchange even the wealthy would shudder to pay.

The bag of coins weighed heavily in his pocket and on his conscience. That Mamna could so easily turn a woman over to demons without proof of her being spawn bothered him. The possibility that the priestess was right bothered him more. If the thief did turn out to be spawn, what might that mean?

Any spawn he'd ever heard of, or seen, were male. And they were always monsters.

He finished his tea. "I should go."

Blade cocked his head. Sand, driven on the howling wind, rang like raindrops against the exterior walls and shutters. "It's going to be a rough night. You're welcome to stay." He frowned, and Hunter knew he was still thinking of those questions about his past and who might be behind them. "In fact, I recommend you do. The women won't mind. You might even be able to talk them into letting you use their bath."

"They'd do that for me?" Hunter's surprise was sincere. Even though Freetown was built on an oasis, its water was tightly controlled. By Mamna. Baths were a luxury few could afford.

Blade's eyebrow shot up. "You've paid for it a dozen times over. Besides, it has a lot to do with your odor. They prefer their men clean. Sapphire especially."

Hunter spent most of his days in the desert alone, so he was used to his own smell, but a bath was always welcome and it was hard to turn one down. But he was more uneasy about those questions regarding his past than he cared to admit, and while Blade could look out for himself, Hunter didn't like the idea of bringing any danger to the women. He was already too fond of them.

And Blade's reference to Sapphire in particular sent a message that he'd spent more time with her than he should. The girl might be hard, and used to this life, but she was young enough to have dreams for the future and he had no urge to crush them. Not to mention, she'd brought dangerous attention to herself tonight.

That alone was a good reason for him to refuse to stay. "Thanks, but I'd better go."

Blade unbarred the back door, the one that led from the kitchen to a small yard behind the saloon, and Hunter slipped like a shadow into the dark and deserted street beyond. Blowing sand stung his cheeks, and he pulled a heavy cotton kerchief over his mouth and nose. He settled his hat back on his head, tugging the wide brim low to shield his eyes.

Mamna and her priestesses had founded Freetown on the outskirts of the ruins of a buried city. The ruins stretched across several miles of desert, and although they undoubtedly contained many treasures, no one dared enter them to find out—the shifting sands left them too unstable, and riddled with deadly sinkholes.

Whoever the original inhabitants of that lost city were, however, they had done their part against the demon invaders before falling. It was rumored the demons had once numbered in the tens of thousands. Now, there were scarcely a hundred.

Even in the gloom of a storm, the streets of Freetown weren't difficult for Hunter to navigate. He knew them well. A market served as the town center. Radiating from it, like the spokes of a wagon's wheel, spread the other main areas—the wealthy, the not so wealthy, the poor, and the various trade shops that serviced them all. Blade's saloon sat at the outer tip of one spoke, near the high wall surrounding the city. The wall wasn't meant to keep demons out. That was impossible. Rather, it allowed Mamna to be selective of the people who came and went.

Most people. Not Hunter. He came and went as he pleased.

He headed for a hidden smugglers' tunnel that burrowed beneath the outer city wall. Mamna knew of the tunnel—she knew everything regarding Freetown—but so far, she'd chosen to ignore its existence. Their conversation had left him more distracted than was probably wise, but the storm should have kept even the bravest of lowlifes indoors. He felt safe in letting his thoughts wander. Only demons would be out tonight and he'd have plenty of warning if any came near. The amulet around his neck, tucked beneath his shirt, lay cold against his skin.

His mind kept returning to those questions about his family Blade claimed people were asking. He hadn't thought of his sisters in a long time. It was pointless to do so. When he'd left the Borderlands he'd gotten as far away from them as he could, covering his tracks and not looking back, because only they knew why he'd killed that first demon. No one else cared as long as he continued to kill them—few men survived such an encounter. Blade, one of the toughest men he knew, had almost died.

He caught a slight movement from the corner of his eye, an unnatural shift of shadow off to his left. Someone was following him.

He stopped, not bothering to pretend he wasn't aware. His amulet remained cold and silent, so it wasn't a demon. He unholstered his six-shooter, praying his stalker was alone, then pressed himself against the false front of a nearby shanty in an attempt to keep the wind-whipped sand from blinding him completely. He disliked using a gun inside the town where it might draw more unwanted attention to him, but tonight, the storm would drown out any sounds of a gunfight.

The attack, although expected, nevertheless took him by surprise, more because of its professionalism and choice of weapon than its aggressiveness. He sucked in his stomach as the knife in his assailant's hand slashed a six-inch gap in his shirt. He brought his gun up, fired, and was rewarded with the hiss of an indrawn breath. He drew his short sword from its sheath with his left. He didn't want to kill his assailant just yet.

Dead men didn't talk.

Lightning-quick, the man came at Hunter again, but Hunter was better prepared this time. He slid to the side to avoid the thrust of the knife, and from behind his back he drove his sword's blade through the other man's extended arm.

Rather than jerk away, the expected reaction, the assailant fell forward. A heavy knife handle protruded from between his shoulder blades.

Hunter holstered his gun, reached down to jerk the blade free, and wiped it clean on the assailant's ruined shirt.

"Thank you," he said. He handed the knife hilt-first to its owner.

You're welcome." The knife disappeared into the sheath Blade wore strapped to his mangled leg.

"Not that I wasn't managing just fine on my own," Hunter added.

"You were doing okay." Blade rolled the dead man onto his back with the toe of his boot. Enough light remained for them to identify him as Scarface. "But increasing the odds in your favor never hurts." His eyes met Hunter's. "Why would anyone risk angering Mamna by killing someone she's just hired?"

"That's what I was hoping to ask him."

Blade rifled through the man's pockets and came up empty-handed. "Nothing. The man's a professional."

"Maybe he's poor," Hunter guessed, without any real hope.

"Even poor people keep things in their pockets." Blade patted down the man's arms and legs and came up with an assortment of weapons, difficult to obtain and worth double their weight in gold. He held them out. "See anything here you want?"

Hunter waved him off. "You killed him. It's all yours."

The weapons disappeared into Blade's clothing.

"How did you know he'd follow me?" Hunter asked.

Blade shielded his face from the stinging sand with the crook of an elbow. "His hands were too clean."

That was a detail a man like Blade would notice it right away. An assassin's hands were his greatest asset, and Blade took pride in his own despite the fact he no longer worked for hire.

"Why didn't you warn me?"

"Because it was something you should have noticed yourself." Demon howls carried on the wind now, still far off in the distance, and Blade checked over his shoulder. "Fresh blood is going to draw them here. Sure you don't want to come back to my place for the night?"

"I'm sure." Hunter grinned at him. "Scared?"

"Terrified," the other man admitted without shame. "While I don't mind dying, being eaten alive continues to bother me. I'm heading for home. If I were you I'd search this guy for markings, but I doubt you'll find anything. He's your problem now."

Blade left, and Hunter took a few extra minutes to search for any tattoos or markings that might give some indication of where the would-be assassin was from. He found nothing, as Blade predicted, but that could have been because of the poor light and blowing sand.

Or it could have been because Blade was right. The man had no markings on him because he was a professional.

Then, because Hunter didn't feel like confronting blood-frenzied demons either, he headed for shelter.

CHAPTER TWO

Goddess Mountain occupied the eastern border of what was known as the Wasteland. It was called a mountain because of its prominence, not its actual size and elevation, and was completely artificial in origin. The goddesses—lovers of nature, creators of life—had built it, seeded it, and made it their home, and over the decades, nature's contributions to their endeavors had also thrived. The result was a dense, beautiful mix of conifer and deciduous trees, flowering shrubs, and colorful-but-hardy desert plants. Wildlife flourished here without predation. Not even the demon fires of some twenty years past had been able to fully destroy its ecosystem.

Airie tipped her wide-brimmed hat forward to partially hide her face, hitched up her scratchy woolen trousers in what she hoped was a manly fashion, and stepped from the concealment of the forest at the mountain's base into the world beyond. Her boots, two sizes too large, were the smallest pair she'd been able to acquire. If luck were with her, she wouldn't trip over them and fall on her face.

This was her third visit in as many months to the mean little trading post at the foot of the mountain because she was hesitant to spend too much money all at once. To do so would attract unwanted attention. She also didn't like leaving her mother alone more than necessary. Desire hadn't been well of late.

And Airie had been forbidden by her to come to this place. But what else was she supposed to do? The offerings to the goddesses and priestesses had stopped a long time ago, and she and Desire had run out of the necessities and small luxuries they couldn't grow or raise for themselves.

A tingle of excitement coursed up her spine. The trading post was no more than a one-room log cabin, crudely constructed, but to Airie it represented civilization. She craved the company of other people far more than the sweets she planned to buy today in the hopes they might help improve Desire's appetite.

Airie's too-large boots thudded heavily on the sagging porch. More than one pair of eyes tracked her progression. She dipped her head, resisting the urge to tug at her hat's brim again, and pushed past the small group of men gathered in the open doorway. Hopefully the dirt she had rubbed into her cheeks and chin would disguise the fact she couldn't grow whiskers. Her height was another advantage.

The men let her pass without a second glance, content to go about their own business.

Inside, Airie's eyes had no difficulty adjusting to the darkness of the long, narrow room. Desire often marveled at her ability to see on even the blackest of nights, but to her, it was as natural as breathing.

Three men crowded together near the squat wooden flour bin, deliberately blocking the room's center aisle. Airie, recognizing trouble, turned to leave, but in this instance, her normally sound instincts came a second too late.

A man with bad skin broke away from his two companions and approached the narrow counter running the width of one end of the room. Smoked meats hung from the crude rafters, swaying in the slight current of air he created as he moved beneath them, almost grazing them with his greasy head. Airie crinkled her nose. She rarely ate meat, liking the taste even less than the smell. Another one of the men brushed past her to bar the door, and she discovered the meats weren't the only source of offensive odors in the room.

The man with bad skin had a gun in his hand. "If you want to stay open for business," he said to the boy behind the counter, "then you have to pay taxes."

The boy was young and badly scared. Airie could smell the fear oozing from him, another scent unpleasant to her, because it stirred her anger, which could be too much for her to control at times.

Losing it here would be disastrous. She clenched her hands in tight fists, attempting to strangle it, and tamped it down as best she could.

"Taxes?" the boy echoed.

He wasn't quite right. Airie wondered where the boy's father was. What would possess him to leave such a child alone, in charge of a store in a land where theft was a way of life?

All three men laughed at his ignorance, unaware of the danger.

"Taxes. The money you have to pay if you want to be in business. You'll be forfeiting it every month from now on," the bad-skinned man said. His words, high-pitched and slow, mocked the boy's ignorance.

Airie's temper cranked up a notch. There would be no assistance from the people outside. If they knew what was happening in here, they chose to overlook it.

So far, the men had paid her little attention. Although tall for a woman she was slight, and no doubt they thought her the boy she pretended to be. She settled her hat more firmly on her head, hoping it would stay in place, and wished her mother would let her cut off the long, dark curls.

The thought of her invalid mother made her pause and re-evaluate the situation. If anyone saw she was a woman, it would make future excursions to the trading outpost difficult for her, if not impossible—and then where would she and her mother be?

She should stay out of this. The world beyond the temple on Goddess Mountain could be a cruel place, plain and simple.

A broom rested against a shelf of dry goods. She inched around with her back to it and reached behind her so no one could see her actions. If they threatened to harm the boy, then she would interfere. His life was what mattered. The rest was only money.

The boy opened a drawer and lifted out a tray of gold and silver coin. The man tucked his gun into his waistband and emptied the tray into a canvas sack, grunting his disapproval at its lack of weight. "This is it?"

The boy nodded and the men, seeming to accept that this was all they could expect, tossed a few more items from the counter into the sack, and then were gone. Both relieved and disappointed, Airie let go of the broom.

Other patrons drifted inside now that the thieves had left, and she quickly gathered what she had come for. She took the merchandise to the counter. The boy's fingers trembled as he collected the coins Airie passed him. And yet the trembling wasn't all due to fear. The danger hadn't completely passed yet.

"Where's your father?" she asked, lowering her voice so that it couldn't be easily identified as a woman's.

The boy's eyes darted to the sides. "He heard they were coming and said that if he were here, they'd most likely kill him. He told me to give them whatever they wanted."

So the man had left a child to be murdered in his place. She pressed her lips together to suppress her true opinion and took a moment to form another.

"I could never have been as brave as you were," she said.

The boy shrugged off her praise, although his shy smile said that it pleased him. "You deal with what life hands you. How you deal with it is up to you."

The platitude was one she'd heard many times, usually applied to some small hardship, and common enough to hold little meaning. Yet, from this simple child's mouth, it resonated, speaking not to her, but to something living inside her. It awakened an awareness—a presence—as if from a long and restless sleep. One that whispered to her.

Change is coming.

Whether good or bad, it couldn't say.

Someone else wandered to the counter then, so Airie shook off the premonition and the voice, shoved her purchases into her backpack, and returned to the sunshine outside.

The peak of Goddess Mountain itself belonged to the goddesses, as did the stone temple carved into it. That was holy ground. Around the mountain's base, however, the people who worshipped them had once made their homes. A wide, shallow river divided the mountain from the desert. One of the goddesses had thought to consecrate the waters before she fled, protecting the people from demon fire and saving their lives.

After the fire, those same people had abandoned their homes and scattered throughout Wasteland. Many of them followed the priestesses to Freetown. Others had gone to the north. All of them sought a place to practice their faith where they could be safe from demons. As the mountain healed, people returned. Not, however, to worship. They came for the prime, unoccupied land and new opportunities. The result was a think but growing population of the best—and the worst—that Wasteland had to offer.

Airie knew no other life. She did know right from wrong.

She was also fearless.

Even though she knew she should, because daylight was fast expiring, she didn't head for home. Instead she walked the perimeter of the outpost, looking for the three thieves. She hated that they were escaping unchallenged.

The newly-awakened presence inside her questioned why this was so different from what she'd done so many times herself.

The difference, her conscience responded, *is that we take only from those who invade our home.* Goddess Mountain was forbidden to all but supplicants, and anyone venturing near the sacred temple should know enough to leave an offering, no matter how small. If they didn't, then it was her duty to enlighten them and see that the goddesses were honored.

When she found the thieves, they were shouldering their packs and preparing to leave. They headed up the mountain rather than away from it. She followed.

They'd built a crude camp for themselves a few miles up a faintly marked trail. She peered out from a tangle of shrubbery, wrinkling her nose in disgust at the mess they had made. These men were definitely not supplicants. Broken tools, scraps of past meals, and other offal desecrated the goddesses' home.

The man with the bad skin set his pack against a ramshackle shelter woven from evergreen branches. He'd removed his gun from his clothing and set it near the sack of stolen goods, a hair's breadth out of easy reach, while he counted the coins. He swatted at a blowfly attempting to take up residence on his pocked cheek.

"That ought to keep the old hag happy for a few weeks," he said with satisfaction when he was done.

Carefully, quietly, so as not to attract attention with her movements, Airie stooped to select a stout branch out of deadfall to use for a weapon. She weighed it for sturdiness with a practiced hand. Her mother couldn't fault her for what she was about to do. Now that the goddesses were gone, people forgot too easily, or no longer cared, that this remained a sacred place. Her priestess mother was too old and ill to confront men such as these, and it fell to Airie to take on her responsibilities whenever it became necessary. She would drive the thieves from the mountain, nothing more.

She tugged at her hat, remembering at the last moment to keep her face partially hidden as she stepped out of her hiding place in the bushes.

"This is the goddesses' mountain," she called out to them, her makeshift staff lying in confident repose across her palms. "You're trespassing. Are you prepared to pay the price?"

Incredulity swept across the leader's face. Airie made special note of him. He wasn't as tall as she, but he was much heavier, and the extra weight on him couldn't be attributed entirely to fat.

The other two men, recovering from their surprise, split up and slowly circled behind her, flanking her on either side, but she kept her eyes focused on the one in front of her. Her fingers curled around her staff, excitement pumping up her heart rate. She wasn't afraid, or even alarmed. Her reflexes were excellent. So was her strength.

"The goddesses are gone," the first man said. "It's time the mountain gives back to the people all that the goddesses once kept from them."

She didn't bother to correct him. The goddesses' physical presences might be gone, but all her life she had felt them in spirit. They remained close at hand, constantly watching and waiting, biding their time—but for what, she didn't know.

One man came in low, from the side, attempting to catch her off guard. With a whip-like flick of her wrist, she brought the staff over her head and down, rapping the man hard at the temple. His eyes rolled back and he dropped like a stone. In a continuous motion, she brought the staff back and caught the other man in the ribs. He fell, clutching at his stomach, and retched into the dirt. Airie's chin shot up and her hat slid off, releasing a thick, dark braid of waist-length hair.

"A priestess, then," the leader said, thick lips curling in amusement. He looked closer. "Too young to be a priestess. And far too pretty. Priestess spawn, perhaps?" He laughed, and it was an ugly sound. "What other services did the priestesses provide when they lived in the temple?"

Airie gasped at the crudity and irreverence of the remark. Desire was too good and kind to be the brunt of this heathen's coarse humor.

The man advanced. "What services do *you* provide to mortal men?"

Kill them, a dark, inner voice commanded.

Airie's temper reacted, so quickly she couldn't catch it back. A red haze slid over her vision, intensified by heat. Sparks from her eyes sprayed the man's face and greasy hair.

He drew back, terror twisting his features.

"Demon spawn!" he spat out, tripping over his own feet in his haste to back away.

His companions, roused from senselessness by the panic in his shout, scrambled upright and stumbled after him. Long after they were gone from sight, Airie could hear them crashing through the brush in a headlong flight down the mountain.

Her normal vision returned, along with a rising dismay. She'd succeeded in ridding the mountain of parasites, but a little too well. Her mother wouldn't be pleased if she found out about this.

Airie would have to see that she didn't.

She picked up her hat, dusted it off, and set it back on her head. Then she cleaned up all traces of the thieves' desecration, tearing down their shelter and putting their trash in a pile before burning it all. She uncovered nothing of any value other than what they'd taken from the trading post. She doused the fire with dirt and slipped the canvas sack filled with money into her backpack before beginning the trek to the trading post to return it.

While the boy was busy with another customer at the back of the store, she set the bag of money behind the counter and left without being noticed. By the time she began the long climb to the temple and her waiting mother, the sun had slid below the horizon, plunging the mountain forest into deep shadow.

Darkness didn't bother Airie. She could see quite well in it and was unafraid of the mountain's nightlife. In fact, there was very little in her life for her to fear.

But some things did.

Demon spawn, the thief had called her.

It was no goddess who had counseled her to kill.

* * *

The doe flowers were in bloom. Their rich scent hung heavy on the damp, moonlit air, pink heads bobbing as the mountain breathed them in.

Desire waited patiently at the open door of the stone temple for Airie to return. Her bones ached and she longed for Airie to help ease her pain, but it was becoming more and more obvious to her that not even Airie's healing touch would work much longer. Her time was coming. When it did, what would become of her daughter?

The goddesses watched over her, and Desire was deeply troubled by that fact. Their mortal forms might be gone from the world, and their gifts now limited within it, but their spirits remained. Desire shivered. She'd once served them faithfully, and continued to pray to them, but she'd seen how they'd turned on one of their own. She'd deny them in a heartbeat if it meant keeping her daughter—their blood—safe from harm.

She heard Airie before she saw her, singing as she climbed the night-shrouded path. The priestess smiled into the inky blue darkness. Airie was a true child of the earth. Her smile faded as quick as it had appeared. She was a child no longer, and hadn't been for quite some time. She was a grown woman. And Desire didn't know what was to become of her.

Airie reached the top of the path. Tall, slim-waisted and long-legged, with sable eyes and coal-black hair, she was the counter-image of her golden mother—dark where the goddess had been fair—yet they had the same features and the same presence. From the way she carried herself to the healing power of her touch, Airie had the bearing of a goddess. It was impossible not to love her—even though Desire knew from long experience how difficult goddesses could be to love at times.

Airie's wet hair, long and loose to her hips and slightly curling at the tips, told Desire she had stopped to bathe in one of the hot mountain springs. She wore a fresh change of clothes. The sleeves of her crisp white blouse were rolled back to her elbows, and her long brown skirt wrapped around her legs with each stride. From her fingers dangled the pack carrying the offerings she'd gone to collect. Desire wasn't misled by the easy way she carried the pack. It would be full, and very heavy.

Despite the singing, Desire sensed something was wrong. The soft glow of happiness normally surrounding Airie was missing tonight.

Airie set the pack at her mother's feet, then bent down and kissed her cheek. Concern filled her voice when she spoke. "You're in pain."

"It's nothing," Desire replied. Just that one brief kiss had been enough to ease her aches. "Sit. Tell me about your day. You're late."

Very late, in fact. Far too late to have been collecting offerings. But then again, Airie often lost track of time. She sat in the long cool mountain grass at Desire's feet, her head on her mother's knees.

"I walked to the far side of the mountain, beyond the lake."

Desire's erratic heart skipped a beat it could ill afford to lose. Airie hadn't gone to the far side of the mountain. If she had, she would have brought back sweetberries and some of the white cedar bark Desire often sprinkled on the fire at night to freshen the temple air. The white lie disquieted her. While kind and gentle, Airie was also fiercely protective, and there was nothing she wouldn't do for Desire, or anyone she loved, if she believed she had no other choice. Desire hoped that protectiveness wouldn't get her in trouble someday.

She chose not to challenge Airie on the lie. Instead they both sat in silence, soaking up the sounds and smells of the evening as she stroked Airie's damp hair.

"When did you first notice my eyes?" Airie asked suddenly.

This time when her heart stopped, Desire feared it might not start again. She carefully considered her answer before speaking. "You were a baby."

She'd been outdoors when she smelled smoke and hurried inside to find the chamber on fire and Airie sitting in the middle of it, shrieking at the top of her young lungs. She'd torn the crib apart with her hands. The angry welts on her neck indicated she'd most likely gotten her head caught between its spindles.

Airie lifted her head. "Were you afraid of me?"

"Not for an instant," Desire was able to declare in complete honesty. She'd never regretted throwing away the protective amulet given to her by the goddess. Any fear she had was for Airie, not of her.

Airie was quiet for quite some time then, gazing out toward the west. Miles beyond the moonlit mountain, visible from the temple in daylight, the flatland settlements served as reminders that there were other people in the world. On calm nights, settlement lights could be seen, but on this night the wind blew across the desert and a sandstorm swallowed the world at their feet. Windows would be shuttered tight against it. And against demons.

Here on the mountain, though, demons weren't a concern. Despite the fire that had forced the goddesses to flee, this place remained forbidden to them. To this day Desire didn't know how demon fire had reached the mountain, although she had her suspicions.

Airie pointed into the blackness that cradled them. "What's beyond the flatlands?"

This was a game they'd played when she was a child, with both of them making up the most ridiculous stories about the world around them, but Desire sensed that tonight Airie wasn't playing a game.

"You've studied your maps. The biggest settlement is Freetown. To the west of it lie the Borderlands, near the far end of the world. To the north are the gold mines and mountains of the godseekers. To the south lies the sea. We live in the east. Together, we're the Wasteland."

"And the boundary surrounds us all." Airie's lovely face, normally all smiles, was unusually pensive. "The world is a very small place."

"Only what we know of it today. Before the immortals it was much larger, and given time, it will be again." Desire didn't doubt that, but it was difficult to explain to Airie when she'd never traveled beyond the mountain, nor studied the buried ruins of a very different civilization from the one she lived in.

"What brought the immortals here?" Airie shifted to look at Desire as she asked the question. "They have no need for a physical world to live in."

Desire didn't like discussing this subject with Airie. She'd tried hard over the years not to influence her. She would never want her to choose sides between her two birth parents. But Airie deserved at least some of the truth, and she wouldn't deny it to her. Not as long as it did her no harm.

"Time," she said simply. "To the immortals it has no meaning. Here, it can run out. We have a beginning and an end, something they don't understand. That makes everything they experience within our world that much more exhilarating." She paused, weighing her next words with even more care. "The goddesses came first," she continued, "a dozen of them, a long time ago. They traveled the Old World in its entirety, bringing life and prosperity with them, and receiving great pleasure in return. Then the demons arrived, numbering in the thousands, to scour the world with demon fire in their hunt for the goddesses. Mortals tried to protect the goddesses from them. They fought back with fire of their own. Before they fell, they decreased demon numbers to the hundred or so remaining today."

Airie didn't appear satisfied. "Demons make no secret of the fact that they hate mortal men. If the goddesses are gone, why would they remain?"

"They have no choice," Desire replied. "The goddesses are stronger against a hundred than a thousand. They built the boundary beyond which no demon can cross, confining them to the Wasteland. No one knows what exists beyond that boundary anymore, or if anything of the Old World remains. All we have of it here are its ruins. But people are stronger and more resilient than the immortals give us credit for. Someday, curiosity is going to win out over fear of the unknown. The boundary will fall, the demons will leave, and the world will be whole again."

Pensiveness touched Airie's tone. "If the goddesses brought life and prosperity to mortals, why did they abandon us to demons?"

"The immortals have always been at war," Desire said carefully. "The goddesses came here to escape demons, and they left to escape them again."

Airie tipped her head to the side, still deep in thought. "I often dream of the desert, even though I've never seen it. It's a vast place filled with heat and sand, and holds the most beautiful sculptures carved from the earth."

Desire caught her breath at the unexpected and unwelcome revelation that the demon in Airie continued to search for its own kind. She'd thought Airie had learned to control it. That she'd left the dreams behind, with her childhood.

Then Airie shifted their conversation yet again. "Do the goddesses mind me being here? In their temple?"

"You're my daughter," Desire said simply, evading the true question. "They watch over us both. Your talent for healing is their gift to you. You'd have no gift from them if you didn't belong."

Airie plucked a slender blade of dew-slickened grass, twisting it around her fingers. "Tell me about my father."

This was the one topic Desire had never discussed with her. Always, when asked, she'd told Airie that she'd been created out of love, which was all that mattered. That answer had satisfied her in the past.

Dagan. Her father's name is Dagan.

But the time wasn't yet right to tell her.

"I have a right to know," Airie said.

"Why do you want to know *now*?" Desire was reminded of the questions she should have asked Airie earlier, and her suspicions grew as to what she'd been up to. "What's happened to make you so interested?" *What have you done?*

"Nothing."

Desire let it drop. They both had secrets they were unwilling to share. Sooner or later, however, she intended to have answers to hers. Despite her declining health, the next time Airie went to collect the offerings, she would follow.

* * *

His real name was Dagan. Only one other person in all of eternity had been given the right to call him by it. To his followers, and the world, he was the Demon Lord.

He came to rest on desert sand still scorching hot though the sun had set many hours before. He balanced his weight on thickset legs, furled his wings between powerfully muscled shoulders, and with a grinding of bones and joints, shifted into the mortal form demons used for hunting women. Plain cotton breeches were all he wore. Most times, he wore nothing. For this meeting, he preferred the priestess's eyes on his face. He wasn't blind to the way she watched him.

He sniffed the air and caught a faint whiff of blood, the coppery tang of it unmistakable. The winds were high. On nights like this one—when the stars and the moon shone their light on the world and the winds blew—demons called to mortal women, beckoning them into the desert for games of pleasure. Few women chosen to play could resist the call. He followed the scent, striding easily across the sands and past plush cacti, the desert wind tangling his hair. Nightlife, both predator and prey, scurried away at his approach.

The woman was not quite dead when he reached her. Her skin was yet warm to the touch, and her lips gaped on guttural screams. Long, sand-clumped fair hair, damp with sweat, pooled beneath her head. She'd been pretty once, which was to be expected, since demons hunted only the best. Now, however, swelling distorted her face and limbs. Her distended belly was ripped open wide.

The smell of her blood ignited a reaction in Dagan that at one time, he might not have been able to resist. Time, however, had affected him in many ways that immortality had not. He'd learned to control even the strongest of his urges. He no longer prowled for either women or pleasure. He came here tonight only because the priestess had summoned him.

"I want his name," he said to the dying woman.

Demon allure—immortal compulsion—demanded she answer him. She heaved it from her lungs on a tortured breath.

Be'el.

Dagan formed a talon from one fingernail and slit her throat to end her suffering. The talon retracted. The true cause of her death lay next to her, panting heavily and blinking its owlish eyes. A bulbous head, too large for a long, ungainly neck, lolled to one side. Wet wings glistened in the pale moonlight, curling and uncurling with each labored breath, clawed fingers and toes moving in unison. It lapped greedily at its mother's blood. It was difficult to believe that something so pitiful had the potential to hold demons chained to this world.

He didn't bother to resume his manhunting form. It wasn't necessary, not with a newborn, although he didn't underestimate it. Spawn were as likely to turn on their demon fathers as they were their unfortunate mothers, and one never knew what immortal strengths they might have inherited—which was another reason why they could not be allowed to survive.

He planted a slim, bare foot on the squirming body, and reaching down, ripped the head from the spawn's scrawny neck before it could bite or scratch him. The blue-green light of demon death rising from its body was fainter than that of a true demon, but evident nonetheless. Immortals didn't die the same way mortals did, not even a monstrous hybrid such as this.

"Nasty business," a voice laden with distaste said from behind him. The priestess, Mamna, stayed well back, her hand covering her nose to filter the stench. Spawn smelled worse dead than alive.

Dagan tossed the head aside and wiped his hands on the hem of the mother's tattered dress, wishing he could do the same to the priestess. She skulked about, always watching, seeing and hearing things not meant for her eyes and ears.

"Demons pursue their promised mates. With mortals, reproduction is sometimes the unfortunate result of the hunt." He faced her. "Have you learned anything?"

"No. I've hired someone to bring her in."

Dagan stilled, instantly wary. "Who?"

Her response took a heartbeat too long. "The Demon Slayer."

Anger built deep inside him, flaring from his eyes as demon fire. The glow glittered off wind-polished particles of sand and shot red shards of light into the night. "You hired the Demon Slayer to do demon work?"

The ugly little priestess didn't flinch. She knew better than to show fear to a demon. The heat of his gaze scorched her homely face. The goddesses hadn't chosen their priestesses for their beauty. If anything, they'd had been chosen to highlight the beauty of the goddesses. The handicap made them safe to wander on such nights when no other mortal woman should dare. Mamna was safer than most, although not because of her looks.

His fingers curled at his sides. If anything should happen to the goddess-cursed amulet she wore, she'd have cause for concern. Her hold over him would be finished. The existence of the amulet she'd stolen from her mistresses, however, was a secret they both kept for now, and for their own reasons. They knew far too much about each other, and neither wished for their secrets to be exposed.

"The Slayer has proven himself to be more than capable of besting a demon," she said. "And even though the thief might wear the form of a woman, she's still a spawn."

The fire in his eyes cooled at the priestess's words. She was right. There would be a certain advantage in having the Slayer involved if the little thief should get out of hand. But if she did get out of hand, and the Slayer was forced to kill her, Dagan might never know for certain if she were his.

He needed to know. He needed to know if she had been born to the one who'd betrayed him. More than that, he needed to know if she was the reason demons could no longer abandon this world and return to the heart of the universe—if, thanks to a mixed immortal heritage, she possessed that kind of strength.

Mamna claimed the spawn on the mountain was that of a priestess who'd survived the fire. She was also the one to suggest that such a spawn—born in mortal form and not as a manhunting monstrosity—might provide the key as to why demons remained trapped in the mortal world.

He didn't trust Mamna. She had her own scores to settle. She hated the goddesses with the same passion he did himself, and if she thought this thief could be used against them in some manner, not even fear of him would stop her. But the goddesses had found a way to keep demons within this world and he intended to figure out how.

"Spawn are mine," he said. "Whether this one's mother is a priestess or not, she's to be turned over to me. And make no mistake. I want her alive."

Without waiting for the priestess's response to his warning, he assumed his manhunting form once more and set his wings free. They billowed like sails, catching and filling, lifting him into the starry sky. He headed for his desert home, away from the unfortunate mortal mother who had once been lovely enough to catch the interest of a demon but was now nothing more than food for scavengers.

Mortal women could be exceedingly beautiful, Dagan conceded as he glided on a bank of warm air. But it was fleeting, and nothing when compared to the light and essence of an immortal goddess.

One in particular.

His mind filled with the sight of her walking across the warm desert sand toward him, a smile igniting her golden face, her translucent white gown outlining the graceful curves of her body. Light had shone from her pores. She was meant to be his.

The memory brought him no joy. The smile and body he'd found so irresistible had masked treachery. She'd fought her battle armed with the weapons she had known would fell him, and the victory had been well and truly hers. In the end, she'd proven stronger than he.

All that was left for him now was to destroy everything she had once cherished, and hopefully, regain freedom for what remained of his followers.

CHAPTER THREE

"What in the demons' land would possess you to use such a mount?" Blade roared. He leaped awkwardly out of range of a sticky, razor-sharp tongue, his hat landing in the dust.

Hunter nudged the squat-legged sand swift into position with his shoulder and swung his saddle onto its back. "Sally's already eaten. She's testing you."

"Testing or tasting?" Blade growled. He kept a wary eye on the creature as he stooped to retrieve his hat, his crippled leg bent outward at an awkward angle.

Hunter understood Blade's suspicion regarding the giant desert lizard and its surly nature. If not properly tamed, they were known to eat their riders on occasion. But Hunter had been raised in the farming region of the Borderlands. He knew how to break a sand swift as well as a hross, and once they'd been broken, they were fiercely loyal and protective. He never had to worry about murderers and thieves with Sally tethered at the mouth of his canyon to watch over him.

Besides, adult sand swifts weren't the real threat. Juveniles lived in these canyons, hiding from the heat amid the rocks and the shrubs. Continuously hungry because of their rapid growth rate, they reached full size within a year. Even though no bigger than Hunter's fist in their first month of life, juvenile tongues contained a protective, paralyzing property that stunned their prey so they could feed on it at leisure. Adults of the species no longer required the poison, for either protection or in order to feed, and their bodies absorbed it at about six months of age.

Hunter drew the saddle cinch tight, fastened down the last of his belongings, and tested the straps. The day was young and the heat of the desert hadn't yet penetrated to the canyon floor. With a week's ride ahead of him, then another back, he was anxious to get started. A crooked blue sky cut between the cliffs above. The mountain beckoned from the east. He'd never been there, had never felt the urge before, although it monopolized the desert horizon—designed by the goddesses to serve as a constant reminder of their presence to mortals and demons alike.

Probably not their smartest idea, given what the demons had done to it.

And to them.

He patted Sally's thick, scaly neck. "Did you come out here to make fun of my mount? Because I have a thief to catch and I'd like to get started before the sun gets too high."

"I came to tell you I took a closer look at the money your friend used to pay for his drink."

Blade held something out and Hunter took it, turning the small coin over in his fingers. At first glance, it was nothing special—a thin gold coin, unrefined and common, with a few tiny threads of impurities. On closer inspection, however, the gold had an odd, fiery cast.

"It's from the gold mines of the north," Blade said.

Definitely an assassin, then. The north was the land ruled by godseekers, the goddesses' favorites. Some called them the goddesses' whores, although never to their faces. Godseekers believed the Demon Slayer was destined to lead their army against demons and return the goddesses to the world. Hunter believed their faith in him was misplaced. Yes, he wanted the demons gone, but he would never willingly bring the goddesses back either. The immortals were one and the same to him. They didn't belong here.

Yet it was unusual for one of the godseekers' assassins to stray so far from home. Demons made certain any mortals who left the north didn't do so through their territory. Blade was the only man he knew who'd survived such an attempt, and he'd paid a high price for it.

Hunter tossed the coin back into his friend's outstretched palm. "Godseekers have never tried to have me killed before, although I must say, it's a nice change. I never much cared for being worshipped."

Blade tucked the coin into a pocket. "Why suddenly decide to kill you right when Mamna has hired you to head to Goddess Mountain? Does the timing not make you at all curious?"

Of course it did. But he wasn't making more problems than already existed. He was far more worried about the priestess's motives for hiring him to begin with. He slammed his hat onto his head. "Perhaps their grudge is with Mamna, not me. You were once an assassin. Why do you think this one tried to kill me?"

"For your amulet," Blade said. "It's what makes you the Demon Slayer. If you refuse to lead their army, they'll find another who will."

"This amulet offers no true protection from demons—simply an equal strength," Hunter pointed out. "Anyone who does manage to take it from me would have to be willing to fight them."

"An assassin would be willing."

"Would godseekers allow any assassin to lead an army on their behalf?"

Blade's sharp features tightened. "If he were also a godseeker, then yes."

Hunter would have to take Blade's word for that. He knew very little about the men of the north. "It's been more than twenty years since demon fire scoured the earth. The youngest of the godseekers would be well into his forties by now. One who's also an assassin would be very rare."

"And yet, they exist. I know of at least one, although he'd be in his sixties today. Ten years ago, he was formidable. But also honorable," Blade added, the concession forced from him with obvious reluctance. The saloon owner harbored no fealty toward his northern brethren.

"Would your honorable-yet-ancient godseeker assassin have had me knifed in the back in an alley thousands of miles from the north, in order to steal my amulet from me, so he could wear it and lead an army against demons?"

Blade's dark brows hooked together. "Unlikely."

"Then we're back where we began."

"I still say Mamna might as easily be the one trying to have you killed. Who knows what drives her logic? Perhaps she wants to keep you and your amulet out of the reach of the godseekers. You could be riding into an ambush."

The possibility of an ambush wasn't what ate at Hunter. He was hunting a woman on behalf of the very creatures he hated more than anything else in the world. He didn't believe Mamna's claim that the woman had demon blood, although part of him hoped it was true. Then he could hand her over to Mamna with an easy conscience, and maybe this knot in his stomach—the one that said he'd finally gotten into something over his head—would go away.

He placed his foot in one stirrup and swung into the saddle.

"We could speculate all day. There's only one way to find out who was behind it, and that's to wait for the second attempt. If it comes."

"It will," Blade said.

* * *

A week later, and many miles from Freetown, there had been no more attempts on Hunter's life.

Once he crossed the river that signaled the true end of the desert region, the land turned greener, becoming resplendent with rolling foothills and grand trees. Here and there, thrusting through fields of long grass and overgrown brush, poked crumbled bits of blackened stone and mortar—all that remained of settlements burned out by demon fire. He'd been a small boy at the time, but to this day he remembered the odd, greenish glow of the sky and the whitefall of ash that had rained throughout all the lands for days.

And yet, despite the desecration, people had chosen to rebuild in the region.

As he approached the base of Goddess Mountain, he began to understand why. The goddesses' presence could still be felt here. The devastation caused by the fire had been replaced by new forest growth, and while not as glorious as it once must have been, the mountain was recovering. Sunshine saturated the surrounding air, warming the sharp scent of pine stinging his nostrils. He breathed it deep into his lungs, and for the first time in many years, was stricken with a wave of homesickness. He'd grown up on a ranch at the far edge of the desert, and it wasn't the smell of the mountain that struck him so much as the freshness of it, and the peacefulness.

The sand swift lashed out with its tongue and caught a saucy graybird that ventured too close, methodically grinding it to pulp before swallowing. A ripple trickled down the length of its body that Hunter could feel beneath his thighs.

"Why a bird?" he asked, patting its scaly hide. "You aren't fussy. If you have to snack, why not on something that nobody likes?"

He rode a narrow path winding upward that he guessed led to the temple. A few miles along, the path skirted a small lake cut from the rock with waters clear and deep.

Movement on the other side of the path caught the sand swift's attention. Its broad head swung around, nearly unseating Hunter. He grabbed at the reins and slid from the saddle, putting the beast between him and whatever had distracted it, his free hand dropping to his six-shooter, swearing at his own inattention. Twice now, he'd been taken off guard.

He was getting too old for this business.

He scanned the scarred rocks and trees, searching for whatever the sand swift had seen, and caught a flash of long black hair and a filmy white sleeve buried in the dappled shadows beneath a tangle of brush. The sand swift, however, wasn't showing any undue signs of alarm. Its color stayed a steady, greenish brown, not changing to the vivid purple signifying danger. Its mouth remained closed. When agitated, its tongue flicked whip-like back and forth, a warning for all to stand clear. His amulet, too, lay silent next to his skin. This wasn't a demon.

"I know you're there," he called out. "Show yourself."

The bushes rustled.

"I need help," a feminine voice said. "I've injured my leg."

Hunter, who'd bested demons in battle, wasn't about to fall victim to such an obvious ploy. He relaxed, loosening his grip on his weapon but not on the reins. If this was the woman he'd been sent to hunt, it amazed him she hadn't been caught long before now.

"I don't help thieves," he said.

"I'm no thief." Indignation quivered in the feminine voice.

The bushes parted and her head poked through. Hunter stared. She had the face of a goddess, with smooth, golden skin and full lips a deep shade of ripe-apple red. Thick black hair absorbed and reflected the light. Her eyes, dark as a moonless night, gazed up at him in silent reproach for his lack of chivalry.

If this was his thief, she wasn't at all what he'd expected. Or been led to believe.

Hunter collected himself. He had seven—no, six—beautiful sisters, and he wasn't easily swayed by a lovely face. He'd loved his sisters. But they were far from the fragile creatures they sometimes portrayed, and even though he hadn't seen them in a number of years, he remembered their feminine tricks quite well. They played most men for fools.

That didn't mean a man couldn't enjoy being made a fool of every once in a while.

"I need help," the woman repeated.

Here was the test.

"You have another leg, I assume, and two arms. Come out where I can see you first."

She emerged upright from the bushes, favoring her right leg, although it was hidden beneath her long skirt so no injury was visible. He noticed no weapon, which meant nothing. The blouse and skirt could hide any number of interesting but dangerous things. Glossy hair hung in curls to her hips. She dropped to the ground, drawing her knee to her chest and rubbing her ankle.

Hunter sifted through his options. She didn't appear badly hurt, which made him more suspicious. On the other hand, if she posed a real threat to him, Sally would have indicated it by now—although granted, a sand swift's interpretation of a threat and his could be two vastly different things.

He dismounted, tossed the reins over the sand swift's neck, and walked toward her. Her eyes contained not even the slightest hint of fear. Rather, she bore an air of innocence difficult for most women in this day and age to feign. Even Blade's ladies, lovely and kind as they were, had faces filled with too great an understanding of a harsh world.

She couldn't possibly be the thief. Not with this guileless, trusting demeanor. For an instant, he had an ugly vision of what it would mean to turn a woman this young and lovely over to Mamna, and by default to the demons, and it wasn't nice. A memory of his sister's swollen belly, and the fear and pain etched on her dead face, also arose.

Miriam might have given her innocence willingly to the demon she'd professed to love, but the relationship had ended badly for her. It had ended badly for the demon, too. Hunter had made certain of that.

He looked at the sand swift standing calmly nearby, and then opted to give the woman the benefit of the doubt. He crouched down beside her, eyes shifting to her ankle. "Where does it hurt?"

That brief opening was all she required. The heel of her palm came up with lightning speed, connecting with the bridge of his nose. His head flew back and red stars burst from the blackness behind his eyes.

Acting on instinct alone, he rolled to the side and shot to his feet. The blow had been well aimed. He wiped his nose with the back of his hand, surprised to find she hadn't drawn blood, and equally certain she'd held back.

She was on her feet now too, no longer favoring her leg. She was tall, he noted. Almost as tall as he, but with the fine-boned delicateness of a woman, making the power behind the controlled blow she'd delivered all the more surprising.

So much for guileless and trusting eyes.

He was more entertained than angry. He could accept that he'd been played for a fool. He'd expected to be.

"I'd prefer not to hurt you," she said to him. "All I want are your packs."

She was good, he granted her that, and her restraint said she hadn't tried to kill him. The pain behind his eyes ebbed to a dull, throbbing ache.

"And if I don't give them to you?" he asked, curious as to how far she'd take this.

Faster than he'd imagined possible, one of her booted feet caught him high in the ribs, toppling him to the ground. His hip landed on his six-shooter, and he forgot the pain in his head in favor of new ones.

She walked to the sand swift and worked at the fastenings that secured his belongings to the saddle. The indifferent sand swift showed not the faintest trace of agitation or aggressiveness toward her.

So much for loyalty and protection, too.

The entertainment he'd been gleaning from the situation vanished. As did his good nature. If she wished to be treated like a woman, she should act more like one. He went in low, intending to hit her in the center of her chest with his shoulder to knock her down.

She was quick—but so was he. He grabbed her arm as she tried to sidestep, hooking her feet from underneath her with his ankle. With a twist of his upper body, he hauled her off balance, rolled her over his throbbing hip, and hurled her into the deep waters of the small lake at the side of the path.

She came up gasping, her hair streaming down her face, her wet blouse transparent. Hunter took the time to enjoy her appearance, and let her know he did, while rubbing his ribs where she'd kicked him. That was going to leave a mark. His hip, he suspected, was already blue.

Enough was enough. Now that they'd both had their fun, he had to decide what to do about her. Wincing a little, he extended a hand to help haul her from the water.

Even though he braced himself, fully prepared for her to try and pull him in too, he wasn't prepared for her strength and he shot headfirst into the lake.

He got his feet beneath him and surged to the surface, flipping his hair from his eyes. His hat floated nearby. He gave her a hard push, sending her into deeper water. It wasn't a gentlemanly thing to do, but this was no lady. Then he grabbed a handful of her wet hair, and wrapping it around his wrist, hauled her head under water. Her arms flailed, but she didn't strike hard enough to bruise. He collected his hat and settled it, dripping, back in place.

A few bubbles drifted up, then a few more. Hunter considered releasing her. Although Mamna hadn't specified alive—that was an assumption—and his ribs and hip hurt like hell, he didn't want her dead. Everyone needed to eat. Being a thief didn't make her spawn.

But he hated having to wear wet boots.

He counted to ten. Before he got to three, the temperature of the water began to rise. Then the surface of the water boiled, stinging his skin through his pants. He dropped his hold on her hair and paddled a few paces backward.

She burst from the water, sleek black hair plastered to her cheeks and breasts, anger crackling like a halo around her. He didn't have a chance to enjoy it this time. The flames shooting from her eyes had him floundering for shore.

As did the amulet around his neck sputtering unexpectedly to life.

* * *

Long before Mamna's time, a temple honoring the goddesses had been strategically constructed over a deep well feeding into a small desert oasis. Back then, the oasis had been little more than a place for travelers to pause and regroup in relative safety when crossing through demon territory. Consecrating the groundwater in its well had been the goddesses' gift to men, turning it into a weapon that could be used against demons because it ate demon flesh like acid.

Of the nine original priestesses who'd fled Goddess Mountain ahead of the fires, six remained. Two had died of old age, and a third, from a wasting sickness. Mamna, now in her fifties, was the youngest of the survivors and the leader the others turned to. She controlled the temple, the water, and therefore, Freetown.

Every evening, she and her priestesses gathered inside the temple. The people of Freetown could be excused in believing they worshipped. In reality, it gave them an opportunity to meet undisturbed and exchange reports of any information they'd gathered throughout the day. Each of the priestesses was well aware that their elevated position in Freetown was thanks to Mamna, demons, and fear—and that knowledge was power.

Market days in Freetown doubled as judgment days. Mamna liked for as many people as possible to witness the power she held.

The woman brought before her for sentencing today was especially lovely. For that alone Mamna would have condemned her to death. Neither of them had had a say in the body they'd been born with, yet Mamna's was a punishment and hers a reward.

But this woman had made sentencing her particularly easy. She'd arrived through the slave trade, destined for one of the remote mining areas, and was well aware of her worth on the market. She'd spoken ill of the priestesses, as if she were superior to them, and been overheard. That was enough.

It had been several years since Mamna's last public demon-raising. That demon had been fueled by the terror of the onlookers to such an extent that the man on trial that day had been savaged and partially eaten before she could call it off. But the people were due for a reminder of the protection she afforded them and the respect she was due.

"Clear the circle," she commanded.

The temple guards, understanding what she intended to do a few beats ahead of the crowd, were slow to obey. Then, as if to make up for it, as well as to avoid the fallout of her displeasure, the crowd was forced back with brutal efficiency.

A shallow trough had been carved from the baked desert earth and lined with tile to hold water. Four points had been marked inside the circular trough—north, south, east and west. The trough of water represented the goddess boundary that surrounded the world. Mamna's dais occupied the land of the goddesses to the east, and signified their mountain. The center of the circle was the desert, the land claimed by the demons. Tied to a pole at the center of the desert stood the woman on trial, limp from both fear and the dry morning heat.

Buckets of water, drawn from the temple's cistern early that morning by the priestesses, were poured into the trough. The consecrated water was a precaution on Mamna's part. The amulet she wore kept demons out of Freetown, but she'd invited this one in. If it managed to escape her hold the artificial boundary would temporarily contain it, but she'd need to be quick in reclaiming it before the water evaporated into the thirsty desert air.

The condemned woman remained defiant in her silence, although her face had lost its color. Mamna might have found it in her heart to pity her if she hadn't despised her so deeply. Demons could be gentle with the innocent, but traders, before bringing slaves through the desert, spoiled their women to avoid having them stolen away.

When the trough was full, the priestesses stepped back and blended in as best they could with the crowd. No one could now cross the circle—not that anyone would willingly try.

The amulet throbbed beneath Mamna's clothing. Summoning a demon took more out of her than she liked. The amulet had been intended for use by a goddess, not a mortal. It drew its power through her, and she wasn't young anymore. Sweat beaded her forehead and streamed down the sides of her face. Her shaved scalp itched under the cap she wore to protect it from the sun. Gradually, the sounds of the crowd and the condemned woman's heavy breathing muted to dull background noises.

She directed her thoughts through the amulet and into the desert territory the demons had claimed. Once inside their territory, she called out the name the Demon Lord had compelled from a dying woman. *Be'el.*

A dark speck appeared on the horizon, growing larger as it approached, then took shape. Giant wings blocked the sun and blackened the sky, casting a shadow that swallowed a crowd immobilized by terror. The demon landed inside the circle where it had been summoned, its clawed feet kicking up dust. It crouched on the ground before the dais, furling its wings tight against massive shoulders. Thick red bone plate covered its body. The tips of the horns on its bent head grazed the hem of her gown, but when it straightened and stretched, its true size expanded to gigantic proportions. The amulet grew hot against Mamna's flesh, and in a spontaneous, defensive response, seared into her skin. She ignored the pain.

The majority of the crowd withdrew several yards, widening the distance between them and the circle. A few brave souls stood their ground, but remained ready to bolt at the first sign of danger.

The demon blinked eyes flaming red with hatred, sweeping them over the crowd before turning its attention on her. A deep, gravel voice rolled from its bone-plated chest. "Why have you summoned me?"

Confident in the control the amulet gave her, Mamna met that fiery, hate-filled gaze without flinching. She'd faced the Demon Lord more times than she could count. This demon paled in comparison. "You don't question me. You are here to see that justice is served."

"I care nothing for mortal justice."

Her bent fingers gripped the arms of her throne. "You stand on priestess ground. By the goddesses' command, you will do as I say."

Slyness entered its eyes. It rolled its head back and forth on its shoulders, examining the silent onlookers, then it slid a long, high-arched foot toward the circular trough filled with a scant trickle of water. Shrieks of terror rippled through the crowd, and the people closest to the circle trampled those behind them in a panicked stampede to escape.

Mamna watched the crowd with contempt.

Then she recognized something was wrong. The amulet around her neck lost its searing heat. The steady throbbing had become erratic. The demon's head whipped around, sensing the sudden shift in dynamics inside the circle, and she cursed her inattention. This wasn't the time to show either fear or a loss of control.

She gestured to the bound woman, who trembled and made small, animal noises deep in her throat.

"This woman is accused of treason," Mamna said to the demon, in a hurry to end matters she began to wish she hadn't begun. "Conspiracy against the priestesses is conspiracy against the goddesses. Therefore, they disavow her. She's yours to do with as you please. What will it be, Demon? Do you want her?"

It stared at Mamna. She stared back. Slow seconds passed. Then it turned to examine the bound woman, opting for an easy reward over a confrontation it might not win. The woman had slumped forward in a faint.

"I will have her," the demon decided, and the glint in its hot eyes said it wouldn't be easy for her when it did. It would feed on her fear, and play with her for hours.

Mamna released the demon, sending it back to the desert from where it came. The amulet regained its steady beat. Her own fear, freed by the demon's departure, licked at her insides. It didn't seem as strong to her as before

She addressed the guards. "Turn the traitor loose in the desert. Give her no food or water."

If the heat or wild animals didn't kill her first, then the demon would return for her tonight. No mortal would dare go to her rescue now that she'd been claimed by it.

Stone-faced guards untied the woman. As she revived, and realized her fate, her low, panicked, guttural wails built to a crescendo of ear-piercing shrieks.

Mamna signaled for a young attendant to help her from the throne. Her legs, unsteady from a combination of age, deformity and unease, wobbled as she stepped from the dais. Pausing for a moment to regain her balance, and annoyed by the fading screams of the condemned, she slid her hand under the neck of her dress and ran nervous fingers over the amulet's varnished surface.

Tiny fractures marred the flaming rainbow's previously smooth finish. Anxious for complete privacy so she could examine the full extent of the damage, she dismissed the hovering attendants with a wave of her hand. She'd make this walk back to her city residence alone to prove she remained strong.

As she stepped onto the weather-beaten, oil-soaked plank sidewalk, a man dared to approach her. He appeared to be in his mid-forties. This one would have been a beautiful man in his youth, and was attractive still. His eyes were slate gray and very direct. He was a tall man, and as handsome as she would expect of a northerner, although his dark blond hair carried more than a hint of silver. His clothes were of good quality, meaning he had to be from the north, a region wealthy because of its gold and silver mines.

But now that the goddesses were gone, demons made it dangerous for anyone wanting to do business with the north. Traders either had to take a direct route through demon territory and hope to pass unobserved, or skirt the border and take their chances on being robbed and murdered by mortals in the lawless outposts between the larger settlements. Northerners, who possessed the greater wealth, rarely found their way to Freetown, preferring to allow traders from other lands to assume all of the risk.

This northerner wore a small, amber-colored amulet around his neck that she recognized as something the goddesses had once given out freely to their favored companions. It also told her he was a godseeker as well as a northerner. The amulet offered no protection from demons, but grew warm if an immortal lurked nearby—which would explain how he'd survived a trip through the desert. Most damning of all, the stench of the goddesses clung to him, and he had a particular light in his eyes possessed by all godseekers who'd serviced them as one of their whores.

Mamna hated godseekers. They considered themselves the priestesses' equals. Or better. Whoring had won godseekers the right to rule in the mining regions, however, and the assassins they commanded were feared throughout the entirety of Wasteland.

This one held his hat in his hands with a deference that didn't quite match his manner. She waited for him to speak, too cautious to simply dismiss him before she knew what he wanted from her.

"I've come to bring you a message on behalf of the north. The goddesses are here," he said. "The godseekers have felt their presence. Priestesses must join with us to gather their army for them. *Change is coming.*"

Godseekers believed the goddesses remained watchful over Wasteland, biding their time until they could return, but that wasn't true. This world had been touched by them and their presence would be felt here forever.

Mamna should know. She had been chosen to serve the goddesses when she was a girl of fourteen. A simple touch was all it had taken to make her their servant. She'd hated them in return, but once touched, no one could resist them, and she wore the taint of their caress like an invisible brand to this day.

"Goddesses are long gone from the world," she said. "You feel the lingering of their presence, nothing more."

The light in his eyes brightened. "One goddess remains," he insisted, "left here to welcome the others back to our world. They'll forgive you your dealings with demons if you join her army and fight for her. Think of it, Priestess. You'll no longer be a slave to the Demon Lord."

"I command demons. They don't command me," she said sharply. Had he not just witnessed how she'd summoned one to dispense justice? How she'd bent it to her will? "The goddesses are gone. I witnessed their departure myself."

"One remains on the mountain," he insisted. He stepped closer, crowding her with his greater height, emphasizing her deformity. She scowled up at him, but he was so wrapped up in his message that he didn't notice how much he displeased her. "She defends against trespassers and collects alms for their temple from the faithful."

The noise from the market faded, overwhelmed by a roaring in Mamna's ears as all of the blood in her twisted body rushed to her head. "A dying priestess and her bastard, thieving daughter live on the mountain."

Stubbornness set the godseeker's jaw in a hard line. "She's a goddess, not a thief. The Slayer will lead her army against the demons. This is our chance to fight back, to send them away. This world doesn't belong to them."

Nor had it belonged to the goddesses, Mamna longed to shout. An immortal was an immortal. Other than gender, there was no distinction between them. But the godseeker's beliefs, like those of all true fanatics, would never change.

"Even if you're right, she's still only one goddess while the demons are many. She can have no hope of standing against them alone."

"She holds the will of all the goddesses," he insisted. "Her army will drive the demons out."

Mamna was truly worried now. Freetown, the center of trade throughout Wasteland, and already a fortress against demons, was the perfect place to raise such an army—and the godseekers wished to make it their base. If that were to happen, and the godseekers and their assassins gained a foothold in Freetown, she'd have a far bigger problem than demons and a cracked amulet on her hands.

"I'd have known if a goddess had been left behind," she said again, although she'd given up hope that he could be deterred. "I was there."

Suspicion backlit the zealousness in the man's eyes. "We thought you, of all people, would welcome this news."

Welcome it?

She'd betrayed the goddesses to the Demon Lord. She'd carried his fire to the mountain for him. She'd fanned the flames. She did not, under any circumstances, wish for the goddesses to return.

Neither did she wish for the Demon Lord to discover how she'd spied on him and his goddess lover, and been the one to gather soil from the desert earth where they'd lain together, then given it to the goddess's sisters. When the goddesses fled the world, she'd stolen the amulet they'd crafted from it. The round disc of polished desert sand was what kept Freetown—and her—truly safe.

But now it was damaged and only a goddess could repair and invoke it again. With her goddess-tainted blood, the spawn might be able to do so.

Mamna's goal in bringing her to the Demon Lord's attention had been to enjoy watching him destroy the offspring he'd created with one of her hated former mistresses. Now she had a reason to want the spawn alive, even if temporarily.

She considered having the godseeker killed so he couldn't spread his story of a goddess and her army. One lift of her finger would make it so. But she discarded the idea. More godseekers would be coming, and they might not identify themselves to her before irreparable damage was done in Freetown.

Something else had occurred to her, requiring more thought. The Slayer wore an amulet that had earned him his title. She didn't know how he'd acquired it, only that it had to have been invoked by an immortal to be as powerful as it was. She'd been content to leave him be. He could never kill every demon—not in her lifetime—and he kept their attention away from Freetown. But his was the only other amulet she knew of that offered any level of protection from demons. Who was to say the Slayer was the only one who could wear it?

If that thought had occurred to her, then it had occurred to others—which explained the attempt on his life she'd witnessed the night she'd hired him. Only one of the best assassins in Wasteland would have dared make such a bold move. That assassin would belong to the godseekers. And if the godseekers wanted the Slayer's amulet, then Mamna wanted it more. The next Slayer to wear it would be one of her choosing.

"What is your name?" she asked the godseeker.

"Pillar."

"Well, Pillar." She gathered the stiff skirt of her gown in one crooked hand. "Come with me. We can talk over lunch."

CHAPTER FOUR

Blade had never been one to concern himself overmuch in the lives and affairs of others. He made exceptions for Hunter and Ruby because they'd saved his life, and for no reason other than that they'd chosen to.

Hunter was why he'd come to the market today. More northerners had arrived on the first wagon train and that didn't bode well. His friend had gotten himself into trouble and needed Blade watching his back.

He hadn't counted on Mamna raising a demon. It had taken everything he possessed to stand his ground at the back of the heaving crowd, but he had. And he'd buried his fear deep. Never again would he allow a demon to feed on it.

He had no love for the gnarled little priestess. What she'd done today spoke of a soul twisted beyond all redemption. Yet he couldn't deny that she served a purpose.

After the goddesses abandoned them, all of Wasteland had fallen into a state of such chaos it was a wonder the world hadn't imploded. Mamna had saved it from ruin. She had the protection of the Demon Lord, which extended by default to the area she claimed as hers, and thus indirectly to its inhabitants. She was the reason Blade, and others, had settled here, and what gave her authority over them. She'd established her own version of law in Freetown.

But what had happened in Freetown today wasn't law. Mamna had a cruelty to her, a disregard for life that Blade, despite his own tainted past, found unsettling. Now that the horror show was over, and the shell-shocked crowd had begun to disperse, he should return to his saloon and open it for business. He suspected a number of people would be after a drink.

He, too, wanted to forget the morning's proceedings, and the fate that awaited a woman simply because she'd talked too much.

Instead, he slipped away from the crowd and toward the main gates of Freetown, which faced the wide expanse of desert and the distant northern mountains. There was nothing Blade could do about her sentence, and little to free her. He had women of his own to protect.

But he knew he wouldn't be able sleep that night if he stood back and did nothing. Perhaps it was because he had once faced a demon and lost. Still, he had to be very careful.

He cut down some side streets, taking a shortcut to the gates. Small buildings skirted the city wall, the homes of workers who'd all be away at this time of day. He scaled the side of one house, digging his toes into chinks in the rough, wind-chewed wood, and swung his long legs onto the clay-shingled roof. His damaged leg screamed in a protest which he ignored. He eased one of the knives he'd taken off Hunter's would-be assassin from the wide cuff of his linen shirtsleeve. With this weapon, there'd be nothing to trace back to him.

He spotted them from his hiding spot on the roof, gathered at the open gate and the worn wagon trail that led through the desert. The three silent guards appeared unhappy, but had little choice other than to do their duty. Blade didn't blame them for this. They would have loved ones to protect.

A few curious onlookers straggled behind the procession. The prisoner dragged her feet, pleading tearfully for her life, and Blade shut his ears to the things she promised to do for the guards if they set her free. She bargained with what she had, and no one could fault her for it.

He wasn't as close as he'd like to be, but at least he had a clear shot. He palmed the unfamiliar knife, thankful he'd taken the time to practice with it and be somewhat used to its weight and balance. He drew back his arm, careful to keep the movement from attracting attention below, and in a smooth, experienced motion, brought it forward.

Despite the distance, the knife found its mark.

The woman let out a small groan of surprise and threw her head back, then slumped forward, limp now in the guards' grasp. Brief panic erupted as the guards and the onlookers all realized at once what had happened—and how exposed they were to danger.

Panic was the reaction Blade had hoped for. He swung from the rooftop and dropped to the far side of the building. An assassin's work was more difficult in daylight, and a successful escape was the mark of a true professional. He'd once been the very best.

First, he had to be certain the woman was dead. Rather than running away, he limped straight into the melee. No one ever suspected a cripple.

She lay on her side in a pool of deepening blood, arms flung out like a discarded doll, her eyes wide and staring—although it was clear that she would never see anything in this world again. Blade didn't waste any more pity on her. She'd known the rules of Freetown. She should have kept her opinions to herself, or at least been more discreet with them.

"What happened?" he asked one of the guards.

The guard was young and unused to his job. His skin was pale and his eyes glassy. "Someone tried to free her but killed her by mistake."

"Someone has terrible aim," Blade said. In reality it had been perfect. He'd severed the aorta and the swelling around the wound indicated she'd died almost instantly. In all the years he'd worked as an assassin, he'd never allowed his targets to suffer. That was the difference between a killer and a monster.

"It's better for her than dying at the hands of a demon." The guard spoke with feeling, voicing an opinion Blade shared.

A second guard unstrapped a rifle from the sheath on his back and cradled it in his arms, his unease with remaining so exposed evident. His gaze wandered the now-empty street, settling on anything that moved. "We'd best clean up here and search for the killer."

Blade left them to close the gates and take care of the woman's remains, confident their search would turn up nothing. Right now, he wanted to get home to the women who waited for him, and to forget about this whole morning.

Hunter could watch his own back for the rest of the day.

* * *

"Airie!"

The single-worded command rang at her from the rocky edge of the lake, whip-sharp and reproachful.

Airie's vision cleared. She'd never heard Desire sound so angry before, and it brought her back to herself faster than anything else could ever do. Water, warm now, swirled around her as she slogged, shame-faced, to shore, her wet skirt dragging heavily behind her.

The stranger had already climbed the rocks to stand near Desire. Water ran from his clothes and spilled over the tops of his boots. His wet denim trousers outlined muscled thighs and buttocks with each jerky movement. He spoke to Desire using words that Airie couldn't quite believe.

"The spawn. Is she yours?"

She expected a denial from Desire, some sort of reproof for the insult, but the terrible slur didn't seem to register with her mother.

Instead, the elderly priestess stared wide-eyed at the amulet around the stranger's neck. She stretched out shaking fingers to touch the jagged lightning bolt etched out of sand. "Where did you get this?"

He lifted one dark blond eyebrow, his puzzlement over her reaction plain, but he kept his response gentle. "I found it a long time ago, floating in a container in a spring."

"How far did it travel," Desire whispered, "and for what purpose?"

Airie pulled herself up the rocks to shore, hampered by the wet weight of her skirt. "He's a trespasser on the goddesses' mountain," she interrupted. "He has to leave."

Desire tore her gaze away from the amulet to look at Airie. "A small token is all that's required. It's not necessary to take all of his belongings from him."

Airie's face flamed, and this time, not from temper but shame. Her mother had seen more than the dunking she'd received. She hadn't wanted for Desire to find out how she collected their alms.

She blamed the stranger for that as well. She turned on him. "Leave whatever you feel you can spare, and then be on your way."

The stranger, water dripping down the sides of his lean face, met her eyes with a look that revealed contempt and a faint surprise, as if he couldn't quite believe who—or what—he was seeing, but that he found her distasteful either way. "Then I'll leave you my name. It's Hunter, but I'm better known as the Demon Slayer."

Desire's face went gray and she grabbed at her chest just as a tremor rocked the ground beneath their feet. She stumbled and would have fallen if the stranger, who was closest, hadn't caught her in his arms and held her steady.

The tremor passed.

Airie righted herself, and with a cry of alarm, she reached for Desire. "Mother!"

"This priestess is your *mother*?" Again, faint surprise, and this time a touch of horror, filled his voice.

Airie was too intent on the woman in his arms to care about him or his reactions to her, although she filed them away to contemplate later. She stroked her mother's cheek. The ashen skin warmed beneath her fingers, but Desire didn't stir.

Her mother was dying. She had to do something—anything—no matter how insignificant, to try and bring her peace in these final moments.

Take her home.

The command came with great clarity. She couldn't permit this woman who had raised her, and loved her, to die here on the mountainside. Desire needed to be home, in the temple, where she could rest and better feel the presence of the goddesses, who would summon her to them when she passed from this life.

The stranger knelt and laid Desire's frail little frame on the cold ground. He headed for the sand swift, standing nearby, its jaws working around something it had eaten. "I'll get a blanket from my pack and—"

Airie began to undress. His head swung around. "What are you doing?"

Her fingers fumbled on the hooks at the waistband of her skirt. She'd thought it obvious. "I can't carry her against my wet clothing. She'll freeze."

The stranger's neck reddened and he busied himself at his pack. He tossed a heavy shirt and pair of coarse trousers over his shoulder at her. Airie caught them. "Put these on. I have a blanket for the priestess."

She changed clothes quickly, not caring if her nudity bothered him. A body was a vessel that contained life. He'd called her spawn. She would never forgive him for the slur. She slipped her arms beneath Desire's shoulders and knees and lifted her easily.

Again, the stranger started, but he said nothing about her strength.

"Here." He reached out as if intending to take Desire from her. "If you aren't afraid of Sally, you can ride and hold the priestess. I'll hand her to you. I'll walk."

She cradled her mother, half turning away to shield her from him. She didn't want him near the temple. She didn't want him to be there for her mother's passing. Grief was an unfamiliar emotion to her. The potential scope of it, already strangling her heart, frightened her, and she was afraid of how she might react to that fear.

"You've done enough. I can carry her home myself."

The stranger dropped his hands to his sides, but he didn't budge. "Those are my clothes and my blanket. I want them back."

He was insufferable. He also served as a buffer against her fear, his hostility rekindling her temper. The anger he provoked, she could control. "Consider them your offering and leave."

"I already gave you an offering," he said. "You asked for what I could spare and I gave you my name."

Hunter. The Demon Slayer.

He had no shame, and they wasted precious time by arguing. Without another word, she passed her mother to him and reached out a hand to take the sand swift's reins to hold it steady.

"Careful!" Hunter barked.

The animal's tongue, hooked with barbs instead of taste buds for capturing prey, flickered out to encircle her wrist. Under normal conditions it might have torn flesh. Airie, however, wasn't so fragile. She rapped the beast's ugly snout with her other fist and it released her. She then scrambled onto its back with less grace than she would have liked, still holding its reins. Hunter's frown darkened as he lifted Desire up in front of her.

Another tremor shook the earth, harder than the first. Beneath her, the sand swift staggered. She clutched her mother tight, digging her knees into the animal's leathery sides to keep them both in the saddle.

The tremor passed. Hunter snatched the reins from Airie's hand. "That does it. We're getting off this mountain."

Panic seized her. "No! If we take my mother away from the temple, the goddesses might not be able to claim her."

"The goddesses are gone."

"If the goddesses are gone, why do I feel their presence in me? Why do they speak to me?"

"That's not the goddesses you feel or hear." He shoved the sand swift with his shoulder so it faced toward the foot of the mountain.

Despite the awkwardness of her mother's limp form in her arms, Airie made a move to slide to the ground.

"Sit still," he commanded.

"Have you no respect for the traditions of the priestesses whatsoever?" she asked, hating that she had to beg but willing to do so for her mother's sake. She swallowed past a painful lump in her throat and blinked back tears of desperation. Already, the first claws of grief tore at her heart. "Please," she whispered. "Does it not bother you that you're making a dying woman abandon her faith at a time when she needs it the most? Have you no decency?"

He stared at her, speechless. His eyes, the deep blue of a mountain lake's crystal depths, swirled with such hostility for her that it took her aback.

"You're a—" His eyes narrowed. "You dare speak to *me* of decency?"

He swore under his breath, but he yanked the beast's head around and they started up the steep path toward the temple.

* * *

Hunter continued to swear as they climbed.

It was the underlying touch of disbelief that, if not for the intervention of the priestess, this spawn could have torn him to shreds or drowned him in the lake that fed his anger.

His amulet had been useless against her.

The priestess's knowledge of the amulet had also caught him off guard—almost as much as the fact that it hadn't reacted to the spawn's presence. Not until her true nature emerged. His ribs creaked with every breath he drew, and he winced. It should have given him her demon strength but it hadn't. Why not?

Anger was the emotion he chose to cling to, because the source of that, he understood. She dared challenge his decency. *His*. His initial attraction to her made him feel somehow unclean. Spawn were an abomination, tolerated in no world. He should walk away now, while he still could, and leave her to whatever fate the mountain dealt her. It was either that, or turn her over to Mamna as he'd been hired to do.

If only she didn't look like a woman, or behave as though she loved the priestess. Was it possible for a spawn to be female? What if there were more spawn like this one in the world, masquerading as mortal women?

The thought chilled him. Demons were one thing. But a spawn born to the mortal world, and mortal in appearance...

He shut his mind's eye against the nightmare vision of his sister's mutilated body, and the grotesque parody of human life that had scrabbled in the dirt beside her remains.

The path to the temple was easy enough for Hunter to follow, even without direction. They crested a rise and there it was—the gleaming white stones of its entrance marred by the scars of demon fire, despite time's obvious efforts to scrub them clean.

The entrance was open. He moved to take the priestess from the spawn's arms, but the spawn slid easily from the sand swift's back and leapt lightly to the ground. She brushed past him, carrying the old woman into the temple herself.

Hunter could leave. He could say he'd seen no signs of the thief, and with the mountain's grumbling considered it unsafe to search. Or he could do as he'd set out to, and take her to Freetown.

And Mamna.

He should at least check on the priestess before he left. He'd never seen the inside of a temple before. He wasn't devout, so it surprised him that no complaint was made when he crossed the threshold. Then again, the argument could be made that he was no more of an intrusion than a spawn.

Light gleamed from the ceiling of the temple's main room. A fire with no discernible source of fuel burned in a grating. A low settee faced the fire. The spawn lowered the priestess to its cushions.

The priestess was awake. "Airie, fetch me my pendant," the old woman murmured, her voice scratchy and filled with pain.

The spawn rose to obey. Hunter, standing close by, caught the fresh, flowery scent of her damp hair. The scent disturbed him even more than her presence. Flowers, to him, were a symbol of all that remained pure in the world, and were out of place on a demon.

He watched the spawn leave the room, unable to help his reaction. She was beautiful, breathtakingly so, and he resented this male awareness of her. This was why so many mortal women fell victim to demons. Physically they were irresistible. Now he, too, had been touched by that same deadly allure.

But it was false, nothing more than bewitchment, and he'd do well to remember it.

He forced his attention back to the priestess. "How do you control her? You wear no special amulet for protection. Is it something about the temple, or the mountain itself? Have the goddesses left that much power here that they can protect you from her?"

If so, and the goddesses' protection was for the priestess alone, what would happen if the priestess was dying, and the spawn was then able to roam free in the world?

The priestess regarded him with something like pity in her eyes. "She's not a monster. She's a young woman who's been sheltered all her life, and she's afraid of what will happen to her once I'm gone."

As well she should be. It would only be a matter of time before the demons came for her. One could argue that his presence here meant they already had.

"That fear alone should have been reason enough for you to destroy her when she was born," he said. "There's no place in the world for her kind. What were you thinking?"

The priestess reached for the sleeve of his jacket, her grip as fragile as the rest of her, although her words were fierce and intense. "I was thinking that she was the most beautiful baby I'd ever seen and that I felt nothing but goodness in her. She was born out of love, and indeed, I love her with all my heart."

His sister had thought her spawn was born of love too—before it ripped her apart. The priestess had been lucky to survive the birthing. Countless other women had not been so fortunate.

Countless more wouldn't be either—not while demons continued to wander the earth. "You understand that the demons will find her and kill her, don't you? That by letting her live, you've made her death a far worse one?"

Pain that had nothing to do with illness crossed the priestess's lined face. "I'd hoped that by raising her to follow the path of the goddesses she would be accepted for what she is. A young woman, with all the failings and graces of any other. She's kind, loving, and knows right from wrong, although she's not perfect and makes mistakes. She made one today. Please don't hold it against her. I could not have asked for a better daughter."

He should cease trying to reason with her. The woman was dying and he wasn't easing her journey. He was too angry, however. He'd thought—hoped—that Mamna had lied to him and he was here on a false errand. "She has a demon inside her."

"She has *Airie* inside her. She decides who she is. She sometimes loses her temper, as she did today, but she's had little experience with the world beyond the mountain. As her experience grows, so will her self-control."

It was too late to make the priestess understand why her daughter could never be allowed to leave the mountain alive, or that what he had to do, he did for both the world's benefit and also for Airie's.

Airie.

He'd already begun to think of her by name. If she were truly good, as the priestess believed, then he would be doing her a mercy, because she couldn't stay isolated here forever. Even if the mountain did continue to protect her, loneliness would eventually make her seek out other living beings. What then?

"I've been praying for a sign from the goddesses." The old woman paused, caught her breath, and continued. "Take her with you. You can teach her control. You wear protection. I never needed it, but until Airie gains full control of herself in the outside world, there may be more times like today when you will. I promise you, they'll be rare. She knows right from wrong."

She didn't know what she asked of him. If he took Airie with him, she'd be passed on to the demons. He tried not to think of what the Demon Lord would do to her before he killed her, because kill her he would. He didn't permit spawn to live, any more than a mortal who stumbled upon one would. It would be better for everyone involved if he killed her now. He'd tell Mamna he'd had no choice in the matter, which was true.

"I'm sorry, I—" Hunter began, but then Airie walked into the room and he could say no more.

She'd changed her clothes and tied her hair into a long, heavy braid that touched her waist. She cradled a rainbow-colored stone on a golden chain in the palm of one hand. The pale, goddess-infused lighting of the temple caught the amulet's colors and shot them to the darkest corners of the room. She carried the amulet to the priestess and tried to press it into her thin fingers.

The priestess refused it. "It's yours now," she said. "Wear it always, and think of your mother often. Remember me in your prayers."

Hunter stood on the periphery of the room, uncertain what to do and feeling more like an unwanted intruder with each passing breath. Airie kissed her mother's cheek as the priestess's eyes slid shut. Moments later, a dry rattle deep in the old woman's chest told him the end was near. Airie clung to her hand, holding it tight against her breast, tears streaming down her cheeks.

Hunter had seen death more times than he cared to remember. He'd experienced it firsthand with his own sister. He'd felt the gut-wrenching pain of its touch. Never before, however, had he witnessed a raw grief such as this. Airie's was something he knew he would never forget—not so much because of its intensity as for its quiet dignity. It was as if she drew every emotion she felt deep within her body and held it there so it couldn't escape.

But it was the gentleness in the touch of a spawn for its mother that unsettled him the most. *She's kind, loving, and knows right from wrong...*

He felt the jaws of a giant, invisible trap slamming shut around his neck. He couldn't kill this woman and call it merciful, or for the good of the world. Not while there was the slightest chance the priestess had been right about her.

He let her sit in silence for a long time, saying whatever goodbyes she felt needed to be said, then placed a firm hand on her shoulder. Time was passing, and this mountain was the last place he wanted to be if the earth tremors began again.

Airie started at his touch, as if she'd forgotten all about his presence.

"We have to go," he said. "Gather your things."

She looked up at him with dark, tragic eyes, and again he was struck by the illusion of beauty and innocence she presented. Instinct had him wanting to reach for her, to take her in his arms and offer comfort.

Then his ribs twitched with pain and he remembered she wasn't all that innocent, no matter what her mother believed about her or how she presented herself. She possessed demon allure. He called to mind an image of his sister and her torn remains, and of the monstrosity she'd died giving birth to, and any pity he might have felt for Airie fled.

She was a monster.

"I'm not going anywhere," she said. "I can't leave my mother." A hint of hysteria tempered her words.

Spawn or not, this was awkward for him, and as always when Hunter didn't know what else to do, he opted for plain, harsh truth. "Your mother is gone. She asked me to take you with me."

"I heard her." A shiver began in her as if she were cold, or in deep, physical pain, but then she pulled herself tight to contain it. "Don't worry. You won't need protection from me because I'm not going anywhere with you. If there's no place in the world for my kind, then I choose to stay here."

So she'd caught his words. The sense of being somehow in the wrong made him angry all over again. "You can't stay here. We'll have to make a place for you elsewhere."

When she looked at him, it was as if she saw inside him and had no liking for what she found. Coldly polite, her contempt lashed him. "First, tell me something, Demon Slayer. What are you doing on Goddess Mountain? Are you on some sort of pilgrimage?"

He was at a loss. He hadn't anticipated difficult decisions. He hadn't thought about having to explain himself to her when he'd set out from Freetown. She was the criminal, not he. While he hadn't intended to tie her up and carry her across his saddle, the way he did when collecting bounty—past bounties had been male—some stupid part of him had assumed that since she was female, she'd accompany him without resistance.

Or that Mamna had lied and he'd go home without her.

Another tremor shook the room, saving him from having to give her an answer. He stumbled against her, knocking her from her chair. They fell to the floor in a tangle of arms and legs and he shielded her with his body. Bits of the ceiling bounced like hailstones off his back.

A second tremor, far more intense, rumbled deep beneath the temple floor, then rammed to the surface. Fine fissures shot up the walls and the temple's odd lighting flickered and dimmed. A loud crack from beyond the open entrance made it sound as if the whole mountain were splitting in two, and Sally, waiting outside, let out a bellow of fright.

Hunter had only a few more seconds before the animal bolted, with or without them. He grabbed Airie's hand and jerked her along behind him through a smokescreen of dust as he ran from the temple to the sand swift, adrenaline lending him enough added strength to override her half-hearted protests. He hoisted her into the saddle and scrambled up after her.

The temple collapsed. A slide of boulders, dirt and debris buried its entrance.

"My *mother*!" she cried.

Hunter didn't waste time contemplating how they'd been mere seconds from joining the dead priestess in her tomb, or responding to the agony in Airie's voice. All of that would come later. Instead, he gave the sand swift its head. He intended for them to make it off the mountain before it fell beneath them.

The ground shook as they hurtled down the narrow path, packs bouncing and swaying.

CHAPTER FIVE

Dagan found the brutal harshness of the desert much to his liking, and so he'd carved his stronghold from its stark red cliffs. Demon fire flickered from sconces lining the earthen walls of the main hall, casting shadows that danced across the gathering and into the far corners.

The stone platform on which he stood placed him well above the restless crowd. As he looked out on them, he was reminded of how pitiful their remaining numbers were. He'd once commanded tens of thousands—and enough demon fire to scorch this entire world. The last time he'd summoned his fire, it had barely been enough to burn a single mountain.

And to do even that, he'd required the aid of a priestess.

He rolled his shoulders. Prolonged periods in mortal form created discomfort, but overall, it was the one best suited for life on this world. Mortality fascinated him. It was governed by the passage of time, heightening the urge to taste life's fleeting physical pleasures such as immortals had never before experienced, and so demons assumed two—one was used for hunting men, the other for pursuing women.

Time, however, had begun to affect them in other, less pleasurable ways. Dagan held up one hand and examined it by the light of the torches. The flesh over the knuckles had stretched and thinned over the years. His hair, once black as onyx, now bore a few threads of silver. Quite often, after prolonged periods of inactivity, his joints stiffened and even ached. Many, although not all, of those gathered around him were faring no better.

The reality was that Dagan now found himself at the head of an aging army. Time had become the goddesses' most effective weapon against them, and he had to find a way to escape before it was too late. If spawn were the key to why they were trapped, then there could be others disguised in mortal form like the one on Goddess Mountain. Until he knew for certain, he was taking no more chances.

He stepped to the front of the platform. The horde facing him gradually quieted. When they were silent and all he could hear was the sputtering flames of the torches, he spoke. "The mating with mortal women ends now."

An angry murmur began at the back of the room, quickly spreading throughout. One of the demons who'd chosen to keep his hunting form for this gathering nudged his way forward through the crowd. Firelight glanced off bone-plated red skin as thick as a sand swift's hide. Ridges lined a curved spine. Two short, sharp-pointed horns sprang from the sides of a broad forehead. His name was Be'el, and in his manhunting form even the bravest among them thought twice before accepting his challenge. His was the name given to Dagan the night of his meeting with Mamna.

Dagan had no intention of letting him live.

"We followed you to this world for the promise of its pleasures," Be'el said. "We fought mortals to earn them. Now you wish to deny them to us?"

Dagan didn't shift to his manhunting form, knowing it would insult and enrage Be'el that he did not. An added advantage to his mortal form was that he wouldn't succumb as easily to bloodlust, and he needed to keep a calm head. He lifted his shoulders and swung his arms in anticipation. "We came here to bring the goddesses to their knees before us."

"And we did."

There was a rumble of agreement. Dagan waited for it to die down. "No. They ran from us. And now they're free while we are stranded here, trapped in time."

"Time." Be'el spat on the ground. "Time is nothing to us. If not for you, we could rule this world and all its pleasures would be ours for the taking."

"For how long?" Dagan asked. "Until the last of us grows old and dies?"

"We are immortals."

Death wasn't a concept any more easily understood by demons than they grasped time. They feared neither. Freedom, however, was something all immortals valued. So was power. To claim one meant to risk losing the other, because when one immortal was killed in battle by another, the victor owned the death and the dead became a slave.

But victory came with its own heavy price. The dead didn't give up freedom willingly. For Be'el to challenge the Demon Lord, he had to believe Dagan weak enough for him to enslave. That challenge could not go unanswered.

"We're bound by the laws of the universe," Dagan said. "While we're confined to this world, we are as subject to time as any mortal."

"Then we should be able to enjoy all of the pleasures time has to offer."

Again, there was a rumble of agreement. Louder, this time. Soon, the crowd would grow completely out of control.

"Clear the floor," Dagan commanded, turning the rumble into a roar of eager excitement as he leaped to the ground. Demons emptied the area in front of the platform, pushing back to the far walls of the cavern. Many of the spectators scrambled to the platform for a better view of the fight to come.

Be'el stepped into the cleared space. Dagan beckoned with cupped fingers for him to approach. Be'el didn't waste time, instead shooting out one massive, fisted hand in a roundhouse blow aimed at Dagan's temple.

Dagan's mortal form was lighter and more agile, and used the thin desert air with greater efficiency. He easily dodged the first blow, and the next, dancing around the floor on the balls of his feet, making Be'el chase him.

Be'el roared with rage and frustration.

The onlookers didn't care for Dagan's tactics either. Their discontent forced him to present one shoulder and absorb the next ham-fisted blow. He swallowed the pain and remained standing. A mortal form wasn't built for this type of abuse. That his could take it served as a reminder to everyone present as to why he was Lord.

He would give them another reminder.

He summoned a ball of red flame to the tips of his fingers that licked up his arms and shot from his eyes. A spray of sparks danced from the ground to the cavern ceiling. He threw the ball of fire at Be'el. It caught him in the chest, ignited, and sent him staggering. Dagan then aimed a kick at his knee.

Be'el's own bulk toppled him. Once he was down, he rolled on the stone floor in an attempt to extinguish the flames, but Dagan didn't allow the fire to retreat until the smell of roasting meat filled every crevice of the cavern and the walls rang with Be'el's screams. He planted a bare foot on Be'el's smoldering chest, and bending, slammed both fists into Be'el's ears hard enough to draw blood.

Now that he'd drawn it, bloodlust made him want more.

Be'el, however, was not yet defeated, and age had slowed Dagan more than he wanted the others to see. Be'el's feet caught him from below, lifting and tossing him to the side. Dagan rolled as he landed, waited for Be'el to follow through with the attack, then grappled him into a headlock. One of Be'el's claws scored a tear down his arm, and the combination of fiery pain and the smell of his own blood made Dagan lose the last of his control. He shifted to his hunting form, bit into Be'el's shoulder, cracking through protective plating, and tore the flesh from the bone.

Be'el howled in pain and anger. Blood dripped from Dagan's chin as he swallowed the mouthful of hot flesh. He crammed the claws of one hand into the wound and wrenched until the exposed bone popped free from Be'el's shoulder. Be'el panted, his agony evident, but still, he didn't cede.

Dagan crooked his arm around Be'el's neck. This would be a fierce death for him to own. The more of these he possessed, the greater the risk they might someday manage to turn on him. It was why demons rarely fought each other, and why they enjoyed hunting men.

But Dagan wasn't a demon. He was their Lord. With a jerk of his elbow, he snapped Be'el's neck. The blue-green haze of the dead demon's soul settled over him, slowly seeping under his skin to join the others already in his possession.

The cheers of the onlookers echoed throughout the cavern, bringing him back to the moment, and he tossed Be'el's limp body aside for the others to finish. Breathing heavily, he shifted back to man form so his lungs wouldn't have to labor so hard for air. He had two of his supporters kneel so he could stand on their shoulders, and they raised him tall above the rioting crowd.

Drawn blood meant that tonight, there would be no holding them back and he didn't want them turning on each other. Their numbers were few enough. Let them turn on those the goddesses had favored instead. Let the demons destroy everything the goddesses had loved, and leave nothing for them to return to once the demons were gone.

"There will be no more mating with mortal women," Dagan repeated, shouting over the crazed cacophony of the crowd. He lifted a blood-drenched fist against their displeasure. "But do what you will with the men."

With that, he released them into the night.

Dagan, however, didn't join them. He abandoned the empty cavern to soar above the cooling sands of the desert. The winds cleared his head. When he'd first come to this world, he'd found the freedom of flying on air intoxicating. He'd believed mortal women were too beautiful to resist.

Then he'd seen a goddess in her mortal form for the first time.

The pull of the wind had been strong that night, he recalled. He'd let it fill his wings and carry him far out into the night, as it did now, closer than he'd ever before dared to travel toward a mountain that was protected against him and his kind.

Something below had caught his attention that night. A sparkle of starlight on water, perhaps. Or on wet, golden skin. A faint hint of perfume. He'd let the wind drop him to the sand, where he'd used his mortal form to carry him to the edge of a small oasis.

He'd known her for a goddess the instant he set eyes on her. No mere mortal could be so perfect, or capture a demon's attention so completely. He'd heard stories that a goddess was as alluring to mortal men as demons were to women and felt nothing but contempt for such human weakness. Seeing this one, however, made him understand.

Clad only in the moonlight and her long, fair hair, her skin shone gold against the pool's glassy black surface. She was alone, she was vulnerable...and in that moment, he'd decided take from her what was his by right. A goddess was the other half of a demon's self, promised to him at the dawn of the universe. The goddesses, however, had refused to be claimed.

Until now.

He took a step closer, and her head lifted from the water in alarm. "Who's there?" she demanded.

Dagan brushed through a small stand of cottonwood and without a word, entered the clearing.

Her eyes grew wide. "You're a demon."

"And you're a goddess." He let his desire smolder for her to see. The west wind had called to him for a reason this particular night. Here, at last, was the one he'd been promised. *"Come to me. I won't harm you."*

She, too, felt the pull between them, even though she hesitated like a gazelle deciding whether or not it should bolt. He moved closer, carefully, so as not to alarm her further, and reached out with one finger to caress the soft, damp curve of her cheek.

With that small touch, the spell shattered.

But not, he thought bitterly, before she'd captured him.

Her name was Allia, or so she'd told him. To this day he didn't know for certain what had drawn her so deep into the desert, and demon territory. He didn't want to believe that it was as Mamna had told him—that she'd been sent by her sisters to seduce and enslave him. He had no reason to believe Mamna spoke the truth—other than that, somehow, Allia had shackled him to her in a way that he could not now escape. He dreamed of her often, and if his own kind knew how he longed for her, they would turn on him for the weakness he displayed.

Mortal life could bring great pleasure, yes. But it also brought indescribable pain. He needed his immortality back. He needed to be free again. If he couldn't have those things, then he wished only for the passage of time to ease this terrible sense of loss that so far refused to abate. Allia might not have been his, but he was hers.

Across the giant dunes of the desert, past the playa and the mesas, the scorched mountain of the goddesses kept silent watch over the mortal world, a stark reminder of what he'd tried to do to them and failed.

A faint rumbling began in the desert earth beneath his feet. The newly-dead demon thrashed inside him. Dagan fell back in surprise as the tip of the far-off, shadowed mountain folded inward.

Then it disappeared from the black, star-littered horizon as if it had never existed.

* * *

Blade had created a quiet haven for himself on the third floor of his saloon. It was sparsely furnished, with a double bed and a single window cut from the sloped ceiling. A plain wardrobe and one heavy chair carved from oak filled the room to capacity.

He sat in the chair in the deep darkness that descended before dawn and stared through the window at the black and empty sky, a cup of lavender tea cooling in his hands. He'd taken off his trousers and shirt, since the heat of the day tended to pool beneath the saloon's rafters. Although the heat was long gone now, he continued to lounge in his underwear.

The street outside was quiet. The wind had died down, but it was far too late for anyone with money to spend to be out. Even the thieves and murderers would be long in their beds.

A tentative knock sounded at Blade's door, followed by a soft voice. "May I come in?"

"If you don't mind the way I'm dressed. Or rather not," he replied.

"I've seen it all before. I doubt if there are any new surprises."

Ruby opened the door a crack and slipped inside before closing it firmly behind her. She placed the small lantern she carried on the windowsill, pulled her wrap tighter, then perched primly on the edge of his bed, her back straight, bare feet dangling a few inches above the plank floor. She was dressed for bed. Her thick red hair swung in loose curls at her shoulders.

The flowery scent of her soap floated around him. He and Ruby had been together a long time. She'd nursed him back to health after Hunter rescued him from the demon. They'd started the saloon together. They didn't love each other. Neither of them was capable of the emotion. But he certainly felt more loyalty to her than he did anyone else, except maybe Hunter, and knew she felt the same.

"What happened in town today?" she asked.

Blade sighed, then scrubbed a hand across his eyes. "Mamna condemned a woman to death."

"I thought you might be the one who threw that knife," Ruby said. Understanding and sympathy colored her tone.

"She was a stupid woman who should have known enough to keep her tongue still. She wasn't worth wasting your pity on."

Ruby reached over and patted the deep, corded scar that ran the length of his thigh. "I wasn't wasting my pity on her."

Blade's lips thinned. He shrugged away from her hand to stare out the window once more. "I don't need it either."

"You're testy because the woman you feel you should have killed is untouchable."

"Mamna's not untouchable. She's as mortal as the rest of us. But I can't go after her the way I should."

"Because of us?" Ruby asked. "Sapphire, Jasmine and me?"

Blade didn't reply, which he supposed was answer enough.

Ruby settled her clasped hands in her lap. "We can look after ourselves, Blade. We had to before we met you and we can do so again. Don't feel as if you have to protect us."

He shrugged. "My time is better spent on you. What would be the point in killing her? If not Mamna making the laws, it would be someone else."

"If you were so worried about our safety, then why did you kill that poor woman? You must have known what would happen to us if you'd been caught."

He placed a palm on the scar on his thigh and made a confession he would only ever say to her because she already knew his weaknesses and didn't think less of him for them. "I couldn't sleep if I'd stood back and let her be raped, then eaten alive by a blood-frenzied demon. Although it's made no difference. I can't sleep now either, so I wasted my time and energy and risked all our lives for nothing."

"It was hardly for nothing." Ruby laced and unlaced her fingers, twisting them. "Despite what you think, you're a good man. You've reaffirmed for me that there are still people in this world who care about others. And as long as there are people like you, it will grow to be a better place. It might take a while, that's all."

How she could be so optimistic, Blade would never know. Ruby's life had been a hard one. The faint light of the lantern softened her face and lent it an air of youthfulness that was long gone in reality. He wished he'd known her before she'd become a whore, and maybe saved her from it, but she seemed satisfied with her lot in life and didn't waste her time dwelling on what could no longer be. She saved her money against the day when she was too old to earn her living on her back, and when that day came, Blade thought he might marry her.

Married women or prostitutes. In the wake of a goddess-ruled world, if a woman didn't serve the priestesses she had to serve men.

Ruby rose to leave, but a slight rumbling began in the floorboards beneath her feet, and she grabbed for the lantern to keep it from sliding off the windowsill and crashing to the floor. She looked to Blade with alarm in her eyes.

"What in the world was that?"

* * *

Airie smelled the fear of the animal beneath her.

The cracking of the earth and the crash of tumbling rocks and trees hadn't abated, so she bent over the sand swift's scaly neck and held on as best she could. Unfamiliar with riding, she slid sideways. Hunter, seated behind her, wrapped his arm around her waist and tightened his grip to keep her from falling. He held the reins in his other hand, although he'd given the sand swift its head.

"The path's gone!" he shouted in her ear.

Airie lifted her head to see what he meant. Fallen pine and rock choked the common path, the one used by the goddesses' faithful. It was impassible. She pointed to her left. "This way. There's a deer path through here that I sometimes use."

Hunter jerked hard on the reins. The sand swift shifted direction too quickly, smashing off the common path into the bushes, and he had to fight to bring the panicked animal back under control.

A branch slapped Airie across the face, knocking her from her seat. She landed on her back in a scratchy thicket, her skirt tangled around her knees. She looked up from her thorny bed to where the moon should have bathed the top of the mountain in its pale light.

Shock numbed her. The mountain peak had imploded. There was no other way to describe it.

Hunter steadied the sand swift, brought it around to where she lay, and offered her his hand. His face tensed when he looked toward the mountain and saw what held her immobile.

"Don't look back," he said.

Airie took his hand and allowed him to pull her into the saddle, behind him this time, and once again they were hurtling down the mountain at a speed that took her breath away.

Without warning, a chasm gaped open in front of them, cutting off their escape. The sand swift reared on its hind legs. It twisted to the side, flipping itself over. Hunter rolled from the saddle, pulling Airie with him, dragging them both clear before they could be crushed beneath the animal's considerable weight.

Airie scrambled to her feet. Panic clawed her throat raw at the terrible sound of the sand swift's screams. It lay on its side, chest heaving, kicking its feet in terror and pain. A splintered pine, broken off by a falling boulder now resting a few paces from the chasm's edge, had impaled it.

Airie forgot her own fear in the face of its suffering. Ignoring the flailing, razor-sharp claws and the heaving earth beneath her feet, she stretched out her fingertips in an instinctive attempt to ease its pain. Hunter lunged from his prone position to snag her skirt and stop her from getting too close to the dangerous animal, but she sidestepped him. He already thought she was a monster. What did it matter if she confirmed his opinion?

She couldn't leave the animal to die in agony.

Making soothing noises deep in her throat, intent on calming its mind, she placed her hand on the sand swift's belly. Immediately, its legs stopped churning and the clear lids of its eyes drooped closed.

Hunter moved to her side. He hadn't uttered a single sound.

"Help me lift it free," she said.

Between the two of them, they raised the animal clear of the splintered and bloodied pine.

Once the sand swift was free, Airie probed the entry wound with her fingers. She sent warm, healing thoughts into the worst of the animal's injuries, along with her prayers, relieved to find that nothing vital had been too damaged for her to mend. Severed muscles, torn tendons and mangled flesh knitted at her command. Moments later, the sand swift was back on its feet, and in a rapture of affection, tried to lick at her face with its rough-edged tongue.

"Here, now!" Hunter caught the tongue in his fist before it could lash Airie's cheek.

The mountain's rumbling had stopped, and a terrible stillness settled over the woods. Airie rubbed her hands over her arms, although the cold she felt didn't come from the air. Something more was missing from the mountain than the usual sounds of animal life. Desolation tore at her, leaving her raw and bleeding on the inside. The presence of the goddesses was gone. The passing of her mother had taken them from her too, and only an empty place in her soul remained. She was alone in a world that wouldn't want her, with a man who disliked and distrusted her. She wanted her mother, and she wanted to cry, but she wouldn't do so again in front of someone who hated her for nothing more than being born.

She looked around. Everything she owned had been abandoned in the rush of their departure. She had nothing—no clothes, no money—except for the amulet her mother had given her. As for Hunter's possessions, only the saddle remained of the things the sand swift had carried. What wasn't smashed and useless had fallen into the newly formed crack in the earth.

"Is Sally okay for us to ride?" Hunter asked.

Airie nodded, unable to speak, and they remounted.

Blackness and silence settled on the mountain. Their descent was slow and frequently blocked by fallen debris. More than once they had to dismount to clear the way. Other than to give direction to each other as they moved what they could and skirted around what they could not, she and Hunter didn't speak.

* * *

Hunter had expected the scent of the sand swift's blood to drive Airie into a demon's frenzy. Instead, she'd saved the creature's life.

Something about that wasn't right.

He asked himself how a priestess, selected for service to the goddesses because of her plainness, had incited the lust of a demon. Her advanced age, ill health and scarred face might have concealed the fact that she was beautiful in her youth, but she would already have been middle-aged by the time Airie was conceived. Certainty had him gripping the reins tighter. The priestess had lied to him, but about what, and for what purpose?

He ducked his head to avoid a low branch, edging it aside so it wouldn't strike Airie, seated behind him. That she believed the priestess to be her mother, he didn't dispute. Which meant the priestess had also lied to her.

He had no idea what to do next.

The heat from her clasped hands spread through his abdomen. When he turned his head, the feminine scent of her skin and hair engulfed him and made him ache in a way he could scarcely believe. One cheek rested on his shoulder, her weight against him suggesting she was close to sleep, and implying a level of trust in him that he didn't deserve. Guilt gnawed at him. He pushed it away. He was the Demon Slayer and she was part demon. If she trusted him it was because she had no one else to turn to, not because he'd misled her. He had no cause to trust her either.

Except that she saved Sally's life, his conscience rebuked him. And she loved her mother, who she'd been taking care of.

He couldn't wait to be rid of her.

They continued down the mountain in silence.

When the first fingers of dawn painted the sky red, they came to a better-traveled path at the foot of the mountain. There, the land leveled off and the forest thinned. Hunter had avoided this path on his way to the temple. It looked well-traveled, and he'd wished to avoid any trouble with the locals. He had no choice but to explore it now. The items he'd lost on the mountain were necessities for travel, and he had to replace them.

"Where does this path lead?" he asked, tossing the words over his shoulder.

"To a trading post." Airie straightened behind him. "I don't want to go there."

Fatigue and frustration, as well as hours of awkward awareness of her pressed against him, sparked an already short temper. "Tried to sell them something you stole and got caught at it, did you?"

"Yes."

That monosyllabic response stopped him and made him wonder as to the real reason she wanted to avoid the place, and if he should be worried, although in the end it wouldn't matter. They'd never make it through the desert to Freetown without adequate supplies. Settlements were too few and far between, with little in them to spare.

"Would anyone at this trading post recognize you?" he asked, without any real hope that they wouldn't. She was unusually tall and very beautiful. She carried herself like a goddess.

Or a demon.

"I don't know," she replied. "When I had to trade, I always went dressed as a boy."

Perhaps there was hope after all. They wouldn't need to be there very long. "Then this time, you'll go as a woman. When we get there, you're to do exactly as I tell you." He could pass her off as a slave.

"I'd rather wait here for you."

She made a move as if to slip from the saddle, but he reached behind him and grabbed her hip to stop her. "I don't think so."

He couldn't let her out of his sight. The world had enough problems without another demon on the loose, especially one who was not at all what she seemed. But she refused to grasp that she was his prisoner.

"I'm not used to riding," she insisted. "I'm tired."

The weary crack in her voice almost swayed him. Then he thought of her flaming eyes and how she'd intended to rob him. While he could hardly blame her for doing what was necessary in order to survive, it made him wary of her motives. He had bruises.

His next words surprised him because, although churlish and grudging, they weren't what he'd intended to say. "Very well. We'll rest for a bit. But we stay together."

His hand was still cupping her hip. He removed it, and she dismounted stiffly. He experienced another twinge of guilt. Throughout the long night, she'd done her fair share in clearing their escape route and not once had she complained. The danger was past, at least for now. She'd earned a rest.

He swung out of the saddle and turned Sally loose to forage for food in the brush at the side of the path. Airie paced, stretching her legs and saying nothing, but her gaze continually returned to the remains of the smoldering mountain.

Hunter could think of no distractions to offer. He reached into a pocket of his duster and found some hardtack, then thrust it at her.

"Here," he said. "Eat something."

She stopped pacing. Her eyes, a soft, deep, feminine brown now, with no trace of flame, fixed on him. "Do I look like one?"

"Like what?" he asked, confused.

"Like a demon. I've never seen one."

"No." He slid the hardtack she ignored back into his pocket. Then, because he didn't want either of them to forget what she was, he added, "Not right now."

Her gaze returned to the crumbled mountain. "This is the way I always look."

She had to know that was a lie. Rumors to the contrary had spread all the way to Mamna, and he'd seen the fire she contained for himself, so it would be foolish to let down his guard. Eventually, her true form would emerge.

He couldn't claim that she'd been using the mortal one she currently wore to seduce him, however. Truth be told, she didn't seem to like him at all, whereas most women did. His jaw tightened. The thought of being judged by a demon and found wanting was far from amusing.

He didn't like inconsistencies, and she was full of them. His aching ribs reminded him of her demonic strength, yet what sort of spawn cried over its mother, then healed a dying animal when common sense and self-preservation dictated it would be better to abandon it?

But what sort of man abandoned a woman to demons?

He grabbed Sally's reins, unsettled.

"Break's over," he snarled. "Get back in the saddle."

CHAPTER SIX

Mamna had forgotten nothing of her time in the temple on Goddess Mountain. It spun inside her head as a collage of thousands of thoughtless little kindnesses and cruelties that often infiltrated her sleep.

As it did tonight.

There was always one particular incident that stood out from the rest. When the goddesses chose the sweetest of their sisters to tempt the Demon Lord, Mamna was tasked with watching over her to see that she didn't fall in return. It never occurred to any of them that poor, deformed, homely Mamna might not be able to resist a demon any easier than other woman, mortal or otherwise. It certainly hadn't occurred to Mamna.

But she'd fallen in love with the Demon Lord on sight, and his blindness to anyone but the goddess chosen for him had cut her far worse than any other slight experienced in a lifetime of humiliations. She'd wanted only to be treated with some of the same gentle kindness he had shown to her immortal mistress. She'd wanted her own chance to serve him. Telling him of his goddess lover's deception had seemed like the perfect opportunity.

He'd been waiting for his lover in their usual place on the night Mamna finally gathered her courage to approach him. She kept her head down, her eyes on the cool, dew-dampened grass beneath her bare, misshapen feet.

"*You have been betrayed,*" she'd said.

At first, the Demon Lord had refused to believe her.

"*Watch and see,*" Mamna declared. "*She will offer you a pendant, a small mountain stone of no obvious beauty or value, with all of the colors of the rainbow. She'll tell you it's a symbol of her love for you. She'll tell you it offers immunity against the goddesses, just as the amulet you gave her protects her from demons. But it is the same stone the*" *goddesses give to their favored mortal men. It is meant to enslave you. It will bind you to her as surely as it binds them."* Mamna held out her hand, raising her eyes to his. She had a handful of the same colored stones, some set into pendants, others as yet unpolished. *"Have you seen these before?"*

She could tell by the look on his face that he had.

Mamna withdrew to a nearby hiding place to watch what happened next. When the goddess had shown up with her offering for him, the Demon Lord rejected it with such violence that the protection of the amulet he'd already given her was all that saved her. The depth of his anger, however, had set the world on fire. Mamna had carried that demon fire onto sacred ground for him, and the goddesses had fled before it.

What he had allowed his demons to do to mortal men in the days that followed the departure of the goddesses still made Mamna shudder, even in her dreams. Betraying immortals, she had discovered, was not for the timid.

She never slept well after the fragments of those memories woke her in sweat-soaked terror, and tonight, when the shaking of the earth began, she was already wide awake.

The protective amulet she wore tucked beneath her nightdress remained silent, but she withdrew it for added reassurance that she was not under demon attack. She rubbed it between her fingers. Its smoothness was gone. The fine cracks that shattered the desert varnish after she'd summoned the demon that afternoon had deepened considerably. Had it lost the last of its power?

Was that what this trembling of the earth signified?

She crawled from the soft, warm depths of her canopied bed and padded across the swaying floor. Thin shafts of moonlight beckoned to her through the slit where the two heavy brocade curtains didn't quite meet. She inched the crack wider and peered outside with one eye.

Her bedroom window, crafted from cut glass and exorbitantly expensive, overlooked the manicured garden of one of the many fortified inner compounds designed to keep Freetown's wealthier inhabitants safe from thieves and murderers. She pulled one curtain farther back and tried to see beyond the city's main walls to the east, where the mountain dominated the horizon, but the night was too dark.

The anxious voices of people swarming in the street outside the compound reached her ears. They, too, wondered what the quaking earth signified. The last time, it had meant the mountain burned and the goddesses had abandoned them.

The tremors slowly died away.

Mamna watched for a long time as the crowds thinned, and eventually, the street emptied. The earthquake might have something to do with the spawn on the mountain. It might have much to do with her damaged amulet as well. The timing was too much of a coincidence, and she didn't believe in those.

She'd become far too complacent about her position. Now, she was vulnerable. She had to act.

Soon.

The godseeker, Pillar, had explained his grand plan to her. He'd said the godseekers would oversee the goddess's army while the priestesses acted as her advisors, and Freetown would open its doors to all who would follow her. In short, he expected Mamna to pay for this war.

She'd committed to nothing. Then when he left, she'd had him followed. He'd taken accommodations in an area of the city with enough room for his northern followers to join him. More were coming. A few discreet questions informed her many were already here. Whether she liked it or not, war was inevitable. And it was on her doorstep.

She hadn't decided yet whose side she'd be on. She did know that the Demon Lord couldn't find out that she was after the Slayer's amulet, so shifting suspicion onto the godseekers would work well for her.

She remained at the window for several more hours.

When night shifted to morning, in an explosion of sunshine, Mamna crawled into her bed.

* * *

Hunter and Airie reached the trading post before mid-morning. They rode into the main yard of a long, low, weathered building constructed of shaved logs. A creaky, sagging verandah lined with barrels ran its full length.

The small trading post was what Hunter would expect to find in a remote location once devastated by fire. The logs for its construction would have been hauled from the far side of the mountain where the fire had not been as rampant. Here, though, on the westward face of the lower mountain region, signs of the fire remained. Fast growing thickets of conifers had squeezed out much of the struggling hardwood in the forests, while a few saplings of the hardier varieties had persevered and thrived.

He hadn't, however, expected to find it completely abandoned. It sat well out of range of any possible landslides caused by the mountain's implosion and would have made a good gathering place for any homesteaders scattered throughout the region. That it was empty suggested people remembered those terror-filled days of the demon fires and most likely preferred to take their chances in the desert.

A part of him was disappointed to find the trading post empty. He'd half-expected Airie's appearance to trigger some sort of riot, and at the moment a good fight would be just the thing he needed to burn off some of the frustration he felt.

He entered the low-ceilinged building with caution, Airie behind him, and made certain that it was, indeed, abandoned. Only the groan of the floorboards welcomed them. Everything appeared to be untouched, so the looting had not yet begun.

Airie gagged, pressing a hand to her face, covering her nose and mouth. "I smell blood."

A few dark patches of viscous red liquid stained the parched flooring. When Hunter looked up, he saw more damp stains on the ceiling where it had trickled through the cracks. The hairs on the back of his neck stood on end. He was alone with a spawn against whom he had no defense. If she went into a bloodlust, he was as good as dead.

"There's a young boy who lives here. He might need my help," she said, her eyes wide and free of flame, her expression reflecting nothing but concern. She caught her skirt in one hand and hurried toward a set of crude wooden stairs, braced against one wall of the room on the far side of the mercantile counter.

Hunter blocked her way. Something was terribly wrong, but so far, she'd kept control of herself and he'd prefer to keep it that way. "I'll check the upper floor. You wait here."

She stood at the foot of the stairs while he climbed them, his hand on the gun holstered at his hip. He'd left his sword strapped to his saddle. The amulet around his neck remained reassuringly cold.

The entrance to the upper floor was barred by a trap door. He eased it upward with the flat of one palm, then cautiously poked his head through the opening. Three bodies sprawled on the floor. Nothing moved. Whatever had happened here, the danger had passed.

He climbed the last few steps, levering his lower body into the room with the help of a handrail attached to the top of the stairs.

It was as if something deranged had been unleashed. The destruction was absolute. Furniture was smashed into pieces.

Bedding and clothes had been shredded. Kitchen cupboards were torn from the walls, their contents strewn from one end of the loft to the other. Two of the bodies belonged to a man and a woman, although it was difficult to determine their ages. They were badly mutilated. The third was that of a boy. He was coated in blood. An angelic, blood-speckled face stared open-eyed at the ceiling. He appeared to have ripped out his own throat.

Hunter had seen a lot of things in his life. Nothing explained this. The scene hinted at demon frenzy, but his amulet gave no indication that a demon had ever been here. Certainly, there'd been none here recently enough to be responsible. And there were no bloody footprints leading to the stairs where Hunter stood. The windows remained closed tight, as they would be at night.

He studied the boy's body for a long time. Then, he backed down into the stairwell and eased the trap door behind him.

"Well?" Airie asked, her face anxious.

"There's a lot of blood on the floor. But the upstairs is empty. The people who lived here likely fled with the others."

She didn't question him, but moved out of his way as he reached the foot of the stairs, then followed him across the room.

He tossed her a sack from a pile he found beside the counter and began to fill one of his own, anxious to be gone. "Take anything you think we might need."

She caught the sack but didn't move. "I have no money to pay for what I take. I left everything behind."

The owner no longer had any use for money. Hunter swept some dried meat from a hook on a rafter and dropped it into his sack. "You're a thief. This isn't a good time to develop morals."

"I told you. I am not a thief."

He stopped with his hand on a jar of preserves. "You tried to rob me."

"I asked only for what the goddesses demand from anyone who enters the mountain. You aren't exempt from that law."

He struggled to be reasonable. "Since the goddesses are gone and you aren't a priestess, I'd say that does make you a thief."

Her expression grew remote, as if she'd closed herself off. "I did what had to be done. My mother is—was—a priestess, and therefore entitled to receive the alms she could no longer collect for herself."

The reference to her mother, reminding him of her loss and her reaction to it, didn't improve his mood. She was a thief and a spawn. Those were the two most important things about her he needed to remember, and what silenced his conscience when he thought about the future waiting for her.

"I'm not getting into an argument with you right now." They had to leave. "Fill that sack, and I'll leave money on the counter—although chances are good that some person other than the owner will help himself to it first." Better than good, in fact.

They filled both sacks and Hunter, true to his word, tossed a few coins on the counter. Airie looked at him.

He sighed, then placed a few more beside them. "There. I've paid for both of us. To repay me for your share, you can tell me why you didn't want to be seen here." He wondered if she would tell him the truth—or if he'd recognize it.

She avoided his eyes. "There might have been a slight altercation with a few traders. And they might have decided to talk about it."

He turned that information over carefully in his head. Wild stories of her had already reached Mamna. The fact that she reddened as she spoke of this particular incident suggested it had been worse than the others. But it bothered him that she could feel guilt or embarrassment over it, and insisted on paying for the goods they were taking, as if she really did know right from wrong.

"Do I dare ask about the reason for this altercation?"

"Does a demon need one?" She shivered, her expression shifting to distaste. "Can we go now? I hate the smell of this place."

Hunter grabbed a bulging sack, slung it over his shoulder, and turned away without another word.

They rode back the way they came. As soon as he could, he intended to leave the common trail and find a place for them to rest for the remainder of the day. He was beyond tired. His muscles ached and his eyes scratched when he blinked. But he had no intention of being found asleep by anyone returning to the small mountain outpost once any initial panic wore off.

As they left the scarred mountain behind them, the trail curled around the jagged foothills. The forest remained thick, tapering off at a point in the distance prior to where the silvery snake of the river and its delta divided sanctified ground from the beginnings of the desert flatlands. The river eventually meandered into one of the many canyons and disappeared into an underground waterway.

"Here," he said, pulling Sally to a halt and pointing into the forest. "See that little patch of light, way back in there? It's a clearing. We can make a shelter, and maybe get some sleep until nightfall." He preferred to travel at night, when the fear of demons kept most men inside.

They dismounted, and as he led Sally through the undergrowth, he took care to erase any traces of their passing, even though so far, they'd seen no one.

Airie proved to be an able woodsman. She required very little direction, and building a shelter out of spruce boughs and saplings went quickly. For Hunter, the difficulties arose once the shelter was complete.

She tossed down the last armload of sharp-scented spruce boughs and made two separate beds on the floor of the shelter. He unfurled the blankets. He wasn't comfortable sleeping with a demon's spawn at his side, although even he had to admit that a spawn who healed animals and became ill when she smelled blood was unlikely to pose any threat to a sleeping man.

But he also knew the only reason she was with him now was because of the cracking of the mountain and their forced flight. He couldn't bring himself to tie her up, or tie her to him, which was what he would have done if she had been a man. She didn't know she was his prisoner, and he had no desire for her to find out just yet.

How, then, did he make certain she was with him when he awoke?

"You aren't to leave this shelter without me," he said to her. "We don't know who else might be around. It's too dangerous for a woman to be found alone."

She wrapped herself in her blanket. The top of her head, and her dark, accusing eyes, peeped out of the cocoon. Her voice was muffled and sounded close to tears. "It's fortunate, then, that I'm not a real woman."

Rather than correcting her, which was what she'd be hoping for, he shrugged. "You give enough of the appearance of one for it to cause problems for you. But by all means, do as you wish."

A sense of wrongdoing on his part—one that he didn't like—intensified, but he'd mishandled everything up to this point and there was no stopping now. The boughs, when he collapsed on them, proved so comfortable that he immediately closed his eyes and decided to take his chances on her disappearing before he awoke. If he found her gone, he could simply track her down.

Or maybe he wouldn't.

* * *

Airie watched Hunter sleep, her hand curled under her cheek and her arm resting on top of the prickly matting. The day had vanished far too soon, and night rapidly approached.

Compared to the men who frequented the trading post, she supposed Hunter was a fine and rare specimen of mortal man. He looked much younger when he was asleep. In fact, he was probably no more than five years older than she, ten at the very most. He had darkly tanned skin, and bleached, shoulder-length hair spoke of many hours spent in the sun. His eyes, when they looked at her, were a shade of blue that could chill like winter's ice or heat with the intensity of a clear summer sky, depending on his mood. Several days' stubble, a few shades darker than his hair, covered his cheeks and chin, but did little to hide the sharp angles and planes. She knew from the hours she had spent in the saddle with her arms wrapped around his waist that solid muscle underlay an otherwise long and lean body. But he'd called her spawn and a monster, and Airie had yet to forgive him for that.

She'd wept again over the loss of her mother and her home while he slept, but now she was ready to move forward. Grief had kept her from taking note of the route they traveled. She hadn't asked him where they were headed because she didn't care. She'd made up her mind as to what she would do, and his opinion on that wouldn't matter because she didn't trust him any more than he trusted her. He hadn't explained what had brought him to the mountain.

He hadn't happened there by chance.

He opened his eyes and blinked, slowly adjusting to the dim light and foreign surroundings.

Then, his eyes settled on her. She wore only her thin chemise and cotton knickers, and the length of his scrutiny told her he noticed them. No man had ever looked at her in a way that made her so self-conscious. Most knew her as a boy, because her mother had warned her constantly of the dangers of two women living alone, even under the protection of the goddesses' temple.

She rolled from her bedding and stretched her stiff limbs. She had no need to worry about protection from Hunter. He saw her as an abomination. Any other impression he might give was a product of her imagination, brought on by the frightening knowledge she was now all alone.

"We should grab something to eat and be on our way," he said, but he didn't move. "We also need to talk about what will become of you."

"I know what I'm going to do."

"Oh?" He continued to watch her with unreadable eyes.

"I'm going to Freetown."

She'd thought it through and weighed the advantages and risks. She was young and strong and reasonably well-schooled. At least, she believed so. The priestesses had once been educators, although only to the finest and most promising girls, and while Airie had no idea if she would have been selected as a student under normal circumstances, her mother had been pleased with her efforts.

She could cook, she could clean, and she could sew. She might even be able to teach. Surely, she could find work to support herself. Her needs were few.

He raised himself to one elbow, propping his head on his hand. "Why Freetown?" he asked.

"I have to go somewhere." She had heard it spoken of at the trading post. It sounded big. Anonymous. She could make a place for herself there. More than any of its other qualifications, it allowed her to remain close to her mother.

There was an uncomfortable stretch of silence. Then, "What kind of work do you think is available to you in Freetown?"

The way he posed the question made her feel ignorant, which in turn left her defensive. "I can do anything any other woman in Freetown can do."

"I don't doubt that."

Airie turned her back on him and the inexplicable sarcasm he'd managed to convey with those four words. His opinion of her and what she was—or wasn't—might not matter, but it stung nonetheless.

The makeshift bedding rustled, and his discarded blanket landed beside her. "Since I'm going to Freetown too, we may as well continue to travel together," he said.

His suggestion filled her with relief. They didn't like each other. They didn't trust each other. She hadn't forgiven him for the things he'd said, and neither of them felt any need to impress the other. The trip would be awkward at best.

But she wouldn't have to make it alone.

"Thank you," she said.

Hunter tugged his boots on. "If you want to thank me, you can try to remember two things the women in Freetown don't do. They don't light themselves—or anyone else—on fire. And they don't get into *slight altercations* with men."

He was so arrogant. Airie reached for the overskirt she'd removed before going to bed. "Then those are two things I can teach them to do."

"Goddesses help them," Hunter muttered to the toes of his boots.

* * *

The early morning sun dispelled the chill of the night.

Dagan wore his mortal form. He squatted on his heels in the shade of a spiny soaptree yucca not far from the entrance to his stronghold at the base of the low cliff, his attention divided between the crumbled remains of the mountain on the horizon and the naked, panting, terrified mortal stretched out and staked at his feet.

As part of the exchange for Freetown's protection, Mamna had agreed to keep Dagan informed of any unusual activity on Goddess Mountain. He considered its peak disintegrating into dust and rubble to be unusual, and had waited several days for her to send word to him of what had happened. So far, he'd heard nothing. Perhaps he was too impatient, but he didn't believe so. She had sent the Demon Slayer to retrieve a spawn living on a mountain that was protected from demons. The mountain had imploded. And now mortals moved about in territory that was forbidden to them.

He disliked being at the mercy of a woman who had once betrayed her mistresses. He'd never fully trusted her because of that, and he refused to sit here and be proven correct while she took advantage of his credulity. Something was amiss.

A stifled moan snagged his wandering attention and drew it back to the matter at hand. The mortal's body hung a few inches over the dirt by the ankles and wrists. He arched his back in an attempt to ease muscles and ligaments stretched taut to the point of breaking, and to relieve the strain on his bonds cutting into his flesh. Dagan had plucked him from the night watch of a wagon train that had crossed too close to his desert stronghold, a bold action that hadn't been attempted since the days when the goddesses reigned in Wasteland. And for what? The wagons had contained nothing but pile upon pile of kyson rawhide, so thick and tough as to be useless.

Dagan could compel him to talk. He could bend him to his will. However, terror was one of the strongest mortal emotions, and a demon soaked it up the way a languid snake bathed in sunshine. It was as irresistible to Dagan as dung was to a beetle, so he preferred to draw out the game for as long as the mortal could withstand it. The white, bell-shaped yucca flowers around the cavern's entrance bobbed on their long stems, nodding their approval.

He flicked a finger and a talon emerged at the tip. He held it up so the mortal could see. The man's eyes widened. His heartrate increased, beating so hard Dagan could see ripples of muscle flinching beneath his chest. His ribcage bellowed.

Dagan inhaled. The mortal reeked of sweat, urine, and fear. He tucked the talon into the mortal's heaving side, beneath his left arm, and dragged downward toward his hip, opening a shallow cut. Blood trickled into the parched dirt. The mortal clenched his teeth. He knew better than to scream, which would only increase Dagan's enjoyment, but the effort cost him.

"Tell me again why so many northerners are crossing through demon territory," Dagan said.

The mortal spat at him, an act of defiance that achieved nothing. The mortal knew what his fate was, and hoped to provoke Dagan to speed it along.

Dagan sank his talon deep into the thick muscle of the mortal's thigh and twisted. his screams could no longer be contained. They washed across the desert, and when they subsided, the entire world hushed in their wake.

The game continued for several more hours. The sun moved until they were no longer in the shade and the mortal was bloodied from head to toe. Dagan had been careful to keep him conscious, but now the heat of the sun, along with blood loss, worked against him. The mortal wouldn't survive for much longer. He had given up as much as he knew, and having passed the point of terror, was no longer of interest.

Dagan dumped the mortal's remains where the wagon train he had been a part of would be certain to find him. Their fear would already be high. One of their men had gone missing in the night. And after they found his mutilated and discarded body?

It was unlikely that this particular group of northerners would reach Freetown. Dagan only had so much control over his demons.

Back at his stronghold, he sat cross-legged beneath the beat of the hot sun and pondered the mortal's revelations. Northerners were moving to Freetown from their mines near the edge of the goddesses' boundary in droves. They claimed a goddess had returned to Wasteland and the implosion of Goddess Mountain was a sign for them to begin building her army.

No goddess had returned. He would have known.

But something had happened.

He murmured a name. *Agares.*

He waited. The world, too, held its breath. A speck of black marred the pristine face of the rising sun peering over the lip of the horizon, growing larger and more irregular in shape as it approached. Seconds later, a manhunting demon wheeled toward him on enormous wings that bludgeoned the air and sent skiffs of cloud skirling in fear.

The demon shifted as it stepped from the sky to land at the mouth of the cavern in mortal form, naked, graceful, and proud. Dagan sometimes wondered if this form accelerated the ravages of time. Agares, however, showed few of its ill effects. His thick dark hair was untouched by gray and his eyes were unlined.

"I want you to find out what has happened on the mountain," Dagan said.

Agares' cold eyes shifted to his, his expression calculating. "What reward am I to receive in exchange?"

There was only one that he'd accept. "You have permission to pursue mortal women." Dagan held up a hand. "Before you go... The Slayer was headed for the mountain. If you see him, and he has a woman with him, you're to bring her to me." He closed his hand into a fist.

"That one is mine."

* * *

Hunter and Airie crossed a shallow ford in the river late on the third day, moving from goddess territory into the desert. Hunter had seen no signs that any of the fleeing refugees had begun to return. He hadn't expected to. Not yet.

But they'd return soon enough.

The moon hadn't yet risen, and they traveled in near pitch blackness, but the sand swift was sure-footed. It was used to traveling the many arroyos and canyons of the desert. Airie was seated behind him. The press of her thighs against his and the occasional warmth of her hands low on his abdomen when she needed to stabilize herself in the saddle didn't permit him to maintain a distance from her, either physically or mentally. He was aware of every movement she made and breath she took.

On the one hand, her decision to go to Freetown meant Hunter hadn't had to force her, but could travel with her as a companion. On the other, it raised a different set of problems. These ones preyed on his conscience.

Despite her unfortunate heritage, she was very much an innocent. While she could, indeed, do the work any other woman did in Freetown, he doubted she understood what such work would entail. She wouldn't be paid directly for it either. Even Blade's ladies were not. Blade gave them back the money they earned, not because any law required it of him, but because it was his choice to do so. Women had no rights in Freetown, nor anywhere else in all of Wasteland. And Airie was worse off than most, because she was something even demons despised. He couldn't decide what she was.

His grandmother had once told him that good and evil were mortal measurements that couldn't be solely assigned to either goddesses or demons, because the immortals were as flawed as anyone. He could picture her still, puffing on a pipe and rocking in her twig chair on the front verandah of the old log farmhouse his grandfather had built for her in their youth. He heard her words.

"Goddess or demon, call them what you will, this world wasn't made for the immortals. Neither belongs here. But they have yet to find a place of their own in the universe, and until they do this world will have to suffer their presence."

Hunter was done suffering. If the world wasn't made for immortals, it wasn't made for their spawn either. What had happened to the family at the trading post was more proof of that. The memory of the boy who'd torn out his own throat gave him chills.

But Airie cried for her mother in her sleep, a fact that also disturbed him. She'd healed Sally. So far, other than her flaming eyes, and an ability to boil water with them, she hadn't done anything that could be considered threatening or dangerous.

What was he to do with her when they reached Freetown?

"Stop!" Airie cried. She slid from the saddle before he or the sand swift had time to react. She hit the ground running, dashing toward what looked to Hunter in the negligible light to be a pile of discarded rags on the side of the road.

They weren't rags, he saw when he dismounted and followed her. A tiny hand emerged from the pile to clutch at Airie's sleeve, and his heart sank. This wasn't an unusual sight for him, although in the past he'd always made the discovery after they were dead and there was nothing left for him to do but bury them—unwanted children, too small or sickly to sell into slavery, abandoned to die. This one was both small and dying. It was a boy, and a very young one, although it was possible he was so malnourished he'd simply failed to thrive.

Hunter tightened the barrier he'd built around his heart. Death was a far better fate for the child than the alternative.

"Leave him," he ordered, deliberately harsh. "He's too close to death."

Airie stooped, scooping the frail child into her arms. The smell of him made Hunter lift his neckerchief over his nose and take a step backward. Desert travel didn't lend itself to good personal hygiene under the best of conditions. The child was undoubtedly ill. He reeked of it.

"I can save him," she protested, smoothing thin, dull-blond hair that appeared gray in the darkness of the night. The child's head lolled against her breast. He was two, perhaps three, years of age. His cheeks were hollow, his belly distended, speaking of slow starvation.

Hunter rubbed his eyes with his thumb and a forefinger. Once upon a time, a very long time ago, he too had believed that life was meant to be preserved at all cost. Experience, however, had taught him that sometimes there was little kindness in doing so.

"Think about what kind of life you're saving him for," he said, unable to suppress compassion even though he knew his words didn't convey it. "He's been starved to the point of death once. If you save him, it will happen again."

Or he would end up sold into prostitution because he was too small for labor. Better the child meet death here and now, rather than damaged and disease-riddled later. Hunter took another cautious sniff of the air. If he wasn't diseased already. What if he carried contagion?

"He won't starve. I'll take care of him," Airie said.

She laid her palm against the child's cheek, and even in the black night Hunter saw the warm flush of life begin to blossom beneath her touch. A sense of inevitability assailed him, but he tried to reason with her anyway. "You have yourself to worry about. How can you look after him, too?"

Her eyes, dark and resolute, met his over the child's stirring form. "By doing whatever I have to."

She had no idea what she was saying, or what it was she might have to do. Hunter tried again to make her see reason. "It's not up to you to decide who lives or dies."

"It's not for you to decide either," came her quick retort. "But if someone possesses the means to save a life, then there's really no decision to be made, is there?"

Being raised by a priestess had left her far too naïve, and that naivety now created yet another problem for him. If he allowed her to save this poor, unwanted child, what, then, would be the boy's future after he turned Airie over to Mamna? How would his fate weigh on Hunter's already overburdened conscience?

This ability to walk away from a helpless child was an unsettling reminder of what he'd become. Blade was right—deciding who was worth saving had done something to him.

Airie waited in tense, pleading silence. The child coughed once, opened his eyes, and looked up at him with such innocent trust that Hunter knew he would now be saddled with two troublesome traveling companions, not one, even though he did neither one of them a kindness by permitting this.

The sand swift had been standing patiently nearby. Its tongue remained firmly in its mouth, probably because the child smelled too awful to taste.

"Keep him, then," Hunter said. She'd learn her lesson the hard way. "But he's your responsibility, not mine. And the first chance you get, you're giving him a bath. He makes me scratch just looking at him."

"Thank you," Airie whispered.

Those two simple words stoked an already ill temper. He wasn't the demon here. He didn't enjoy feeling like one.

She positioned herself cross-legged on the ground, the child in her lap, and stroked his cheek while crooning soft words under her breath. Listening to her, Hunter realized she was praying.

She looked up at him. "Can I have a little water and a piece of dried bread?"

He got them for her. She broke the bread into small fragments and dipped one in the tin cup, then held it to the child's lips. She was patient, repeating the steps several times until the child had swallowed enough to satisfy her. She gave him a sip of water, cradling the back of his head in her hand as she held the cup to his lips.

Hunter took the cup from her hand and putting it back in a saddlebag. If she gave the boy too much, he'd be sick. "We need to go."

When he turned, she was beside him. Her lips curved in a smile, the first he'd received from her, bright in the clear light of the rising moon. Impulsively, she kissed him. It was a light touch of her lips to his cheek, and over in an instant, but it shot an unanticipated lick of heat straight to his groin and stole any more protests he might have made.

"Thank you," she said again, her words infused with a breathless warmth that left a knot in his gut.

Before he could recover, her attention was once more on the child still in her arms, and he was forgotten.

He helped Airie remount, but in front of him this time. He settled into the saddle and slipped a free arm around her waist to steady her while she held the child. Her skirt had slid up to bare long legs, warm against his, and impossible for him to ignore. He jerked at the reins, even more unsettled by an unwelcome and surprising truth.

It wasn't thanks he wanted from her.

CHAPTER SEVEN

Blade limped to the end of the bar, wiping the counter and half listening to the conversations going on around him.

Sapphire, the youngest of the whores, was taking her turn waiting on tables, and he kept one eye on her. She was exceptionally pretty, with blond hair and blue eyes, and she had ambitions. That was why he'd warned Hunter he'd spent too much time with her. She'd begun to show a distinct preference for him, and asked far too many questions about when Blade might expect him again. The gown she wore, a bold, shiny blue, was too tight at the hips and chest and exposed one long leg when she moved. He would have to talk to Ruby about the way the girl dressed when in the saloon. He preferred to avoid trouble.

Noon was a busy time for business, more so these past few days because people were edgy about the fall of the mountain. Everyone wanted to drink. Some chose to eat. In fact, the spicy smell of Ruby's stew reminded Blade to grab a bowl before it was gone. No one wanted to discuss what the collapse of the mountain might mean. Conflict between the immortals had far-reaching repercussions.

He tossed the cloth beneath the counter and watched Ruby disappear upstairs with a client. He really should marry her and give her security. They'd been friends a long time. He owed her that much.

While most people remained cautious of saying anything too loud that might draw unwanted attention, a few could always be relied on for indiscretion. Blade had discovered a long time ago that being a cripple made him invisible. At one time, the limp had embarrassed and humiliated him. Now it worked to his advantage, and he wasn't above exaggerating it. People assumed he was simple because he was disabled.

"Mamna isn't getting any younger," someone said. "What if the next time she raises a demon it escapes her control? What will happen to us when she's gone?"

Blade limped closer, careful not to appear unduly interested in the conversation.

"The Demon Slayer was seen meeting with Mamna," a second man said. "I heard he can fight ten demons at once. Maybe he plans to take her place."

Blade hoped Mamna hadn't heard that kind of speculation. She wouldn't care for it, and neither would Hunter. But he, too, couldn't help but wonder what would happen to Freetown if Mamna were gone. Perhaps it was time he planned for a different future than saloon keeping.

The first man spoke again. "I heard the Slayer is really a demon. That he hates them because he once challenged the Demon Lord and lost."

"If he'd lost to the Demon Lord, he'd be dead, wouldn't he?"

A different conversation by the fire caught Blade's attention. Three travelers, one of them heavyset with bad skin and a loud mouth, had pulled their chairs close to the hearth as if they owned the place. They had the look of tax collectors, technically illegal here in the city but sanctioned in the outer territories, and tax collectors were good at putting their fingers in places they didn't belong. They were bullies and thieves, and Blade hated both. He made a mental note to keep an even closer eye on his till.

"I hope the mountain fell on her," said the loudest of the three. He gave an exaggerated shudder. "Monsters like that shouldn't be allowed to live."

"What monsters are you talking about?" a stranger at another table—a northerner, judging by his clothing—interrupted him to ask.

Blade had noticed an increased number of men from the north in Freetown of late. He wondered what it meant. For him, nothing good. He shrugged off his paranoia. It had been a long time.

"There's a demon on the mountain," the loud one replied. "At least there was. She's likely buried under a ton of dirt and stone by now." He said the last with an air of satisfaction.

"You've made a mistake, my friend. Demons aren't female." The inquisitor turned back to the men at his own table, no longer interested in what, to his mind, had to be a fabrication.

The loud one laughed, and the two men sitting with him looked uncomfortable at the turn the conversation was taking. No one liked to be called a liar, or worse, stupid. Blade didn't believe the loud one was either of those. He moved closer so as not to miss anything, but stayed within a few steps of the shotgun he kept behind the bar.

"This demon was female," Loudmouth said. "We saw her up close."

The two men with him nodded, and a few more people around them shifted their chairs to pay more attention. One of the trio had a long, fading bruise down the side of his face. Another had a split lip and moved carefully, as if his back and shoulders hurt. Blade recognized damage caused by some sort of bludgeon.

Demons didn't use bludgeons. They had no need for them. So why would these men make up such a lie?

"How could you tell it was female?" someone asked.

"It started off in mortal form. Then its eyes glowed red and it turned into a demon. Big one. Hideous. We were lucky to make it out with our lives."

Blade noted the two companions didn't nod in agreement over the description of the so-called demon. They kept their eyes down. Their loud-mouthed leader was lying about at least part of his story, then.

But not all of it. Blade made a living out of reading people, and he believed they had indeed been attacked by a woman. She would need to be a strong one to inflict the damage he saw. She'd also have to have considerable fighting skills. But why was Loudmouth making up stories about her being a demon?

"You should tell Mamna," a wide-eyed believer advised him.

Loudmouth looked smug. "Mamna already sent the Demon Slayer to finish it off. If the mountain didn't kill it, the Slayer will."

Blade didn't like what he was hearing, or the conclusions that could be drawn from it. Hunter had gone up on that mountain well before its lid blew off. There had been one attempt on his life already.

And Mamna was about as trustworthy as a sun-stroked goldthief snake.

The room went silent. Bringing Hunter into the conversation changed several opinions. "It must be a demon then, if the Slayer went after it. He wouldn't do any other kind of work for the priestesses. I heard he once turned down an offer of twenty gold pieces to go after a wagonload of stained glass stolen by outlaws near the Borderlands. He said he wouldn't risk his life for anything so useless."

"Whatever he's after on Goddess Mountain," someone declared, "it can't be a demon, male or female. No demon would dare go near it."

A few people agreed, but even more looked uncertain.

One older man, with a wrinkled face resembling sun-baked dirt, shot a wad of chewed tobacco into a nearby spittoon. He wiped his mouth on a dust-crusted sleeve. "Something had to blow the top off that mountain."

Jasmine, the third whore who'd come to take Ruby's place clearing tables, swatted away a groping hand, gathered some empty plates, and with a sway of her hips and swish of her skirts, carried them through the swinging doors at the back of the saloon to the kitchen. Blade watched her go, lost in thought.

Whatever had happened on that mountain, he didn't like that Hunter had been sent into the middle of it.

* * *

The desert was far from the oceans of endless sand Airie had expected to see. There was sand—plenty of it—but also pillars of granite and basalt, and patches of shrubbery.

And in vast stretches, underneath the earth, odd ridges and patterns could be discerned that were too symmetrical to have happened by chance. They never rode too close to them, though, but skirted around.

"They're remains of settlements from another time," Hunter said when she asked what they were. "Before the demons came. Those are old rooftops you see."

"Can we look closer?" she asked. They'd passed ruins in the foothills too, but these appeared enormous by comparison, stretching for as far as the eye could see.

"No. They aren't safe. They've caused sinkholes to form under the sand, sometimes a thousand or more feet deep. If you fall in one you'll never come out."

She had to content herself with imagining how they must once have looked.

They'd been traveling for more than a week now. She'd chosen to walk so she could explore. Hunter rode, carrying the child on the saddle in front of him without complaint, a small blond head bobbing against his arm as the rolling motion of the sand swift lulled the little boy to sleep.

Hunter persisted in calling him Scratch because he claimed he was so dirty, he made him itch. She didn't bother arguing the point, even though he might equally have called him Shadow since he followed Hunter wherever he went. He must have had a real name once, but so far, guessing at it had produced no results.

She would choose a special one for him when they began their new life. To her, he was a gift from the goddesses as compensation for the loss of her home and her mother, and she loved him already. When she held him, he brought peace to her heart. He should have a powerful name to reflect that.

For now, Scratch was as good a name as any. She wouldn't think about where he might have come from, and what he might be, because she knew beyond doubt that he wasn't mortal. At least not entirely. She would not have him called spawn.

She found clusters of dull crystals scattered in places where the wind had worn the ground bare, and held one out for Hunter's inspection.

He was unimpressed with her find. "It's called desert rose."

She stroked the brittle edges of the stone petals with her fingertips. "It's beautiful."

He looked away. "It's a clump of gypsum that has no value."

Airie slipped it into a pocket of her skirt. "Other than being beautiful."

By mid-afternoon, Hunter hadn't shown any indication he planned to make camp. That meant there was no need of one, and that their journey was almost over. Soon, they crested a rise.She was both excited and panic stricken that they were nearing their destination.

She lifted a hand to shade her eyes from the glaring sun. "Is that Freetown?"

Hunter grunted *yes*.

From this distance, where she could look down on the city, she felt a certain degree of disappointment. It looked shabby, dirty, and crowded inside those fortified walls, and ridiculous when compared to the wide open, vast spaces surrounding it. Very little green touched the streets, an absence disconcerting after a lifetime spent living in the mountains.

"What's that in the center?"

Hunter looked to where she pointed at a tall spire rising well above the surrounding buildings. "A temple."

Airie's drooping spirits lifted. "They have a temple to the goddesses?"

"This temple is to the priestesses, not the goddesses."

She didn't understand. "How can priestesses have a temple to themselves?"

"They call it a market. But no matter what they choose to call it, it's where people go to worship them."

He was in a strange mood today, and she didn't know what to make of it.

"I thought a city this size would have more people traveling to and from it," she said. The road leading to Freetown didn't look well-traveled to her.

"It's a desert city surrounded by demons. Supplies are brought in from the border regions on a regular schedule, and only after careful planning. Smart people travel as part of large wagon trains. Demons are lazy opportunists. The large trains put up too much resistance."

Yet Hunter traveled alone. She was curious why, but she didn't ask.

Instead of following the road to Freetown, he turned his mount off the trail and into rougher terrain. He extended a hand down to her. "You'd better ride with us the rest of the way. There are lots of little things living under rocks and bushes that don't like to be disturbed, especially during the day."

Airie stepped into the stirrup and swung onto the sand swift's back behind Hunter. She slid her arms around his waist and tickled Scratch, who rode in front, making him wriggle away from her fingers. "Where are we going?"

"My cabin."

She didn't dare ask him why. Instead, she rested her cheek against the back of his duster so that she shared the shade of his wide-brimmed hat. His shoulder muscles moved with a fluid rhythm as he guided the sand swift with the reins. She liked the way he smelled of desert and sun-warmed skin, and the feel of his flat stomach beneath her clasped hands. It was easier to enjoy his company this way, when he wasn't watching her. She could pretend he didn't resent her, or find her presence a trial.

A short while later, they reached the ridge of an enormous chasm that cut for miles and miles across the desert, as far as they eye could see. In some places, the bottom rose in jagged chunks to become almost level with the desert floor. In others, it dropped away into blackness. They followed a ridge past deep cuts in the chasm's bank that led to lesser canyons for several hours.

Late in the day, Hunter led the sand swift through a long crevice leading into a smaller, hidden canyon, where he'd blocked off a natural paddock. At the front of the paddock, he'd built a cabin beneath a rocky overhang. Fine lines of erosion ran like tears down the canyon wall's rock surface, feeding into an underground cistern used to collect rainwater and minimize evaporation. Everything was neat and tidy.

And isolated.

"Why don't you live inside the city?" she asked.

"I prefer my own company."

Airie had never spent a lot of time around people, so she didn't know which she'd prefer. At the same time, she had never been completely alone. Her mother had always been with her.

She wondered what she and Scratch were supposed to do now. Hunter had made no secret of the fact that he didn't like having her around. It was possible he expected her to make her own way to Freetown, and that this was as far as he planned to escort her.

"Thank you for everything," she said. "We can walk to the city from here."

Hunter set Scratch on his feet. The little boy scampered off to play in the piles of fine sand accumulated along the base of the canyon's rock wall.

"It's too late for that today," he said. He didn't meet her eyes. "Distance can be deceptive. Freetown's a lot farther off than you think. You'll stay here for now. Help me with the packs."

He'd left them in a pile on the ground where he'd unsaddled Sally before turning her loose. He caught up Airie's small, makeshift bag and headed for the cabin, the loose back flaps of his leather duster rippling around his ankles as he strode across the flat sandy floor of the canyon.

Airie started after him.

"Why is it too late to go into the city today?" she asked, touching his arm to get him to face her. His steps slowed but didn't halt.

"Because the gates of the city will be closing soon. And because I may have a contact for you, who can get you started on a new life."

Airie examined his words. Something was wrong. Hunter had been surly all morning—even more so than usual—and now acted as if he didn't want to see her go. He'd never apologized for the names he had called her, or admitted to being wrong, so why would he choose to help her?

She wanted to say she had no need of his contact, and could make her own arrangements in town, but the sight of Scratch playing in the sand stopped her from doing so. She did need Hunter's help, and that contact of his—for Scratch's sake, if not her own.

"Thank you," she said.

He stopped at that, his back stiff, and whirled to face her. "You have nothing to thank me for."

He left her standing in the middle of the canyon's mouth, uncertain and feeling utterly alone and abandoned. He didn't want her thanks. She wasn't welcome in his home, but neither was she free to leave.

So what was she?

She played with Scratch for what remained of the afternoon, keeping him out of Hunter's way while he worked, until the wind picked up and darkness settled in.

Hunter came to the door of the cabin. "Come inside."

Airie brushed at Scratch's clothes, removing as much sand from them as she could. Hunter watched her, his expression unsettling, so she turned her back to him.

"Here," he said in her ear, and Airie started. He moved very quietly. She was unused to anyone getting so close without her being aware of their approach. He nudged her aside. "You need to peel off his outer things and shake them."

The child lifted his arms obediently over his head so Hunter could remove his shirt. As he did, Hunter got a strange expression on his face.

Hunter held up a small, bright yellow box that had no openings on it that Airie could see. She didn't recognize the material it was constructed from. Scratch always had an assortment of rocks and other treasures he came across hidden in his clothing, and she would set them aside for him to reclaim later in case he remembered.

"Where did he get this?" Hunter asked.

"I have no idea."

She held out her hand to take it from him so she could have a better look, but he pulled it out of her reach. He carried it fifty feet into the canyon, to a more open space, and set it on the ground, his movements careful. He picked up a large rock, hefted it for weight, and walked back to Airie and Scratch.

"Cover your faces," he said.

He hurled the rock at the yellow box. The box exploded with a loud bang, sending clumps of dirt and fragments of rock into the air to shower around them. Airie drew Scratch against her to shield his face, while Hunter wrapped his arms around them both to shelter them with his body. When the dust settled, the box was gone. A hole, almost a foot deep and three feet wide, had replaced it.

Airie's heart thumped hard in her chest as she thought of what that might have done to a small child if it had gone off in his pocket. And to Hunter and her too, for that matter. "What was that?"

"It's a bomb," Hunter said, "from three or four hundred years ago. I've found similar things planted around the old cities. The wind sometimes unburies them." He frowned, but as if puzzled, not angry. "I didn't think we'd passed close enough to the ruins to find anything, let alone something like this." He shrugged. "No harm was done. I have soap and water inside the cabin. You can give him a bath before we eat."

Airie couldn't remember seeing Scratch pick up the box, but, as she led him off for his bath on shaky legs, promised herself she'd be more vigilant in the future.

The inside of the cabin was as neat and tidy as the yard, only very small. There was a counter and cupboard for food and cooking, a potbellied stove, a rough wooden slab table with a single low bench, and a narrow bunk along one wall. A wicker rocker took up an entire corner, and a few clothes hung from hooks on another wall.

"I'm mostly on the move," Hunter said, a faint edge in his tone.

"Don't you worry that you may come back some day and find someone else living here?" Airie asked.

He hauled a small tin bucket of water off the stove and handed it to her. The water was clean and looked fresh. "There's an underground river that flows beneath this canyon and feeds into Freetown," he said, seeing her surprise at the water. "My well is hidden." He passed her soap and a cloth from a cupboard under the counter. The cloth, too, was clean. "And no, I don't worry about finding someone else living here," he said in answer to her question.

"No one in their right mind would try. People live inside walls where there's safety in numbers."

"You live here alone."

He didn't answer that.

She bathed Scratch in a basin on the table. When she poured a pitcher of water over his head he crumpled his face and scrunched his shoulders, making her laugh until she noticed Hunter watching her again. The moment grew awkward, and he turned away.

She dried Scratch thoroughly and wrapped him in one of Hunter's old undershirts. The worn cotton fabric felt soft and smooth to the touch, and smelled of fresh air and soap.

"If you want to wash up, I have a shower outside." Hunter's gaze slid away from her face. "It's not very private, but the water will be warm. I filled the tank earlier."

Airie had been raised by her mother to believe her body belonged to the goddesses, and it was her duty to care for it, but it was what was inside that made it special. Modesty and vanity had never been important to her. She did, however, wish to feel clean again, and said so.

Hunter kept the covered tank, and a large basin that sat beneath it, behind the cabin. The basin had holes in it for drainage.

"You stand in the basin," he said, showing her, "and release water over you by pulling this cord." He passed her another of his undershirts and a pair of trousers before he left. "These will have to do for now. Tomorrow, you can wash your clothes."

Airie, used to cold mountain lakes, found the spray of water glorious, but her hair created a problem. She dragged her fingers through it to remove the worst of the tangles, and left it loose for the desert air to dry. The undershirt Hunter gave her fit well enough, but the trousers were too large at the waist. She fastened the buttons, then rolled the waistband down so that the trousers sat comfortably low on her hips, and turned the cuffs up several inches so they wouldn't drag in the dirt.

When she was done, Hunter took his turn bathing.

He re-entered the cabin with his shirttail hanging free and his blond hair, dark and wet, loose so that the tips dampened the fabric draping his shoulders. The amulet he never removed dangled from a gold chain around his neck. He'd shaved earlier, and it surprised her how different it made him look. How much more approachable he seemed.

The goddesses had been kind when they crafted him. It was too easy for her to forget he was the Demon Slayer, and that his reputation was both deserved and widespread. Even on the mountain Airie had heard of him, and how demons trembled at the mere mention of his name.

Perhaps that was why she trembled at the sight of him now.

She fed Scratch his supper while Hunter sat at the table and watched. When she finished, he held up a long-toothed comb and a leather hair lace, his expression unreadable.

"Come here," he said, patting the bench between his thighs.

After a brief hesitation, Airie did as he said.

He ran the comb through the heavy length of her hair, untangling it as best he could, and then to her surprise, he twisted the strands into a complex braid. The caress of his knuckles against the nape of her neck did little to relax her. Tension coiled in her stomach and made it difficult to draw regular breaths. She had no reason to be so affected by a simple, everyday act that her mother had performed for her many times.

Yet this wasn't the same.

When he was done they sat side by side on the bench at the table, and ate by lamplight. Shadows in the corners made the room seem smaller than it was, and the meal more intimate.

Hunter wasn't inclined to talk. His thoughts appeared to be miles away. While they were traveling, Airie hadn't worried about making conversation with him. They had little in common. This, however, was his home, and despite the fact he'd insisted she stay here, she felt an obligation to be polite.

Scratch had fallen asleep on the floor behind her, and she bent to stroke his baby-fine hair.

"If you give me the name of your contact in Freetown, Scratch and I will be on our way in the morning," she said. "I'd like to get started before the worst of the heat." The heat didn't affect her, but a small child would never survive it.

"Not tomorrow." Hunter stared at his plate of half-eaten corncakes. A damp swathe of blond hair shielded his expression from her. "I have things to do here first, but as soon as I find the time, I'll go to Freetown and speak with them for you. After I've done that, I'll take you into the city."

"That means you'll have to make two trips," she protested.

He jabbed his corncakes with his fork. "Then that's what I'll do."

Everything about the stiff way he held his body, and how he didn't look at her when he spoke, made her uneasy. "What aren't you telling me?"

"I told you before. Freetown isn't a welcoming place, especially for women."

"You told me nothing of the kind. You said the women don't have altercations with men." *Or light themselves on fire*, but she thought it best not to bring up something she'd prefer he forgot.

"They don't argue either." The corner of his mouth curled upward as he spoke, and he tipped his head sideways to look at her.

He was trying to distract her by making light of it. Airie placed her fork on the table beside her plate and dropped her hands to her lap. She examined her fingers, her thoughts spinning further and deeper in unpleasant directions that led to only one possible conclusion. "Am I your prisoner?"

Her quiet question crouched like a hungry wolfcat between them, and he hesitated a breath too long before answering. When he did, his response sounded forced and overly emphatic, and did nothing to ease her disquiet.

"Of course not."

Her supper flipped over in her stomach at his blatant lie. She turned on the bench, jerking her knees sideways from beneath the table so she could stand. Hunter seized her wrist.

"Why would you ask me that question? Did I do something to make you think you are?"

She'd given the possibility of being a captive no thought before today. She felt stupid for not having done so. "You think I'm a demon."

"You're only half demon. That makes you spawn."

"Are they such different things to you?" she asked. "Demons and...?" She couldn't summon the word to her tongue. It was an impolite, derogatory term, and he used it so casually in relation to her that it stung.

"No," he admitted. "They're not."

She drew a sharp breath. What gave him the right to insult her this way? What had happened to him to make him so rigid in his prejudices?

She wasn't perfect. But neither was she the monster he professed her to be.

"My mother was mortal, and a priestess. I was raised to respect life and the teachings of the goddesses. I think for myself, and I make my own choices. What I am and what you believe me to be are very different things."

"Are they?" He frowned at her. "In Freetown, women have no right to protection other than what men or the priestesses offer them. If you reveal yourself there, you'll die. Can you swear to me that you can control the demon in you? Even if you feel threatened? Because I've seen proof to the contrary."

"Of course, I can control it." She knew she could. There was no need for her to be anxious. "It was different with you."

"Really?" His eyebrows went up. "In what way?"

"You're the Demon Slayer. I felt threatened."

"You didn't know I was the Demon Slayer at the time."

"I sensed it," she lied.

He laughed softly. The pad of his thumb scuffed against the delicate flesh of her wrist, which he hadn't released, and her anxiety shifted to an awareness of him as a male. She had never been touched like this before, in a way that stole her breath and made her awkward. She didn't know how to interpret his mood or his actions. Or how to respond.

"What are you sensing about me right now?" he asked.

This time, she answered honestly. "That you're playing with me."

His expression closed over. "Perhaps I am. Would you like me to continue?"

Yes.

No.

While she'd never been averse to a challenge, she was uncertain of the rules of this game. He was very beautiful. The clear, deep blue of his eyes on her made it difficult for her to think. "I have a feeling that playing with you would prove far more dangerous to me than I could ever be to anyone."

"Maybe. Maybe not. You haven't answered my question."

"If you continue to play," she said, "I insist on an equal chance for victory. I intend to defend myself."

She leaned closer and dragged a finger down the side of his cheek, then along the line of his smooth-shaven jaw, and watched his flaring pupils with interest. She kissed the corner of his mouth, then his lips, before straightening to put space between them again.

He didn't smile at her as she had hoped he might. Instead, he continued to regard her with an unreadable expression that held a hint of hunger. Excitement shivered down her spine.

"You've made your opening move. Now, it's my turn." He cupped her chin in his palm and drew her mouth to his.

His kiss was far different from the light tease of hers. It made her heart beat faster and her limbs shake, to the point where she wondered if he could feel them, too. Heat flushed through her as she became lost in the sensations the touch of his mouth aroused in her. Even though he held her face lightly, she could not have pulled away from him if she wanted, which she didn't.

"Look at me," he commanded, his breath soft against her mouth. She had closed her eyes.

When she opened them, the blue of his had darkened to midnight in the lamp-lit interior of the cabin. "Do you still want me to keep going?"

She couldn't speak.

Idly, he hooked his finger through the chain around her neck and lifted her rainbow-hued amulet in his palm. He held it next to the one he wore, then looked more closely at them both. He turned them back to back. With a faint click, they attached like two magnets.

She didn't know what to make of that.

Neither, it seemed, did he. A thoughtful frown crossed his lean face as he worked to twist the amulets apart. Once free, he rose from the bench and reached to take their empty plates from the table. He straightened, the plates in his hands.

"I don't believe you can control your demon instincts. But I do believe you can make a man forget about them," he said.

CHAPTER EIGHT

Hunter unrolled his bedding near the mouth of the canyon, careful to scour the ground around him for any potential and unwelcome sleeping companions. Juvenile sand swifts might not be common in the area, but they weren't unheard of. And there were plenty of snakes and scorpions.

Out of long habit, he placed his short sword alongside the six-shooter beneath his bedding. He pulled the collar of his shirt tight around his neck against the cool night air, then hunched down with his back against the canyon wall so he could sit and think. The winds were light. It wasn't a night for demons. His amulet lay silent against his skin. It had been a rough day for him, filled with guilt and indecision.

He'd had no business playing such games with Airie. The flare of her eyes when he kissed her had been far more erotic and sensual than abhorrent, as it should be. The unexpected fit of their two amulets had also caused a strong jolt of desire for her in him, making it impossible to lie to himself any longer. She was beautiful and alluring, and even though she was spawn, against all common sense he wanted her for himself.

Perhaps it was because he had yet to see her in full manhunting form. Maybe when he did, he could hand her over to Mamna. As it was, when he looked at her, he was stricken with the memory of a beloved sister who had been equally innocent, and betrayed by someone who'd toyed with her in a similar manner. He kicked at a tuft of desert weed with the toe of his boot and closed his eyes. Airie trusted him more than she should. She thanked him for any grudging crumbs of kindness he tossed her way. It left him feeling little better than the demon who had ruined his sister.

He'd give her a week to reveal her true self. He could find a reason to keep her here with him for that much longer. The decision gave him some peace.

He settled into his bedroll, soon so close to sleep he almost missed the black sole of a boot descending toward his throat.

Acting on instincts honed by years spent hunting demons, he grabbed his assailant's foot and twisted it to the side, toppling the boot's owner. In seconds, he was free of the twisted bedding and on his feet, his short sword in one hand and the six-shooter held steady at the stranger's head.

The spread-eagled assailant threw up his hands in surrender. "I wish only to speak with the Demon Slayer."

The man was lean and fit, although the thin sliver of moon didn't give off enough light for Hunter to note much more than that. He pressed the tip of his sword into the assailant's flesh, careful not to draw blood just yet. When he did draw it, he would kill the man. Running a blade through his heart would cause him no loss of sleep, especially now that he had Airie and a small child to protect. It would be far kinder than setting him free in the desert with the scent of fresh blood on him.

Then again, he would have to be in the mood for kindness.

He pressed the point of his blade deeper. "You have to the count of three to tell me who you are and why you're here."

The man seemed untroubled by the sword in his side, the gun at his heart, and the unfriendly tone of Hunter's voice. "I bring a message. The mountain has fallen and it's time to prepare for the goddess's coming. The godseekers are building her an army and request that you join it."

This second attempt on his life suggested Blade was correct—the godseekers wanted his amulet more than they wanted him.

They couldn't have it. Or him either. But giving Airie to the northern godseekers might solve his current dilemma. It was a far better solution than handing her over to Mamna. They'd care for her as if she truly were a goddess—until they realized their mistake.

A piece of amber around the man's neck began to glow, casting warm light into the darkness. Hunter had seen this type of amulet before. It was a gift from a goddess, and it warned of an immortal's approach.

His own amulet grew hot against his skin as he scanned the night sky for demons. In that split-second shift of his attention, the assassin rolled free of the tip of his sword and vanished into the shadowy desert night. Unwilling to shoot him in the back, Hunter let him go.

But where was the demon?

He cocked his head, listening for sounds of its approach, and then realized he'd made a mistake. A demon wouldn't come after him when it could have a woman like Airie—and she was at the cabin, alone with a small child.

Worry hit him, hard. He slid the six-shooter into the waistband of his trousers and tightened his grip on the sword. A gun might be useless against demon hide, but a sword wielded with a demon's strength, and rammed between the chinks in its bone plating, was not.

He loped toward the cabin as quietly as possible, counting off the minutes in his head since the amulet had flared, and prayed he'd be in time.

* * *

When Hunter had stated that he preferred to sleep outside, Airie hadn't protested. His puzzling actions and words had been too unsettling for her to want him too close.

But once he was gone and she had Scratch tucked into bed, she was unable to sleep. The future was a frightening unknown. Who knew what tomorrow would bring?

She wandered onto the verandah and into the darkness, intending to sit and enjoy the moonlight and the sounds of the night in the hopes of finding a small measure of peace. She sat on the stoop, her bare toes peeping from under the cuffs of Hunter's too-long trousers, and absently played with her amulet, running the stone back and forth along its chain. Since Hunter had touched it to his, it felt different to her in an indefinable but important way.

A wolfcat howled in the desert, then another. A hybrid cross between Old World mountain lions and wolves, other than demons, the wolven were the most dangerous predators in Wasteland. Goosebumps chased across Airie's flesh, although not from fear. Now that she was here, and her childhood dreams of the desert a reality, she found it couldn't compensate for the loss of the goddesses who no longer responded to her, even though she prayed to them faithfully every day. With her mother gone, had the goddesses had turned from her?

A soft breath of wind began to rise, scattering dust before it. A low voice called to her from the shadows.

"Well, well, little beauty. What have we here?"

The voice was deep and very masculine, holding a hint of quiet amusement, and Airie's heart began thumping madly beneath the borrowed undershirt she wore. A man stood not twenty feet from the foot of the steps. Tall and broad shouldered, with a mass of curling black hair, he had dancing gray eyes. His chest and feet were bare, a pair of faded cotton trousers his only clothing.

Her breath caught. How had a stranger gotten so close when there was a small child's safety to consider?

Where was Hunter?

"Smile for me, beautiful." A wide grin cut across the stranger's handsome face to display white, even teeth.

It would be very easy to become lost in that smile. The voice, too, mesmerized her, and her suspicion began to fade. How could someone so beautiful be anything but harmless?

He came closer, and she descended the wooden steps to face him, although warning bells rang wildly in a far off, secret part of her head. She tried to dismiss them but found she could not. Something about this situation wasn't right. She hadn't intended for him to get this close. Uncertain how he'd managed it, she took several cautious steps backward.

He halted and lifted his hands, palms outward, in a gesture of placation. His smile widened. "Don't be afraid, little beauty."

She wasn't afraid. Sensing it would be dangerous for her if she were—that he would take advantage of any weakness she exhibited—she chose to confront him with boldness instead. "Who are you?"

"Agares."

His gaze on her was too warm. She had liked that hungry look when she received it from Hunter earlier. Now, she wasn't so certain.

Hunter. She struggled to dredge up an image of his face in her mind. When she did, there was no heat in his expression. Instead, he was scowling. *He wouldn't like this.*

There was no uncertainty in that thought at all. She didn't know why it should matter to her, only that it did. She sensed real danger, too—something she'd never felt from Hunter.

"*The desert is very beautiful, Airie,*" her mother had once warned her. "*But nighttime brings out its predators, and demons are the most dangerous predators of all.*"

She was being stalked. A dark voice spoke to her before she could retreat.

You know what you are. You can stalk, too.

Her smile mirrored his. "I'm not afraid of you, demon."

She saw the glint of surprise in his eyes, quickly hidden, although not fast enough. He had expected a shy, feminine resistance to his demon charm. Had known what to do to overcome it. This was a game he'd played with mortal women many times before. A hot ember of anger tingled to life, shooting ripples of fire through her flesh. He hadn't yet realized that she wasn't mortal.

Or that he, too, could be prey.

You know what you are.

She did. She was half demon.

And it was the demon awakening inside her who offered her guidance. *Let him discover what it is like to walk into danger, unable to resist it.*

"Come to me, Agares," she said, the soft, seductive words barely recognizable as her own. Her extended hand and naked arm gleamed with a fiery golden light.

He dragged one foot forward, then the other, while she waited for him. He reached to take her extended hand. Then, quick as a goldthief snake's strike, he seized hold of her.

Too late, as she tumbled into his arms, Airie discovered that even though she might be able to compel him, he was a demon nevertheless—and with a great deal more practice at it.

She was the one playing with fire.

"Whatever you are," he murmured, his lips hot on her cheek and ear, an enormous erection pressing into her hip, "the pursuit has become far more intriguing."

In a contest of wills, her instinct insisted she was his equal. In one of pure strength, she wasn't as certain of victory. What she refused to offer freely, this demon planned to take from her by force. She didn't know if she could fight him off.

A hand moved to her breast, startling her out of uncertainty. She didn't like to be touched in this manner by a male not of her choosing. Angry red flames clouded her vision as the fire inside her built to an uncontainable level. She had to release it, or it would consume her. How *dare* he touch her this way?

Her eyes blazed, searing the demon's neck and chest. He reared back, releasing her, roaring with pain and surprise. He shook the hand that had touched her so intimately as if it, too, had been singed.

"How..." he breathed.

He stared at her, and past her anger and his sudden caution, Airie saw recognition. His self-preservation kicked in and he shifted, assuming his manhunting form. The handsome face disappeared, swallowed by a mashed snout, a long, wolfcat-like jaw, and fiery eyes. Bony plates covered the thick red hide of its hunched torso, protecting vital organs. The sheer size of it should have inspired awe in her.

Airie's anger, however, was far from spent. The demon had touched her. She would touch it too, in a manner it didn't like. It towered over her, but she faced it without flinching.

Fear is for mortals, that inner voice whispered.

The demon dipped its head toward hers. She had no ready weapon. As the ugly snout approached her face, she stooped, grabbed a handful of sand, and threw it at the demon's eyes in an attempt to blind it, even as her other hand slashed out to seize it by the windpipe. The fire in her palm sheared through its thick hide, and it bellowed as it tried to shake itself free of her grip.

She didn't let go, instead re-directing her fire into its throat to cut off all air. A talon sliced her arm open as the demon struggled, but she barely noticed the sharp sliver of pain. Instinct again warned her of its intentions. By drawing fresh blood, it hoped to summon a battle rage in an effort to gain added strength against her.

It wouldn't get another opportunity to try for it. The fire on her skin cauterized the cut on her arm, sealing it shut before it could bleed. She squeezed her fingers closed around the demon's windpipe, completely enraged and beyond reasonable thought, and watched with hungry triumph as life slowly seeped from its eyes.

"I own your death and your strength," she said. "You will do as I say."

A green-blue haze shimmered in the air around it, then moved to envelop her, too. *I am yours to command.*

The submissive words shook her, a reminder that this was no game. She might have a demon inside her, but she wasn't a monster, and she wouldn't become one. She didn't take life. *Any* life. An echo of her mother's voice overrode any urgings of her demon instincts. *You control your anger. It doesn't control you.*

She released her grip on the demon's windpipe and it staggered backward, scratching at its throat and gasping for breath as the green-blue haze returned to its body, reabsorbed into its skin. Cunning returned to blood-red, glowing eyes. It looked to where a familiar presence watched from the black shadows, and for the first time since the demon approached her, Airie experienced real fear.

Hunter.

The demon sensed him too.

* * *

Hunter, rushing headlong in panic to Airie's defense, skidded to a halt in disbelief as she grabbed a demon in manhunting form by the throat. He watched her fingers tighten, and send fire into its flesh, then saw the demon's eyes cloud over. He recognized the telltale, bluish green haze that preceded the death of a demon as it settled around Airie.

And then, she released her hold on the demon's windpipe. The bluish green haze disappeared. Hunter's heart skipped several beats. What was she doing? Why had she stopped?

The demon lifted its head and looked in Hunter's direction.

"Hunter!" Airie cried, following its gaze. "Look out!"

Hunter looked to her instead—a distraction that cost him a fraction of a second and the element of surprise. The demon drove itself at him on broad, leathery wings, striking him in the chest with splayed feet, knocking him thirty feet backward into the canyon wall and sending the sword spinning from his hand. Air exploded from his lungs on a painful and protracted exhale as he slumped to the ground, stunned by the impact, only alive thanks to the protection his amulet gave him.

The demon paced toward him. Hunter wheezed into the dirt as he reached for his sword, feigning more serious injury to lull the demon into false confidence even as the amulet siphoned strength from it and into him.

He caught a flurry of skirts from the corner of one eye. Airie had grabbed a shovel standing against the side of the cabin and now brandished it like a cudgel, the rough wood rolling easily between her palms.

Her movements diverted the demon's attention from him. Hunter, abandoning his desperate search for the sword, brought his elbow up to ram into its groin. The demon backhanded him across the face in rebuttal, and Hunter's head snapped back. Airie delivered a sharp crack to the back of the demon's head with the flat of the shovel.

It turned on her.

"Get back!" Hunter shouted at her. He hauled himself across the ground by his elbows to his sword and grabbed its hilt.

Airie, however, like a golden, glowing, avenging goddess, rammed the handle of the shovel into the demon's stomach at the point where the bone plates protecting its internal organs fit together. Then she swung the flat end up and under its chin with enough strength to bring it to its knees.

Scrabbling in the loose dirt, it got its clawed feet beneath it and launched itself into the sky. Its dark shadow blocked out the splinter of moon before it disappeared from sight.

Hunter's gaze never left Airie. She couldn't know how impossibly beautiful she appeared in this moment, with her golden skin on fire, and yellow flames, not red, dancing in her dark eyes.

The flames died. She dropped the shovel and hurried to Hunter's side.

"Are you hurt?" she asked.

He spat a mouthful of coppery-tasting saliva onto the sand. The demon had drawn blood, yet it had run away. It knew what Airie was. Nothing good would come of this night.

Anger was the emotion more easily expressed. He directed it at Airie. "The next time I give you an order, you do as you're told."

She drew back the hand she'd been about to place on his arm. When she found her voice, it was soft and full of hurt. "I was afraid for you."

He could have handled the demon on his own, but it didn't change the fact that she had come to his rescue with no regard for her own safety. He should be grateful, not angry with her. And yet it was his anger he continued to lash her with, flaying tiny pieces off her with well-honed words. "The demon escaped. Now it will bring others. I would have killed it if you hadn't interfered. *You* should have killed it when you had the chance."

She twisted the front pockets of the old pair of trousers she wore with her fingers. "I don't kill."

"Not for any reason?" He didn't believe her. "Not even if killing is the only way to rid the world of something that doesn't belong here?"

"As you would have killed me if my mother hadn't interfered on my behalf?"

The quiet observation, filled with scorn, cut him down. He could think of nothing to say, no way to refute it, because he didn't know if what she said was true or false. He did know that if she'd been male, she would be dead by now. He would have killed a male spawn—in mortal form or not—without hesitation.

Turning on her heel, she marched with stiff dignity back to the cabin. The door closed behind her, and he heard the wooden lock bar snick into place.

The metal blade of the shovel had been bent by the force of her blow against the demon. He kicked the shovel across the ground as hard as he could.

Then he gathered up his bedding and moved it to the front of the cabin so he could guard the door in case the demon should decide to return.

* * *

"The young goddess is in the company of the Demon Slayer. She helped him drive off a demon."

Mamna, seated in the lush garden beneath her living quarters, and sheltered from the morning sun by heavy arbors of palm and thick drapes of multicolored, sweet-smelling desert blossoms, regarded Pillar with cool eyes. An artesian well fed a fountain nearby, spilling consecrated water from a pitcher cradled in the arms of a winged cherub. The soft noise of the water effectively distorted any conversation that might otherwise be overheard. Frustration simmered inside her at the satisfaction in her companion's tone. Every passing moment brought the spawn, and the Slayer's amulet, closer to him and his cause.

She had yet to decide who she'd join.

The fanatic lounged in his chair across the delicate, round glass table from her as if he belonged here. As if they were equals. Despite the heat of the sun beating down on him, he'd removed his hat. The silver strands in his blond hair glistened in the light. The toe of one boot tapped terracotta tiling.

A hint of wistful longing edged out the satisfaction. "My assassin tells me she's very beautiful."

Mamna ran her finger around the lip of her dainty porcelain teacup. She had no patience for the envious ramblings of aging men who'd once been favored by the goddesses and who wished to recapture a place in time that could no longer be revisited.

And she was more than a little disappointed in the Slayer. She'd thought he hated demons and their spawn beyond anything. She had assumed he'd be immune to a beautiful face if it belonged to one of them. She had also expected the amulet he wore to offer him some protection against any immortal allure the spawn might exude.

But the Slayer, it seemed, was as susceptible as the next man to a pretty face, proving physical beauty remained the most powerful asset a woman could possess. That was the only explanation Mamna could think of for why he hadn't brought the spawn directly to her as she'd paid him to do. Or, for that matter, killed her outright—which until now had been her biggest concern. The Slayer wasn't famous for mercy.

If the spawn had helped him fight off a demon, however, it meant she'd aligned herself against them, which wasn't entirely unexpected. She'd been raised by a priestess on Goddess Mountain. She had goddess blood in her too. And if she had enough of their power to repair the amulet they had created, then Mamna should be making a friend and ally of her, not an enemy.

As for the Slayer...

If he brought her the spawn, she would forgive him for this weakness. Otherwise she would have him killed—deservedly so—for taking payment and not delivering the promised results. No amulet made him immune to a bullet to the back of the head. Once he was dead, she would take his amulet to keep it from ending up in the godseeker's hands.

The spawn wouldn't end up in Pillar's hands either.

The sun had shifted and her stunted legs were no longer in the shade. She straightened the folds of her light linen trousers, unable to adjust the position of her chair without help and refusing to ask for it. A black-winged shrike snatched at a tiny lizard that scuttled within its reach from under one of the low shrubs.

She picked up the teapot and refilled both cups. In order to keep the spawn close, she had to keep the northerners closer. "Her looks are of no matter, as long as she has the same abilities as her sisters," she said. "Why would you have an assassin approach the Slayer? That hardly seems the way to earn the Slayer's goodwill."

"The assassin was tasked with delivering a message. No one else was willing to do it."

Mamna wondered what sort of messages the godseekers were sending the Slayer. The last assassin had tried to kill him. "If you want the Slayer to lead the goddesses' army, wouldn't it have been better to have someone less threatening approach him?"

"He's the Slayer." Pillar said it as if it were answer enough, but his gaze evaded hers. The Slayer was mortal. They both knew he fought demons, not men.

Assassins, on the other hand...

"You should have come to me," Mamna said. "I could have gotten a message to the Slayer for you."

Pillar took a sip of his tea, then carefully returned the cup to its delicate saucer. "It's already done. The message has been delivered."

And yet the northerners didn't have the spawn in their possession, meaning the assassin was unsuccessful on all counts. The godseeker had to know he'd made a mistake in how he'd dealt with the Slayer.

Meanwhile, he'd done Mamna a favor. "It seems the message was poorly received." Her shaved scalp prickled with heat under the protective scarf wound around her head. Eagerness fluttered in her belly. "Now that demons have discovered this goddess, they'll pursue her. It's their nature. Her best protection from them would be here in the temple, with the priestesses to care for her—as we've done for centuries."

"You and I have yet to come to an agreement as to whether or not priestesses and godseekers are allies in the coming war," he reminded her. His gaze wandered the garden before settling on the consecrated water spilling from the cherub's arms. "You've carved out a new life in Freetown for yourselves that has little to do with worship of the goddesses."

"They abandoned us. We've had to make do with what they left behind."

"They were driven out," Pillar corrected her gently, "and their gifts of consecration were meant for the world, not a single garden. Freetown was once a place of sanctuary for all."

"Freetown was once empty. Now it thrives."

And the northerners planned to take advantage of everything she'd built?

No. Pillar had lost the right to bargain with her when he'd mishandled the Slayer. The scales were once again tipped in Mamna's favor. She signaled for one of the servants hovering nearby to come clear the table, indicating the meeting was over.

"Produce this goddess. Then, we'll discuss the terms of our alliance."

CHAPTER NINE

Hunter jerked on the sand swift's harness, pulling it to a halt a short distance from a bend in the arroyo he'd been following.

The overhanging rock and occasional scrub offered only slight protection from the desert heat, and Sally was out of sorts. The animal had developed an attachment to Airie that made it reluctant to travel too far from her side.

Hunter, on the other hand, had seized on hunting the demon that attacked her as an excuse to escape the hurt in her eyes. A hurt that he'd caused.

But now he'd found something out here in the desert, and the circling of vultures in the barren sky overhead, and the sand swift's sudden increase in surliness, didn't bode well. Neither did the smell.

He tugged his neckerchief over his nose and mouth and slid to the ground, wrapping the reins around the saddle horn to leave his hands unencumbered. He could hear nothing, which was another bad sign.

The amulet around his neck flickered dully, then darkened again, confirming what he'd already suspected. A demon, possibly the one he was tracking, had been at work here, but now it was gone. The arrival of vultures meant other natural scavengers would soon follow, and his amulet gave him no protection from coyotes and wolven emboldened by the safety of numbers and the prospect of an easy meal.

He should turn around. Whatever was ahead was beyond saving. Sally didn't protest as they neared the bend in the arroyo, however, so Hunter felt confident he faced no immediate danger. The weight of his sword against his leg offered a measure of comfort. So did the repeating rifle he carried in his saddle scabbard. Morbid curiosity won out over common sense, along with an urge to reinforce his hatred of anything demon. Including their spawn.

He rounded the bend. Although he had been prepared for it, still, what he found was no easier to accept. He inhaled sharply.

A small wagon train, no more than five units all told, had made an attempt to cross the desert through demon territory. They had chosen the flat-bottomed arroyo as an easier path to travel than the drifting desert sands, and for the moderate protection it offered from anything flying the skies above.

Hunter wrapped the sand swift's reins around a thorny bush and approached the wagon train cautiously, even though he knew there would be no survivors. Pity and anger filled him at the sight of the blackened remains of a campfire that would have acted as a beacon to anything hunting at night. Its scattered ashes indicated that, when the attack began, the wagoners had tried to circle their wagons, an action which would have been of little help against an enemy that struck from the air.

He'd seen similar scenes before. These had been small-time, inexperienced traders trying to make fast money. He'd occasionally hired out his services to escort such people through demon territory in the past. Their wagons would have been filled with whiskey worth its weight in gold in a place like Freetown, isolated as it was from the rest of the world. The wagons would be empty now. Demons, pleasure-seeking bastards that they were, liked alcohol almost as much as they liked women.

The hross that had hauled the wagons—long-legged, sturdy draft animals with enormous, thick-hoofed feet suited for the hot sands of the desert—had been cut loose. Their tracks showed where they'd scrambled in panic up the embankments of the arroyo.

The dismembered and partially eaten remains of the wagoners, however, littered the campsite. Hunter's stomach lurched. He knew from Blade's experience that demons cared little if the men were alive when they started to feed. It wasn't about hunger. They hated men, believing them to be poor copies of the immortals, and held them in little regard. This was their way of showing contempt. They enjoyed the taste of mortal fear.

He would have liked to bury what was left of these people, but the ground was too hard, and he didn't have that much time. The sky had begun to darken on the horizon, and an arroyo wasn't the place to be when the rains came. It would revert to a river.

That temporary river would have to take care of the wagoners' remains.

A vulture, its droopy, malignant eyes gleaming, dropped to the ground and hopped toward a trail of drying flesh. Hunter turned away, fixing his gaze on the abandoned wagons instead. He would see what the demon had left behind with regard to staples.

The first two wagons were empty, much as he had expected. The third, however, came as a surprise. It contained common household goods.

Hunter's stomach plunged lower, bile burning his throat. This wagon had belonged to settlers, probably too poor to join a proper wagon train, and with hopes of earning back the cost of their passage through trade. He flipped open the lid of one of the trunks. It was filled with women's clothing.

Thoughtful now, and already suspecting what he might find, he leapt from the running board on the wagon box and looked beneath it. A young woman, more of a girl, lay curled on her side, her arms tucked under her head as if in sleep, a crusted pool of dried black blood staining her dress and the ground around her. A narrow gold wedding band circled one slender finger. A stray blond curl escaped her bonnet to lie against her waxen cheek.

Hunter knew what had happened to her. When the demon struck, her husband shot her. He didn't blame him for it. She would have had to watch the slaughter, and since as a married woman she wasn't untouched, the best she could have hoped for was to be raped and abandoned in the desert to die. If her husband was at fault for anything, it was for bringing her into demon territory in the first place.

Hunter looked at the sky, still clear above him, and decided taking the time to bury her would be worth the risk to him. He couldn't leave her for the vultures and the coyotes. The blame for this fell on his own shoulders. He should never have allowed the demon to escape.

He carried her body out of the arroyo, and using the sand swift to haul stones from the dry creek bed, spent the next several hours erecting a crude cairn over her remains. Sand from the rising wind stung his eyes, and he wiped his face with his sweat-soaked neckerchief. Despite the scorching rays of the sun, he had discarded his hat and his shirt while he worked.

The makeshift burial complete, he turned back to the wagons. The woman's clothing, he would take with him for either Airie or Blade's women to use. They didn't need to know where he'd gotten it. Any nonperishable food he would take with him as well.

As he returned to the wagons one last time, he spotted something lying on the ground near one wagon wheel. He stooped, brushing the dirt away with his fingertips.

It was an amulet. He picked it up. It had been carved from desert sandstone to look much like the one he wore, although it was a very poor copy and had no real power. His lips thinned. He squeezed the fake amulet, crumbling it into pieces. Whoever had worn it had led these people to their deaths, letting them believe they had protection from demons. And whoever it was, he'd gotten what he deserved.

The young couple had not.

A quick look in the final two wagons also yielded a surprise. They were loaded down with kyson rawhide. The hides were a puzzle, since the true value of kyson was in the meat. As far as Hunter knew, the only market for the skins was in the finished product. It was too tough, too heavy, and too difficult to handle, and required a master leatherworker. The cost of the tools to work it was exorbitant. Why would a small wagon train such as this, which should be traveling as quickly as possible, bother transporting two full wagonloads of worthless rawhide that would only slow them down?

Hunter crammed the food and clothing from the third wagon into his packs, removing his duster from one and putting it on as raindrops began to fall. He needed to get out of the arroyo and find shelter. Part of him worried about Airie, who was unfamiliar with desert weather and its dangers. What if she had decided to explore the canyon on her own? What if she'd decided to head into Freetown without him, and gotten caught in the storm?

He settled his hat on his head to shield his face from the rain as he and the sand swift passed the newly erected cairn. He shouldn't worry about her, but he did. He knew what she was, but at some point, had finally accepted it made no real difference to him. He'd had seven sisters whom he'd loved beyond reason. One of them, thanks to her beauty and innocence, was dead. Airie, despite her heritage, was an innocent, too. And also beautiful. She'd attracted the attention of a demon, and it would return for her. Hunter had to find her a place where she could be safe.

But it was one thing for him to protect her from danger. How would he keep her from becoming a danger to others?

* * *

As Airie unpinned their bedding from the clothesline where she'd hung it out to air, she kept an eye on the darkening sky. Heavy black storm clouds gathered on the horizon, shifting the colorful sandstone carvings peppering the desert landscape from shades of fire to a dull, lifeless gray.

Hunter had been gone for hours now, hunting the demon she'd allowed to escape, and in spite of everything, and his terrible moodiness, she was worried about him. He hadn't liked that she'd interfered in their fight, and he was angry with her, but she hadn't been able to stand back and allow him to battle the demon alone.

She folded a blanket, bending to lay it in a colorful woven basket, brushing strands of long dark hair that had worked free of its braid away from her face. She had no problem with fighting. She'd done it often after the offerings had stopped and her mother grew sick, and she'd needed to feed and clothe them both.

But she'd been raised to believe that all life was sacred and not to be taken without reason. Feeling the demon's life in her hands—knowing she'd own its death—had awakened something inside of her that had *hungered* for it.

She missed her mother, who'd helped keep that part of her silent. She sniffed back the sudden threat of tears. She owed it to her mother to remain strong, and do what was right. She didn't kill.

The sting of sand on the rising wind prickled her skin. Scratch had been playing a game with two sticks, shuffling a stone back and forth in the dirt. He set the sticks aside and came to stand beside her, his worried little face turned up to the sky and his tiny fingers clutching at her skirt.

"Hunter will be back soon," Airie assured him, stroking his head. "It's just a little rain coming. Nothing for us to worry about."

She hoped she was telling the truth. Rain in the desert was unlike rain in the mountains. She didn't know what might happen once it started to fall.

She lifted Scratch in her arms and kissed his cheek. He patted her face, his eyes looking deep into hers for reassurance. Here was one person who didn't see a demon when he looked at her, and she loved him all the more for it. She didn't see a demon when she looked at him either. She'd raise him the way her mother raised her—to be kind and good.

"Do you know what raindrops are?" she asked him. "They're the goddesses' tears. When it rains it means the goddesses are thinking of us. They cry because they take all of our sorrow for themselves and leave us nothing but happiness. Their tears make things grow for us, so we can have life."

The rain was well timed. It reminded her that tears for her mother helped wash away the pain of loss, but eventually, the memories of her would strengthen and grow bright. She carried Scratch to the cabin and set him on the step under the shelter of the verandah roof, then went back to gather her bedding and the basket.

As she picked up the basket, the sky opened up and the rain fell in thick, dirty sheets, the fine, wind-driven sand mixing with the drops of moisture. She raced for the cabin. It was only a distance of a few feet, but she was wet to the skin by the time she reached it. She carried the basket on one hip, and seizing Scratch's hand, hurried him inside and shut the door against the storm. She dropped the basket on the table.

The rain pounding on the roof and the walls was loud, and Scratch covered his ears against it. Airie cuddled him in her arms. She loved the rain and didn't want him to develop a fear of it. The poor little soul had been damaged enough.

She had an idea. She was wet already, and Scratch always seemed to be dirty. The rain wasn't cold.

"Lift up your arms," she said to him, and then peeled his shirt over his head. She stripped down to her shift. "Come on."

They dashed back out into the rainstorm. At first Scratch didn't like it, turning his face into her shoulder as she held him, but then she began to dance with him, and before long he was down on the ground, ankle deep in the slippery mud and squishing it between his toes.

Airie showed him how to slide in the mud by taking a running start and letting her feet shoot out from under her. They were drenched and soon very dirty, and the smile on Scratch's face was worth every minute of it, but it was impossible to see more than a few feet in front of them through the heavy rain. She began to understand why Hunter had built the cabin at the mouth of the canyon rather than deeper in. Much of the canyon floor was a river now.

She refused to worry about him and spoil this fleeting moment of pleasure. He'd survived on his own in the desert for years. He could look after himself. The rain was a gift to a burning land and shouldn't be wasted. She cleared her mind, lifted her face, and murmured the prayers of thanks that her mother had taught her.

The rain gentled but didn't stop. Without the driving force of the wind to mix them with sand, the drops cleared from opaque to shimmering glass that fell around Airie like curtains of tiny, glittering crystals. A figure appeared, outlined in the backdrop of rain, and she caught her breath, afraid at first that the demon had returned. But the figure was that of a woman, and Airie's concern turned quickly to awe. She was in the presence of a goddess.

At least one of them hadn't turned from her.

The goddess's lips moved, but Airie heard nothing other than the patter of the rain on the mud-slickened ground. The goddess stretched out a hand in invitation and she accepted it, her own fingers trembling. The goddess's touch had no substance to it, and yet that it was real was indisputable.

The rain parted around them, leaving them isolated in a sparkling oasis of sunlight. The goddess was golden and glorious, dressed in a gown crafted from a rainbow of colors, and the warmth in her eyes as she examined Airie from head to toe was palpable.

All worry for the future was forgotten, banished by an opportunity Airie had never believed could be hers. Hope grazed her heart and overrode any disinclination to beg. She asked the question most important to her. "Please," she implored, "can you tell me if my mother is at peace?"

The goddess went still. Grief flashed across her face. "She wants you to know that she's with you. And that she loves you."

Airie closed her eyes and absorbed the goddess's words. She had never been given a chance to properly mourn her mother. She'd left no offerings with her body, or dressed her in fine clothes so she could stand with pride before the goddess she'd served. Airie had left her alone, discarded in a temple even the goddesses had abandoned.

But now she knew beyond doubt that her mother was at peace, and she owed it to her memory to try to do something worthwhile with her life, as she would have wanted. The sorrow she'd struggled against ever since leaving the mountain surged, then abated, although it didn't disappear completely and never would.

"Thank you," she said.

"You have no reason to thank me. The immortals watch you. But they don't favor you. You're the product of her upbringing, not theirs, and I've tried not to interfere before this. But you'll have to make a choice. Not now, but soon. You were born on this world, but you weren't born to it. It was never meant to be yours. If you wish to make a place for yourself here, you must be welcomed into it. If you aren't, you'll then have to choose between the world of your mother or that of your father."

"I choose this world," Airie said.

The rain began to thin. Bursts of light shone from the goddess's pores. "You can't. In order to become a part of this world, you'll have to be welcomed by someone born to it." She began to fade with the thinning droplets of rain, her form becoming translucent. The golden light dimmed. "Desire did very well with you," she added, her gaze intent, as if memorizing Airie's face. "Know that your mother loves you. Know, if you need me, I'll be here for you. My name is Allia. You have only to call me."

The rain ceased and the goddess was gone.

As Airie glanced at the rain-soaked mud and rivulets of water streaming down the craggy canyon walls, sudden panic filled her. Scratch was gone as well.

* * *

The rainstorm had forced Hunter to seek temporary shelter in a yucca grove, which meant he'd had no real shelter at all. His miserable day was complete.

Once the storm let up enough for him to judge that the slippery terrain was again safe for travel, he and the sand swift started for home. He rocked in the saddle, settling his hat farther back on his head. Water trickled from its brim down the back of his neck. Why that irritated him he had no idea, because he was already soaked to the skin.

He'd had plenty of time to think while he waited for the rain to abate. The godseekers really were the best ones to take Airie in. He'd tell them she'd healed Sally and Scratch, and they could make of that what they chose. They'd care for her and keep her safe. Before he gave her over to them though, he'd return Mamna's gold. The thought of doing so gave him great pleasure. It had weighed too heavily on him.

He crested the bluff overlooking the canyon, then wiped water from his face, puzzled by what appeared to be two shadows in the canyon where there should not be any at all. Not in this weather. One shadow belonged to Airie. The owner of the second was unidentifiable from this distance because of the rain. What quickly became obvious, however, not only from the halo of unnatural golden light surrounding Airie, but also from the sudden responding warmth of the amulet around his neck, was that the second figure was immortal.

His heart lurched in his chest. The thought of her facing a demon alone for a second time caused him far too much concern, since it appeared to pose no immediate threat to her. If it had, his amulet would warn him. Instead, the amulet sent a gentle heat seeping through him, chasing away the dampness that had permeated his skin for miles.

But threats came in different guises. Unwelcome memories of his sister, vibrant, beautiful and trusting, resurfaced. His fingers tightened on the reins and his vision blurred. Airie was beautiful too, and a demon had seen her last night. That it would return for her was expected. He'd been a fool to leave her alone.

She stretched out her hand to the faint figure before her as if in supplication, and Hunter's shoulder muscles bunched in response. The rain eased, then stopped entirely, and suddenly, she was alone. Her hand went to her chest, clutching into a fist over her heart. She spun around in frantic circles, searching for something that was no longer there.

Hunter had seen enough. He gave the sand swift its head and allowed it to pick its own way down the other side of the steep, muddy slope, aware that the potential for landslides had greatly increased and the rocks were no longer secure.

And then he was at her side. The man in him admired the picture she presented even while the part of him that hated demons wished she didn't look quite so appealing. Clad in a thin white cotton shift, its wet fabric clinging to her curves and far too transparent, she swiped damp curls off her flushed cheeks and tucked them with shaking fingers into her long, thick braid of black hair. She looked fresh and innocent—except for the fear filling her wide brown eyes.

Fear was an emotion he didn't associate with her. Remorse wrenched at his heart, twisting and squeezing. He'd left her alone and something bad had happened. He slid from the sand swift's back and caught her by the shoulders, searching her face. He wanted to ask what the demon had done to her, but didn't know if he could stomach the answer. She was alive, and that was enough. It was more than could be said for anyone else who'd faced a demon that day.

She threw herself into his arms, sending him stumbling backward a step. He quickly regained his footing. His comfort took him a few seconds longer to retrieve.

"Thank the goddesses you're back," she cried, sounding both anxious and relieved, burrowing her face in the crook of his neck. "I only took my eyes off him for a few moments, and now he's gone. We have to find him."

Hunter's arms tightened around her. Did she think he'd help her find this demon? Did she think he would do anything other than kill it if he did?

She was crying now, with intense, shuddering sobs that he'd never heard from her, not even in that first night after her mother passed away. He hadn't been kind to her then. She hadn't seemed mortal to him, not even in her grief. He felt helpless in the face of it now, her mortality no longer an issue.

He held her close and rocked her, resting his cheek against her crown and rubbing the heel of his palm in slow, awkward circles between her shoulders. She smelled of fresh air and innocence, and deep down inside, the protective shell he'd erected around his memories of another life whose innocence was cherished began to crack.

"He's just a little boy," Airie was saying into the collar of his shirt, and the circling motion of Hunter's hand stopped as the extent of his stupidity sank in.

She was talking about Scratch. Of course she was. But then what of the demon?

The child was the more immediate problem.

"Airie," Hunter said firmly. He eased her out of his arms. When he was certain he had her attention, he asked, "Where did you last see him?"

"Here. In the yard. Not ten minutes ago."

"He's got to be somewhere nearby, then. He couldn't have gotten far."

Her breath hitched. "He was afraid of the rain. I wanted to show him there was nothing to fear."

He wondered if Scratch had been afraid of the rain or the sudden appearance of a demon, but he didn't say it. Not yet. Later, he would have a talk with her. She might be half demon, but she knew nothing about them. She was as innocent as her priestess mother had claimed.

Hunter started for the cabin. "Perhaps he tried to find cover."

He checked first beneath the steps, where there was a small crawlspace of the right size to attract a child wanting to hide. Nothing. He looked inside the cabin, under the bed, and inside the cupboard, where it was less likely he could fit. He then searched the corners of the yard where an outcropping or crevice might conceal him. After that he, too, began to worry.

Where could the boy have gotten to?

Airie watched Hunter with an expression of hope and trust on her face. She expected him to find Scratch, but other, more alarming thoughts niggled at him. Coyotes and wolven roamed the canyons. There was also the danger of sinkholes, if one didn't know how to avoid them, and the boy had a habit of picking up things he shouldn't. Worse, what if Airie's demon had found him?

Sally waited where Hunter had left her. He crossed the yard to her side and unloaded the packs. Steam rose from the saddle. Already, the heat of the sun and the dryness of the earth wicked away excess moisture. The desert would be in full bloom for a few days following the rain. Airie would love that.

Once he found Scratch, he'd take them out for a ride so they could enjoy it. After that, he'd make plans to get them both to the godseekers. He couldn't look after them out here. He couldn't watch over them. He didn't lead that kind of life.

Most importantly, the godseekers lived to the north, well out of demon territory, and once she was far away, perhaps the one now pursuing her would forget her. He couldn't bear the thought of her in the possession of a demon.

Or anyone else.

"What are you doing?" she asked.

He continued to place the supplies he'd retrieved from the ill-fated wagon train in a neat pile, his movements mechanical. "I'm going to search for the boy."

He didn't even know where to begin. The desert was vast, expanding in all directions, and he had no idea which direction Scratch might have taken. The rain would have washed away any traces. But he couldn't stand here with Airie looking at him with such expectant trust and do nothing.

He grabbed the bony prong of the sand swift's neck and put his foot in the stirrup. He was about to swing his leg over its back when a small noise behind him caught his attention. Scratch crawled from under the steps, rubbing at his eyes with the knuckles of one tiny fist as if he'd been startled from a deep sleep.

With a cry of relief, Airie swooped him into her arms and showered his ruddy, sleep-stained cheeks with kisses. The sand swift shied to the side, tipping Hunter to the ground and flicking its tongue in an excited reaction to her joy.

Hunter, too, was relieved. He'd developed an unexpected affection for the child. But as he got to his feet and wiped the dirt and drying mud from his clothes, a growing unease dominated his emotions. The boy showed up in unexpected places, often carrying things he shouldn't possess. Whenever Hunter thought to ask questions, however, or investigate, he became distracted by other matters.

Not this time. As soon as he could, when Airie wasn't so emotional, he'd discuss this with her.

Because he had looked under those steps and Scratch hadn't been there.

CHAPTER TEN

It was night. The storm had passed hours before, and already the scents and sounds of a desert newly awakened filled the air.

Agares blinked pig-like, bleary eyes. Something had left him in a foul mood. He was drunk, and wore his manhunting form, and was therefore inclined to belligerence. Leathery wings drooped over his bulky shoulders, and his elongated snout dipped abruptly toward his heaving chest. He crouched on a rock near the entrance to Dagan's stronghold, and appeared in imminent danger of passing out.

Before he did so, Dagan needed to hear everything. Other than that he'd happened on a wagon train of unfortunate travelers hauling whiskey intended for Freetown, so far, he'd passed on nothing of value.

"What happened before the wagon train?" Dagan asked again, for the third and final time. His patience had ended. He also wore his manhunting form, because Agares, in this mood, was too unpredictable. The long, talon-like toes of his bare feet gripped the earth as he balanced his weight on well-muscled legs.

Awareness dawned in Agares's eyes as he finally seemed to appreciate the precariousness of his position. He made an effort to drag himself upright, and shook his head in an attempt to clear it. Droplets of blood-red saliva glistened on his muzzle. The words rumbled from his chest.

"The mountain is gone and there are no signs of the goddesses, except for the one with the Slayer." The rumbled words turned to growls of pleasure. "She could rival the fairest of them, and yet the fool hasn't touched her." He paused as if an unwelcome thought had only now occurred to him. "At least, he hadn't as of last night."

Beauty alone didn't make her a goddess. "There are a lot of untouched, beautiful women in the world."

"Not like this one." Agares's eyes focused. "She fought with the strength of a demon." He zeroed in on Dagan and issued a challenge. "I claim her as mine."

"You can't have her." Not until Dagan knew who had fathered her, or what it meant that she even existed.

The other demon's expression sharpened and grew ugly. He was drunk, but not stupid. Eventually, he'd come to the correct conclusion that the woman was spawn. He'd also begin to wonder at the fact she was a female. And he'd begin to question where she had come from.

"I had permission to hunt."

Weariness swept over Dagan. They'd been too long on this world. Their impulses became more and more difficult to control, and their enforced proximity had them fighting each other. They had one purpose—to find their mate—and by insisting on claiming this woman, who might or might not be Dagan's spawn, Agares issued a challenge Dagan couldn't ignore. He was the Lord and there was only one way this would end.

Agares launched himself from his perch and Dagan, anticipating it, rolled away, taking the brunt of the hit on one shoulder. The crest of one wing bent, igniting Dagan's volatile demon temper.

The fight was as brutal as it was short.

Dagan stood over Agares's savaged remains, breathing heavily while Agares's demon's death fought hard against his possession of it, but in the end it was no match for the demons Dagan already possessed.

Thirst for more blood clouded his thoughts and his vision, and it took time for him to recover. The burning rays of the sun would turn Agares's mortal form into ashes and dust, but Dagan's biggest problem had yet to be resolved—he'd dispensed with Agares before finding out where the Slayer was harboring the spawn. Since the Slayer was known to hate spawn as much as he hated demons, if he was keeping her alive, it meant he intended to use her in some way. But against the demons or Mamna?

Unfurling his wings, Dagan took to the night sky.

As he glided silently above the desert's darkened landscape, he decided it was past time he confronted Mamna and received the truth. If he had to beat it out of her, then so be it. He'd grown tired of her demands and impatient with her motives. She wouldn't hesitate to use the spawn to her own advantage—and only she knew what that advantage might be.

A short while later he circled the night sky above the gated walls of Freetown. He rarely ventured here. He didn't like men. When he looked at them, in particular the ones considered old in mortal terms, he saw what time held in store for him if he couldn't escape it.

Guards patrolled the walls of the city near the gates. They served no real purpose other than to be Mamna's eyes and ears against her own kind, since demons attacked from the sky and didn't stop at the walls for permission to enter.

Mamna's home shrieked her wealth to all of Wasteland. It was a square, flat-roofed building with thick walls built from stone, and a balcony that wrapped around the entire upper level. The windows, opened to the cooler night breeze, were made of real glass imported from the Borderlands. He'd allowed the wagon train carrying it to pass through his territory unmolested at her behest.

She'd profited from his benevolence for far too long.

Dagan cleared the railing of her balcony, landing lightly on his feet. Then he shifted to his mortal form and stood at the window, staring out at the city while he waited for her to awaken.

* * *

Tonight, Mamna's dreams were pleasant.

At first.

When a noise at the window jolted her from sleep, she awoke to a nightmare. She shot upright with a start, her hand clutching the lacy coverlet to her bony chest. The fractured amulet grew hot against her skin. Terror settled in when she recognized the man silhouetted against the moonlit sky. This was it, then. The beginning of the end for her. She wondered what she might say or do to make him spare her life.

He climbed through the window, his long, bare legs and feet sliding easily over the frame. He straightened, wearing nothing but a short pair of breeches molded to muscled thighs.

Mamna averted her eyes, but it was a false pretense of modesty and they both knew it. Despite the fact he had begun to age—slowly—he remained a beautiful man. She both hated and feared him, but she loved him as well, and had for years.

She'd long ago given up hope that her love would fade, or ever be returned by him. Instead, she allowed jealousy and resentment, and hopes for revenge, to twist and taint it. She could find no other way to bear the rejection.

He walked to the canopied bed and drew back the filmy curtain, looking down at her with inscrutable eyes. Grasping her throat, he tried to tighten his grip, but when he could not, he ran a finger beneath the chain around her neck and gave a light tug. His smile threatened to liquefy her insides, but he was a demon who fed on fear, and so she struggled to hide hers.

"Why do you suppose it is," he asked, "that I can get so close to you tonight despite the amulet you wear?"

She dared not brush his hand away, instead covering the amulet with her palm so that he could neither see nor touch it. He already knew it had weakened. She didn't want him to see the full extent.

He straightened, apparently tiring of his game. "The mountain has been destroyed. Why didn't you send word to me?"

"I don't know what happened to it," Mamna managed to reply, and with honesty. "But the Slayer would have been on or near the mountain at the time, and he should be able to give me a report as to what happened when he returns."

The Demon Lord's eyes narrowed. "If the Slayer was on the mountain, how can you be so certain he survived?"

He knew something and was trying to find out if she knew it too. She suspected her answer would mean the difference between life and death for her. She gripped the coverlet tighter. "He's the Slayer. The goddesses favor him. If demons can't harm him, Goddess Mountain is unlikely to do better."

"When will he return?"

"After capturing the spawn." That, too, was the truth.

He continued to watch her, his face dark with suspicion. She kept her own bland.

Long moments passed. "This is your final chance to tell me the truth," he said, breaking the silence. "Is the spawn mine?"

If she said yes, he would kill her. He would probably do so, no matter what. The cracked amulet she wore couldn't protect her if he was truly enraged.

And yet she wanted to wound him. "Who could know that for certain?" she asked, almost spitting the words. "The goddesses were whores. They gave amulets to their favorites. How many of these do you think I've seen on mortal men?" She withdrew the stone she'd worn during her service to the goddesses from the small table beside her bed and tossed it at him. It struck his chest and fell to the floor, disregarded. "These buy them the bearer's loyalty. I have seen hundreds of them. Thousands. Do you think your whore was any different than her sisters? Or that you were the only one of your kind she slept with?"

He laughed as if amused instead of angered by her words, but his laughter soon faded, and his eyes became harsh. "Perhaps not mine, then. But was the spawn hers, and not that of a priestess, as you've tried to claim?"

She was too cautious to lie outright. "I couldn't say. She went into seclusion after you turned from her. Only her scar-faced handmaid was allowed to attend her in those final weeks before the fire." She twisted the knife. "The whore was sent to trap you," she reminded him. "Who is to say a pregnancy wasn't part of that plan?"

The fleeting glimmer of pain in his eyes said she had managed to hurt him at last.

"Since the whore, as you call her, kept herself hidden from all of the priestesses but her own handmaid, then it stands to reason she had something to hide. But over the years you seem to have forgotten to mention that detail to me."

He leaned over the bed, his manhunting form flickering like a shadow around him as a reminder of what he was, and of what he was capable. Hot waves of anger washed off him, banishing the coolness brought on by the rain, and the air in the room became stifling. Terror seized her again and for an instant, she thought she was dead.

"When the Slayer returns, the spawn is mine. If she isn't handed to me at once, keep your amulet close, Priestess, and prepare to use what little power remains to it. What you are about to taught is a lesson you had best never forget."

He let the curtain around the bed fall back into place and crossed to the window, gripped the sill in one hand, then vaulted into the darkness and was gone.

Mamna closed her eyes. Her fingers, still clutching the coverlet, had long since gone numb. The amulet cooled, although it remained warmer than normal, and she suspected if she checked she would find fresh cracks marring its surface.

Her relief at her own survival was short-lived, soon followed by dread. He wanted to believe the goddess had betrayed him because to believe otherwise meant he had betrayed her in return. If he found out that the spawn was indeed his, there was no telling what conclusion he might draw or what he might do in response.

Mamna knew two things. He didn't make idle threats.

And the last time she'd seen him this angry, he'd set the world on fire.

* * *

"You baby him too much."

With bare feet propped against the wall, Hunter sat at the table, his long blond hair, damp from a shower, grazing his shoulders. As Airie moved about the small cabin, restlessly tidying, his eyes followed her.

She didn't know what to make of his scrutiny. Her presence bothered him, more so than usual, and the knowledge left her feeling awkward and too aware of his presence. She knew he disliked her for what he believed her to be, but the look in his eyes this evening was more complex than usual. It was as if he wanted something he could not—or should not—have.

He'd also been staring at Scratch most of the evening, but his face when he did so was easier for her to read. He worried that she wouldn't be able to look after a little boy on her own.

So far, she had proven him right. It didn't help that Scratch wasn't a normal child. As much as she didn't want to see it, she knew he was not.

But normal or not, he was still a child.

"He *is* a baby," she replied. She tucked the blankets around Scratch as he lay on the small cot and stroked a gentle knuckle along his cheek. The steady light from the oil lamp on the table gave his skin a soft, golden glow. In sleep, he looked so innocent. Her heart constricted with residual panic at the thought she might have lost him today. Hunter was right to worry about her ability to care for him. "I would never have imagined a little boy could disappear so quickly. I'll have to find work that allows me to keep him close, at least for the next few years."

Hunter's feet hit the floorboards. "You should think about finding a family for him. There's always some homesteader in the north needing a boy to help out with manual labor."

In her head Airie knew he was right, but her heart told her differently. She couldn't give Scratch up now. They were both alone in the world. They were different from everyone else, and they needed each other. She'd already fallen in love with him. How could she abandon someone she loved and who needed her?

She didn't respond to Hunter's words or look at him. She didn't want to talk about this, or any of her concerns. Instead she said, "We should give him a proper name. We can't call him Scratch forever."

"Airie." He sounded tired, resigned, but not unsympathetic. "Let someone else give him a name. You saved his life. Now give him a chance to have one worth living. Give yourself one, too. It won't be easy for you to look after a little boy. It won't be easy for him either. Not if you baby him all the time."

It wasn't what she wanted to hear. "Caring for him isn't babying him."

Hunter's lips curved into one of those brief smiles. It transformed his face, making him seem less intense. The odd, troubled expression he'd worn all evening disappeared.

"I had seven older sisters. Believe me, I know babying when I see it."

"*Seven*?" This was the first real bit of personal information he'd shared with her, and Airie seized it, her annoyance with him vanishing in an instant. This explained why he was good at braiding hair. "I can't imagine what it must have been like, growing up with so many sisters. You're very lucky. Where are they now? Do you see them often?"

"I haven't seen them in years." He ran his fingertips over the table's surface as if polishing the worn wood with them. Airie held her breath, hoping he'd reveal more. "One of them is dead. I don't know about the others." He looked up at her, catching her off guard with his next words. "Who were you speaking with when I rode into the canyon this afternoon?"

Understanding, followed by sympathy, overcame her surprise at the shift in conversation. He was trying to distract her because he did not want to talk about his sisters anymore, especially the one who had died. His face when he'd mentioned her said it all.

Airie thought it best if she didn't know for certain what had happened to that particular sister. The possibilities were too ugly, and might explain why he'd taken such an immediate and intense dislike to her—aside, of course, from the fact she'd tried to rob him.

She debated the value of honesty in her response to his question. It might make him think kindlier of her to know that a goddess had deigned to speak to her. *Allia.*

But Airie knew better than to reveal a goddess's name. Her mother had refused to speak the name of the goddess she'd served out loud, claiming that immortal names held immense power that was dangerous to mortals.

"My mother taught me that rain means the goddesses are thinking of us—that it's their offering to us, and it brings us life. When it started to rain I called out to them, hoping they might hear me give thanks, and they did. A goddess responded."

"I see."

The quiet, thoughtful statement reminded her of the few times she'd been questioned by her mother with regard to her activities when collecting alms—as if he wanted to believe her and was going to pretend that he did, although they both knew better. Wind pattered against the walls and Scratch sighed in his sleep.

"I'm telling the truth."

"I know you believe you are," Hunter replied. "But what you saw was an illusion. The goddesses are gone."

He'd once called her a spawn. Now he called her a liar—and worse, he thought her naïve. That hurt almost as much. "This was no illusion."

"This is the second immortal to approach you. Immortals are shapeshifters, Airie. They can take on a mortal form to suit their own purposes. It's one more way demons prey on women—by appearing to you in a form that makes you susceptible to their deceit." He got to his feet and the room grew very small. "Promise me the next time an immortal appears to you, you'll call for me." He moved closer, his eyes penetrating in the lamplight. "Promise me you won't talk to one without my knowledge or permission."

The audacity of the request burned within her. She didn't need his permission to speak to beings she'd been raised to respect. She wasn't his servant. Her throat tightened. She didn't know what she was to him. "How could I make such a promise? How could you expect me to?"

His gaze hardened. "I came across the remains of a small wagon train today. One or more demons attacked it. There were no survivors." He stared at the sleeping child for a long time before speaking again. When he did, he was blunt. "Try to understand why no one can find out what you are, Airie. People in Freetown won't welcome you. Not if they know."

"Those people in the wagon train were killed by the demon I allowed to escape, weren't they?" she guessed, and saw by the way his eyes flickered from hers that he believed they were. The possibility that she was to blame for those deaths sickened her. She'd wanted to help Hunter. She had given no thought as to what her revulsion for killing anything might mean to others. Her fingers curled in the front of her dress, creasing the fabric. "You must hate me."

"No. What happened to them had nothing to do with you. They were killed by ignorance, greed and stupidity." He sighed, then spoke to himself, his frustration evident. "You are nothing like what I expected."

"What did you expect?"

She wished she could take back the question. There had been enough honesty between them for one night.

He reached for her hand. She didn't know how to interpret the small gesture. His touch wasn't so much unwelcome as bewildering. The slight squeeze of his fingers on hers brought back the awkwardness she'd experienced all evening as he'd pretended not to watch her.

"I expected a thief." He picked up the lantern with his free hand. "Come outside so we can talk without waking the boy."

He hung the lantern from a hook on one of the verandah's pillars, creating a warm cocoon of light that enshrouded them between the thick layers of night shadows. He sat on the top step and she sat down beside him, smoothing her skirt neatly beneath her. He continued to hold her hand, brushing the backs of her fingers with his thumb as if distracted by the feel of her skin. She wondered if she should withdraw her palm from his but decided against it, liking the sensations he created.

"I'm not a thief," she said, breaking the silence between them.

"While you may not think so, there are many in Freetown who would disagree." He laced his fingers through hers before resting their joined hands against his thigh, pulling her closer to him so that their shoulders touched. He seemed unbothered by the intimacy so Airie relaxed, ever so slightly, against him.

"How can people who are governed by priestesses have forgotten the goddesses and the alms that are theirs?" Her mother would never have allowed them to forget. "Anyone who enters the mountain is expected to leave offerings."

"They aren't called offerings if you take them by force," Hunter said, his tone dry. "They're called loot."

She refused to admit his point was valid. "They could also be called the price of a lesson learned."

He shrugged. "Fair enough. Let's call them that. But if you go ahead with your plan to settle in Freetown, you'll find there are a few lessons for you to learn as well. And I doubt if you'll like their price."

"I don't understand." She tried to put more distance between them, but he slung one arm around her shoulders so she had to tilt her head to the side to avoid pressing her cheek into his chin.

"Do you know what sort of life women lead in Freetown?" His voice took on a quality difficult for her to define. "Did your mother teach you nothing of men?"

"I think I've proved to you that I can defend myself."

She felt the rumble of a laugh build from deep in his chest. "In some ways, I'm sure you can. In others, I'm not as positive." His arm slid from her shoulders to encircle her waist, and he bent his head. He meant to kiss her. Her palms came to rest on the thick cotton front of his shirt, although she didn't push him away.

His lips found hers. She remained motionless beneath the gentle caresses that rained lightly at first, and demanded nothing from her. The heel of his hand began to move in slow circles, rubbing the small of her back, but again, demanding nothing.

The scent of freshly laundered clothing that had been dried in the desert sun lingered around him. She breathed deeply, closing her eyes. The tip of his tongue brushed her mouth, and she tilted her head back, relaxing against the strength of his arm as he cradled her. His other hand found her hip. Kisses, not so light now, trailed along her jaw before dipping lower. She sighed, the roughness of his unshaven cheek teasing the delicate skin of her throat, sparking a sense of restlessness in her that she didn't know how to resolve. She wanted to touch him too, to kiss him in return, but she also wanted to stay just as she was and enjoy the moment.

He lifted her onto his knees. "Put your arms around me," he said. "The way you did this afternoon."

She opened her eyes. At the time, she'd been so afraid for Scratch that she hadn't thought about what she was doing. She'd merely expressed her relief at Hunter's arrival. But she remembered the way she'd felt at the time. All her worries had dissolved. She'd trusted him to find Scratch, and he had.

"I never thanked you," she said, dismayed.

Again, a slow rumble of laughter that never quite escaped shook through him. "You can thank me now."

His eyes challenged her. Airie had a sudden awareness that an imbalance existed between them, and that she was obligated to him, although she'd never gotten the impression that he believed her to be. Until now, he'd seemed to want to be left alone. She didn't know what had changed in him, but something had.

She nestled sideways between his thighs and slid her arms around his neck, pressing her face into his collar. With great daring, she touched her lips to the skin at the base of his throat. Tightly tensed muscles flinched beneath the light caress, an indication to her that she wasn't completely at his mercy. Emboldened, she tasted him with the tip of her tongue. His rumble of laughter became a low purr of surprise.

"Thank you," she said, tipping her chin to look at him.

The wick in the lantern sputtered above their heads, sending its smoking flame dancing. He sifted his fingers through her hair, then held her head in his fingertips. "That was nice enough," he admitted. His eyes smoldered with heat. "But I'm sure you can do better."

His lips again found hers, although this time, they weren't as gentle. One of his hands cupped her head. The other traced its way down the side of her breast. She gasped as his touch lingered, lifting its weight in his palm. Her restless tongue met his. In the back of her mind, a cautious voice warned that this was how a demon had played with her. Another, more adventurous one urged her to enjoy the sensations that the touch and the taste of him aroused in her.

She returned his kiss, clumsily at first and then with more passion. Her hands grew impatient and she fumbled with the buttons on the front of his shirt until she was able to ease them inside. She traced raised welts that crisscrossed his ribs with her thumbs, and she frowned.

"Demons," he said, as if that one-word explanation should be enough.

It was not.

"Why do you do this to yourself?" she asked, her palms resting flat on his bare skin. "You can't rid the world of them single-handedly. They are too many, while you are one man. Who is to say that, sooner or later, they won't come for you?"

Sighing, he raised his head and looked up at the night sky, but he didn't release her. Instead, he trapped her hands with his elbows so she couldn't withdraw them from his shirtfront.

"They don't belong to this world," he said, "and I will do what I can to drive them back to wherever they came from."

He straightened her clothing. She hadn't even noticed that he'd begun to undress her.

"The goddess told me I would have to make this world mine, and that I'd need to be welcomed to it," she said. "Do you believe I don't belong here any more than demons do?"

"Your priestess mother had a lot of faith in you. She worked hard to prepare you for life on this world. I would have to say the real question is, where *do* you belong?" He eased her from between his thighs and onto the step beside him and buttoned his shirt. "You know nothing of men, Airie." He shot her a soft, rueful smile. "Although a few more minutes of this and you'd have learned far more than I'd intended to show you." His smile faded. He lifted a handful of her hair and touched it to his lips before letting it slide through his fingers. "Freetown isn't the place for you. Let me take you north."

Her mother might have had faith in her, but it seemed Hunter had none. She felt betrayed, which was foolish. A few light kisses held little significance to him. He was correct. She knew nothing of men.

Not this one, at least.

"My mother is buried on the mountain," she replied, quiet but firm. "I have to at least try to make a place for myself in Freetown so I can be near her. She didn't raise me to choose a path because of its ease."

The flame in the rocking lantern swelled, growing too large for the chimney to contain and cracking its glass. Within seconds, fire licked the dry timbers of the verandah post, threatening the roof.

She caught her breath. Had she done that?

With a curse, Hunter tore off his shirt to beat at the fire.

"Get Scratch out of bed!" he said sharply.

She roused at his command. Instead of obeying him, she extended her hand toward the spreading flames. The fire blazed brighter, then, reversing its course, skipped from the smoldering wood to the tips of her fingers and into her waiting palm. She curled her fingers closed and the fire vanished.

Darkness, and a faint whiff of smoke, embraced them. Hunter's mouth opened, then closed, whatever he'd been about to say forgotten. He stared past her shoulder at something in the distance.

Airie turned to see what had deflected his attention. An orange glow lit up the night above the narrow walls of the canyon.

The sky over Freetown was on fire.

CHAPTER ELEVEN

Another small group of northerners had made it through the desert to Freetown unmolested by demons, and they wanted to celebrate.

Blade eyed them from his position behind the bar. Six of them were drunk. The seventh was an assassin. He sat off to one side, drinking little, absorbing as much from his surroundings as he could. He wore his sandy blond hair overly long in the front so that it hung in his eyes.

No one else would have known him for what he was. Blade, however, had spotted the weapon he wore tucked into the collar of his shirt when he'd bent over to adjust a knife in his boot. That inability to conceal small details revealed more of his story. There were only two ways to become a godseeker assassin. The first was by reputation. The second, recruitment. Recruits were better trained.

Blade guessed this assassin had maybe eighteen winters behind him. He'd probably earned a reputation around his hometown, made a lucky kill, and decided to turn it into a profession.

Well, they all had to start somewhere. Blade had been about fourteen, and his first kill was an uncle who beat him. He'd practiced with knives for months beforehand because that had been one big, mean son of a bitch, and he knew there would be no second chances.

The northerners brought news with them. They'd traveled partway across the desert with a large wagon train filled with traders, then broken off and traveled ahead once Freetown was within a day's ride. The train's size meant it was well defended. Since demons hunted alone, they tended to treat the larger trains with more caution.

For an isolated frontier such as Freetown, the arrival of these wagon trains was crucial. It took careful planning to move a train the size of the one the northerners reported, which meant it wouldn't be leaving Freetown any time soon. The saloon would be busy in the coming weeks.

Blade polished shot glasses with his apron and listened to the drunken northerners talk. They hadn't come to trade, and if their trip wasn't for profit, then it had something to do with the fall of Goddess Mountain.

One of the men hoisted his glass in the air. "To the goddess."

A chorus of "To the goddess," rang out in response.

A glass smashed on the floor, and Jasmine moved to clean it up with a whisk broom and dustpan. When she bent over, one of the men slid a hand beneath her skirt. She straightened and shoved the man's hand away, knowing she had nothing to fear with Blade in the room.

"If you plan to pay for it, then show me your money," she said. "Otherwise, keep your hands to yourself."

Blade limped to the table. There was going to be trouble, and he hated trouble. He made his voice friendly, distracting the men while Jasmine escaped.

"Perhaps you should keep it down. Public places have eyes and ears, and Mamna can become a little ill-tempered when she's reminded of the goddesses," he said.

One man spat on the floor in contempt. "Mamna can hang. We've crossed the desert to greet the goddess born on the mountain, and to join in her fight to drive the demons from this world."

Blade's fingers itched for his knives. "You'd be better advised to avoid demons instead. A single goddess won't stand a chance against them. There are too many."

"She will lead us. She will lend us her strength. We will be her army." Six heads bobbed in drunken agreement. "She will have the Demon Slayer with her," someone added. "Once he has joined her, other men will follow."

Hunter would no more throw in with goddesses than he would with demons—but Blade had been raised in the northern mountains and knew there'd be no changing the minds of fanatics. He didn't bother to wish them luck in making converts for their army in Freetown either, because they wouldn't find many. People here had lived too long in fear, both of the demons and of Mamna. They were broken.

So was he.

He returned to his position behind the bar. Sapphire picked up a tray filled with drinks from the counter. Worry touched her eyes as she looked from Blade to the table filled with fools.

"You don't like those men, do you?" she said.

He shrugged. "Liking them or not is a waste of my time. They're dead men if they continue on as they are."

She bit her lip, drawing the attention of a number of prospects in the room. The saloon had grown more crowded.

"Stay away from the boy sitting alone," Blade advised her. He'd never interfered with her clients before, but the assassin would be more trouble than all his companions combined. An air of entitlement hung about him.

Her eyes widened in curiosity. "Why?"

"Because he doesn't know shit about the world beyond the north. And he's not going to be satisfied with a half hour of your time."

She turned her head and met the boy's eyes. He smiled at her, and Blade knew he'd wasted his breath trying to warn her.

"He's handsome," she said.

The undercurrent of wistfulness he heard in her tone made him wish he'd said nothing. Who was he to keep her from spending time with someone her own age, pretending to be something she should have been but was not?

"I've misspoken." He filled a row of shot glasses with practiced efficiency while the girl loaded them one by one onto her tray. "What you do is your own business."

A short while later he watched her go upstairs, hand in hand with the boy.

Ruby drifted up to the bar not long after, smoothing the muslin of her gown over her hips. She wore her red hair high on her crown, with a few long, loose curls trailing against the creamy skin of her neck. The fine lines around her smoky gray eyes made her look wise rather than old. Blade often wondered at her true age. Not that it mattered to him.

"Sapphire has gone upstairs with a young man her own age," he said to her.

"There's going to be trouble, then," Ruby sighed, interpreting what he didn't need to say. "If she were as smart as she is attractive, she'd know enough to leave the young ones to the older women."

"Maybe he'll take her away from all this." Blade kept a neutral expression. He was curious what Ruby's reaction to that statement would be.

She didn't laugh. Instead, she appeared to mull over his words. "It's possible. But I'm very much afraid that Sapphire enjoys being a whore too much."

Blade had always assumed women whored because they had few other options. It had never occurred to him that they might like it.

"Do you enjoy it?" he asked. They knew each other too well for him to worry that the question might offend her.

She leaned on the bar, propping her chin in one of her hands. Her gray eyes grew thoughtful. The sounds of the saloon dimmed around them. "I like being a businesswoman. There's a difference."

She lifted her tray and went back to work. As he watched her move around the room, her head dipping occasionally to talk to someone, he thought again about asking her to marry him. He could do worse.

She could do better.

He wished the evening was over, but it seemed to be just getting started. People came and went, the opening and closing of the door drawing in wafts of air still fresh and cool from the earlier rain. The steady stream of customers so late in the day, at a time he'd normally be closing his doors, told him that news of the coming wagon trade had spread and they wanted to celebrate. The safety of idiots wasn't his concern.

Soon, he was too busy to worry about things over which he had no control.

An hour or so later, the young assassin slid onto a stool at the bar. He had all the arrogance associated with youth and his chosen profession. Blade remembered the days when he'd been the same. He looked up from searching under the counter for an unopened bottle of rye and met the boy's eyes.

"I know who you are," the boy said.

Another glass shattered on the floor. Blade's hand hung beneath the bar for a split second, then he grabbed a bottle by its neck and set it on the bar's counter.

"You know who I was. And I was a fool." He leaned on the bar and gave the boy his most chilling stare. "I thought I could change the world. I thought I could cross the desert alone because I was good with a knife. Demons don't care about knives. They care even less about mortal men. Would you like me to tell you how it feels to be eaten alive?" He straightened and nodded to the other northerners. "Then you can share the information with your friends, who are so intent on going to war against them."

"Perhaps you could also tell me how it feels to be a coward," the boy replied.

Not that long ago, Blade would have killed anyone who dared speak to him in such a manner. Now, he accepted that the boy was right. Self-awareness took much of the insult from the words. "It makes me appreciate breathing."

He might have said more, but was given no chance. A disturbance broke out at the front of the saloon. The door flew open and several people gathered around it, pointing at the night sky.

Patrons spilled onto the steps, then into the dusty street. Blade followed more slowly than the rest, partly because of his limp, and more because he wanted to keep an eye on the drunkest and meanest in the crowd.

Out in the street, however, the drunks weren't what caused him the greatest concern. Against the backdrop of the city's wooden palisades, and the deep cobalt night sky, bright orange fingers of flame lit up the heavens.

From out of the flames swept a demon.

* * *

From the mouth of the canyon, Hunter watched the flames rise in the desert sky. His thoughts had leapt immediately to Blade and the women.

"It's a wooden city. A fire will spread fast. I have to go."

Airie touched his arm. Her face glowed like red gold in the flickering light of the lamp overhead. "I can help."

"There's nothing you can do."

He started to shake her off, to go back to the cabin for his sword and his weapons, but then he stopped. He was no longer alone. He had her safety and Scratch's to consider. He'd brought them here. If anything happened to him, what would become of them?

Torn, and wasting time his friends might not have, he shot another look at the burning sky over Freetown and was forced to accept the truth. There was nothing he could do either. It was too late. The town would burn to the ground long before he arrived.

And then a thick gray mass rolled over the horizon, blocking the flames from view and obliterating the stars, plunging the night into a deeper darkness than before. Hunter recognized the changing texture of the sky, and what it meant, even under the blanket of the night.

"Is that rain?" he said out loud, incredulous. "Twice in one day?"

It was unheard of.

A howl of rage split the night sky, echoing across the desert sands and shaking the earth. Airie edged closer to him, and he slipped an arm around her shoulders.

"What is that awful noise?" she asked. Tension rippled in her eyes.

But no fear.

"That," Hunter said grimly, "is the battle cry of a demon."

* * *

Dagan swooped from the fire-seared sky over Freetown, flames shooting from his eyes and the horned tips of his wings. The first strokes of demon fire scorched the tops of the city's palisades. A building burst into crackling flames.

He had placed Mamna where she was. Had given her position and power. He couldn't harm her directly, not yet, but he could take everything away that he had given her, and she needed to be reminded of that. This was the last time she held things from him.

The sight of mortals spilling into the streets to stare up at him, slack-jawed and uncomprehending, enraged him further. The goddesses had favored these creatures. That alone was enough to make him hate them. That one goddess in particular had found them to her liking was more than he could bear. He had once loved her more than his own life and arrogantly assumed he had been loved in return.

A part of him had hoped she would return to him. That she would confess her role in her sisters' deception and beg for his forgiveness. But if the spawn were his, and had survived all these years in the care of a priestess on the goddesses' mountain, where demons were unwelcome, Mamna was undoubtedly correct. The spawn was a weapon to be used against him and his kind.

He would turn his anger on those Allia had loved more than him.

Bells rang at the walls and more people swarmed outside to see what was happening. He plunged downward, his attention on those mortals foolish enough to remain in his path. They'd assumed Mamna kept demons out of the city. Dagan was no ordinary demon. They scattered before him, scrambling over each other and screaming in terror.

A spray of bullets from a shotgun bounced harmlessly off Dagan's bone-plated body, ricocheting into the crowd. The spray of bullets didn't slow him, but the boldness of the act had him seek out the shooter.

The man lifted the shotgun again, but the weapon jammed in his hands. His eyes widened when he saw the demon's attention on him. He tossed the shotgun aside and turned to run. Dagan's claws grazed his shoulder, tearing a chunk of flesh and muscle from bone and knocking him to the ground, shrieking in pain and terror.

The scent of fresh blood drove Dagan on. He banked to the left, coming around for another kill as two more men, braver than wise, stopped to help their downed companion. Dagan tore the head off one and grabbed the other in his talons to carry him high, then dropped him, screaming, to the earth.

Fire had caught the roof of a second building by now, and licked up the side of a third. Dagan plunged through the flames to emerge in a display of splendor. He would show the world what they faced if they disregarded his presence. It had been too long since they'd last seen what he was capable of.

Are you watching, Mamna? Do you see what happens when you conspire against me?

The first sheets of rain struck, fierce and unexpected. Smoke and steam sizzled in the air as the fires of the burning buildings died beneath the onslaught.

He tumbled backward, his wings beating the sky, and forgot the mortals bleeding to death in the street. Droplets of water pocked his thick hide as if they were made of acid.

Goddess rain. Dagan shot above the roiling clouds and the downpour, and circled the city. Goddess rain had been called against him. *Him.*

Rage filled him. He had once brought this world to its knees. Even now, the goddesses protected it. Demon numbers might be small, no more than a hundred all told, but they would still be enough to destroy this entire world if he chose.

The battle cry he let loose shook the heavens.

First one, then another, and eventually a score of demons responded to their lord's summons, filling the night sky above Freetown. They took turns darting under the clouds in an attempt to ravage the city, but each was forced back by the driving rain.

Once Dagan's initial anger was spent and reason returned, he called off the demons. As long as the rain fell they were unable to take action. But the rain couldn't linger forever.

And if the spawn had done this, then she would die.

* * *

Hunter had everything packed and was ready to leave by the first light of day.

The problem then became Airie. She would attract far too much attention in Freetown.

His feelings toward her remained mixed. He'd already decided to tell Mamna that he hadn't found any thief, and that she had undoubtedly perished when the mountain collapsed. He would return the gold that made him feel so unclean.

But Airie's demon blood couldn't be ignored. Taking her to Freetown with him meant risking exposure if she couldn't control it. However, he didn't dare leave her behind. She'd said she could pass for a boy. Though he had his doubts about it, they had no choice but to try.

He handed her some of his clothes. "Wear these."

When she was dressed, he had to admit that she was tall and lean enough, and the clothes suitably bulky, for her to fool most people. His boots, however, proved too large, so they stuffed socks in the toes. He tried not to smile. She walked like she'd spent too many hours in a saddle.

Her hair posed another problem.

"We could cut it," she said.

She offered the solution with such enthusiasm that a smile escaped him. Cutting it would make things far simpler. However, when he looked at the gleaming black masses of curls, he couldn't bring himself to do it. He liked it as it was, and once the weight was removed, those curls would become ringlets. He'd have to cut it too short to compensate.

"Your braid will work well enough," he said. "Lots of men wear them, although not quite as long and thick as this."

He helped her tie her hair. The smooth tresses slid like silk over his palms, and he couldn't resist pressing a light kiss to the gentle curve of her neck when he was finished. A flash of sunlight lit her eyes as his reward.

He would have liked to kiss her with more thoroughness. Last night it had been very difficult for him to stop. The next time it would be twice as difficult, if not impossible, and while he believed she wouldn't object, it would only be because she didn't understand the repercussions. He wasn't certain he fully understood them all either.

He found her an old hat he'd intended to throw away, and the disguise was complete. Then, he inspected her. Since he already knew her, he would never be fooled. But unless someone looked closely, for all intents and purposes she could indeed pass for a boy.

A very effeminate one.

There was little to be done about that. His options were to escort a strikingly beautiful woman into town or a strikingly pretty boy, and he was less likely to have to kill someone over the latter.

"Let's go."

They emerged from the hidden canyon into a desert that was almost unbearably hot, although neither Airie nor Scratch seemed to mind. Joshua trees, normally dressed in layers of dust, had been washed clean by the rain. With upraised arms, some standing as many as forty feet tall, they gave a hearty—if illusory—appearance of welcome to travelers approaching Freetown.

Hunter and Airie took turns carrying the little boy on the sand swift's back. Occasionally, Scratch squirmed to be let down so he could walk too, most often when Airie was on foot. She held his small hand and sang to him, swinging his arm as they trudged along the wind-bared trail.

Other, less-travelled trails converged with the main one at several points. Around midday, Hunter spotted a telltale cloud of dust in the air ahead of them that signaled a wagon train of significant size approaching.

A new plan occurred to him. If the wagon train was reputable, he could enquire about having Airie and Scratch join it while he rode ahead into Freetown. The wagon train would make her invisible. She could meet him after dark at a predetermined location inside the city gates and Mamna would be none the wiser.

The plan had merit. A quiet entry into the city would be best for everyone.

As they drew close enough to see the wagons at the tail end of the train, Hunter, who was walking, caught the bit with his fingers and drew Sally to a stop. The sand swift shook its flat snout, leathery sides heaving, displeased at the delay when it scented both food and water so close. He counted thirty-two wagons.

"Wait here," he said to Airie. He lifted Scratch from the saddle. "I want to see what's ahead."

She dismounted too, her long legs sliding elegantly to the ground, and he groaned out loud. She looked at him with puzzlement in her dark eyes, his reaction arresting her movements. "What's wrong?"

He set Scratch on his feet. "You move like a woman."

"I do. I'll try to remember not to do so in the future."

His lips slid into a slow grin. "Only when you're dressed like a man. Otherwise, having you move like a woman is preferable by far." He nudged the boy toward the shelter of nearby rocks where he could escape the worst of the midday heat. "I won't be long."

By the time Hunter reached the lead wagon, the entire train was within sight of Freetown's gates. When he saw that its wares included a brace of slaves, he almost turned back.

The term *slave* was somewhat misleading. They were almost always women, intended for trade in the mining towns where life was hard and pleasure scarce. Hunter never dealt with such traders, although his reluctance at the moment stemmed more from uncertainty as to how Airie might react than from any personal preference. Then he thought of Mamna and the demons, and decided he'd take his chances. Airie would only have to travel with the wagon train for a few hours.

The wagon master, a middle-aged man with skin eroded by the elements and a thick dusting of red desert sand on his face and clothes, rode a long-legged, black-haired hross alongside the wagons. He kept a sharp eye on the wagon train's progress, and the sky. His eyes noted the amulet Hunter wore around his neck as Hunter approached.

"Slayer," the man acknowledged him, touching the wide brim of his hat with the tips of two fingers.

"Master," Hunter nodded in return. He squinted at the cloudless blue sky. "It's a beautiful day."

"It is that."

They exchanged a few pleasantries while the wagon master's hross flicked its ears back and forth in displeasure at Sally's proximity. The sand swift responded by licking her sharp tongue across its rump, creating immediate chaos. The hross hauling the wagons closest to them shied away from the sand swift, too. It took a few moments for the men to regain control of the animals.

"I acquired two young travel companions on the trail," Hunter said to the wagon master once calm was restored. "Brothers. One is a small child, perhaps two and a half or three years, who can't walk very far on his own. The older boy is maybe sixteen, and stronger than he looks, but he's already carried the little one a long distance in this heat and refuses to leave him behind. They're both too tired to walk any farther, and my sand swift can't be trusted to carry them." He patted Sally's neck and she obliged him by darting out her tongue at the wagon master, who dodged it like a man who'd had plenty of experience. "Would it be possible for the boys to hitch a ride the rest of the way into Freetown with you? Neither one of them talks much, so they're no bother." He'd have to warn Airie to remain silent and not ask so many questions so as not to give herself away.

Hunter expected the wagon master to express no interest in anything other than compensation, but the man was no fool. His request for payment was high. The only gold coin Hunter possessed belonged to Mamna, the weight of it heavy in his pocket and sore on his conscience. He contemplated paying the wagon master from it, but returning it to her in its entirety was the wisest option. He wanted to be done with her, once and for all, and without obligation—either real or imagined.

"Your price is too steep, my friend," he replied, injecting a note of careless regret into his words that said this wasn't his problem. "The boys will have to walk the rest of the way on their own."

He tugged on the sand swift's reins as if to withdraw.

"Wait a moment." The wagon master rested his arm on his knee, the reins loosely wrapped around one wrist. He spat in the dirt. "Word has it that Freetown was attacked by demons last night. That only rain held them off. We aren't stopping any longer than necessary in a place the demons have marked. If you stay with us for protection while we're in Freetown, then escort us the rest of the way across the desert, I'll take those boys into town for you."

If the demons were banding together, not even the size of this wagon train—which snaked a mile back down the trail—guaranteed the traders safe passage. The Demon Slayer would be no guarantee either, although better than nothing.

"You'd have to pay me more than a short ride for two boys," Hunter replied, and named a price twice as high as the wagon master's original demand.

He didn't want to seem too eager for this deal, but it had given him an idea. He was rushing to Freetown out of fear for his friends. Abandoning Airie there had never been his objective. Agreeing to accompany the wagon train would give him a way to get her safely across the desert and away from the demon who'd discovered her.

"The boys can ride in the last wagon," the wagon master said, once they'd agreed on a price. He eyed Sally. "Try to keep your sand swift from eating any hross."

Hunter went to collect Airie and Scratch. After giving her instructions as to where to meet him once she passed through the gates, he deposited them both in the last wagon.

The wagon belonged to a trader carrying stained glass and other high-end building materials. The goods were of little interest to thieves, who would go for more practical items such as food and tools, and was why this wagon brought up the rear. Its wagoner wasn't pleased with having the extra weight added to his load, and therefore was disinclined to be communicative, and after a short time riding alongside them, Hunter no longer feared Airie's disguise might fail.

Satisfied he had secured their safety, he rode ahead, anxious to learn what had happened in Freetown during the night.

CHAPTER TWELVE

Mamna spent the early hours of the morning wondering how she might turn the terror of the previous night to her advantage. By the time she took her lunch in her garden, now exploding with colorful blossoms and rich, earthy fragrance, the warm puddles from the rain had long since evaporated.

If the Demon Lord called his fire against Freetown again, her amulet alone wouldn't be enough to prevent the destruction of the city, not even if it was intact. The goddesses themselves hadn't been able to withstand demon fire. That meant he'd need to be placated. Giving the spawn to him was the only thing that would do. Only she could have called goddess rain against him and he'd know it.

But Mamna didn't have the spawn.

The delicate pastries turned to dust in her mouth, and she pushed her plate away in annoyance. The head of the night watch had waited all morning to speak with her. She called for one of the servants to admit him.

He walked with stiff-bodied abruptness along the narrow path, his wide shoulders nudging aside the tendrils of greenery and the draping flowers. He stopped by her chair, waiting for her to acknowledge him.

"Well? What do you have to report?" she demanded.

"One civilian was torn to pieces, another decapitated. Three guardsmen were killed by fire on the ramparts." His face remained impassive. "The walls are scorched but still stand strong. Three buildings burned. The rain came in time to prevent more from catching fire."

Mamna took a sip of her drink, feigning unconcern for his words, but a slight tremor in her fingers threatened to give her away. She set the glass down abruptly. "What is the mood in the streets?"

"Fearful. Uncertain." The head night watchman clasped his hands behind his back and took care not to look at her. The bobble in his throat worked up and down. "There's talk that the demon attack was provoked by the rain earlier in the day. The fact that the rain came again in the night is considered further proof of deliberate provocation."

"Who do people believe is responsible for this provocation?"

"They believe only a priestess could call the goddesses' rain."

Mamna's hold over the citizens of Freetown was based on their fear of demons, and of her—and in that order. She'd have to remind them of the role she played in their safety.

"Is it true that a wagon train approaches from the north?" she asked.

"Yes."

"Lock the gates against them, then." That should provide enough of a distraction for the demons for one more night. "The gates can be re-opened tomorrow morning."

She dismissed the night watchman. All wasn't yet lost. With demons harassing Freetown, the Demon Slayer would come. He might already be here.

He'd accepted money from her. Sooner or later, he'd come to her.

* * *

"They've locked the gates."

The wagon master's anger wafted thick and sour on the hot, sere afternoon air when he delivered the news. A vein flexed at his temple. Blackened scorch marks ran along the top of the palisade where demon fire had flayed it before the rains came the previous night.

Hunter looked at the sky. It was a good three hours until sundown. The gates shouldn't be closed yet, let alone locked and barred. "Did the guards give any explanation?"

"They said only that the gates will be re-opened in the morning."

They were being used as bait. Mamna hoped that by locking them outside, demons would go for easier prey. Hunter debated as to what they might do. The tunnel was the only way into the city now, and an entire wagon train of people couldn't enter through it without being noticed. They'd be driven back or killed. Either way, they were dead.

The wagons ground to a halt. Several of the men rode forward to find out what caused the delay. People were hot and thirsty, and had counted on Freetown for fresh water. Many had run out. Weary after days spent rationing, they'd grown reckless with their supplies.

Word of the locked gates began to spread. Soon a small, hostile crowd formed. No one wanted to spend a night in the open when demons were expected to rampage.

"We'll stand and defend ourselves," the wagon master said. "We may have to sacrifice some of the women."

A spark of anger caught fire inside of Hunter. "No. You know what demons will do to them."

"The lives of ten slaves compared to those of a hundred men?" The wagon master sounded tired. "If we don't make some sort of offering, the demons will take whatever they want when they return tonight—including the women—regardless. What would you have us do, Slayer? Not even you can fend off an entire army of demons."

Hunter had nothing to say to rebut. The wagon master was right.

He turned the sand swift and rode back to the last wagon, where Airie sat with Scratch on her lap. Thank the goddesses the wagon master didn't know she was a woman, but being dressed as a boy wouldn't be of much help to her during the coming night. She was unclaimed, and therefore, more attractive to demons than a few slaves who'd been spoiled before being brought into the desert.

Her presence would bring disaster down on these people—and on herself. She couldn't stay here, but it was too late in the day for them to put any distance between themselves and Freetown. Their only chance for safety would be within the city walls, meaning he would have to get her and the boy into the tunnel without being seen. Once he got them to safety, he'd return to help with the wagon train's defense.

"What's happening?" Airie asked when he approached, her dark eyes wide and curious. "Why have the wagons stopped?"

"The gates are locked."

The shortness of his reply, and the anger he couldn't hide, worked to keep her from asking more questions, but he sensed her concern. She glanced toward the gates and the activity of the wagon train's men in front of them.

"Come on." He slid from the sand swift's back. "The little one should stretch his legs." He reached up and took Scratch from her arms.

She vaulted one-handed off the side of the wagon and landed cat-like on her feet. If he hadn't been in such a foul mood he might have laughed. There had been nothing feminine at all about her dismount.

He stepped closer to her, set Scratch on the ground, and issued orders in low tones. "Take the boy and head around the right side of the wall. About three hundred feet in, you'll find a cluster of sage buttressed against the footings. Pull the sage aside and smooth away the sand. You'll see a handle and a trap door. There's a tunnel beneath. Go inside, but don't go all the way through. Wait there for me. I may be a few hours." He eyed the blue sky, deepening to purple and then to red along the horizon. "Maybe longer."

He could see the stubborn determination rising in her eyes. She knew what was coming at nightfall and she didn't want to leave him behind.

"Please," he added, not wanting to sort out his feelings for her right now. "Think of him." He looked at Scratch, who squatted at their feet and was chasing the trail of an insect through the sand with a dried twig. "I can't help these people if I have to worry about the two of you."

"But I can help."

"No." He was becoming too protective of her, and at some point, she was going to have to stand on her own, but that time wasn't now.

She caught the inside of her lip with her teeth. She took Scratch's grubby fingers in hers and averted her face. "I'll worry too much about you."

She uttered the words so softly he wondered if he was meant to hear them. They touched him nonetheless. How long had it been since a woman had worried over his welfare? Did it matter?

He'd chosen this life. He had known what to expect. Still, he would have liked to hold her and ease her fears, but he could hardly do so with her dressed as a boy.

Colorful sage and stands of cottonwood ringing the palisades offered some privacy from prying eyes as Airie led Scratch away. He watched them out of the corner of his eye, making certain no one followed them. Once he was confident she'd done as instructed, and wasn't coming back, he went in search of the wagon master.

"There's a small arroyo not far from here," Hunter said to him. "It will offer some protection for the night, but it's narrow. The wagons will have to remain where they are."

The wagon master took off his hat and rubbed his face with his sleeve. The sun remained fierce in the heat-rippled sky, although it would set in a few short hours. "I won't leave them behind. We traveled prepared to fight demons. We have barrels of pitch, and bows and arrows."

Hunter understood his reluctance to abandon the wagons. These people had traveled a great distance, many of them carrying all they possessed, while others had invested heavily in trade goods in the hopes of making their fortunes. Their lives were more important.

"Bring a wagon to haul the pitch and weapons. Nothing more. If anyone refuses to follow my orders, I walk away." He looked at the sky. "Make up your mind. We don't have much time left."

The expression on the wagon master's face said he was angry, yet had no other choice but to agree.

There would be too many people in a confined space for a sand swift to resist, so Hunter led Sally to the trail and slapped her hindquarters with his hat, sending her lumbering for home.

The arroyo took a half hour to reach on foot.

It was a narrow desert wash dappled in scrub with steep banks about the height of a man. Hunter averted his eyes from the slave women in chains who trudged stoically past him to sit in a line against a rock embankment. He was doubly glad Airie wasn't here. She didn't need to see this. He had no time to deal with her reaction.

The wagoners built a fire to heat the pitch. After that, there was little for anyone to do but watch and wait. It was going to be a very long night. All the while, Hunter worried about Airie. If he was to get her out of the tunnel and to Blade before demons attacked, he had to act now.

Armed with a sword, a backpack, and several well-hidden knives, he sought out the wagon master. "I'm going to scout the area around us and make certain nothing approaches on foot," Hunter said. "I'll be back in a few hours."

He then slipped through the scrub at the mouth of the arroyo. Once out in the desert, he began to run.

* * *

The tunnel was black inside, very narrow, and smelled of sour, stale dirt and other, even less pleasant things.

Airie sat on the ground and cuddled Scratch on her lap, burying her nose in his hair and breathing his little boy scent. Dark places held dark creatures, tiny but deadly, and she did not want him inadvertently provoking anything. He liked to examine things too closely sometimes. She wondered where he came from.

Kissing his cheek, she murmured, "Poor baby."

He snuggled deeper into her arms and fell asleep within seconds, his thumb in his mouth, leaving Airie with her thoughts.

She wasn't patient, particularly when afraid, and she was afraid for Hunter. He had refused her help. He still didn't believe a goddess spoke to her.

She removed her hat and set it on the ground, pulling her braid free of her shirt with relief. Her hair itched her skin.

Several hours passed before she heard a scraping noise, then Hunter lowered himself into the tunnel, and Airie could have wept with relief.

"We don't have much time," he said to her. "I have to get you both to a friend's place. He lives nearby. He'll watch out for you until I return."

"We can leave Scratch with him," she replied, "but I'll stay with you. I can help."

"We'll talk about it later." He took Scratch from her. He was awake now, although silent as usual. "Follow me."

The tunnel was short. Hunter eased open the trap door on the other end of it, listened carefully, then slid it aside. They emerged onto a street, near the back door of a silent building.

Airie could see well enough in the darkness. She looked around, curious. The street was long, straight, and wide enough for a single wagon to pass through. They stood at the end nearest the city wall. Another, narrower street, more like a path, looped the wall's inner perimeter.

Footsteps thudded above, approaching on the wall. Hunter grabbed her hand and pulled her into the shadows, out of sight, as a figure swinging a lantern came into view.

The guard paused above them, angled the light in different directions, then after a few long moments, continued on.

"Night watchman," Hunter whispered to her. He examined her. "What happened to your hat?"

She'd forgotten it on the floor of the tunnel. She made a move toward the tunnel entrance. "I'll go get it."

"Never mind," he said, his words stopping her. "We need to hurry. There's no one around other than the night watch."

There wasn't, she noticed, examining the street where they stood with growing unease. It was as if the entire city had been abandoned. She had seen more signs of life back home in the mountain's sparse trading posts than here.

And suddenly, a presence inside her grew restless. Her skin itched as if it were now too small for her body, and stretched unbearably tight. Compulsion, as if someone called her name, drew her toward the west end of Freetown and away from the direction Hunter indicated they were to travel.

She reached for his fingers to lead him. "We have to go this way."

Hunter shifted Scratch in his arms so that the little boy sat on the crook of one elbow. "Impossible. The demons will be here at any moment and I have to cross open desert to get back to the wagon train. The sooner I drop you off with Blade, the better."

The compulsion grew stronger. Not even the threat of being separated from Scratch helped her to fight it.

Airie shook off Hunter's hand and darted away. She heard his spurred boots clicking on clay cobblestones behind her, then his soft swearing. "Damn it all, Airie, we're announcing to the entire city where to find us. Slow down and try to make less noise."

She halted in the shadows of a long archway that led into a small cobbled courtyard encased by four two-level buildings. Inside the courtyard, a small crowd had gathered. In the midst of the crowd, one speaker stood out. A faint amber light glowed at his collar.

"The goddess is here," he was saying. "I feel her presence."

The glowing amulet he wore around his neck was what had drawn her to him. The goddess she harbored had responded to it. Now that she knew what compelled her, she found it easier to resist.

The light infusing the amber amulet flickered and went out. Murmurs of disappointment spread through the gathering. Hunter pinned Airie to the wall of the archway with his body. One of his knees blocked her path.

"Northerners," he breathed into her ear. "The one speaking is a godseeker. We don't need this kind of attention right now."

"If the Demon Slayer is with her," the godseeker continued, "we will ask him one last time to join us. If he refuses again, we will kill him."

"If I remember correctly," Hunter muttered beneath his breath, "they went straight to trying to kill me."

"Why would they want to kill you?" Airie whispered.

"For my amulet. Whoever wears it becomes the Slayer."

The goddess inside Airie flared a denial at his words. *The Slayer is my champion. There will be only him.*

Scratch, still in Hunter's arms, squirmed to be let down. The moment of inattention he caused was enough for Airie. She pushed past Hunter and stepped boldly into the courtyard, guided again by the tug of compulsion on her amulet.

"Who's there?" the godseeker demanded from his place at the head of the gathering.

Airie's skin warmed. She looked at her hands, flipping them over to examine her palms. Her skin was glowing. Her head went up and her voice rose so that all present could hear. "No one harms the Slayer."

The words rolled from her chest like a clap of thunder, startling her as much as anyone. The goddess had spoken, joining her thoughts and her voice to Airie's.

Her audience stilled, gaping at her in wonder and fear. One by one, they dropped to their knees.

She turned to Hunter, who had stepped into position beside her, his hand on the hilt of his sword. Scratch remained hidden in the alley. She could feel him behind her in the shadows.

"Congratulations," Hunter said to her, keeping his eyes on the men in the gathering. "You have just been deified."

But from the corner of his eye he was looking at her strangely now, too. The soft golden glow from her skin warmed the angles of his face so that she could read the caution creeping into his eyes. She didn't like it.

The glow of her skin dimmed with the shifting of her mood.

"She has come to lead us," the godseeker said, starting toward her through his small crowd of followers.

"No, she has not." Hunter stepped in front of Airie.

The godseeker reacted as if the move were a threat. He dropped his hand to his hip in a blur, too fast for Hunter to react to the gun being drawn on him.

Airie's world slowed, the faces around her distorting, sound waning to a dull background roar. Her own movements, however, became lightning quick. She pushed Hunter aside. The bullet shot past her ear to embed in one of the buildings behind her.

He tried to kill the champion. This is not to be tolerated.

Anger set in. She felt the heat rise in her eyes. She turned her head, needing something to burn, and narrowed her gaze on a target. The godseeker's boots smoldered. With profound disbelief on his face, he danced as he tried to stamp out the fire.

"Airie. Stop!" Hunter seized her by the arm and shook her.

The godseeker wrenched his boots off his feet. Smoke rose from the insoles.

"If you wish to fight demons," Airie said past Hunter to the now silent gathering, "you first need to know your allies." She let her eyes flare again. "And your enemies."

Hunter backed away from the mute northerners, pushing her behind him and into the alley where Scratch sat in wait on the cobblestones. Hunter snatched him up, then turned on Airie.

"Start running," he said to her, his voice quiet and grim. "And do not utter one more word until I say you can."

CHAPTER THIRTEEN

Blade carried the bucket of food waste into the small, unlit compound off his kitchen, heading for the alley beyond. A skittering of loose gravel immediately inside the locked gate let him know he wasn't alone.

He stepped out of the thin wash of light streaming from the open doorway behind him and reached for the knife he carried beneath one arm, but a long, low whistle stayed his hand.

Hunter.

The light from the kitchen was enough for him to identify the wriggling bundle Hunter carried in his arms, and Blade could not have been more surprised if his friend had appeared naked and dancing by moonlight before him.

What in the name of the goddesses was Hunter doing with a child?

Blade cleared his throat. "Well."

"Well, what?" Hunter plunked the child on the ground at his feet.

The toddler looked up at him, all wide eyes and wariness. The dark expression on Hunter's face left Blade with no idea what to say next.

"Hungry?" he asked the child, figuring that to be a safe topic, and if the answer was yes, one easily addressed.

The little boy nodded.

Ruby appeared in the kitchen doorway, no doubt wondering what was taking him so long.

"Well," she said, echoing Blade's surprise. She glanced sharply from Hunter to Blade. "We don't deal in children." Her tone left no doubt as to her opinion of those who did, an opinion Blade shared.

Surely Hunter wouldn't—

A woman moved out of the shadows into the soft light, surprising Blade even more than the child Hunter had carried. Hunter owed his life to his ability to move silently, so Blade wasn't concerned that he hadn't noticed his presence until Hunter wanted him to. But it bothered him that he had not been aware of the woman's.

She was very tall, but with a delicate femininity of frame. Her hair was as black as pitch, long and thick, and tied in a simple braid that dangled neatly to her narrow waist. Long legs, trim hips and high breasts didn't escape his attention, although the men's castoffs she wore were far from flattering.

Yet it was her face that took his ability to breathe.

She had the smooth, golden features of a goddess. He'd never forgotten their visits to his childhood village, infrequent though they had been. No one who had seen them could possibly forget.

Ruby had crossed over the threshold to stand in the compound beside him. "Put your tongue back in your head," she said in an amused undertone. "You've seen women before."

"The little boy's hungry," Blade replied.

Ruby smiled at the woman. "I imagine you are, too." She extended her hand in welcome. "I'm Ruby."

"Airie."

Airie took the offered hand and when she did, Ruby started at the touch, as if she had received a jolt of some sort and wasn't quite certain whether she liked it.

The older woman recovered her hand and her poise with equal speed. "Let's go get you both something to eat, shall we?"

She stepped aside. Airie took the boy by the hand and led him into the light and warmth of the kitchen.

Blade watched them disappear inside, then turned his attention back to his friend. "Who is that?"

"That," Hunter said, slinging the pack from his back and dropping it to the ground with a grunt of pure weariness, "is a demon."

Blade drew back and stared through his kitchen doorway in shocked disbelief. "No."

"Oh, most definitely yes," Hunter said. "So keep your voice down or she'll hear you."

Blade's initial disbelief turned from shock to a slow burning, incredulous anger. "So you brought her here? To my home?"

Hunter mounted the single wooden step and closed the door to the kitchen, throwing them into darkness, shaking like a man badly in need of a drink despite the fact he never drank. Not to Blade's knowledge.

"She's not one hundred percent demon. I don't know what she really is, except that she is the spawn I was hired to bring in. After we saw the fire last night I had to find out what was happening with you, and leaving her behind wasn't an option. What would you do in my place?"

Some of Blade's anger faded with the dawning awareness that Hunter's shock and disbelief surpassed his own.

What *would* he do?

Blade had no ready answer as Hunter sat on the back step and told him everything, starting with his first meeting with Airie, their flight down the mountain, and ending with the altercation with the godseekers.

"Let's say she really is half demon," Blade said, although the thought of it made him ill. "Do I want her here? Do I want her near the other women?"

Hunter lifted his shoulders in a shrug of bewilderment. "She healed Sally with the touch of her bare hands. She saved that scrawny kid, who was starved to the point I could have sworn he was the next best thing to dead, and the next day he was fine. She wouldn't let me leave him behind, although you and I both know that would have been the kindest thing to do." He sighed, letting his hands drop. "She set a godseeker's boots on fire. Although to be fair, he was trying to kill me."

Blade remembered Ruby's flash of surprise as she touched Airie's hand. He would ask Ruby about that later, and about her impressions of her. Ruby's instincts regarding people were usually sound.

"Can she be a good demon?" Blade asked. Hunter shot him a black look, which he returned. "Then why have you brought her here?"

Again, Hunter lifted his hands helplessly. "I wanted her to be safe."

Blade didn't want any demon, good or otherwise, male or female, in his home. But the memory of the woman he'd been driven to kill wouldn't leave him, and that Mamna would turn Airie, too, over to the demons wasn't in doubt. What the demons would do to a spawn wasn't either.

But what the demons would do to a spawn who looked like Airie before they killed her was the uncertainty that made Blade hesitate. That was the real reason Hunter had brought her here—uncertainty had made him hesitate as well.

"You should have killed her when you realized what she was," Blade said.

"I know." Hunter passed a hand over his face. "But it's too late for that and now, I can't turn her over to Mamna with an easy conscience. Not until she does something...I don't know. Demon-like."

Setting a man's boots on fire wasn't demon enough?

Blade sensed his friend's tiredness despite the thick darkness. It was unlikely that he'd had a moment's rest since first meeting

Airie, and how he'd managed to get her to Freetown was a complete mystery. She did not act as if she had come against her will.

"What do you consider 'demon-like'?" Blade asked. He settled on the step beside his friend, his leg aching fiercely. "Will she have to kill someone? Because you and I have both killed people, but you and I have never brought anyone back from the dead. What demon display would it take to make you turn her over to Mamna?"

"I don't know!" Hunter all but snarled. He kicked a heel into the dirt. "I don't know what I'm supposed to do with the boy either."

Responsibility for others wasn't something men like Hunter wore with ease. It fit like a poorly made shirt, too tight at the neck and shoulders. Blade knew all about it. "You've gotten yourself into a lot of trouble this time."

"What's worse, I've brought the trouble to you."

Blade was honest. "And I can't say I'm happy about it. But what's done is done, and until you come up with some plan, we aren't going to sleep at the same times. I'm not letting a demon run free around here without one of us watching her."

"Thank you," Hunter said. Relief thickened his voice.

"Don't thank me yet," Blade warned him. "These two aren't the worst of your problems. Sooner or later you'll have to deal with Mamna, and that's the one thing I can't help you with."

"Can you keep Airie and the boy for me for the night?" Hunter rose to his feet. "I have to go back. I left the people from the wagon train in the canyon where I usually camp. They'll be frantic by now. I've been gone too long as it is." He rubbed the back of his neck.

"You think the demons will come back tonight?" Blade asked. He tried not to think of the man's screams as he'd been torn apart in the street the night before. He tried not to remember his own when the demon had torn flesh from his leg.

"Yes. So does Mamna. The gates were locked about three hours before sundown," Hunter replied. "I'm guessing she wanted to offer them a diversion."

Blade looked at him. "You don't have to go back out there. You don't owe those people anything."

Hunter handed the pack to Blade. "Give this to Airie. I do have to go because I made a promise to them. Besides," he added with a lopsided grin. "There will be demons to kill."

"I'll kill this one if I have to," Blade warned his departing back.

Hunter froze but did not turn around. He appeared to be thinking Blade's words over with careful consideration.

"I know," he admitted finally, then opened the gate and stepped through it. "But you won't have to." He latched the gate behind him.

Blade sat for a long time on the step listening to the cold desert night, hoping his friend's instincts were good ones. If he did have to kill her, it would be the death of a friendship as well.

* * *

Who was Mamna, and why would Hunter turn Airie over to her?

She'd tried not to listen to the conversation outside because she suspected it wouldn't be to her liking. But the tone of Blade's voice, and the reference to Mamna, had turned her skin to ice. That Hunter also didn't trust her around his friends—that he thought she might somehow harm or endanger them—hurt her deeply.

Yet she couldn't deny the possibility existed.

The gate latched behind Hunter, and she turned her attention back to the lovely woman named Ruby with the gleaming red hair. She puttered around the large kitchen, exuding a gentle kindness and chattering quietly to Scratch, who sat on a bench at the long wooden table.

"Does he not yet speak?" she asked Airie, glancing up from a small plate of some sort of stew she'd set on the counter to cool. She ladled up another plateful from the pot on the stove and gestured for Airie to sit, then placed it in front of her.

"No," Airie replied, and wondered if it was as unusual as she suspected. The slight frown on Ruby's face indicated it was. Airie touched his hair, brushing it back from his cheek. "I don't know what his life was like beyond a few days ago. Perhaps he has nothing he wants to speak of." The possibility broke her heart.

"He's young," Ruby said. "He'll forget his past life, and he'll speak when he's ready."

The man named Blade limped into the kitchen, his presence a dark cloud of thunder that nevertheless did not diminish Ruby's light.

He had straight black hair that met his shoulders, dark, brooding eyes, and a hawk nose over a harsh mouth. Despite an overall leanness, his arms and chest were well muscled beneath his linen shirt. He could not, however, disguise the pain that she sensed had been a constant companion to him for a very long time.

Airie understood chronic pain and that each individual dealt with it differently. The pain, she suspected, Blade could endure. Its limiting effects, he could not. Sooner or later his lameness would eat away all that he had been and leave nothing but bitterness behind, and what a waste that would be. This was a man whose friendship Hunter valued. Ruby, too, obviously respected him.

Airie could help.

He limped to a large chair near the stove and eased himself into it.

"What happened to your leg?" she asked.

Ruby stiffened.

His eyes met Airie's. "I battled a demon and lost," he said, his words flat and cold. Dispassionate. "It ate most of my thigh."

Ruby gasped. "Blade!"

Airie had heard Hunter tell him what she was, and the anger in Blade's response. She had braced herself for a revelation like this. Not much wonder he hated her and had said he would kill her if he had to.

It didn't change the fact that he was suffering and she had the ability to help him.

Scratch slid from the bench and toddled the short distance to Blade. He did not wait for assistance, but climbed onto the man's lap without invitation. Blade's surprise and uncertainty as to what to do next defused the tension permeating the room. He did not seem to know what to do with his hands. Wincing, he set them under the little boy's arms and shifted his weight off his injured leg.

Airie needed to touch Blade in order to determine the extent of his injury, and Scratch had given her an opportunity to get close. That it was an old injury would make repairing it more difficult, although not impossible. It would depend on how willing he was to accept her help.

During her mother's last days, she had refused help from Airie. She had known she was dying, Airie now knew, and Airie could not cure what nature decreed. Only slow it.

Demons, however, were not natural to this world, and she believed she could heal an injury caused by one. But only if Blade let her.

He continued to watch her, his hostility not as open, but neither was it completely hidden. Airie pushed the food around her plate with her fork.

"You're tired," Ruby guessed, noticing her lack of interest in the meal. "Let me feed the boy, then I'll show you where you'll be sleeping." She looked at Blade, daring him to argue. "They can use your room. You'll stay with me."

Scratch remained on Blade's lap while Ruby fed him, and as he held the boy, the man's mood seemed to shift. It softened. And saddened.

Airie's heart ached for him. Blade wanted this. He wanted domestic, and normal, and he believed he could never have it. He was wrong. He could have this if he wanted. His leg wasn't what kept it from him. It was the excuse that kept him from having to try. Even if she healed the physical wounds, he would have to deal with the deeper scars on his own.

The kitchen was warm, and a knot in the kindling snapped, sending sparks crackling around the inside of the stove. She yawned and started to rise, intending to take Scratch from Blade and use that as an excuse to get close, but Ruby was faster. She lifted Scratch from Blade's arms.

Blade stood too, and without warning, his weak leg went out from beneath him. He tumbled to one knee, Ruby helpless beside him, her arms filled with little boy. Blade's hand hit the stove's hot surface palm down as he fell, and he swore.

Airie darted forward and grabbed his burned hand.

"Don't touch me!" Blade growled. He tried to jerk his hand free from her grasp, but Airie was strong and refused to release it. Blisters, thick and watery, had begun to form. She poured healing into his hand. And then, she extended its reach. She did not ask his permission. He would not want the help of a demon, not even a half one. His revulsion for her was plain, and made her hesitate, but for no more than a second. She could not bear to see him suffer when there was no need for it.

The extent of the damage done to his leg filled her with a deep sense of dismay. She closed her eyes. Not much wonder he, too, hated her for what she was. It was a testimony to his inner strength and whoever had tended him that he had survived such a wound.

That he could walk at all defied belief.

A flicker of awareness for what she was doing dilated his eyes. "Stop," he said, his voice harsh and tight. "I don't want this."

He meant he didn't want the help of a demon.

She continued to knit the nerves and tissue anyway, and reconstructed what she could. His skin remained scarred. She would leave him that much because she knew he would want the reminder of an important event in his life. But he didn't wish to be a cripple. That, she could take away.

Finally, Airie opened her eyes to meet his.

He was angry, she saw. Furious, although he hid it well. Ruby stood nearby, clutching Scratch to her breast, uncertain what to do or whom to help. Worry etched her brow. Blade's gaze shifted from Airie to her, and when he saw the expression on Ruby's face, some of his anger faded. But not all.

"Take them away," he ordered Ruby, not rising from his one-kneed position on the floor. He held his burned hand to his chest. His breath came in small gasps, as if he were in great pain, but any pain he experienced was no longer physical.

Ruby wanted to go to him, but Airie read her indecision. After a visible struggle, she seemed to decide that he was best left alone.

"I'll be right back," Ruby said to him. "Don't you dare try to move."

Ruby handed Scratch to Airie, lifted a lantern from one of the hooks on a ceiling joist, and ushered her up a staircase at the rear of the kitchen.

The saloon had three stories, unlike many of its meaner neighbors. Three women lived in rooms on the second floor. Blade kept the attic for himself.

The room Ruby led her to was large but spare. A double bed filled one corner. A sturdy wardrobe stood in another. A cushioned bench lined a deep window well beneath a skylight. Airie could see the night stars above her. A screen in the third corner indicated a chamber area.

"There are clean linens in the wardrobe," Ruby said, distracted and obviously in a hurry to return to Blade. She lit a lantern on the nightstand. "A nightdress, too. If you need anything else, my room is directly below this one. It's the first off this set of stairs."

"I didn't hurt him," Airie said, wanting badly for this woman to think well of her before Blade told her the truth about what she was and changed her mind.

"I know you didn't," Ruby said. She smiled, although it was tainted with sadness. "I knew the minute you touched my hand that you could heal."

She left, closing the door behind her, and Airie no longer felt as if she had done something good.

* * *

Disregarding Ruby's instructions not to move, Blade pushed himself to his feet and steadied his breathing.

In and out, in and out.

He looked at his palm in the flickering light of the lanterns hanging about the low-ceilinged room. It was unburned. A recent nick on one of his knuckles was also gone.

But it was the absence of pain for the first time in almost a decade that left him dizzy and made his knees unable to hold his weight. He staggered into his chair and probed his bad leg through the heavy fabric of his trousers with nerveless, shaking fingers.

He was afraid to look. Beyond a doubt, the leg was whole.

He could hear the soft voices of the women above him, drifting down the stairwell. Ruby would be back soon and Blade was not ready to face her.

He kept his array of knives beneath the counter. He rose, and began the slow limp to collect them, then realized he no longer needed to do so. A fresh wave of dizziness assailed him, and he grabbed for the table. He shifted his weight to his bad leg.

It held him.

He gathered the knives and slipped them into his clothing with practiced speed, listening hard for Ruby's footsteps on the stairs. Then he walked to the door, gingerly, remembering those mind-crippling days after the demon attack when he had thought he might never walk again. Only Ruby had kept him from taking his own life. She had also forced him to take his first steps.

His brain disengaged, overwhelmed. He had to get away, to think, but he had nowhere to go. He strode into the small courtyard off the kitchen, then crossed to the gate with increasing confidence. His leg was as good as new. Better, in fact.

Once outside in the empty street and under the protective cover of night, he walked without any clear destination. Instinct led him to the city wall and the hidden tunnel Hunter used for his comings and goings.

Blade slipped into the tunnel, needing the privacy, not knowing what to do next and feeling as if his entire world had keeled on its side yet again. He'd made a new life, far different from the first. He rested his back against the dirt wall, then slid to the ground.

He sat in the darkness and wept.

* * *

When the first demons appeared on the horizon, blocking the moon with their numbers, Hunter was well within sight of the arroyo.

He quickened his pace, and as he ran across the shadowed desert, he thought about strategy. Demons didn't play well with others. Of the estimated hundred or so in existence, probably no more than thirty would form any kind of alliance. Even that would be of short duration, because they would turn on each other as easily as on men.

A force of thirty demons was still formidable. Three times the size of a mortal man in their manhunting form, with bone plating protecting any vulnerable areas, they could tear an inexperienced fighter apart in seconds.

While Hunter's amulet gave him his opponents' strength, outsmarting them was up to him, and demons weren't stupid. *Sluggish thinkers*, was how Blade once described them. Perhaps it was because their manhunting form was predatory, distracting them with the scent of blood and the heat of battle. If the wagoners were to draw demon blood first, it might create enough of a distraction within the demon ranks to help them survive the night.

Hunter ducked through the scrub and into the arroyo. He called out to alert the wagoners of his identity so he wouldn't be shot, or run through with a blade or an arrow, as he approached.

"They're coming," he said, telling the men on watch what they wouldn't have been able to see. "I have a plan."

They would begin with flaming arrows. Hunter needed the majority of demons kept at a distance while he lured one or two from the sky. Then, he would draw blood. Once they were in frenzy, they'd be less careful about protecting their vulnerable spots.

He waited at the head of the arroyo, the archers behind him and the hot pitch nearby. The first demons appeared. The first volley of flaming arrows flew in response.

One of the demons broke free of the others, as Hunter had hoped. It landed on the desert floor, out of range of the arrows. "Slayer!"

Hunter, his sword in his hand, stepped out of the canyon. The desert night was cold. Stars sparkled in the sky. There was no sign of rain tonight, and the archers were keeping the rest of the demons at bay as best they could. Adrenaline surged. He enjoyed fighting too much. Eventually, that would be his downfall.

The demon on the ground shifted. Became mortal.

"Slayer," it called to him again.

Its voice was hypnotic, even to Hunter, who was a man and supposedly immune to it.

Not immune. Rather, not so deeply affected, and not in the same way. It had challenged him, and he was responding to it. His sister hadn't stood a chance against this.

Neither would Airie, despite any demon traits she might have inherited.

The quiet of the night was broken by the steady hiss of released arrows and the whisper of wings. Hunter, his sword in his hand, strode out to meet the one who challenged him. He stopped a few yards away.

"What have you done with the spawn the priestess paid you to bring to me?" the demon demanded.

So this was the Demon Lord. The moon and the stars lit up the desert landscape and Hunter could see his opponent quite clearly. With long black hair and direct eyes, he was larger than Hunter—heavier, and better muscled.

Hunter's amulet glowed fiercely, blistering his skin, a warning that even in mortal form, this demon was dangerous. He spread his legs and moored his feet more firmly in the dirt, bracing himself for attack. The thought of Airie in those hands turned his stomach to stone. "She's dead."

"She was seen with you." The demon remained unmoving, watchful. "I would imagine she's very beautiful. Tell me about her."

"When the old priestess died, the mountain would no longer tolerate a spawn's presence and it collapsed, taking her with it. She is dead," Hunter repeated.

"She's not." The demon's features hardened. "I want her. If you don't give her to me, I will rip these people apart. Then I'll burn the city to the ground. I will show no mercy."

"Why do you care about her?" Hunter asked. "Why is she so special to you?"

"Because she's one of mine."

Airie belonged to Hunter. He wasn't giving her up.

He tightened his grip on his sword and advanced. His amulet flared another warning. A second winged demon broke free from the legion soaring above to land lightly behind him, and Hunter now had two demons stalking him. The amulet indicated that the Demon Lord remained the greater threat, so that was where he kept his attention.

And then a shadow, moving silently across the dark desert, came to his aid, running toward him in a crouch. Knives flew from fingertips with unnerving precision, aimed at the second demon and the vulnerabilities between those bony plates. Several of the well-aimed blades hit their marks, and the demon grunted in surprise as blood poured from the wounds. It turned on itself, biting and clawing at the protruding knives, before retreating into the night sky.

Hunter went after the Demon Lord with his sword. The Demon Lord flashed a feral grin. Any other mortal would have felt terror. Not Hunter. Not when Airie had been threatened. All he felt was fury.

"This is your final warning. I want the spawn," the Demon Lord said. "Then, you can have your fight. When it's over, I'll give her your head as a gift." He shifted, resuming his manhunting form, and shot into the night sky to rejoin the others.

"I'm not used to running anymore," Blade complained, resting his hands on his knees in an effort to catch his breath.

Hunter might have questioned his ability to do so now, except he'd seen Airie's healing skills before and could guess what had happened. For his friend's sake, he wasn't sorry.

He bent to retrieve Blade's knives. "I suggest you get used to running again," he said, "because we have to move fast." He looked at the blood staining the ground, then at the swirling sky. "More company's coming."

They spent the remainder of the night in the canyon, taking their turns with bows and arrows. Blade wasn't as good with this weapon as he was with his knives, but Hunter's aim was respectable.

During a lull, he and Blade sat together. Blade polished his knives with sand to remove the demon blood. Hunter didn't ask him about his leg. They did, however, speak of Airie.

"The Demon Lord wants her alive," Hunter said.

Blade frowned as he worked. Each cleaned knife vanished into his clothing. "Have you touched her?" he asked. Hunter shot him a dark look. "I don't mean in that way." He paused, reconsidering his question. "You haven't, have you?"

"No," Hunter said. "Not that it's any of your business."

"When she touched me to heal my leg, I felt nothing but good coming from her."

"She set a man's boots on fire," Hunter countered. He doubted if the godseekers would welcome her as their goddess after that.

"His boots. Not him. And the man tried to kill you first, did he not?"

"He did."

Hunter traced a figure in the ground between his bent knees with a small rock. He'd considered himself a loner for many years now. An outsider. And yet, he had places he could go if he chose. Even family, if he wanted or needed them. What would it be like to be in Airie's position—a woman alone, unwelcome, and feared by all?

"I want to believe the best of her. But she's half demon. That won't change. No one who discovers it will ever accept her."

The dissonant howl of frustrated demons echoed off the canyon walls. The enslaved women huddled closer, no doubt afraid that one of them might yet be chosen as a peace offering. But despite the unnerving noise, Hunter knew the wagoners were holding their own. A few more hours and the ordeal would be over for another night.

"Are you afraid of her?" he asked Blade, his thoughts again returning to Airie.

"I wouldn't have left her unguarded in my home if I believed she was a threat to anyone." Blade looked at Hunter. "Are you? Afraid of her?"

"No. I'm afraid *for* her."

Blade slipped the last of his knives back into his clothing. "Then you, my friend, have a problem."

He did indeed. He thought of her constantly. He dreamed of her. His compulsion to be with her—to protect her—was great, and he wasn't a man given to impulse. She had a beautiful smile and a kind heart. But how much of his attraction to her was because she was demon, and had its allure?

"Do you find her attractive?" he asked Blade.

His friend froze. The sidelong look he sent Hunter was loaded with speculation. "Will an honest answer get me killed?"

"No. Possibly," Hunter conceded. He couldn't be sure, and now he wished he hadn't asked the question.

"Yes. She's beautiful. Any man would tell you the same thing. But I can resist her. I'm not as certain the same can be said for you." Blade stood, ready to take another turn with a bow and arrow. He tested his leg as if still not quite trusting its soundness. "Do the world a favor—If you want her, then act on it. Don't think so hard about the reason for it. And don't tempt other men by asking such questions. Not unless you're willing to fight them for her."

When he considered the matter from a practical perspective, who would be better able to protect the world from a spawn than the Demon Slayer?

But a small, ugly part of him couldn't forget that he would be making a spawn a permanent part of his life.

He returned to his position at the mouth of the canyon, aimed a flaming arrow at a shadow above, and released it. A scream rang out in reward. The demon he struck reared back, wings beating hard, its feet scrabbling at air, although it didn't fall from the sky.

Hunter watched it break rank and fly off, an arrow protruding from beneath its ribs.

Airie might have demon blood in her, but she wasn't one of them. She never would be. He wouldn't abandon her to them.

CHAPTER FOURTEEN

Airie sat by the window all night, watching the sky, with Scratch on her lap. She stroked his hair. There'd be more children like him, and the young boy at the trading post, in the world. If there was no place for her, then what was to become of innocents such as these?

She'd been so lucky. She'd had a mother who'd loved her to teach her right from wrong.

When Scratch fell asleep, she moved him to the bed, then returned to the bench in the window well and her vigil. What if Hunter was hurt? What if he needed her?

She knew the instant he returned. Light had begun to seep over the tops of the city walls. She heard him enter through the courtyard and the back door, but he didn't immediately come upstairs. Low voices rumbled in the kitchen two floors below, although not loud enough for her to distinguish what was being said. Something heavy scraped across the tile-d kitchen floor.

The wait was agony.

Then, he stood in the doorway.

Airie flew across the room and into his arms, the too-short nightdress she'd found in the wardrobe tangling around her shins. Relieved beyond measure that he was safe and in one piece, she rained kisses along the lean lines of his fresh-shaven jaw. That was the scraping she had heard on the floor in the kitchen downstairs—the washtub. He'd stopped to clean off the violence of the night.

Ruby trailed behind Hunter, her fiery hair loose around her shoulders, wearing a thin cotton robe over her nightdress. Her slipper-clad feet made very little sound as she eased past him and gathered a sleepy Scratch into her arms.

"You'll sleep better if you don't have a little boy under your feet," she said. She cradled the boy's head against her shoulder and turned to leave. "I'll take care of him."

"No." Airie had worried all night over Hunter. She wanted Scratch where she could see him, and know he was safe.

"Let them go," Hunter said.

Something unsettling in his eyes as he looked at her made her obey. It didn't frighten her. But it made her cautious. The door closed behind Ruby, the soft snick of the latch echoing loudly in the sparsely furnished room.

"What's wrong?" Airie asked.

"Well-timed rain showers. Godseekers shouting about the return of a goddess. Miracles." He traced a finger along her cheek, then brushed her lips with his thumb. "Forget I said anything. They're not important."

But she could see they were important to him.

"I told you that the goddesses hear me when I call to them. That I spoke with one," Airie reminded him. "I told you the rain chased the demons away."

"You told me, but I wasn't listening to your meaning," Hunter said. "I've heard it now."

He was speaking in riddles. She pulled away from him. "Then you can explain it to me because I don't know what it is you think you've heard me say other than that the goddesses bring rain."

He wouldn't allow her to withdraw, capturing her hand. "Please, Airie," he implored her, tiredness apparent in his whole manner. It blanketed his features and shadowed his eyes. "I need you near me. Innocence is such a rare thing in this world."

A few short days ago he had called her spawn. While she disliked that he thought of her as such, she did not care for him thinking her innocent either.

And yet she knew she was both.

Perhaps it was the demon in her that made her more daring. It had been a long, frightening night of worry, and she was glad to touch him. If it was her innocence he wanted, he could have it. She had no real interest in preserving it.

Not where Hunter was concerned.

She pressed against him, her hands on his chest, and lifted her lips to his. Heat shot to her apex on contact, sparking into flames that spread through her body until fire consumed her. She made a soft sound of pleasure.

The effect on him was like setting a struck match to dry kindling. His tongue thrust between her lips, boldly stroking the insides of her mouth.

She met his tongue with the tip of her own. He tasted warm and sweet, and Airie wanted more of him. Tangling her hands in his shirt, she fumbled with the buttons. His hands covered hers, helping her, then the shirt dropped to the floor.

The pads of his fingers caressed her bare flesh at the open neck of the wide-collared nightdress she wore. He inched the smooth fabric off her shoulders, then hesitated. He broke off the kiss.

"I need you to understand what we are doing," he said to her, his breathing unsteady as he struggled to speak. He closed his eyes, then opened them again to meet hers. His thumbs swiped across her collarbone so that she had difficulty focusing on his words. "If we go much further, I won't stop."

"I don't want you to," she said. "I'm not stopping either."

He dropped a kiss to her forehead, and suddenly, she wanted him. All of him. She wanted him in her, as close as they could possibly become. She shrugged out of the nightdress. It slipped from her shoulders to pool at her feet. She stepped out of it, then kicked it aside.

Hunter cupped her face, tipping her head back so that she met his gaze. His eyes were blue and very intense, and any concern she might have had as to whether or not he found her attractive solely because of her demon blood vanished.

"You are so beautiful," he said to her, with just enough wonder in his tone to stoke the fires of desire. She'd never thought of herself as such, had never had a reason to think about it, but he made her feel as if it were an indisputable fact.

She liked that he thought of her that way.

One of his palms slid down her arm to her waist. His fingers trailed across her bare hip, then he tugged her against him. Again, he kissed her. Slower this time, deeper, and so thoroughly she lost all sense of their shifting surroundings.

He had drawn her to the bed. Soft morning light enveloped them as he pressed her into the rough blankets, the springs of the mattress groaning beneath their combined weight. He shrugged out of his trousers, sliding them off his muscular thighs and casting them aside.

She had never seen a naked man before, although she'd been told what to expect.

He lay down beside her and propped his head on his elbow, looking at her with understanding. "Go ahead and touch me," he invited her. "Wherever you'd like." Desire darkened his eyes. "If you're not ready for that, close your eyes and I can touch you."

"I'm ready." She smiled at him.

Teasing the arch of her foot along one of his calves, she enjoyed the texture of his skin. Her hand went to his hip, then the tips of her fingers traced the curve of his buttocks. The amused expression on his face disappeared.

He bent his head forward and placed a kiss on her neck. The next kiss feathered her breast. Then he drew the rosy bud of her nipple into his mouth, tracing the tip with his tongue, and she gasped with pleasure.

She touched the hard planes of his stomach and he sucked in a breath. She drew her hand away, uncertain of what his reaction meant, but he caught it.

"You surprised me, is all," he said. "Surprises are good." She ran her hand lower, felt tufts of curls, and encircled him with her palm. He let out a low groan. "*Very* good." He kissed her mouth, his tongue tracing her lips. "And very surprising."

He reached between them and wrapped his fingers over hers, showing her how to move her hand. She loved the sounds he made as she did so, his eyes closing in deep concentration as she found a rhythm that pleased him.

He released her hand and moved his own to the mound between her thighs. He inserted a finger, stroking her gently to the same cadence she caressed him, and she cried out in amazement.

"I told you surprises are good," he said, sensual satisfaction curving his lips as he watched her face.

She could no longer speak, lost in the sensations he'd created, arching her back to press against him and force his touch deeper inside her. He shifted his hips so that she could no longer hold him in her hand. He leaned over her, guiding the tip to her opening.

"I'm sorry, Airie," he said. "This often hurts the first time." He slid his entire length inside her in one thrust, then lay still, holding his weight on his arms until she could breathe again. "Give it a moment. You'll get used to the feel."

He distracted her with silly words, mixing them with tender kisses. His tongue again found her mouth, thrusting in and out, until suddenly, she realized he'd started to move inside her as well.

Any pain was forgotten, replaced by an indescribable pleasure. Sweat beaded on his forehead as he established a slow, deep tempo that gradually built. Within moments she was writhing beneath him, begging him for more, to make it faster.

"Airie, honey, if I do that, it will be over too soon for you." Pleasure and regret mingled in his eyes as he gazed down at her.

"I don't care," she gasped, the slow build of an impending climax clenching her muscles around the hard length of him. Color exploded behind her eyes and she cried out, wrapping her legs around him. He gave in to her demands, thrusting harder and deeper, and groaned as he came, although Airie barely heard him past the waves of pleasure engulfing her.

Hunter did not withdraw afterward, but anchored his weight so that he did not crush her and watched with an air of intense satisfaction while she recovered. He traced the curve of her cheek with the backs of his fingers.

"The first time is the worst," he said.

Airie caught his hand in both of hers. She pressed his fingers to her lips. "If that was the worst, then I don't dare dream about how wonderful the next time will be." He frowned, and some of her pleasure dimmed, replaced by uncertainty. "That was presumptuous of me," she said. "I enjoyed it so much that I assumed you did, too. You don't have to do it again if you don't want." She tried to push away from him.

"Stop." He pinned her down and kissed her until she went quiet beneath him. "I'm flattered beyond belief that you enjoyed it. Believe me, I did too, every bit as much, if not more. I'll be able to think of nothing else now until the next time, which may be far too soon for you.

"But did you know," he added, continuing to frown, "that your eyes are on fire?"

* * *

The fire in her eyes quickly cooled.

He had made a mistake, he saw at once, both in what he had said, but more importantly, what he had done. Claiming her hadn't diminished her appeal. In fact, the opposite was true.

The shift wasn't subtle. Sensuality seeped from her, her bare skin gleaming like brushed gold beneath the spray of morning sunshine on the rumpled bed. Gone was the innocent beauty, replaced by a glowing woman who was too desirable by far.

He couldn't say he fully regretted it. He wanted her again. And he wanted her far from demon territory, where she'd be safe. But first he had to explain, because he could see that she'd misinterpreted his words.

"Your eyes are beautiful. I like that I can make them flame."

He said the last with more satisfaction than intended, but it achieved the desired effect. Her smile returned, more radiant.

"For the most part I can control it. But you make me forget."

She made him forget things, too. Important ones. At their first meeting, her eyes had shot fire when he'd thrown her in the lake. They had also flamed when she confronted the godseekers.

Which brought him back to the matter of his second mistake. A level of sensuality that could only be attributed to her demon blood had been awakened in her. The effect was magnetic and didn't appear to be lessening with the passing moments. Regardless of where she eventually settled, her mixed heritage would never go unnoticed. Not by men, and most assuredly not by demons. But better for her to be noticed by mortal men, who she could defend herself against, than by demons, who perhaps she could not.

Absently, he stroked her neck and shoulder while he thought matters through. His fingers brushed against the amulet she wore, and his own warmed pleasantly in response. The two fit together. He wondered if they magnified his and Airie's reactions to each other.

Natural or not, whatever the source of his attraction to her, he'd already made the decision that she was his. He'd convinced himself that he would be protecting mortals from her. In reality, Airie was the one who needed protection the most. He had to get her away from demon territory and that part of her heritage. He'd take her to the Borderlands, to his childhood home. It wouldn't be far enough—a demon had managed to find his sister there—but it would be a start.

He was tired of fighting demons. His sister was dead and nothing would bring her back, while Airie was alive and he had the ability to keep her that way. He no longer cared who had fathered her. She'd been raised well. Her tendency toward petty thievery aside, she was open and honest. She had empathy for others. He liked those qualities in her, and they had nothing to do with sexual attraction—although that, too, was high.

"We're leaving tomorrow," he said. "You, Scratch and me. As long as we stay here, you're in danger."

She'd started to drift off to sleep. Her eyes, now their natural dark, chocolate brown, fluttered open. "What do you mean?"

He twisted a lock of her hair around one finger, rubbing it with his thumb. "You once asked me what I was doing on Goddess Mountain and I never answered."

She sighed and rolled to her back, dragging the sheet with her to cover her breasts. "I no longer want to know," she said, staring at the ceiling.

Guilt consumed him, forcing him to continue. "I was hired by a priestess to bring you to her. She intends to turn you over to the Demon Lord."

Airie tilted her head toward him, her soft exhalation of breath heating his skin. "And you agreed to do it because I'm spawn."

Her calm understanding cut him, almost as much as her use of the slur. It sounded ugly coming so casually from her lips. How many times had he wounded her by using it himself in the same manner?

"I agreed to it because if I didn't go after you, she would have found someone else to do it. I couldn't in good conscience see a woman turned over to demons."

"Unless the woman was spawn," Airie added. Her fingers tightened on the bedding, their tips whitening.

Yes. That was to have been his justification. He despised himself for it. "I tried to keep you from coming here."

"Yet here we are." She shifted to face him. "What will you do with me?"

"You aren't listening." He wanted the fire back in her eyes. "I said that you, Scratch and I are leaving."

"When the goddesses and the Demon Lord all want me dead? Why would I endanger the two of you too?"

"Mamna doesn't represent the goddesses." Hunter needed her to understand that. "She's an evil, hateful little woman who has made a position for herself by using her connection to the immortals to her advantage." He cupped her chin so that she had to look at him. "I don't believe the goddesses want you dead. You told me that one speaks to you. What of that?"

Airie's gaze remained steady and unreadable. "You were right, and I was mistaken. It was a demon."

Hunter drove a hand through his hair. He had a lot to atone for. He had done nothing to make her believe in her own worth. "Do you trust me?"

Airie bit her lip.

"*Do* you?"

She finally nodded, and the weight crushing his lungs eased.

"I never told you what happened to my sister. I've never told anyone." He swallowed against the painful lump in his throat that always accompanied her memory and forced himself to continue. "We grew up in the Borderlands. She was closest to me in age, and very beautiful, even more so than my other sisters. I'd gotten used to them sneaking in and out of the house to meet boyfriends over the years, so when she started doing it too, I didn't think anything of it. Not until she got pregnant. And even then, when she begged me not to tell, I kept her secret for her. We lived so far from demon territory that the possibility never occurred to me. I thought the father was some local boy."

He brushed the backs of his knuckles up and down the side of her neck, and she closed her eyes as if knowing how the story would end.

"She disappeared one night, and when I finally tracked her down in the desert, the spawn she gave birth to had already torn her to shreds. I killed it. I tracked the father down and I killed him, too. Now you know why I hate spawn, and why I hate demons."

Airie looked away. "I see."

"No, you don't." He shifted one leg, turning her to face him. "You aren't spawn and you aren't a demon. You are Airie—nothing more, nothing less—just as your mother said. And nothing will ever change that. I won't allow anything to happen to either you or Scratch. We'll find a place for the three of us. In the meantime, until we're ready to leave Freetown, I want you to stay here, remain out of sight, and let me take care of everything."

He kissed her, felt her lips part, then deepened it briefly before drawing away. She had been up all night, waiting for him. They were both exhausted. He had things to do, but nothing that couldn't wait. Right now, he wanted to make certain she slept.

He settled onto a pillow and spooned her against him, her back to his front, his hand at her waist. Once she fell asleep, he'd return Mamna's gold. Then, they would leave Freetown. In his head, he ran through the things they'd need. Crossing a desertful of demons with her wasn't going to be easy.

Staying in Freetown, however, would be disastrous. For everyone.

* * *

Sleep eluded Blade.

He'd have thought the opposite would be true, considering this was the first time in years he had approached it without pain.

Perhaps it was because he was alone in Ruby's bed. Each of the women who lived at the saloon had two attached rooms at their disposal. One, they used for working. The other was private. Blade was in her private room.

Alone.

He punched a pillow to distribute the feathers more evenly. He didn't know what to make of Airie. Or her relationship with Hunter. He pitied his friend though—and envied him, too. Not because of her looks, which were stunning enough, but for the way she seemed to occupy his friend's thoughts so completely. He couldn't remember Hunter ever allowing a woman to distract him to this extent before. The fact that she had done so told Blade far more about her character—who she was, rather than what—than her healing of his leg.

Hunter's hatred of demons, however, ran far deeper than his. He didn't know what had happened in Hunter's past to make this a truth, but he did know that Airie was going to have a difficult time getting beyond it.

He stretched out on his back beneath Ruby's plain cotton sheets, resting his head on his bent arm. Faint light trickled through the drawn muslin curtains, but he could see the contents of the room clear enough. A small writing desk with a ruffle-skirted chair, a chaise longue adorned in many multi-colored silk cushions, delicate oil paintings on the walls he suspected she'd created herself in another lifetime. She was feminine but practical.

Now that he had a life to offer her, he was going to ask her to marry him. Together, they would run the saloon. They'd offer a haven to women. And now that he could protect them properly, the women wouldn't have to work on their backs unless they wanted to—which, Ruby assured him, some of them did.

It was early yet. He rolled from the bed, drew on his trousers, and took the back stairs to the kitchen where he knew Ruby would have taken the little boy so she could work. At this hour, she'd be alone and they could talk—something she'd been avoiding.

The scene he walked in on was what he'd expected. She stood at the stove, her hair caught back with a scarf and her face shiny from the heat, while Scratch—Hunter needed to do something about a real name for the boy—sat on the floor near her feet. She'd given him a pot and spoon to play with. The boy smiled up at him.

Ruby, too, glanced up from the stove, although she didn't smile. Her eyes darted to his leg, then away, as if she didn't want to be caught staring. As far as Blade was concerned, she could stare all she liked. She'd seen him at his absolute worst. Now she could see him as a whole man—one he hoped had grown better over the years. He wasn't proud of his past. Before he asked her to marry him, he planned to tell her about it. He cleared his throat, nervous now, and she stiffened as if she knew he was about to say things she didn't want to hear.

"I was an assassin before you met me," he said to her back.

Her tone, when she replied, was neutral. "That's not a surprise."

Of course it wasn't. She'd seen him practice with his knives. She knew he'd murdered the woman Mamna had condemned. What she didn't know was how he had become one. Why.

"I killed my uncle when I was fourteen." That earned him a bit more of her attention. "He raised me after my parents died. I hated the bastard. He beat me and made me work in the mines like a slave. There wasn't a bit of kindness in him."

Some of the stiffness went out of her spine. "Then it sounds as if he deserved it."

Blade had always thought so. The rest of the community, however, hadn't shared his belief. The mining tunnels his uncle owned had collapsed shortly after, leaving them unworkable, and he'd borne the brunt of the blame for the bad luck.

"My uncle was a godseeker. I had no choice as to what I'd become after I killed him. Only the lawless would do business with me."

For the first few years he hadn't asked questions regarding who he'd been contracted to kill. Women and children, usually runaways or thieves, had been among their numbers. Those had been speedily done. As time went on and his skills improved, he'd been given more voice.

But when he'd tried to cross the desert on his own, his lost battle with a demon meant he again had no choice with regard to his future. What money he'd managed to save had gone into the saloon.

Now, he had choices.

When he finished talking, and laying out the bare facts, he waited a long time for any response. She continued to stir the pot on the stove, a frown on her face, and beckoned for him to remove the fresh bread from the oven. Above them, he could hear the other women starting their day.

She banged the spoon on the edge of the pot before setting it on the counter and turning to face him. "Does Hunter know you killed a godseeker?"

"He knows I came from the north. He knows I killed my uncle. The pieces are easy enough to put together." He gave her a half-hearted grin. "Apparently I babble when I'm feverish."

"You do."

Blade didn't ask what he'd babbled to her about. Her manner suggested he might be better off if he didn't. "What does it matter?"

"Your uncle was chosen by the goddesses," Ruby said.

Blade couldn't hide his distaste. "He was a handsome man, who was nothing more than one of their pleasurable toys, and so arrogant he couldn't see the truth of that."

"Is it true that a goddess will lead the Slayer against the demons?"

He shifted his weight, forgetting his leg no longer needed to be favored, and straightened. He felt as if he had grown several inches taller overnight, and his back was stiff from the change in his posture. "You can't believe stories that are told second hand."

She watched him with thoughtful eyes as he stretched his back muscles. "What if Airie is that goddess?"

"She's not."

"She healed your leg."

"That doesn't make her one of them." He exhaled. "I grew up on stories of the goddesses. I remember their visits to the northern mountains from when I was a child. They were never what the world would have you believe. Call them goddesses or demons if you like, but in the end, they are all immortals, one and the same." He heard doors opening and closing and knew he had to hurry. "I have something I've wanted to ask you for a long time," he began. He wouldn't ask her now, not when privacy was no longer assured, but he'd give her an opportunity to think about it rather than spring it on her unannounced. "Perhaps tonight?"

Her smile became fixed and falsely bright. "We'll see," she said. "The last few days have been poor ones, moneywise. If business picks up, I may be working. If not, there's a child in the house to consider." She nodded at Scratch, who had been so silent Blade had forgotten his presence. "You should go back to bed for a few more hours," she advised him. "There will be plenty of time for questions in the future."

A sense of unease assailed him, but he let it go. "You're probably right."

He climbed the back stairs to her rooms. Instead of her private bedroom, he slipped into her working area.

She'd chosen red as a color scheme, an obvious play on her name. The room was decorated in satins and silks, with lush dressings hanging from the walls and varieties of intimate lace strategically spilling from open drawers. Beneath the king-sized bed she kept a box filled with what she referred to as the *tools of the trade*.

She'd never offered to use them with him.

He sat gingerly on the edge of the bed, mentally comparing this room to the one he occasionally shared with her. He realized that he knew very little about either her or her background. In fact, she knew far more about him. He rubbed his leg out of long habit. She knew what he wanted to ask her. She was going to say no.

And he, fool that he was, was going to ask her anyway.

CHAPTER FIFTEEN

Hunter dressed. Then, for a long time, he stood beside the bed and watched Airie sleep.

She was golden-skinned and painfully lovely. Her long hair, loose across one naked shoulder, gleamed like a waterfall of black diamonds caught in a shaft of sunlight. The rainbow-hued amulet around her neck exuded a palpable contentment. The one he wore emitted a similar sensation.

He wished he could share in it. He felt as if he'd stolen something irreplaceable from her. He'd taken what he wanted, and told himself it was in her best interests, but by doing so, he'd tied her to him without regard for her wishes. He couldn't let her go now, and while he no longer had any objection to having her as a permanent part of his life, who was to say she wanted him always in hers?

He left her sleeping, and with his boots in his hand, crept silently down the back stairs to the second floor.

As quiet as he tried to be, Blade heard him. He stopped Hunter at the landing, beckoning him into the hall so their voices wouldn't carry. He looked like hell, but Hunter likely looked no better. They'd both shared in a long night spent fighting demons, and another, similar, night approached.

"Where are you going?" Blade asked him.

"To return Mamna's money." He met his friend's gaze. "Then Airie, the boy, and I are leaving. It's not safe for anyone in Freetown with her here."

Blade inclined his head. "That's probably wise."

It could hardly be called wise to take a beautiful, half-demon woman and a small child of questionable parentage on a cross-country trek through the heart of demon territory. And it ate at Hunter to leave Freetown defenseless, without his skills as the Slayer to help them, knowing that another attack was imminent. "I'll be back in a few hours. We should talk about what will come tonight, and how to protect people against it the best way possible."

Again, Blade nodded.

Hunter yanked on his boots and left through the saloon at the front of the building to avoid the women he could hear laughing together in the kitchen.

* * *

Airie huddled at the top of the stairs with her chin resting on her bare knees, hugging her legs, listening to the voices of the two men a floor below.

She made Freetown unsafe for its inhabitants. The grimness in their tone when they spoke of Mamna also made her uneasy. Why would a priestess want to turn Airie, who'd been raised in the goddesses' very own temple, over to demons, whom the goddesses despised?

Because she was spawn. There could be no other explanation.

Did you know that your eyes are on fire?

Pain filled her heart. No matter how Hunter felt about her at this moment, deep down, she would always be spawn to him. When he looked at her he would forever be reminded of a sister he'd loved, and how that sister had died. She didn't delude herself into believing that sleeping with him was enough to surmount such an obstacle. She wanted a place in the world, yes, one with Hunter, but she wanted one that was real. Always, she would wonder when his hatred for what she was began to outweigh his desire. She'd worry over it. Neither did she want to be the reason he left an entire town defenseless.

You deal with what life hands you. How you deal with it is up to you.

Hunter could help these people, and so could she. She was the one the Demon Lord wanted. If she left the city, the demons would follow.

But Hunter would try to follow her too. She'd have to put as much distance between them as possible. And she'd have to leave Scratch behind. She blinked back a few tears at the thought, but Ruby already loved him enough to see to his welfare.

The older woman had left a clean change of clothes for her on a chair next to the bed. Airie dressed in the simple brown skirt that tied at the waist, and long-sleeved, light cotton blouse. The skirt was several inches too short, and the blouse too tight across her breasts, but they were clean and reasonably comfortable. She tied her hair in its braid, then took a few coins from where Hunter had hidden them. She needed to buy a few things in the market. She should also replace the old boots of his she'd been wearing.

She made her way out to the street unseen by Blade or the other inhabitants of the saloon.

* * *

The Slayer had come at last.

Mamna received him inside her home. He entered the front parlor, stooping his head slightly to avoid the crystal chandelier affixed to the ceiling in the center of the room.

He tossed a familiar, draw-stringed bag onto a polished mahogany sideboard. "I wasn't successful. I've come to return your money."

Without another word of explanation, or begging her permission, he turned to leave.

Mamna choked back her anger. Her amulet hadn't yet failed completely only because it hadn't been truly tested. When the Demon Lord attacked Freetown again, and she was expected to respond, the people would soon see the full extent of their vulnerability. And hers. The spawn was her final hope. She had to be here, or somewhere close by. The Slayer wouldn't take that away.

"Wait," she said.

He paused, exhibiting the sleek tension of a sated predator. The indifferent eyebrow he raised infuriated her. She'd paid him well. How dare he stand in her presence and pretend not to have the very thing she wanted?

"What happened on the mountain?" she asked.

His eyes became glittering, blue chips of ice—cold, and difficult to read. "I never reached it. I was a few hours away when the summit collapsed. I met a number of people fleeing for their lives, but none of them was a woman fitting the description you gave me. I assume she died in one of the landslides. Those were especially spectacular, even seen at a distance."

"You're lying."

His expression hardened. "Be careful what you say to me. I've returned your money. I owe you nothing."

"The spawn was seen with you."

"By whom? A godseeker assassin? A demon who slaughtered a small wagon train of innocent people in one of the arroyos? One of your guards who denied entry to another wagon train, which was then forced to defend itself against a demon attack led by the Demon Lord himself? On second thought, I deserve compensation." He retrieved the bag of coins, opened it, and withdrew five gold pieces. He slipped the gold pieces into his pocket and returned the bag to the sideboard. "Don't contact me again. Rely on your other resources to do your dirty work for you."

The man had no fear. Not of demons, and certainly not of her. She would find a way to make him pay for his arrogance. "So you know nothing of a woman who set a man's boots on fire?"

"No."

There were no obvious tells in his body language. He stood at ease, his hands loose at his sides, giving nothing away. Certainty that he was lying galvanized her into recklessness. He had the spawn. She had until nightfall to claim her.

"You've slept with her." It was a stab in the dark, but a very slight dilation of his pupils gave him away. If she hadn't been watching for it she might have missed it. The unwelcome discovery enraged her more. "You foolish, mortal man. You have no idea what you've done."

He shrugged. "Did you know that the Demon Lord made me an offer for her as well?" he asked. "Last night, when I helped those wagoners fight off the demons you'd abandoned them to?" His face was a hard mask. "Let's say I do have her hidden somewhere. Why would I want to turn her over to either one of you? Why wouldn't I want to keep something so valuable for myself?" His cold eyes stabbed her. The temperature in the room dropped ten degrees. "I can live with my choices. I suspect you're the one who has no idea what she's done. Good luck in your battle with the demons."

Fear threatened to eviscerate her. She had to persuade him. Otherwise, he would walk out the door and everything she'd worked for would be gone.

"The spawn has two birthrights," she spat at him. "Aren't you the slightest bit interested in the second?"

"No." He headed across the tiled floor to the door.

"Her mother was a goddess who whored herself to a demon," she shouted after him, too angry to care who in her household might overhear. "She betrayed him. She betrayed her sisters, and the priestesses who served them. She betrayed the entire world. Enjoy your spawn while you can, Slayer. Being a whore will come naturally to her. So will betrayal."

His eyes bored into her. She thought she might have him.

"If she's half goddess and half demon," he said, his hand on the door latch, "that would make you one hundred percent her servant, would it not?"

The door closed behind him.

Mamna was left shaking with anger and fear. She didn't doubt that after tonight, despite the presence of the Demon Slayer, and the godseeker Pillar, Freetown and the majority of its inhabitants would be lost. Why should she be lost too?

She had until nightfall to find the spawn. If the Slayer had brought her to Freetown with him, then Mamna had a good idea of where she might be.

* * *

Airie had no worries about becoming lost. All major streets in Freetown led to the city center and ended at the outer wall. Once she finished in the market she had only to find her way to the wall, then follow the street that encircled it to the tunnel. From there she could make her escape.

Layers of desert dust coated the board sidewalks and the wooden fronts of the buildings of Freetown, although the sun shone bright and hot overhead, and the sky was an endless blue. There was tension in the streets as people struggled to maintain a pretense of normalcy during the day despite what happened at night.

She wasn't oblivious to the stares she received—she, too, had seen the golden cast to her skin—but she held her head high even as her spirits plummeted. Was she fated to be so very different, then?

Once in the market, a degree of anonymity returned as people's attention gravitated toward a high platform in the middle of an open courtyard. A few of the traders from the wagon train peppered the crowd. No one recognized her dressed as a woman as she worked her way into the throng.

Hundreds of voices, all talking at once, blended into a dull, distorted roar that made her ears ache and her heart beat a little faster. The majority of the spectators were men. The crush of bodies, combined with the heat, fast became stifling. Whatever sort of market this was, it wasn't for her.

"What's happening?" she asked a man with thick, gray-streaked hair and heavy white eyebrows over a broad nose.

"Slave auction."

He spared her half a glance, then another, longer, look, as he took in the hue of her skin. His eyebrows disappeared into his shaggy hairline before he sidled away.

She tried to push back the way she came, but the number of people had now swelled to the point that departure was impossible. The crowd carried her forward, not away, and she was swept to its front where ten or so naked women stood shackled together at the back of a platform. Most kept their heads down, averting their faces, although a few held their chins high and stared at the crowd in defiance.

Anger woke the darkness she carried inside her. Fire flared in her eyes. She felt its heat. A dull red crawled beneath the gold of her skin as it sought an escape. *Burn the temple. Burn the entire city to the ground. Make them* fear you.

Then another, gentler voice interceded. *Rain is a part of you, too. It too is yours to command.*

Airie closed her flaming eyes and lifted her face to the sky. *Bring me the rain.*

The sky darkened, opened up, and a downpour began. Chaos erupted as people scattered and fled, seeking shelter. The streets soon flooded with rushing torrents of dirty water.

Someone draped an oiled leather duster over her head to protect her from the driving rain, and Airie could see once again. She wiped water from her face with her free hand and looked into steady, familiar blue eyes. Her demon purred, happy to see him. *Mine.*

She waited for recriminations. Braced herself to receive them. But this was an action she gladly claimed and couldn't regret, because Hunter was wrong. The goddesses did speak to her. And they'd been as angry as she was at the fate of those women.

A huge grin creased his face.

"Nicely done," he said, and kissed her deeply as the deluge continued around them.

* * *

He'd stumbled on her scant seconds before she opened the skies.

The wet taste of her, the wary hope he saw in her eyes, made him wish they weren't standing beneath his coat in an open market. He shouldn't have needed Mamna to point out the obvious. Airie was every bit as much goddess as she was demon. Maybe more so. She could call fire, but chose to call rain. She could destroy, but preferred to heal. She'd been granted refuge on Goddess Mountain.

He thanked those same goddesses that he'd come to the market to purchase supplies. Considering the fire that still burned in her eyes, rainfall wasn't the reaction he would have expected, but it was confirmation that she could, indeed, control what was inside her.

The rain continued to fall, although more gently now. She was soaked to the skin. There was little to be done about that as he hustled her through the empty streets. With the newly acquired golden glow to her skin, and the subtle sensuality, she looked every inch a goddess now. Word of her presence would already be spreading.

"Did you see what was happening?" Airie demanded as he hurried her along. Indignation quivered in her tone.

"I saw." He'd tried to warn her that her expectations of Freetown were too high.

They reached the small compound behind the saloon. He hustled her through the gate and into the kitchen, where he found Blade sitting at the table. Blade paused with his coffee cup halfway to his mouth, surprise in his eyes. He looked from Airie, with her wet, clinging clothes and golden skin, to Hunter, who was equally sodden.

"Don't ask," Hunter said, then spoke to Airie. "Go dry off. I'll join you in a few minutes." He took her hand to draw her back to him again, and looked into her troubled expression. "You'd better be waiting for me. Don't think I don't know you were running away."

Fire sparkled in her eyes.

He watched as she left the room. When the door closed tight behind her, he slid into a seat beside Blade at the table and dropped his forehead into his hands. "I found her at a slave auction in the market. She took exception to it."

"Was she noticed?" Blade asked.

He lifted his head. Incredulity seeped into his tone. "What do you think?"

Blade shrugged. "We have greater problems. The city has been sealed off. The gates are closed and guards have been posted near the tunnel."

Hunter rubbed his tired eyes with the heels of his palms. Demons waited outside the walls and Mamna waited within. The situation wasn't good. Running had never been a real an option. Wherever they went, Airie's father would come for her.

An idea began to form. "What if the Slayer agreed to head the goddess's army?"

"Wouldn't we also need a goddess?"

"According to Mamna, we have one. Or half of one." Hunter repeated what the priestess had told him.

"Do you think word of what happened in the marketplace will spread quickly?" Blade asked.

"I'd imagine word has already reached the Borderlands."

Blade tapped his thumb on the table as he stared at the wall, lost in thought. "We have to convince the godseekers that you're ready to lead them on their goddess's behalf, and get them back out on the streets to spread the word that the Demon Slayer now heads their army." He pushed away from the table. "I know someone who can deliver a message."

* * *

Sapphire had been reluctant at first to admit she knew where the young godseeker assassin she'd spent too much time with was staying. But Blade could be persuasive.

Frighteningly so.

While the girl delivered the message to the northerners that Hunter wished to speak with them, Hunter joined Airie.

She sat on the bed wearing only her shift, watching Scratch play on the floor. Hunter threw himself on top of the blankets beside her. The springs creaked beneath his weight. He wanted nothing more than a few hours of sleep with her in his arms, knowing that she and Scratch were both safe and close at hand.

Fire spilled out of her eyes. It was odd that not so long ago, he'd viewed those same flames with suspicion. Now he recognized it as passion, and an integral part of her personality that he'd come to appreciate and value. He didn't fear it. It entranced him.

"Why were those women being auctioned off in the market?" she asked.

"Freetown supports the sale of women to outlying areas. They usually end up as wives to men working in the more remote mines." But not always.

"Priestesses would never allow such a thing."

Airie sounded more as if she wanted him to confirm the truth of her statement than that she believed it. He wished he could do so, because he liked that she was so innocent of the terrible things that went on in a virtually lawless land. Immortals had once ruled Wasteland completely. Now, it struggled to find a new path.

He rolled to his side and rested his head on the heel of his hand so he could better see her face. He traced a finger along the outside of her thigh, from the curve of her hip to her knee, lifting the edge of the thin cotton shift in an attempt to tease a smile from her. "The priestesses are the ones who began the tradition. They said the slave trade honored the hardworking men of the north by giving them wives made in the image of the goddesses."

"How could the priestesses have strayed so far from the goddesses' teachings?" Airie asked in dismay. "My mother never taught that the goddesses were perfect, but said they bring life to the world. Mortal women do too, and for that alone, women should be respected and honored."

She was such an innocent.

He stopped playing with the hem of her shift and braced himself for whatever storm he was about to unleash. "Blade and I have a plan for fighting the demons. I'll need your help."

"I can call rain against them. That will chase them away, just as it did before."

"Chasing them off is no longer enough. They'll keep coming back. The time has come to take a stand against them. The northerners believe you're a goddess. We can use that to our advantage."

She was so still she could have been carved from stone. "How?"

"Blade has gone to speak with them. He'll tell them I'm willing to lead their army—which I am—and that I'll fight on your behalf." Which he would. Always. "We need you to speak with them too, to help persuade them that you're who they believe you to be."

"You want me to pretend to be a goddess so you can convince people to die fighting demons?" She folded her arms. "No."

She truly didn't know what she was—and he had no idea how to explain, or how much to tell her, to win her support. Northerners expecting to be addressed by her would soon descend on the saloon. He had to persuade them to fight beside him rather than against him. They would only do that if it was a goddess's army he led.

He was bone-tired already from too little sleep and he had another long night ahead of him. Fatigue fueled frustration. Turning her over to the demons would end this standoff for Freetown. It was her life he was trying to protect. He betrayed his own kind for her. She didn't understand that she wasn't mortal, and mortals owed her nothing.

Whereas he would walk through fire for her.

"Have I ever asked so very much of you," he said, "that you can't find it in you to help me now when the people of Freetown need me the most?"

He might as well have slapped her. The hurt in her eyes made the sensation a thousand times worse. But his words couldn't be unspoken.

"I'll gladly help you save lives. But I'm half demon," she said quietly. "Fighting is one thing. Killing them makes me something I don't want to be. There must be another way."

He'd forgotten the conflict her mixed heritage must cause her. Goddesses created. Demons destroyed. She walked a fine line between them. But killing demons was what he did, and what he would continue to do as long as they remained in the mortal world. He'd compromise, but he wouldn't yield. Not on this.

"Make an appearance, that's all I ask. You won't have to do anything. I'll speak for you."

She finally nodded, and the heavy weight inside him eased, but he saw the doubt lingering in her eyes. He took her in his arms. Whatever happened with the demons come nightfall, he'd make certain Airie played no part in it.

What happened in the future, however, remained to be seen. He knew who her father was, even though that was something else of which she was unaware.

And that was good, because Hunter intended to kill him.

CHAPTER SIXTEEN

Steam rose from the muddy streets, only to disperse almost immediately into the dry desert air. The red earth cracked beneath the hot sun. Creosote-soaked sidewalks had dried enough that they were no longer greasy, although treacherous pockets of water continued to pose a hazard to the inattentive.

Mamna settled the hood of a weathered, oiled canvas cloak forward so that her face was in shadow. She'd donned the cloak not so much for disguise—an impossible feat thanks to her deformity—but because her bald scalp and face required vigilant protection from the sun's rays.

She also carried a gun in one deep pocket. The weight of it pressed reassuringly against her thigh. People remained too afraid of her ability to summon demons to openly express hostility toward her, but while many still believed she could protect Freetown, she was well aware of the rebellious, hate-filled glances directed her way as she walked the street that encircled the city inside the wall.

She overheard whispers that the northerners spoke the truth, and a goddess walked in Wasteland again. A third cloudburst in as many days was the proof. Some people swore they'd seen the goddess in the market shortly before the afternoon shower began. Many held out hope that the rains would recur tonight to save them from more demon attacks.

Mamna could have told them that goddess rain, falling in demon territory, wouldn't withstand demon fire for long. Not when Goddess Mountain hadn't survived it. Once the Demon Lord had what he wanted, he'd burn Freetown to the ground.

Mamna would be long gone from the city by then. She'd use the last bit of power her amulet possessed to bring the spawn to heel. She'd tell her of how the goddesses had planned for her birth in order to rid the world of demons forever. She'd force her to repair the amulet.

Then, once darkness descended and the demons threw the city into frenzy, Mamna would make her escape.

There were two gates into the city—one to the north facing demon territory, and the other the east, where Goddess Mountain had fallen. At the north gate, Mamna left the circular thoroughfare and entered one of Freetown's meaner districts. Pillar and his northern followers had taken shelter here. This particular district was used mostly by teamsters who accompanied wagon trains. Its residents were transient and Mamna was less recognizable here. Unless they looked closely, which they'd have no reason to do, most who saw her would assume she was a child.

This was also where the saloon the Slayer favored was located. If the spawn was in the city, then a whorehouse filled with women, and run by a former godseeker assassin, was the perfect place to hide her.

Mamna reached the saloon on the edge of the city, not far from the north gate. The street was busy. Far busier than it should be, considering another demon attack was expected. People should be in hiding. Instead, northerners abounded. She remained in the shadows, watching and waiting, trying to decide how to gain entry unobserved.

Several large open wagons, hauled by straining double teams of sturdy black hross, trundled past the alley where she hid, so heavily laden with kyson hides that the axels creaked and groaned. Sweat stained the hrosses' broad flanks. Their long manes and tails had been plaited, and the beadwork worked into the designs rattled and clattered. Thoughtful suspicion pinched at her lips. Hross were valuable animals. It made no sense to abuse them this way, and for such a poor cargo. At one time she would have investigated. Now it no longer mattered.

She'd been watching the saloon for less than a half hour when a blond-haired woman emerged and crossed the street, as if headed for one of the many narrow alleys in the city that served as shortcuts between the districts. She was young and very pretty, but despite that, had the hard-edged look of an experienced whore. Mamna had seen her before. She'd been waiting on tables in the saloon early on the night Mamna had met with the Slayer to hire him.

All Mamna needed was a few hours of the whore's time. Fear and money should be enough to buy them.

"Girl," she called, beckoning to the whore from the alley entrance. "Come here. I'd like a word."

The girl turned. The basket that hung from the crook of her elbow bumped against her hip. The widening of her eyes and the slight stiffening of her posture said she recognized Mamna. She approached slowly, her steps dragging and her gaze darting side to side, as if expecting an ambush. She halted far enough away from the priestess that she had room to bolt if she sensed danger. Smart.

"Do you know who I am?" Mamna asked.

Calculation slid into the girl's eyes. She nodded.

Mamna's hopes soared. This one would do nicely. "How would you like to earn a gold coin?"

* * *

Airie helped Sapphire serve coffee to the men in the saloon who'd come to hear what Hunter and Blade had to say.

Hunter had wanted the northerners to see her, but the curious scrutiny of so many strangers left her uncomfortable. She was used to avoiding attention, not seeking it out.

And while she'd agreed to help Hunter, she didn't like being presented as something she wasn't. Serving was her silent act of rebellion—something no godseeker would expect a goddess to do.

The men sat in half-circles at the round tables they'd drawn together in the saloon, all facing forward so that they could see and hear. She thought there might be fifty men in total, maybe more. Most were northerners, but according to Sapphire, some were locals. Hunter, Blade, and a godseeker sat at a table before them. Hunter refused to look at Airie, despite her having chosen a position near the center of the room, so she'd be in his direct line of vision as a reminder that she'd agreed to be seen. That was all.

The godseeker in charge of the northerners was older than Hunter and Blade, but handsome. Airie remembered him. He was the one who'd threatened Hunter—although the two men appeared to bear each other no ill-will over the incident.

"We have a system for communication set up throughout the city," the godseeker said. "There are plenty of men who will fight demons if we call them. More will fight if they believe the Demon Slayer does too." His eyes slid to Airie, then away, but he made no mention of goddesses.

"The demons will attack from above, and they'll use fire," Hunter added. "Every available man or woman who can use a bow and arrow or sword should be positioned on the rooftops inside the city, and the walls surrounding it. Only the best shots should be using rifles. The chance of ricochet is too high."

The godseeker concurred. A number of men in the crowd nodded as well.

"I have fifty wagonloads of kyson hides distributed around the city walls," the godseeker said. "It's thick and naturally resistant to demon fire, and can be used as a shield for the marksmen. Those who can carry water for fighting fires should do so. We'll need access to the well in the temple. I'll arrange it. Mamna won't help us, but others will." He exchanged a long look with Hunter. "Not all of the priestesses have forgotten who they serve."

Airie's heart beat with gladness. The goddesses might never return, but the gifts they'd left behind should be remembered and the priestesses played an important part in retaining them.

Hunter leaned forward in his chair, resting his forearms on the table. "We don't want the demons to accurately guess our numbers. Let them think we're paralyzed with fear, which is what they'll expect. They haven't met with organized resistance in over three hundred years. We'll draw them in as close as possible, then let the sharpshooters take over. Demons are most vulnerable here, here, and here." He indicated points on his body. "Where the joints in their bone plating expose flesh."

"What will you be doing?" someone asked.

"Demons have no more liking for each other than they do for us, and they don't fight well together. I'll challenge the Demon Lord. If we take away their leader, they'll lose any organization. That's to be our real advantage."

Thankfully, the copper tray Airie carried was empty. The walls and the ceiling of the saloon rippled and danced, leaving her dizzy and grasping at the back of a chair for support.

Hunter saw her falter. He partly rose, checked himself, and shifted the action so as to turn and lean across the table and whisper something to Blade.

She fled to the kitchen behind Sapphire and tossed the tray on a counter. It made a tinny clatter that reflected her thoughts. The wave of shock passed. Anger settled in. He had no right to place himself in danger this way. If anything happened to him, she and Scratch would have no one.

Sapphire caught her arm.

"A priestess has asked to speak with you privately," the blonde girl whispered. "She says with the help of a goddess, the priestesses can prevent more bloodshed. Will you meet with her?"

Having a priestess believe she was a goddess scandalized Airie. Her first instinct was to go to Hunter and insist he explain the true situation to everyone. This farce had gone too far already, and yet, it had barely begun.

Knowing that he didn't trust priestesses, and he'd never change his mind now, had her say yes to Sapphire instead. The goddesses had once allowed men to stand between them and the demons, and as a result, Wasteland had been almost destroyed. Never again.

Not in her name.

If Hunter would make no effort to avoid bloodshed, then it was up to her.

"Where and when does she want to meet?" Airie asked.

* * *

Around the city, people prepared for battle and the defense of their homes. Airie had been told to meet the priestess in the courtyard near the temple within the hour after sunset.

Nothing moved here. The temple, a narrow, spired structure constructed of baked clay and wood, showed no signs of life. Stalls had been curtained off, their wares locked away. Street lanterns remained unlit. The temple guards, positioned around the courtyard earlier that day for the market, now walked the walls with the city's night watchmen and the northerners under Pillar's command. Their attention was occupied by the sky as they waited for the demons to attack. Whatever happened inside the city tonight wasn't their concern.

She heard the faint scrape of footsteps on stone behind her and spun around, fists clenched, to find a small figure hobbling toward her. At first, she thought it was a child. Then the figure lifted the hood of its cloak and she saw the telltale shaven head above a plain, broad-featured face.

A priestess.

"You wished to speak with me?" Airie said.

Instead of answering, the priestess clutched at her throat. The same sense of compulsion Airie had experienced the night the godseeker called to her slammed through her, and the goddess inside her surged to life. Outrage forced her back a step. The priestess was using an amulet against her.

Her.

Her skin began to glow, bathing the ground at her feet in a golden light. "You dare try to use an amulet of the goddesses against me?" The question, posed by a goddess, thundered from Airie through her demon's voice.

The old woman recoiled in terror. "I only wished to confirm that you are who the godseeker claims you to be. Forgive your servant for doubting you, Beloved. I meant no disrespect."

Airie might carry the will of a goddess inside her, but she was a person in her own right. That was how she'd been raised, and who she'd remain. But if the priestess truly believed her to be a goddess, then why was she so afraid?

She placed her fingers against the priestess's throat. The urge to choke her was strong. Instead, she felt for the chain. She drew the amulet into her palm and examined it in the golden light cast by her skin. The amulet depicted a flaming rainbow, and looked very much like the ones she and Hunter both wore. She didn't know the significance of the image, although seeing it caused the goddess who protected her a great deal of pain. Airie felt it as if it were her own. Deep, tiny fissures marred the smooth desert varnish.

"This amulet protects the world from demons," the priestess said. Her breath brushed Airie's hand as she spoke. "With your help, it can be used to free the world of the immortals forever."

The demon in Airie objected to the throbbing amulet in her palm. The goddess rejoiced. "Of what help could I possibly be?"

The priestess's eyes hardened. "You can heal the amulet. Give it life."

"And who would become responsible for such a gift if I do?"

"I've been its custodian for years. I've used it to build this city and protect it from demons. Now that the goddesses are gone, it belongs to me."

Airie clenched her fist. The amulet crumpled to dust. She sifted the dust through her fingers and let it trickle to the ground. "You are free of the immortals, Priestess." The goddess's voice echoed with that of Airie's demon, both of them speaking as one. "No one protects you now. Betrayal brings its own rewards. Enjoy them."

The presence of the goddess faded, along with the golden brightness of Airie's skin. The priestess dragged in a raw breath. She knotted her fingers in the now-empty chain around her neck.

"If you pray for forgiveness, the goddesses will hear you," Airie said. The goddesses had once touched this priestess and claimed her as their own. Whatever betrayal the priestess had committed, her connection to them would never change.

The priestess's lip curled in contempt. "You think I'm the one who should pray for forgiveness? A demon spawned you and a goddess whore gave birth to you. You are an abomination. The goddesses fear you and the demons despise you. Your death would banish the demons from this world for good. If not for you, they would be long gone—the same as the goddesses." Her ugly face twisted into an even uglier smile. "But the Demon Slayer never told you that, did he?"

* * *

Mamna had hated the spawn on sight.

Although she had her mother's face, there could be no mistaking who had fathered her. She was dark-haired like him. She bore his eyes, and despite the ugly, ill-fitting clothing she wore, also his bearing.

"My mother was a priestess, the same as you are," the spawn said.

But Mamna heard the uncertainty underlying her words. "I watched you grow in your mother's belly for months. I heard the goddesses plan for your birth so that they could use you against your demon father. The priestess who raised you was left to ensure you were delivered to him when the time came. That time was the collapse of Goddess Mountain."

The demon-dark eyes turned the angry red of denial. "My mother would never do such a thing."

Mamna leaned close, enjoying the pain she was inflicting. The spawn had destroyed Mamna's amulet, and with it, any use Mamna might have had for her. "When the Slayer arrived, she turned you over to him immediately, did she not? Did she fight for you? Warn you of danger? Or was she faithful, and unwavering in her loyalty to the goddesses?"

"You're lying," the spawn said, but again, with a tremor of doubt.

"Am I?"

"It's so hard to tell," a cool voice said from the darkness surrounding the entrance to the temple. "I find it easier to assume that you are."

The Demon Lord stepped away from the shadows. The contents of Mamna's stomach shifted at the expression on his face. Without her amulet, she hadn't been alerted to his proximity. Neither had she expected to see him here, inside the city walls in his mortal form, when the entire city anticipated a show of strength from him. He would have had to walk in through the main gate during the day.

Years of angry frustration boiled away any fear Mamna felt. She'd wanted nothing more from him than that he favor her with a small portion of the kindness he'd once shown to a goddess.

But Mamna wasn't beautiful, and by nature, he wasn't kind. He was a demon, with no pity or thought other than for his own superficial wants and desires. She'd wasted so much of her life harboring impossible hopes and dreams.

No more.

Desperation forced her thoughts to coalesce a plan of action. She didn't want to die, but if she did, she wouldn't make her death easy for him. Her hand inched toward the pocket in the seam of her cloak.

"Would you really try to kill me?" the Demon Lord asked. He had flames in his eyes now, fed by an unleashed hatred for her. "After everything we've meant to each other?"

That he could speak those words to her with such malice made her hate him even more. He didn't deserve her love and never had.

"I've meant nothing to you," she said, "while you were once everything to me. I betrayed the goddesses for you. I would have done anything you asked of me for no more reward than the chance to serve you. Instead, you've spent years blinded by the loss of a whore who cared so little for you that she abandoned both you and your spawn. Good riddance to her. To both of you."

She fumbled for her gun.

The Demon Lord raised his hand, palm out, but she managed one shot at the spawn before the flames of his fire engulfed her. Pain and sheer terror wrenched shrieks from her throat. Along with her own screams, she heard those of the spawn.

Rain began to fall, faster and harder, and for an instant, Mamna thought it might save her. Then the rain turned to billows of steam, and all she could see or feel was fire.

* * *

Dagan watched Mamna burn.

She'd never wanted to serve him, as she'd tried to claim. She wished to manipulate and control. She'd lied to him about the existence of his daughter for years, which forced him to consider the possibility of other lies he'd accepted too readily, and of truths he'd perhaps spurned.

He turned his back on the dying priestess to examine his daughter. She looked so much like her mother. His breath hitched at the flood of memories. Too much of the past had bared itself already today. He didn't care to see or hear any more.

The girl needed to be taught her place.

The burst of rain had stopped. Beyond the wall, near the city's gates, the first of his demons dove from the heavens, a great shadow that plunged in a free fall before twisting to one side and soaring away. An answering wave of fiery arrows from the ramparts dragged streaming tails of yellow across the deepening indigo sky. The city was undefended on this side, dark and silent. It wouldn't remain so for long, once the attack began in earnest.

Dagan tossed back the hood of his slicker. "What's your name?"

She didn't flinch from him as he'd intended her to. Dark emotions lashed at him instead—anger and contempt—overriding the gentler, goddess-driven ones that had fueled her defiant attempt to save the ugly priestess from his fire. This daughter despised him, which he found intriguing. Demons didn't show fear and she had none.

"Airie," she said.

Rainbows and lightning.

The meaning of her name was a slap in the face. The rainbow pendant she wore around her neck dealt another harsh blow. It had once been offered to him, and he had thrown it back at its owner. He reached out and touched it now, rubbing it between his fingers, not wishing for her to see how much she'd unsettled him.

"Where did you get this?" he demanded.

Her unwavering, fearless eyes held his. "From my mother. She told me to wear it, and to think of her often, and more importantly to remember that I was born out of love." She twisted the pendant from his fingers as if afraid he would somehow taint it, and tucked it inside her cloak. "At least I was born out of love on her part."

His throat ached. Allia had given this token, once meant for him, to their daughter. She'd had some true feelings for him, then, or she wouldn't have done so. Yet she had also allowed the Slayer to take possession of the amulet he'd given to her, and that was not to be forgiven.

At least I was born out of love on her part. He didn't dare to dwell on the meaning behind those words.

The wind had risen with the arrival of his demons, dispersing the remainder of Mamna's bitter, smoldering ashes as it wound its way through the narrow streets of Freetown and past the tightly shuttered houses.

He couldn't decide what to do with this unwanted daughter. He had planned to kill her. He still might, but his curiosity regarding her was far from satisfied. "It's possible that it's as the priestess said, and your existence is what keeps demons trapped here within the confines of time. It's equally possible that your death would be my destruction. Her words aren't to be trusted."

Flames rippled beneath golden skin, and crackled in blazing eyes. Lifting a hand, an orange and yellow ball of fire formed in his daughter's palm. She drew her arm back and released it at him with a great deal of force.

Fire was his. Rather than dodge, he called the flames to him and fanned them until they embraced them both. He felt a subtle difference in the fire she wielded, however. It was almost as if it had been tainted by the goddess inside her. He slowly absorbed the heat until the last of her flames died away and only the golden gleam to her skin remained.

"Never use demon fire against its lord," he said to her. "I own it all, even yours, and I can call it to me as I choose."

She took one step toward him, and bracing her foot, balanced her weight over her bent knee for impetus. She shot a blow to his chin with the heel of her fist that rocked his head back. While he remained off balance, she followed up with a strike of her other knee to his hip that nearly felled him.

Impressive.

She was fast as well as strong, and the blows hurt. Her skirt, however, hampered her. He grabbed her leg, flipping her onto her back on the ground as they both fell, so that he landed on top. He dropped his knee to her chest, then pinned her with one forearm across her throat. She struggled to get her arms between them in an attempt to unseat him, but he blocked that move, too.

If he intended to kill her, now was the time. But what might it mean for him, to own such a death as this?

He didn't want her dead yet. Although, with the way her skin glowed in his presence, there would be no hiding what she was from the others. And while he now had his daughter in his possession, he wanted his amulet back, too.

The Slayer would come for her.

"I think," Dagan said slowly, "that I'd like to know what other surprises you might possess."

He lifted her in his arms, shifting to manhunting form so quickly that she couldn't fight back as he leapt into the air. He climbed steadily and circled the city. Faint shouts carried to them over the wind as mortals rallied against demons. Archers on nearby rooftops who witnessed his ascent from within the city walls released a fresh volley of flaming arrows. A few struck the buildings. Confusion broke out below as people ran toward the creeping flames, shouting for water.

With his enormous wing muscles pumping, he glided through the billowing clouds of smoke forming high above Freetown, using it as cover, then flew off into the desert. He left the demons behind to do as they wished.

Demon fire, however, would not be called again this evening. He had no wish for harm to come to the Slayer. Not tonight.

When it did, it wouldn't be fast.

Or merciful.

CHAPTER SEVENTEEN

Beneath the ocean of endless stars that glittered in the night sky, Hunter paced the walls of the city, making certain the Demon Slayer was seen by everyone who'd turned out in defense of Freetown.

Northerners had spent the remainder of the day going door to door, casting a wide net throughout the city in order to recruit as many as possible who were willing to fight. The final numbers had been both surprising and heartening. The godseeker Pillar had been right. Once word of Airie began to spread, and with the Demon Slayer to fight for her, hopes had risen. The city guards and the night watch had chosen to join in. So had the priestesses, although not out of any loyalty to the goddesses. They feared demons more than Mamna, who they claimed had gone missing. After tonight, no matter the outcome, her hold over the city was done.

Enormous kyson-hide shields lay in wait on the ramparts, ready to be hoisted into position at the first sign of attack. They'd protect the archers from any demon fire directed at them, but required two men, each armed with spears for fighting in close quarters, to lift and support them. Hundreds of buckets of consecrated water sat at the ready, supplied by the priestesses, as Pillar had promised. The water served not only to keep fire from spreading, but also as another form of defense. In buckets, it couldn't be used to keep demons out. The buckets, however, could be hurled at any demon to venture too close.

On rooftops throughout the city, women and children settled in to defend their homes against any demons that might get past the men on the walls. The bright sparkle of their lanterns winked in and out of the darkness as they moved about, reminding Hunter of the quick flash of fireflies flitting on the open fields of the Borderlands he recalled from his youth.

Once this was over, he'd show Airie the place where he'd been raised. He hadn't made amends with her before he left the saloon, and it ate at him. She'd promised him she wouldn't leave him again, and he believed her, but because he wasn't trusting by nature, he'd asked Ruby to watch over her for him as an added precaution. He couldn't fight at his best if his mind dwelled on her safety.

Despite his worry, anticipation built steadily inside him. He loved fighting demons. It made him feel invincible. Alive.

Yet he couldn't continue to fight them forever. He'd grow old, and someday, he'd lose. He refused to think of what might happen if he lost tonight.

Tonight, Hunter intended to make a statement to all of Wasteland. Everyone had heard of the Demon Slayer. Very few had seen him fight. Tonight, he would fight on Airie's behalf. He'd kill the immortal who led the demons. People would see it, and they'd remember. He'd walk through those gates alone, and he'd issue his challenge. He'd remind men that mortals were also to be feared. Wasteland had belonged to man first, and soon, if not tonight, it would be theirs again.

Pillar stood on had his arms raised in supplication. He was leading the kneeling northerners and the priestesses in prayer. They were giving thanks for the goddesses' gift of one of their own. The city guards and the night watch didn't join in, but showed respect by stopping whatever they were doing so as not to interrupt. In fact, the entire world had gone very still. Even the restless tumbleweeds held their breath.

When the prayers were finished, Pillar came to stand beside Hunter. "The archers are in place," he said. "On the wall, and then on some of the rooftops scattered throughout the city. Whenever you're ready, I'll give them the signal." He stared out at the desert. "You've fought demons. What are our chances?"

This was no time for second guesses. "One-on-one?" Hunter shrugged. "Slim to none. But they stand to lose more than we do. Never forget that man once fought a thousand demons in possession of enough fire to raze the world. We cut those numbers down to little more than a few dozen. Our numbers from that war have recovered. Theirs haven't. And won't. The Demon Lord barely managed to summon enough fire from his survivors to route a few unarmed women from a mountaintop. If we remain organized, and show them no fear, then demons are the ones who should pray."

The amulet around Hunter's neck flared to life. Pillar's, too, began to glow. An alarm sounded. A black form sailed across the face of the quarter moon, cutting its light like a lunar eclipse. Its wingspan had to surpass twenty feet. It was followed by two more shadows. The three demons circled overhead, staying well out of range of the weapons, the whisper of their wings the only sound to be heard other than the jagged breathing of men trying to wrestle control of their fear.

Fear would be man's undoing.

High above them, one demon broke away, diving swiftly at the wall, earning a high-pitched, panicked wail from its intended prey.

"Now," Hunter said.

From behind the kyson-hide shields, a volley of flaming arrows streaked trails of orange and yellow into the sky. The arrows bounced off the demon's plating, showering thousands of rainbow-hued sparks in their wake before falling harmlessly to earth.

But a single demon had kindled terror in them, and these men would have to hold steady against as many as thirty. Hunter scanned the sky for some sign of the Demon Lord, but it was impossible to distinguish him from the others.

Another demon spun out of the night. It rolled in the air, evading the flaming wall of arrows, and snatched one of the guards from his post. The man's screams broke off as the demon tore him into pieces, spraying the raised shields with blood. Chunks of flesh rained down on a section of the rampart.

Horror, so thick Hunter could taste it, washed through the men. When the wagon train had fought demons off, they'd done it from the cover of a canyon. These men had nothing but kyson hide, and despite Pillar's claims, it was untested. They had to see for themselves that they could rely on it. They also needed to see what consecrated water could do to a demon at close range.

Ten more demons approached. Three descended, attacking the wall. Hunter sprinted toward the one closest to him. He grabbed a bucket, sloshing water over one pant leg. With inhuman strength, he hurled the bucket and its contents at the demon. The demon let out an unearthly squeal that rang in Hunter's ears. It plummeted downward, one wing badly burned, to crash onto the rampart. Hunter snatched a spear from the hands of a guardsman rather than take the extra seconds to unsheathe his sword. The demon rose to its full height, well over ten feet, and the damage to its wing left it angry. It came at Hunter. He thrust the spear into the chink in its armor between its groin and thigh, hitting an artery. Blood gushed. The demon clawed at the shaft of the spear. With a roar, it toppled off the rampart and crashed to the ground below, where it lay still.

It was the victory the men needed to see.

Fire erupted within the city's market behind Hunter, raising shouts of alarm from a few men on the wall, but it failed to catch hold on any of the nearby buildings. Moments later a demon exploded into the sky, before disappearing into the smoke-shrouded night. It carried someone in its arms. Hunter closed his eyes for a second, but there was nothing he could do. Whoever the victim was, they were already dead and nothing he did could save them.

More demons circled, but they'd become cautious. As Hunter had told the godseeker, they had more to lose.

For the remainder of the night, they were content to harass the walls.

When dawn arrived, Hunter stood back and listened as Pillar received reports. Freetown lost twenty-three men. Only the one demon had been brought down. The night hadn't been a success.

Hunter scanned the horizon. A brilliant yellow dawn blanketed the city. They'd driven the demons back, but the Demon Lord had failed to appear.

Wearily, covered in soot and sweat, he walked through the emptying streets to Blade's saloon. Mortal losses throughout the night had been heavy and discouraging, but the demons hadn't burned the entire city, as it had been feared would happen. The fire brigade had performed its duties admirably. Freetown remained standing, although not unscathed.

At midday, the battle's leaders would meet again. In the meantime, he wanted Airie. He craved her smiles and her touch. When she was near him, his world seemed brighter and filled with hope.

Hunter knocked off the dust at the door, then entered the kitchen to find Blade and Ruby sitting at the table. Ruby's hair was unbound, and she'd been crying. Neither looked as if they had slept. Hunter headed for the back stairs.

"Airie is gone," Blade said to him.

There must be some mistake. She had promised him she'd be here. "Impossible."

Fresh tears filled Ruby's eyes. "Sapphire said Airie went to meet a priestess last night. I made her tell me where she'd gone and I went after her. Mamna was waiting."

Hunter went cold.

Ruby told him of the priestess's words to Airie, of the terrible things she had said, and of the Demon Lord's appearance. "After he killed the priestess, he took Airie with him," she finished.

Mamna was dead. The Demon Lord had Airie.

That explained why he hadn't made an appearance last night. He'd already gotten what he wanted. The enormity of what all of it meant had not yet fully hit Hunter. He felt frozen inside. Numb. That would change. When his anger unleashed, he intended to be far from here.

"You should have come to me at once," he said to Blade.

"I only just found out, myself."

Hunter headed again for the stairs.

"Where are you going?" Blade called after him.

"To pack my bags. I've already lost too much time." The Demon Lord had too great a head start, and could travel much faster than Hunter.

"Wait." Blade surged from his chair. He came to stand by Hunter but didn't block his path, which was wise given Hunter's mood. "You need to think about this. You could be walking into a trap."

Or Airie could already be dead and he was wasting time better spent defending Freetown. Blade said none of that, and Hunter was grateful. His insides had begun to thaw. He had to get moving. He wanted to be alone when reality settled in. It would be better for everyone. "I'm not leaving her with demons. Do you know what they will do to her?"

Blade's jaw worked. "Better than most." He scrubbed at his face. "Did you hear what Ruby said to you? Did you understand it at all? Airie's not mortal, Hunter. Do you really want to involve yourself in this?"

Hunter rounded on him. "I know what she is, and who. She's Airie, and that's all that matters to me. I can't abandon her to demons, any more than I abandoned you—and I knew nothing at all about you."

There was silence. "No, you didn't," Blade said, his voice quiet. "Neither did she when she healed me. She's certainly worth far more than me. But this is immortal business."

Ruby inserted herself between them. "She isn't dead," she said to Hunter. "She fought him. If he'd wanted to kill her, he could have done so."

Of course Airie would have put up a fight. What she couldn't have done was kill, even to defend herself, as she should have.

How quickly his opinion of her had changed.

But there were other things demons could do to her that were worse than death, and thinking of them offered no comfort. As long as the Demon Lord lived, she would never be safe.

A muscle worked at the base of Blade's jaw. "If you're doing this, I'm coming with you."

Ruby made a small sound of dismay. Her anxious eyes fixed on Blade, who refused to look at her.

Hunter understood what the offer cost his friend, and was moved by it. He wouldn't accept it, however. "You coming with me won't make any difference. Taking a whole army of mortals deep into demon territory wouldn't defeat them. I have some protection, but you have none."

He touched his amulet. He didn't say what they all knew. He couldn't abandon Airie to demons, and yet he was abandoning an entire town. Come nighttime, Freetown was as good as lost.

"Take the boy and the women, and head to my cabin," he added. "At least there, you'll have some protection."

Blade looked from Hunter to Ruby, and nodded, yet Hunter knew that while Blade would take Scratch and the women to Hunter's cabin, he'd then return to fight in Freetown with the others.

That decision was his to make.

Hunter looked in on Scratch before he left.

The child was asleep on the floor in Ruby's private bedroom, snuggled into a thick nest of blankets, and he didn't wake him. He could hardly explain to a child what was happening.

He left the saloon, then made his way out of Freetown through the tunnel.

From there, he headed into the desert toward demon territory.

CHAPTER EIGHTEEN

Hunter took a short break to avoid the worst of the midday heat. He awoke to small fingers prying open one of his eyes. A solemn, accusing face stared into his.

He shot upright in a tangle of bedding, his gun in one hand, his sword in the other, and his heart pounding beneath his ribs like an animal intent on escape. *Scratch.*

How on earth had the boy followed him?

He set the weapons down. His heart rate steadied. The boy gave off an air of innocent satisfaction at having found him. "Sometime soon, you and I are going to have a little man-to-man talk."

It was too late to turn back now, and even if he did Scratch would only come after him again, meaning he had no choice but to keep going and take the boy with him. The prospect should displease him, when in fact, he found just the opposite was true. How many people, other than Scratch and Airie, actually sought out his company for no purpose other than to be with him?

One companion had been returned to him. Now, he wanted the other.

He untangled himself from the bedding and stood, tucking in his shirt tail and slipping his suspenders over his shoulders as he did. A quick glance at the sky told him the afternoon was still young. He shielded his eyes and checked the landscape for familiar markings, squinting against the hazy heat dancing in waves off the uneven desert terrain. There were many little dips and valleys, as well as patches of low vegetation and pillars of sand and rock, and it took him a moment to place them.

He experienced a brief disorientation. He'd traveled a lot farther into the desert than he'd thought.

"I don't suppose you'd know anything about that?" he said to the boy. Scratch sat beside a clump of sage, dribbling dirt through his fingers, and didn't answer. Hunter rubbed the top of the boy's head. "Of course not."

He packed his bedroll and settled his hat on his head. A few miles to their east lay a canyon cutting a deep ribbon through the desert. Its nooks and crannies would offer them hiding places from demons in the coming night.

Even though he slowed his steps to accommodate the boy's shorter stride, they walked the few miles to the canyon's lip and began their descent to the bottom in what seemed like no time at all. Midway down, a gently sloping shelf jutted out over the canyon floor far below them. When they reached it, they followed the shelf gradually downward. Walking was far more comfortable here than above, where they'd been exposed to the full heat of the desert.

Late in the day, Hunter's amulet grew warm against his skin. The skin between his shoulders prickled, as if it were shrinking. He looked up.

They were being followed.

He took off his hat and wiped the sweat from his forehead with his sleeve. The canyon now had them at a disadvantage. The sheer walls at this point made climbing ill-advised, effectively boxing them in. If he'd been alone he might have tried anyway, but Scratch, agile as he was, would never make it.

The canyon, however, was not one straight crevasse. The gorge at the bottom, where the floodwaters flowed, was fed by a number of smaller arroyos. Some were dead ends. A few led back to the desert surface.

He'd feel more confident facing a demon on the level ground above rather than down here, where his footing was uncertain. He took the child by the hand and headed into a passage barely wide enough for him to fit through, hoping that would make it even more awkward for a bulkier demon, forcing it to change to its mortal form.

"We're going back up," he said to Scratch.

The boy bobbed his chin up and down, his eyes widening. He knew, too, that they were being followed, and that their situation wasn't good.

The arroyo proved so narrow in places that Hunter had to turn his shoulders sideways and carry his pack in his hand. It narrowed again so that the sky appeared as a thin blue sliver of ribbon above them. The temperature, however, dropped a few welcome degrees, the thick granite walls dispersing much of the heat.

Around a bend, disaster awaited them. There had been a rockslide here at one time. Rubble blocked their path, and the opening above it was too small for Hunter to climb over. The amulet around his neck grew hotter, shining in the gloom, and any hope of escape died.

They could try to outwait the demon tailing them by staying where they were, and pray it was too large to come into the arroyo after them, but Hunter wasn't about to put his faith in that approach. Besides, there was always a secondary danger of paralysis from juvenile sand swifts hiding in rock crevices. He didn't much care to suffer that fate either.

"Climb up and tell me if you can get past the rockslide," he said to Scratch.

The child did as he was told, climbing nimbly up the mound of rock and debris. When he reached the top, he looked down at Hunter and shook his head.

"Stay up there. No matter what, you don't come down from there until I tell you to." He reconsidered that order. "If I'm not back before dark, you're to return to Blade's." He'd have to draw the demon away from him. At least then the boy would have a chance.

Hunter set his pack against the rubble and withdrew his sword. His gun would be useless. If a bullet struck bony plate, the ricochet off the stone in the canyon walls might kill either him or the boy.

He refused to think of what would become of Scratch if something should happen to him. The boy had made it through the desert and found him on his own. He might be able to find his way back to Freetown.

And as for Airie...

He concentrated on the amulet, drawing as much power from it as he could as he worked his way back the way they'd come.

Then, he stepped into the open.

And discovered two demons hunting them, not one.

They came at him on foot. Massive, with ugly heads bulging forward from bunched, rock-solid shoulders, their leathery skin and bone plating shone a dull red in the filtered light. Meaty fists hung from heavy arms and their footsteps shook the ground when they walked. Although their wings were their main weakness in a fight, when not in use those wings furled inside the protective bony humps on their backs, as they were now.

Hunter had to strike first. Having a demon's strength was of little help to him when he was outnumbered. At least he had the sun at his back and it would be in their eyes, not his. He rushed forward, a move they didn't anticipate, and struck the demon closest to him with a closed-fisted blow to its throat. The demon staggered from the force of it. Hunter ducked to the side, careful to keep the first demon between himself and the second, mindful of their talons. If blood were drawn, he didn't want for it to be his.

As the first demon choked, clawing chunks of flesh from its damaged throat, Hunter followed through with a well-placed knee to its groin. Only then did he thrust his sword into the soft point under the demon's arm and into its heart. The demon collapsed, then lay still.

Hunter whirled, yanking his sword free, prepared to face bloodlust from the second demon, but this one had greater self-control than the first. That made it all the more dangerous.

Regardless, now that there was only the one left to deal with, Hunter's confidence in his chances rose.

It was short-lived, however. A heavy fist connected with the side of his head and his thoughts splintered into pain. The ground and the sky spun together, fading to gray before righting themselves. But, rather than move in to press its advantage the demon stepped back, looking at a point beyond Hunter's shoulder. While Hunter knew better than to turn to look, the shadow that fell across him from behind made him do so despite his best intentions.

This third demon was even bigger than the first two.

He was a dead man. Of all the years he'd hunted demons, why had his luck run out now, when Airie and Scratch were depending on him?

He could take at least one more demon with him. He danced to the side, trying to draw the second demon between him and the third as a shield, but they both circled, flanking him. The third demon's taloned fist shot out, and Hunter thought, *This is it*.

But instead of the crush of those talons around his neck, leathery knuckles brushed his skin and the talons closed around the amulet. The demon snapped the gold chain, curling the freed amulet into its fist.

It scooped Hunter up in one arm and in seconds became airborne, carrying him off into the dusky sky.

* * *

The Slayer had come to him even faster than expected.

Dagan held the amulet restored to him in his hand, rubbing one thumb over its jagged surface. He remembered the pleasure on Allia's face the day he gave it to her. It brought him no joy.

He had the Slayer, too, imprisoned in a large metal cage that swung from a chain in the cavern ceiling near Dagan's throne. The sight of him entertained those demons preparing for another long night of attacks against Freetown.

Such organized attacks wouldn't last for much longer. He'd allow the demons to go back to their solitary hunting patterns. And then, Freetown could genuinely begin to worry.

"Fight me, you bastard," the Slayer shouted at him. The cage swayed beneath his shifting weight as he shook the bars in an attempt to free himself.

"You'll get your fight." He held the amulet aloft. It glittered as it spun on its silver chain. "What do you think your chances of victory will be?"

The Slayer's fingers ground into the bars of his cage. "Do you think I need that trinket to best you?"

For a mortal, and a prisoner, he was arrogant. Dagan enjoyed his lack of fear. What would it take to instill some?

"Did you think it would work against me? Did you not know that it's mine? That I crafted it?" He watched the Slayer's expression change to one of caution, and knew he hadn't. "I know what it is. What it can do. And it's no ordinary trinket."

"It's not," the Slayer conceded. "But I found it in a stream, buried in the mud, so it's something someone discarded as having no value to them."

The game lost its pleasure. Dagan closed his fist around the amulet. "Why didn't you turn my daughter over to the priestess as you were hired to do?"

The Slayer continued testing the bars, searching for weaknesses. "I have a liking for women. I wouldn't turn the worst of them over to demons."

"She is a demon."

"I hear she's as much goddess. Maybe more, if one judges her by her nature." The Slayer's grin filled with insolence. "Mamna likes to talk. Sometimes she even tells the truth."

"We'll see how much demon is in her when I have you torn apart in front of her eyes." Dagan leaned forward. "Blood tells, Slayer. In more ways than one. Do you think her demon can resist the smell of yours when it's spilled?"

The Slayer held onto his grin. "I think," he said, his words slow and deliberate, "that you have no idea what she is, or what she can do. You know nothing about her."

"I know she was born inside of time, which gives her limitations that make her of little use to me." Dagan watched the Slayer carefully. "But not, perhaps, to one of my demons. She'd make a fine reward to the one who captured you."

The slight heave of the Slayer's chest and his quickening breath were all that gave away his anger. "Ask the last demon who dared to touch her what her limitations are."

"I would prefer to discover her limitations on my own," Dagan said. She would join him, or she would die. She couldn't survive amongst demons if she were unable to defend herself. He signaled for the demon standing closest to his throne to come forward. "Bring my daughter to me."

* * *

The room where Airie was imprisoned had been carved from the earth. It contained sparse, bulky furnishings. She lay on an enormous dirt bench that doubled as a bed. Demon fire burned from brackets carved to represent nude figures contorted into impossible and confusing sexual positions. There was no natural light.

She stared at the stone slab that passed for a door. It could be opened by using a single word of command, which she'd been given. It wasn't entirely accurate, then, to claim she was a prisoner—but the one time she'd ventured from her room, the number of demons roaming the halls had discouraged her from wandering too far, even though none of them approached her.

She didn't take their restraint as a good sign.

She had no idea what the Demon Lord intended to do with her. She didn't expect a loving family relationship to develop, nor did she want one. She certainly didn't feel safe in his care. More than anything else, she felt anger and worry.

Her anger came from the number of lies she'd been told, particularly by Hunter. He had known who had fathered her, and yet he hadn't communicated it to her. The worry was for precisely the same reason. Hunter had known, but continued to protect her. By now he would have discovered she was gone. He would come for her. What would the Demon Lord do to the Demon Slayer, the one man all demons feared, when he did?

She tucked a hand beneath her cheek and wondered, too, if the priestess's words were true, that she'd been intended as a weapon to use against demons. Perhaps that was why the goddesses had watched over her all these years. She'd hoped it was because she was loved. The possibility of being nothing more than a tool chilled her and left her feeling more alone than she had since her mother—the one who'd raised her—had died.

But what of the mother who gave birth to her? What if she'd been watching over her, too? Was she the one who spoke to her?

She uttered a soft prayer. *Please. If you're my mother, speak to me now.*

A soft voice whispered back. *Are you ready to hear?*

The question gave Airie pause. Desire, who had raised her, would always be her mother, and Airie had never wanted to know more than that, even when it was clear that Airie had abilities immortal in nature. She couldn't blame others for her ignorance when she'd never pushed for the truth.

Yes.

A gleaming golden light took shape in the room. Part of Airie recoiled. Another part gazed on the apparition with a desperate longing, as if she had found a broken or missing piece of herself, only to discover that she could never be restored and made whole.

"My loved ones call me Allia," the goddess said.

Allia. Her birth mother had a name.

"Is what the priestess said true?" Airie asked. "Was I created by the goddesses to be used against demons?"

Allia clutched her hands to the slender waist of her gown and appeared to choose her words with great care. "First, you need to understand the relationship that exists between the immortals. Demons search the universe for the other half of their souls. Goddesses bring life to the universe, but also restrict demons' movements within it. My sisters wanted to craft an amulet that would bind demons to us and give us more freedom from them, and I was part of that plan. But the moment your father first touched me, I knew I was the one he searched for, and that we were meant to be together. You're the result." A wistful smile lifted the corners of her lips. "You were created from love." Her smile warmed. "And you are loved."

As much as Airie longed to believe her, she couldn't forget Mamna's ugly words. "If you're the other half of his soul, why would he accept a priestess's word over yours?"

"Because the priestess told the truth," the goddess said. "She simply didn't tell him the whole of it." Deep blue, beautiful eyes met Airie's. "I was meant to betray him. In the end I couldn't do it, but how was he to know that? We were at war. Neither one of us trusted the other enough to be honest. We share the responsibility for the destruction of our love. And now you're caught in the war between us. You were born to immortals, but also inside of time. You're bound by its laws. Through you, so is your father—and through him, the demons."

Airie's stomach tightened. She represented betrayal and punishment, not love. She had no place in the mortal world, nor amongst the immortals either. It would have been better for everyone if she had never been born. "What do you want from me?"

"Not *from* you, *for* you," Allia gently corrected her. "I want you to find peace. I want you to be free. I want you to find the kind of love your parents should have treasured, but didn't. I can help you do that."

It was difficult to think of the Demon Lord as her father. She'd seen him burn a priestess to death before her eyes, and the reminder that she had the capacity for the same sort of violence made her afraid—not for herself, but for others. Not much wonder Hunter had been repulsed by her when they first met. He, more than anyone, knew what a demon could do.

"What would I have to do?"

"Give me your trust." Allia smoothed her palms over the folds in the front of her gown as if nervous. "A priestess once had enough faith to stand by me when everyone else abandoned me. She loved you enough to ask me for your life, and I gave it to her, even though you're half demon. She reminded me you're also half goddess, and swore to me she felt nothing but goodness in you. For her sake, can you trust me with your life now?"

No one had possessed as much faith in the goddesses as Desire. To know she'd asked one of them for her life made Airie's heart ache with love for her, because the request would not have been made lightly. She could do this one last thing and give the goddess her trust, not for herself or the immortals who'd created her, but to honor Desire's memory and what she would have wanted. She would have wished to repay the goddess for the trust placed in her to raise a half demon in a mortal world.

"Yes," Airie said.

The goddess glimmered brighter, as if some long-lost hope had been restored to her. "The Demon Lord will send for you. When he does, you'll permit me to face him on your behalf."

And Airie, despite her remaining misgivings, placed her trust in Desire and agreed.

* * *

Airie entered the main cavern. Her footsteps caused a faint brush of sound against the dirt floor in the otherwise heavy silence.

The demons gathered in the hall watched her walk the length of the large room. Several shifted away as she passed so as not to come in contact with the golden light enveloping her. The amulet slipped from Dagan's fingers. The similarities were much more pronounced. If not for her dark hair and eyes, he would have thought it was her mother who approached.

She stopped in front of him. Her eyes didn't hold flame, as they had last night. Instead they were deep, vivid pools of blue that he'd seen often in his dreams, and now, seeing them in his daughter's face, he couldn't speak.

"Why?" she demanded of him. The fierce golden glow of her skin forced those standing closest to her to abandon their manhunting forms for mortal ones and to back farther away. "Why did you turn from the one who offered you half of her soul?"

This voice, too, he'd heard in his dreams.

"Allia?" He whispered the name, hardly daring to believe it was true. He could see her now, hidden in the faint shadow of gold surrounding their daughter.

Her face tightened, reminding him too much of how stricken she'd looked the last time he saw her. He'd been cruel, his words harsh in the backlash against her betrayal, although he could no longer recall all that he'd flung at her.

"Don't call me that," she said. "You have no right."

He'd once had every right to use her given name—the one only her sisters had known. Had he truly thrown that right away?

No. The blame for the bitterness of their final parting wasn't his. Allia had fled the mortal world with her sisters a long time ago. His gaze sharpened. This girl before him now was a spawn, preying on the weaknesses of her demon father—yet another trick of the goddesses being played on him. He should strike her down and be done with their games.

But what if Allia truly spoke to him through her?

He couldn't keep from pursuing the possibility any more than he could squelch the swell of hope it raised that she'd finally returned to him.

If so, she would have to earn his forgiveness.

"You plotted against me," he said.

Her chin lifted. "Until the first moment I set eyes on you, that night by the pool in the desert, and I knew we were meant for each other. After that, I was yours."

He'd always known their first meeting wasn't by chance—just as he had known she was his. But to admit that would mean to accept a share of the guilt, and he wasn't to blame for this. The goddesses were. That meant Allia was, too.

"Our daughter is another part of your plot."

"Never," she said. "I swear to you, I never anticipated her. She's innocent." The golden light grew brighter still. "I gave up everything for her at the time of her birth. She now owns the soul you refused to accept. I am hers."

It took two breaths of time for him to understand what she was saying to him. Even then, he was unprepared for the desperate sense of loss and the bone-chilling despair that accompanied the knowledge. A part of him had assumed he would one day find her again. He'd nursed thoughts of revenge, and of how he would make her pay for her betrayal. Those thoughts had all involved her belonging to him.

She would never be his again. She'd never be able to assume a mortal form. She'd never experience the world's pleasures. He closed his eyes against the pain. She'd been so beautiful and gentle. He hadn't wanted her dead.

And now, he had no idea what to do with their daughter.

He opened his eyes. She was an abomination. Something that was never meant to exist. If she was what kept the demons trapped in this mortal world, then by rights he should kill her.

He sat back in his throne with one leg extended. "If what you say is true, then her death would free you."

"What would it change for you and me?" Allia asked. "I don't want freedom. Not at her expense. You and I are responsible for the death of any love between us. We alone own that. She's the true innocent in all of this. She might have been born inside of time, but immortality can still be hers if she wants it. You can set her free if you choose."

Of course. His daughter's death would free him from time, but the bond would work both ways. His would also free her.

And yet, either way, they would remain connected to each other forever.

"You hate me so much that you want me dead?" he asked the other half of his soul—the golden goddess who no longer loved him, and who stood with their daughter against him.

Allia's eyes gentled. "I would see you at peace."

The bitterness of loss burned in his throat like hot bile. What was peace to him now, when he could have had so much more than that?

He hated the priestess who'd lied to him. He hated the goddesses who'd used Allia against him. He hated, too, the daughter responsible for the death of the one woman he'd been meant to love and protect for eternity. Because of her, Allia was lost to him forever.

And a tiny part of him hated Allia as well. She should have told him of the plot from the beginning. If she had, things would have turned out very differently for them. This was as much her fault as anyone's.

He gripped the arms of his throne, his thoughts conflicted. If his daughter wanted a place amongst the immortals, she'd have to fight for the right to claim it. If she didn't earn it, then she would die.

But if she died, he would own her death. He didn't know what that might mean for him, or to the others he commanded. Was this yet another part of the goddesses' plot against demons? Was the risk worth it to him?

He no longer had anything to lose.

"If she wants immortality," he said, the challenge ringing clearly throughout the cavern so that all in attendance could hear, "then she will fight me for it."

* * *

Torches filled the room with a smoky light that illuminated striated walls of red sandstone blackened with soot.

The cavern was high-ceiled and relatively narrow, tapering to a single entrance through which faint light could be seen, so it must be day—although Hunter couldn't begin to guess at the time. That tiny entrance was also the only exit he'd been able to discern.

He peered through the bars of the cage, making no sudden movements, careful not to draw unwanted attention as he watched Airie walk—golden and beautiful—through the crowd of demons and straight to the Demon Lord's throne. All eyes remained on her, including his.

Not once did she glance at him.

Blood pulsed at his temples. He had never in his life wanted to kill demons more. He promised himself he would have the opportunity soon enough. But for now, he forced his mind to separate rational thought from emotion. He'd be of no help to her if he couldn't pay attention and form a plan. She was alive and unafraid, and although that calmed him somewhat, he knew that she was far from safe even if she did not.

A small sound beside his cage, a slight shuffling, caught his attention. He didn't dare turn his head, but from between the slats of his prison floor, he saw the top of a child's head.

Scratch.

The boy had crossed miles of desert—twice—and walked through a den of demons, avoiding all observation. Even now, no one seemed to pay him the slightest attention.

Hunter could no longer deny it. The child wasn't mortal.

Acceptance slid through him with an ease he didn't bother to question. Whatever Scratch was, he loved Airie as much as she loved him. There was no threat in the boy, only the same innocent kindness Airie possessed, and that was all that mattered to Hunter. He could no longer summon the hatred he'd once felt for all demon offspring. He had come to love them both.

Scratch stood on his toes and slid an object into the cage, pushing it under Hunter's hip and out of sight. Searing heat seeped through his clothing.

His amulet.

A spark of hope ignited. If he put up enough of a fight, he could force the demons to kill him rather than have them tear him apart and eat him alive. He didn't want either Airie or Scratch to witness that.

Hide, he mouthed to the child.

Scratch disappeared from his line of vision. Again, Hunter tried to hear what was happening with Airie.

Immortality can be hers if she wants it.

He'd missed important information. What did that mean? What else had been said?

If she wants immortality, she will fight me for it.

No.

Hunter surged to his feet, hurling his whole weight at the bars of the cage, again and again, the rage pounding against the inside of his skull matching his frantic efforts to free himself.

CHAPTER NINETEEN

Fire sputtered in the sconces anchored high on the soot-streaked cavern walls.

Doubt squeezed Airie's heart over the wisdom of the deal she had made. She'd drawn on a lifetime of faith by granting the goddess permission to speak through her, but the sight of Hunter in a suspended cage in the demon-filled hall, and the whispers of those demons and their plans for him, meant that his life was also at stake now, and she was no longer willing to rely solely on the faith she'd been raised with.

She had goddess blood in her. She had demon blood, too.

Release me, she demanded. *I'll accept the challenge.*

Her request, however, went unheeded.

The Demon Lord came around to the front of the platform and stood not five feet from her, staring at her face as if searching for something familiar in it.

Again, the goddess addressed him. "I have the right to fight for my daughter's freedom."

His eyes shuttered. "I refuse to fight you."

"Then another will fight you on my behalf." She looked to Hunter, wild now inside the swinging cage, his chest heaving with the enormity of an anger that threatened to burst loose at any second. "If the Demon Slayer wishes, he can fight for me."

Airie tried to scream for him to refuse. This wasn't his battle. She, however, was trapped as effectively as he was, and was every bit as angry, because she'd trusted the goddess with her life, but hers wasn't the one most precious to her. She hadn't thought to safeguard Hunter's. She'd been so naïve. She would never forgive the goddess for this betrayal.

Hunter's knuckles gleamed stark white against the bars of his cage as he tried to bend them with his bare hands. "I do wish it. I want to fight. More than anything."

"Very well," the Demon Lord said to the goddess. Cunning entered his expression. "But remember, Allia, if he wins, he won't be the one to own my death. It will be hers to struggle against for eternity."

He turned to his throne as if in search of something. At the same time, Hunter stooped to retrieve an object from the floor of the cage. It dangled from a gold chain snarled around his fingers, and flushed a dull red in the firelight when he straightened.

"Looking for this?" he asked, holding the amulet up for the Demon Lord to see before fastening it around his neck.

"How..." The Demon Lord recovered. "So be it, then. Slayer!" he thundered, his challenge shaking the cavern. The cage swayed on its chains. "Fight me!"

The demons gathered around roared in anticipation.

And Airie, helpless through her own misplaced trust, could do nothing but watch.

* * *

The cage dropped to the stone platform and Hunter exploded from inside, ready to fight anyone who approached too close to Airie. As he landed in a crouch to stand between her and the press of demons, thrusting her behind him, the rumble in the cavern rose to a level that shook the earth beneath his feet.

He didn't fully understand what had just transpired. The conversation he'd overheard had been confusing at best. All he knew beyond any doubt was that Airie had been threatened, she was in danger, and he was going to kill the demon responsible for it.

Yet he despaired of getting her to safety once it was finished. Even if he won this challenge, he couldn't fight all of the remaining demons. The odds were hardly in his favor. His weapons had been confiscated. He calculated at least a hundred demons present, which meant nearly, if not all, of their numbers. A memory of the poor young woman from the ill-fated wagon train attacked by demons intruded. Grimly, he acknowledged the reality of their similar situation and its inevitable outcome, and that a dark decision had to be made. Better for Airie to receive death by his hand than face these monsters alone. He didn't want her to witness what they would do to him either.

First, however, a challenge had been issued and accepted. He'd take the Demon Lord and as many more demons with him as he could.

He groped behind him with one arm to catch her around the waist and draw her to his side, careful to keep one of his hands free and not to turn his back on the demons, and took one last look at her face, hoping she'd recognize in his own some of what he was thinking. The touch of the bright golden halo of light surrounding her calmed him. There was so much he wished he'd said to her—words of the profound love he felt for her but had refused to recognize until too late. He wished he'd been kinder and gentler with her. It was hard to acknowledge that the last thing he might ever bring her was death.

She met his eyes. "I'd like for you to wear this. But please, return it when you're done. It was a gift to my daughter."

The words made no sense. Or perhaps he simply didn't want to understand. As she lifted the rainbow amulet from her own neck to place it around his, it struck him that something else wasn't right. He stared harder into her face. Her eyes were blue now, not brown, although familiar gold fire flickered in their depths. In his rage he had, indeed, missed important information. Whoever this was, it wasn't Airie.

If the Demon Slayer wishes, he can fight for me.

She smiled at him, an apology in the soft arc of her lips. With a politeness of manner, she extricated herself from his embrace. "Be quick," this Airie-who-was-not advised him. "She's very angry. I can't hold her back for much longer." Her voice turned wistful. "I hope someday you can convince her to forgive me."

Immortality can be hers if she wants it. Understanding edged past his confusion, like the sun sliding from behind clouds. Airie was the child of two immortals, not one. A goddess did, indeed, walk with her.

Which meant she didn't have to die by his hand. As long as he won this fight, she would have immortality to save her.

His relief was followed by another, more painful, awareness. When this was over, whether he lived or died, he would lose her. Regret stung at the backs of his eyes. He'd wasted their valuable time together by worrying over things that didn't matter. It was Airie, the woman, whom he loved. Would always love.

Whereas Airie the immortal could never be his.

"Whether she forgives you or not," he said, his throat thick, "know that I thank you for this. She could never have killed him, not even to save herself."

Sadness touched the edges of the goddess's smile. "She would have, for you. But she'd never be able to forgive herself for it after. He wouldn't forgive himself either, if he harmed her. I'd rather they both be unable to forgive me."

She took both amulets in her hands, and in a sweet, rich voice so much like Airie's it made his chest ache, she offered him her blessings. Then, with glowing fingers that trembled slightly, she fitted the two amulets together, just as he had once done with them.

"Goddesses offer a different type of strength," she said to Hunter. She leaned closer to whisper in his ear. "When the Demon Lord fights, he doesn't fight only you. He battles the demons whose deaths he owns, because they fight him for their freedom, too."

She drew away before Hunter could ask her what she meant.

"Slayer!" the Demon Lord shouted. "I grow impatient."

Hunter lifted Airie onto the low platform and out of harm's way. Then, as he turned to face his opponent, he put her firmly from his thoughts.

He had a fight to win.

The demons had begun to assemble into a tight half-circle around the front of the platform, forcing the Demon Lord and Hunter into its center. Many wore full manhunting forms. Hunter chose not to dwell on what would happen when first blood was spilled. He only hoped it wasn't his.

He held his hands low and ready, prepared to defend himself against attack, and breathed deeply as he blocked out everything except his opponent.

The Demon Lord had chosen to fight Hunter in mortal form, stripping down to expose a broad, bare chest, wearing nothing but a pair of faded trousers. Thick black hair, shot through with threads of gray that glinted red in the firelight, swept his shoulders.

While impressive enough, this wasn't the form Hunter would have preferred to confront. He'd meant to goad the Demon Lord into using his greatest strengths first, so that the amulet could absorb and transmit them to him.

"You excel at fighting women," he said. "A goddess, a crippled old priestess, and now your own daughter. I hope a mortal man won't prove too much of a challenge for you." As he spoke, he watched carefully for any opportunity to strike.

The demon's face darkened. "Her goddess mother was a pleasure-seeking, faithless liar. Did my daughter tell you she loves you, as her mother once swore she loved me? Did she compel you to believe her?"

"You should be more concerned with why I'm known as the Demon Slayer," Hunter said. "When I kill you, you'll die screaming."

"We'll see if my daughter screams, too, when she dies. Although you'll already be dead, so you'll never know for certain." He smiled. "You'll have to imagine it."

Hunter had chosen his weapon poorly. Airie was his weakness, not her father's. The Demon Lord cared nothing for her, but perhaps he did for the goddess. The demon spoke of her with too much anger and contempt for it to be otherwise. "I wonder if Airie's mother also died screaming."

He had little time to prepare himself against the furious response. A shimmering ball of searing flame the size of his head caught him high in the chest, igniting his shirt and hurling him against a living wall of demons. Blinding pain scorched through him so that it was all he could do to keep from screaming himself.

Then his amulet compensated, caught the power behind the demon fire, and gave it to him. The flames died. The pain, too, ebbed away as fast as it had risen. Rough hands and grasping demon claws thrust him back to his feet. Hunter's shirt hung in smoldering tatters from his body, but other than that, he was unharmed.

The amulet the goddess gave him could heal.

The Demon Lord walked the edges of the semi-circle, pumping a fist in the air while the crowd roared, but his complete attention wasn't on the fight, Hunter saw. His eyes drifted to the platform. Hunter, seizing an opportunity to use the distraction against him, rushed at his swaggering opponent.

The Demon Lord whirled, dropping into a crouch. In a blur of speed, one fist shot out.

Hunter blocked it and ducked, following through with a foot to the back of the Demon Lord's knee that spilled him to the ground. Another roar arose from the spectators.

The Demon Lord surprised him again, and Hunter found himself on his back, looking up at a ring of faces—too many of them demonic now, not mortal, as they shifted in reaction to the fight.

The Demon Lord's knuckles slammed against Hunter's cheek, narrowly missing his nose, and for a second, Hunter thought his cheekbone had shattered. Agony blossomed in his eye socket and shot through his temple before his amulet absorbed it and turned it to strength.

But the Demon Lord had not gotten as much force behind the blow as he'd intended. The flash of awareness in his eyes as his glance flickered to the dual amulet on Hunter's chest said that he hadn't expected for something he'd crafted to work against him. Now that he knew it would, he would find a way to circumvent it once he got over his shock.

Hunter had to draw blood while he still had a chance. He hooked his feet into the Demon Lord's hips to lock him in place, then grabbed the amulet in his fist and used its edge to gouge at the Demon Lord's face. A thin line of red streaked from the demon's left eye, down his cheek, to the corner of his mouth.

He bellowed in outrage and pain. He tried to shift, but the amulet had drawn too much from him and he couldn't do so completely. Claws sprouted from the tips of his fingers.

Those were enough to be deadly.

He slashed at Hunter's throat, and thick spurts of warm, copper-scented blood sprayed out to stain the Demon Lord's face and bared chest in reward. Still straddling Hunter's body, both his fists flew high and his shouts of victory rang off the cavern walls.

A woman's screams pierced through the howls of the demons as Hunter's hands went to his torn throat in an effort to stop the heavy flow of blood. He fought to stay conscious, fear for Airie the only thought in his head.

The Demon Lord drew his hand back, prepared to deliver a second blow to Hunter's chest to tear out his heart with his claws, but the attempt to shift had cost him more strength than he seemed to realize. Hunter's reinforced amulet shot out great streams of blinding golden light that flung the Demon Lord several feet backward. He struck the edge of the stone platform and slumped to the ground in a daze. A chunk of rock the size of a demon's fist split away and toppled past his bent head.

As Hunter struggled to right his blurring vision, the bleeding at his throat stopped and the sting of the cuts disappeared. A sense of urgency, and of time slipping away, roused him to action. The second amulet was growing weaker every time it had to heal him.

A larger threat reared its head.

Hunter froze in the act of rising, one hand on the ground and legs bent at the knee, and looked up. The demons closest to him had caught the scent of his blood. Hunger glittered in their red eyes. He dared to steal another glance at Airie, who had fallen to her hands and knees when the Demon Lord struck the platform's edge.

She was no longer alone. Beside her, outlined in gold light, stood the silhouette of a second woman. Her lips moved as she spoke words to Airie he couldn't hear, and she placed one hand on Airie's arm.

His heart went still. Airie had freed herself. If her goddess mother couldn't contain her when she was this agitated, it wouldn't be long before she threw herself into the fray. She possessed no natural fear for herself. She'd let nothing stop her from coming to his aid.

He didn't trust goddess light to protect her from blood-frenzied demons. Not when the goddesses had been unable to defend themselves against the fury of the Demon Lord as he burned their mountain.

The Demon Lord was on his feet again, although staggering as if drunk. A bluish green haze enveloped him.

Hunter blinked, thinking at first that his vision had been damaged by one of the blows he'd received, but then the haze wavered and separated into a number of shadows.

The goddess's words returned to him.

He battles the demons whose deaths he owns, because they fight him for their freedom, too.

The Demon Lord was weakening, and the change in the tone of the crowd's rumbling told Hunter the others knew it, too. The cheers for their leader died away. Their thirst for blood did not. Both the Demon Lord and Hunter were coated in it, and Hunter watched warily as their attention shifted between them, trying to decide which of them was the weaker.

He couldn't claim to be in the best of shape either. Much of the strength he'd gained from one amulet was lost in his healing to the other, and while he thought he could manage one demon, a hundred would be ninety-nine too many.

Low chanting began, gradually gaining strength and momentum.

Blood. Blood. BLOOD.

Pushing and shoving from the spectators at the back as they tried to move to the front triggered a brawl. One sledgehammer-sized fist missed its target and pummeled a hole into a cavern wall. Another demon slammed headfirst into a stone pillar. Fine cracks splintered upward and fanned across the ceiling in intricate, spidery webs. Without their leader to keep them in check, whatever discipline remained to them was about to be lost.

The fire guttering along the cavern walls gave Hunter an idea. Airie needed something to do that would be of benefit to them both, yet also keep her from harm.

"Airie!" he shouted to her. "Surround us with fire!"

CHAPTER TWENTY

Fire was her weapon, too.

Her inner demon, straining against the confines of a goddess upbringing and the will of her demon father, told her all she needed to know. The fire she held was hers. She'd been born with it. And she was also the Demon Lord's daughter. If he could call her fire to him, she could call his to her.

So she did.

It danced up the walls in great ropes of yellow flame, twisting and swirling along the rifts in the cavern's ceiling before dropping to form a thick sheet of fire between the two combatants and the mass of demons.

As it fell, Hunter shot from his crouched position like a bullet from a gun, ramming his shoulder into the Demon Lord's chest and bearing him to the ground.

Both were on their feet again in an instant. The Demon Lord grabbed Hunter by the arms, then grimaced, unable to retain his grip as blue-green shadows undulated and writhed beneath his flesh. Hunter took immediate advantage, and brought his head forward to smash it into the demon's face before driving a knee into his groin.

Bloodied and weakened, doubled over in pain, the Demon Lord's eyes went to the golden figure of light on the platform beside Airie. Loss and sorrow crossed his face, followed by resignation. Airie knew he was beaten, and moved to shield her goddess mother from the sight of what was to come.

He wiped at the blood streaming from his nose and mouth with the back of his hand as he squared off against Hunter to deliver one last affront. "My demons won't be held back. Will you battle them all, Slayer? Is she worth that much to you?"

"Yes," Hunter said.

He shot his fist into the Demon Lord's broken face, knocking him down one final time. Then, he crushed his throat beneath his boot.

A thick, blue-green haze slid from the fallen Demon Lord to Airie, filtering through the pores of her skin, its weight and a sick comprehension driving her to her knees on the platform. She owned his death now, as he would have owned hers if he'd won the challenge instead of Hunter, and her demon instincts whispered that it wouldn't be as easy to bear as her mother's had been.

The sound of the goddess's sobs echoed in the otherwise silent cavern as the demons watched their leader fall. The wall of fire Airie had summoned at Hunter's request faltered and slipped from her grasp.

She lifted her head.

The mood in the cavern had shifted from ugly anticipation to an even uglier threat. Hunter stood to her right. Blood stained his tattered clothing and smeared his skin, but for all that, he appeared unharmed. He flung sweat-dampened blond hair from his eyes and glared around, chest heaving, primed for the next demon to step forward and challenge him.

They divided their attention between her and Hunter, as if deciding which of them to pursue first. Raw anger exploded inside her as her demon burst free. She possessed fire. And rain. She would kill them all, one by one if she had to.

She dragged herself to her feet, then the edge of the platform, as the goddess's sobs turned to screams. *No, Airie. This isn't the way!*

Ignoring the warning, Airie leapt to the ground to meet the first of those demons brave enough to approach her. Hunter started forward to protect her, his expression murderous, but she wouldn't have him facing more danger on her behalf.

Stronger now, and becoming acquainted with the additional weight of her father, she reconstructed the wall of fire around them.

Four demons, however, had gotten too close to her and were now trapped inside it, too. She slapped her palm to the bone-plated arm of the first one to reach for her, and mixing demon fire and goddess rain together, drove them deep into its flesh. Steam billowed beneath her touch. The demon shrieked in agony as it boiled from the inside out. She turned her face from the stink of cooking meat.

The demon fell to the ground, clouded eyes staring upward. The haze of death rose from its body to settle around Airie, coating her skin in a sickly green light. In her head, she knew horror. This was her first step toward immortality—although she'd taken it in a direction she'd never intended.

She didn't want to be a demon.

Neither did she want for Hunter to die.

She brought the flat of her hand against a second demon, sending another burst of fire and water into its flesh. More screams, and a second blue-green haze joined the first. This death was stronger, and the weight of it sent Airie to her hands and knees again so that the wall of flame she'd built to protect Hunter faltered, but she couldn't stop now.

She groped blindly and caught a leg above the ankle. The thick, clinging haze of this third death when it came drove the others a little deeper. Panic scalded her. She didn't know if she could carry the weight of too many more, yet she had to find a way to drive them away so Hunter would have a chance to escape.

Then her mother was at her side, draping her in golden, goddess light, but even that couldn't displace the eerie glow of the dead demons clinging to her.

"Listen to me," Allia said. "You have a choice to make. You own your father's death, and therefore his strength. You can command demons. Or you can take my place with my sisters. They will welcome you." Her cheeks sparkled with golden tears. "But choose quickly, while you still can. They won't wait for you. Now that the demons are freed from the boundaries of time, my sisters will go back into hiding."

"And if I don't make a choice?" Airie asked her. "What happens then?"

The goddess wiped the tears from her cheeks. "The number of deaths you own will decide the matter for you."

That was why her mother had tried to stop her from fighting them. Already, she felt the enormous surge of power that full demon immortality would bring her. It was heady, and difficult to resist, and she knew it wouldn't be long before she could not. She tried to organize her thoughts, and examine her options so that she made a decision that was of benefit to others, and not herself. It had to be something her mother—her priestess mother—would have approved of. She'd always encouraged Airie to do what was right.

Choosing either immortality meant her parents would never be free again. She would own their deaths forever.

If that was the price they paid for her immortality, she didn't want it.

"I have a third choice," she said. "You once told me if I wanted a place in this world I would have to be welcomed to it. But even if someone does welcome me, I don't want my place here to be as an immortal."

"You can live inside of time and be subject to its laws, but you'll never be truly mortal," the goddess warned her. "You can't give up the deaths you now own. They will be with you throughout your lifetime." Her eyes were anxious. "Think carefully. The goddesses will accept you. So will the demons. Are you as certain of your welcome here in the mortal world?"

One person would welcome her. In her heart, she knew with absolute truth that Hunter held the other half of her soul. She could search for all of eternity, from one end of the universe to the other, and never again find an equal.

"Yes," she said.

Their fingers touched, a brief clasp, her mother's little more than a soft stirring of air against Airie's skin.

Golden light laced with streaks of vivid blue-green shot through the cavern as her mother's image was joined by the shadowy haze of another, larger one. While Airie might command her demon father's death, and have his protection, it was Allia he would forever follow. Perhaps his defeat was more of a kindness than she'd understood. Her throat tightened, and she looked away from them to find Hunter.

More blood had been spilled. He'd won this fight, too, but he wouldn't win many more. Agitated beyond reason now, on the other side of the wall, several dozen demons hurled themselves into the fire in an attempt to get at him. More had scaled the cavern's walls to the cracked ceiling, thinking to break through at the top.

Yet Hunter, with one knee on the ground and breathing in deep, heaving gasps, his body battered and bloodied, his face dripping in sweat from the heat of the blaze around them, had eyes for no one but her. He pressed his hands to his thighs and pushed to a standing position.

Airie ran into his arms.

He cupped her face in his hands and scanned her anxiously from head to toe, then finally, satisfied she was unharmed, kissed her. He paid no attention to the shadowy forms of her father and mother standing close by, or the demons roaring for the Slayer's blood.

"Surround yourself with fire," Hunter said to her. "Then I want you to run." His mouth settled in grim resolve. "They want the Demon Slayer. They can die fighting him."

* * *

Airie stood straight and tall as she curled her fingers to fists and took a step back. Her eyes flashed with fire. "I'm not running from them. From now on, they run from *me*."

Gold and blue-green light encased her. The wall of shimmering flame she held curled inward as it collapsed, then ran like fingers of fire along the ground.

A roar came from the mouth of the cavern, building in intensity. At first, Hunter couldn't place the source. Then he recognized the pounding of heavy rain.

A wide stream of water gushed toward them, forcing demons to take to wing. Those who weren't quick enough found they didn't have room to spread theirs out, and they screamed in agony as the water washed through, ankle deep, to flood the floor of the entire cavern. The fire met the rain, and the cavern filled with a thick, scorching steam.

Sweat streamed down Hunter's face.

Scratch.

His heart pounded. Airie didn't know he was here, and Hunter had no idea how demon flames and goddess rain might affect him. He glanced around frantically, trying to find his hiding place, and shouted for him, hoping to be heard over the rain and fire and demon screams.

The child crawled from under the platform, near Hunter's feet. Steam penetrated every corner, every crack and crevice, making it impossible to escape its touch. Hunter snatched Scratch up in his arms, turning his body in order to shield him as best he could.

Something hard pressed against his chest, and he looked down to see what it was. Scratch had a rock of some sort in his hands. It was egg-shaped and rough, colored a drab shade of green similar to the areoles of cacti, with a pin at the top to lock its detonator.

Not a rock.

Hunter's heart pounded harder. With the bomb cushioned against his chest, and Scratch in his arms, he grabbed Airie by the hand and ran, following in the wake of the demons who'd managed to flee.

Out in the open the rain continued to fall. It ran down Hunter's face and soaked his tattered clothing. Blood trickled in thin rivulets from his chest and arms to drip to the ground in pale, watery splotches. Thankfully, it had no effect on the child. He set Scratch on his feet and eased the bomb from his tiny fingers.

Hunter examined it. It fit the curve of his palm, and was heavier than he'd expected. The head of the pin was round, as if meant to fit a man's finger. He wondered whether it was still live, and if so, how stable the detonator might be after all these years. He didn't want either Scratch or Airie near him when he pulled the pin.

"Stay right here," he ordered the boy. He took hold of his chin and looked into his face to make sure he had his full attention. Rain clung to the boy's lashes. "I want you where I can see you. No hiding. No more touching things you find if you don't know what they are. Do we understand each other?" Scratch nodded, and Hunter ruffled his wet hair. "Sit down and cover your head until I tell you it's safe to move."

He jogged a short distance away, then closed his eyes and prayed as he yanked the pin.

Nothing happened.

He threw the bomb into the mouth of the cavern. Again, nothing happened. Less than ten seconds later however, the earth shook, knocking him to his knees. He covered his head with his arms as chunks of dirt and rock pelted him.

When the ground steadied, he lifted his head. The mouth of the cavern had crumpled. Then, as he watched, the cliffs above it collapsed inward. Streams of smoke drifted up through fallen rock and rubble, intermingling with the immortal mist Airie had unleashed. Hunter wiped mud from his face, grimly satisfied with the devastation. The goddesses' temple was gone. The demons' lair was, as well.

He looked around to see what else might have been destroyed, or what danger remained.

As near as he could tell, the demons were gone.

Hunter checked on Scratch, who was sitting where he had been told to wait. Then he went to Airie, who had not yet released her hold on fire and rain, or the steam that billowed into the sky and rolled through the yucca trees, twisting around and under everything it touched, layering the desert in a thick, hot fog. Rain slid down her hair and off her cheeks, like teardrops that sparkled as they fell. Mud spattered her slim, bare feet. The flames in her eyes were gone, leaving them soft and beautiful, and shining with flecks of light. He read anxiety in them and reached for her, wanting to hold her tight and reassure her that all would be well, but he couldn't be certain yet that it was.

He did know, however, how much he loved her. She'd fought demons for him, and she would always do so, and it was best to accept it. They would fight them together.

She stepped away from him, not letting him touch her. His heart retracted into his throat.

"Time has run out for me," she said to him. "I have to choose who I am. What I will be." The fire in her eyes disappeared, replaced now by gleaming tears of gold that made him ache for her. "Immortals are no longer welcome here."

He didn't know what she meant. She was Airie. Nothing more, nothing less. Her place was with him. Then he saw the entire situation with greater clarity, and a part of him died. She was also an immortal—but she could be only demon or goddess, not both.

There seemed little contest in that decision. Or consolation, for that matter. Either way, he had lost her.

"I understand." He swallowed hard. He cleared his throat, embarrassed by the emotions he couldn't hold back. "I love you. Before you go, I thought you should know that."

A smile lit her face. "I have a third choice, but it's not mine to make. If you could, would you welcome me to your world?"

"Always." Hope flickered to life in his heart. "Whether you're goddess or demon, I want you by my side."

She was in his arms, hers tight around his neck, a sodden bundle who kissed his rain-washed face over and over. "I want you, too," she said. "I love you. Wherever you are, that's where I belong."

The sun peeked out through the rain. A rainbow, brilliant and multi-hued, arced across the desert from one end of the horizon to the other. He hated himself for what he was about to say. He would have hated himself more if he didn't.

"I don't want you to give up your immortality for me if that's the price you'll be paying."

She took the back of his head in her fingers and drew his mouth to hers. The golden sheen to her skin slowly faded away beneath the steady patter of rain.

"What good is immortality to me," she said against his lips, "if my heart remains mortal?"

CHAPTER TWENTY-ONE

It was three days before the heavy mist dissipated and the sun returned. By that time, everything in Freetown was sodden. Nothing had escaped its touch. It flowed under doors and through the tiniest of cracks.

On the afternoon of the third day, Blade knocked on the door to Ruby's private room.

"Come in."

She sat in the chaise longue, surrounded by colorful cushions, a book upside down on her lap. She smiled, but it didn't quite reach her eyes in the way it once had when she looked at him. She didn't offer him a seat either, or ask what he wanted with that little lift to her voice that told him he could have anything. Their relationship had changed, and he didn't know why.

He did know. He simply couldn't believe that it mattered.

"Marry me," he blurted out, and felt like a fool. This wasn't how he had intended to ask her.

She carefully lifted the book, marked the page, and set it aside. Then, she sat up straight and looked at him. "Why?"

A wagon rolled by outside in the street, its wheels clattering noisily over the slickened ruts. Her response wasn't what he'd expected. *Yes* and *no* were straightforward answers. He hadn't anticipated having to explain himself. He wasn't certain he could. "I should have asked you a long time ago."

"Why didn't you, then?"

Ruby deserved the truth even though he didn't like going down this road. "You deserved better than half a man."

She studied him. "Maybe now I think it's you who deserves better."

A fine-edged knife of pain slid into his chest. "I'm whole. I'm not perfect."

"Neither one of us is." She patted the seat beside her. He sat, careful not to crush her skirt, feeling clumsy and awkward on the feminine piece of furniture. Her eyes had gotten suspiciously shiny. "When I first met you, you worked very hard to walk again," she said.

The pain eased. "We can be married inside of a week."

She took his hand, linking their fingers, and spoke with a gentle grace. "You aren't that man anymore. But even then, you never worked hard enough to turn a relationship between us into anything more than friendship. I'm not sure why you should want to, now."

"Why do women always have to think things to death?" Blade asked.

She laughed. "If we didn't do the thinking, nobody would."

"Marry me," he repeated, more desperately this time, but she was shaking her head.

"I would never have said yes, even if you'd tried harder." She took a deep breath. "I'm a whore. It hasn't been a bad life. I have more independence than most women. But if I ever change my mind about marriage, it will be for someone who's never known me as one." She held up a hand when he would have interrupted her. "I'll tell him. I'm not ashamed of it. What's important is that if the time ever comes, this life will be in my past and it will never have been a part of his."

"My timing was bad," Blade said.

Ruby squeezed his fingers. "Terrible. But there was never going to be a good time, so it doesn't matter."

He'd known all along she'd say no. That was probably the real reason he'd never asked her before. But he should have, if only to show her that he cared.

But by asking her now, he'd freed them both to move on with their lives. He touched her face with the fingertips of his free hand, then kissed her, somewhat ashamed of the relief he felt. He got to his feet. His heart wasn't unscathed, but he would survive. He knew she would, too.

"I would have made a good husband," he said.

She clasped her hands in her lap, looking lovely in the light filtering through the muslin curtains. "And someday you will. But not for me."

He left, closing the door behind him.

* * *

Hunter heard the sound of a door opening and closing a floor below him and was instantly awake.

It was nothing, just one of the saloon's restless residents, because Airie still slept—she would have awakened otherwise—but the stealth in the movements he'd heard made Hunter uneasy. He slipped from the bed, careful not to awaken her. She rolled over in her sleep and flung her arm over his still warm pillow, pulling it close to her, and he smiled in the moonlight.

Blade was right. He was a lucky man. More so than he deserved.

He found his friend in the kitchen, filling a large pack with canned goods and utensils. He was dressed for travel.

Blade looked up when Hunter entered, his face shadowy in the glare of the single lantern hanging from the ceiling joist behind him. "Sorry if I woke you."

Hunter sat down at the long wooden table and watched him as he continued to work. "Going somewhere? Without saying goodbye?"

"I don't like goodbyes."

Neither did Hunter. But omitting this one didn't sit right. Packing and leaving in the middle of the night indicated to Hunter that Blade didn't intend to return.

"Where are you going?" he asked.

"Not sure."

So his friend was running away from home. Granted, Hunter had once done the same thing, but he'd been a kid. Blade was a little old for that. And settled. With Mamna gone, and the full use of his leg restored, he had a real chance for his business to grow.

Hunter waited for Blade to elaborate. When he didn't, he said, "I guess what I really want to know is, why?"

With the pack bulging, Blade flipped the canvas flap closed and tightened the leather straps. He lifted a careless shoulder, not meeting Hunter's eyes. "Now that I have my leg back, I'm restless to see the world." He sighed, looked at the ceiling, then finally at Hunter. "I asked Ruby to marry me and she said no."

"I see."

And he did, far better than Blade. Hunter knew his friend, he knew Ruby, and he knew something of women. The two weren't suited to be more than friends. Perhaps with a bit of distance between them, that might change. If not, it was never meant to be.

"Change is coming," he reminded him. He and Blade had spoken of it. Of the children like Scratch, and the boy at the trading post, whose demon heritages had begun to fight free with the fall of Goddess Mountain. Now that the immortals were gone, more would come out of hiding. Who knew how many, or what they might be capable of?

"Let it. Until I find trouble, I don't plan to borrow it." Blade shrugged into the pack's shoulder straps and tied it tight around his waist. "Do me a favor. Make sure Airie understands that me leaving isn't a bad thing. She's given Ruby and me a chance at new lives."

"Speaking of Ruby... What about her? And the others?"

Blade tapped an envelope on the table behind Hunter. It had Ruby's name on it. "She'll run the saloon. It's in my name, so she should have no problems. And if the laws change, it becomes hers."

So that was it, then. Blade was a grown man. Hunter wasn't about to try to change his mind.

But he was going to miss him far more than he'd expected. When he'd decided to take Airie back to his home, he hadn't thought he'd lose all contact with his closest friend. He held out his hand. "If you're ever in the Borderlands, look me up. If you need me, send for me. I'll come."

Blade's grip was solid and familiar, and far too brief. "I will."

He let himself out through the kitchen door and was swallowed by the night.

Hunter continued to sit, thinking back over their years of friendship. Blade had provided him with a place to return to. But the saloon had been a temporary home. Now it was time for him to make a real one with the woman he loved.

He extinguished the lantern and went back to bed, and to Airie.

* * *

Normally Airie loved this time of day, when night began the slow descent into day and both the moon and the sun touched the sky. It spoke to both parts of her nature and brought them into balance.

But she cried when the remnants of the collapsed mountain disappeared beneath the desert horizon behind them. She couldn't help it. She didn't want to leave her mother behind—but she didn't want Hunter and Scratch to see her cry either, so she did her best to hide her tears.

Hunter, who was walking, knew immediately what was wrong. He drew Sally to a halt and eased Airie from the saddle. She slid to the ground with Scratch in her arms. Hunter took him from her and set him on his feet. Then he pulled Airie close.

"She wouldn't want you to feel this way," he said. "She wanted you to be safe and happy. That's why she asked me to take you with me before she died. I promise you, we'll come back to visit her."

Airie rested her head against his chest, feeling the steady, reassuring beat of his heart. He meant well, and he intended to keep his promise, but it was a trip that took several months when traveled both ways. She knew they wouldn't be back for a very long time, if at all. She was leaving her home for the unknown.

While Hunter loved her, she worried what his family would think of his choice in a mate. She would never be truly mortal. Her parents remained with her—two silent presences—both content to wait out her mortal life in order to regain their freedom. She also possessed demon deaths, although her father fought those for her and kept them under submission.

"What if your family hates me?" she asked. She wanted to add, *because of your sister*, but she didn't have to. Again, he understood her concern.

His arms tightened. "It was a long time ago. My family will look at you and see someone I love, and they'll love you, too. Besides," he added. "No one could have a better reason to hate demons than Blade, and he wants you to keep him in mind if you ever get tired of me."

She hadn't wanted a reminder of Blade. She'd tried to speak with Ruby about him before they left, to say she was sorry for causing her pain, but Ruby had refused to listen to any apologies.

"You gave him back something that was worth far more to him than I ever was," she'd said, offering Airie a bright smile that fooled neither of them. "And I deserve better in a marriage than a comfortable friendship with a man filled with regrets."

Scratch tugged on one leg of the trousers she'd worn for travel. Hunter had bought her clothes and boots that fit. The little boy, too, was comfortably dressed, although no matter how hard she tried, she couldn't seem to keep him clean. And although he'd been warned time and again not to pick up things he didn't recognize, they had to conduct periodic and thorough searches of his pockets.

She bent to receive the grimy kiss he offered her, then looked up at Hunter. "He's the same as me, isn't he?"

While it was unlikely his mother was a goddess, there could be little doubt that his father was demon.

"We'll worry about it if there's ever a need to," Hunter replied, his tone light. "Until then, who better to be his parents than us? He's ours now, and that's all that matters. We'll give him a new name. A good one. We'll raise him right."

She couldn't help but worry. "What if there are more people like us?"

"The world should be so lucky." He pointed to Sally, who was impatiently flicking her tongue. "It's time to move on. Saddle up."

She curled her fingers in his shirtfront and pressed her lips to his.

"I hope you told Blade that I'll never get tired of you," she said. "I love you, and I'll follow you to the four corners of the earth if I have to."

His eyes were a deep, startling blue in his suntanned face.

"I know," he said, a satisfied grin creasing his cheeks.

Airie swung into the saddle and settled Scratch in front of her, feeling better already because in her heart, where it mattered, both of her mothers smiled, too.

THE END

NOTE TO READERS

I hope you've enjoyed this first installment in the **Wasteland** series.

Reader opinions make a huge impact. Reviews increase an author's visibility, and I'd greatly appreciate a few short lines on the retailer of your choice, other any online site where you like to hang out.

The immortals may be gone, but **Wasteland**'s problems are only beginning. The world will be undergoing a transformation in the coming books.

Read on for previews of **Boundary**, coming March 2018, and **The Forgotten**, coming in May.

Visit our website at www.paulaaltenburg.com[1]

Cover design by Stacy Veno

Ebook ISBN 978-0-9937166-9-0

Manufactured in the United States of America

First Edition November 2013

Revised Edition January 2018

---

1.   http://www.paulaaltenburg.com

ABOUT THE AUTHOR

A former manager in the aerospace industry with a BA in Social Anthropology, Paula Altenburg lives on the East Coast of Canada and writes fulltime. She's written for Tor, Entangled, and Tule Publishing.

As well as THE WASTELAND series she's authored over seventeen books, including two contemporary romance series—SPY GAMES (complete four-book series) and THE SWEETHEART BRAND (third book available February 6th from Tule Publishing).

To learn about Paula's upcoming releases, you can follow her on social media or sign up for her newsletter at www.paulaaltenburg.com[1].

---

1.   http://www.paulaaltenburg.com

~ Coming March 2018 ~

Boundary

A Wasteland Novel ~ Book 2

Previously published as Black Widow Demon

Preview

CHAPTER ONE

Tidy towns often concealed dirty secrets. And this small mining town was too tidy for Blade's taste.

Nestled among the foothills of the Godseeker Mountains, it suffered from a too-uniform construction and a general lack of aesthetic design. But after several months of crossing the desert, and with winter fast approaching, Blade's standards weren't high. He wanted a bath, a hot meal, and a soft bed.

A bed he could wake up in alone. The two-foot goldthief—one of the more dangerous variety of snakes in these parts—in his bedroll that morning had been an unwelcome surprise. Fortunately, Blade was neither a restless sleeper nor easily startled, and he possessed a great deal of natural patience. Once the sun came up on the desert, the well-rested serpent had slithered off on its own without incident.

From an outcropping of weathered sandstone, Blade continued to study the mining settlement deep in the valley below him. A lone, open wagon hauled by a sway-backed, listless hross clattered along a dirt trail that broadened into a street where it met the town limits. Layers of desert grime coated flat rooftops, painting the entire town a dull shade of gray. Beyond it, jagged foothills crashed into a vast rocky mountain range speckled with juniper and yellow pine like the stubble on the chin of a pimple-faced boy. Narrow ribbons of silvery water trickled from snow-capped peaks, filtering into thousands of cracks and crevices to vanish before reaching the parched valley floor.

Behind Blade, and above, past the top of the mesa where he stood, stretched the desert.

The world was changing. For three hundred long years, up until a few short months ago, immortals had ruled all of Wasteland. The goddesses had been benevolent, and worshipped by many, whereas the demons had killed mortal men for sport and lured mortal women to them for pleasure.

This bold new settlement had sprung up arrogantly close to what had, until recently, been demon territory. It possessed no protective ramparts, a serious oversight on the part of its founders. The demon occupation might be over, and the immortals scoured from the earth, but any number of mortal dangers remained.

Blade was bone-deep weary of death and destruction, and of the strong who preyed on the weak. His instincts screamed for him to keep moving. When he considered his near-empty pack, however, and that this was the first sign of civilization he'd come across in several weeks, its underwhelming neatness and lack of defenses weren't enough to deter him.

The past was behind him. He was looking ahead. He was no longer a saloonkeeper, an assassin, or a cripple, and a far cry from the helpless, abused boy he'd been long ago. He would be none of those things again. Deep within these mountains lurked a boundary that the goddesses had created to keep demons confined to the desert regions. He would test that boundary and see what, if anything, lay beyond it—or if the Old World had been completely decimated during the Occupation, leaving Wasteland all that remained. He thought that just once in his life he would like to see the sea, something he'd only ever read of in books.

A slight breeze stirred the chill, late afternoon air and he made a face—he stank, no doubt about it. Dust caked the thighs of his denim trousers and stiffened the broad brim of his hat. If he didn't get that bath he could forget about finding a hot meal and soft bed, although waking up alone would be guaranteed. He patted his clothing to confirm that his knives were secure and at hand. He'd been away from the north and the Godseeker Mountains for ten years. He doubted if he would be recognized here, or that it would mean much to anyone anymore if he were, but it paid to be prepared.

As he turned, he detected movement at the far edge of the town, nearest the foothills. From this distance it was difficult to say for certain, but it looked as if they were building a very large bonfire. He wondered what they were celebrating.

Shrugging his pack higher on his shoulders, he picked his way off the outcropping. Once on the valley floor, he carefully circled the town to approach via the main street that cut through its heart.

A neatly lettered sign, not yet worn by wind and blowing sand, proclaimed it Goldrush.

* * *

Fair trial, be damned. Without the arrival of some sort of miracle, come nightfall the townspeople intended to burn Raven at the stake as a spawn.

Until then, she languished in a jail cell that reeked of stale urine. She perched on the edge of a rough wooden bed, its wool blanket scratchy beneath her flattened palms. Her bare feet dangled well above the whitewashed pine floor. The jailor's chair and a desk with a crooked leg were the only other furnishings in the room. Both were well out of her reach on the other side of the iron bars. For the hundredth time, she mentally raced through her options. All of them involved killing her stepfather.

But her first attempt at that was what had gotten her into this trouble.

She toppled to her side and tucked her clasped hands beneath her cheek, staring at the bars. It was his own fault that she'd stabbed him. He'd slipped his hand down the front of her dress, and when she defended herself, had the nerve to blame her for his wrongdoing. He claimed she had tempted him. Then, he'd told others her mother had slept with a demon and that Raven was nothing more than spawn. Fire was the test that would prove it. If she burned, she was innocent.

The injustice of her situation quivered through her slight frame. She wasn't a whore, and she'd rather be tried as a spawn than become one for him. If Creed knew how her stepfather had touched her, he would kill him on her behalf. But her friend wasn't here to help her now. And unfortunately for her, her accuser was also the godseeker who represented the law in this town. No one would come to her aid.

Time crept by and the shadows deepened.

The front door of the jailhouse creaked open and she sat up with a start, her heart hammering in her chest. She blinked her eyes against the sudden stream of light from outdoors.

Justice appeared before her—Justice in the form of her stepfather, and not any sudden righting of wrongs. Hate unfurled in her stomach at the sight of him. She rose from the bed and stood at the bars of her cell. His gait was stiff as he walked into the room to set a lantern on the desk. She had jabbed the knife into his thigh and the fact that the wound pained him filled her with joy. Although, he had been lucky—that was not where she'd aimed.

"There's still time to change your mind," he said to her, speaking softly so as not to be overheard by anyone lurking outside the jailhouse door. "I can withdraw the charges. I can help you exorcise the demon in you."

Raven met his eyes. It was a talent of hers that she could sometimes read people's darkest thoughts, particularly when emotions ran high, and his mind was darker than most. She no longer had any reason to disguise her contempt for him. "You would love to see me humiliated, stripped naked, and flogged to within an inch of my life. Then you would take me, because you believe breaking me will give you a demon's strength."

His face flushed with anger. He had been a handsome man once. Still was, in fact, despite the silver threads lacing his brown hair and the deep creases around his eyes and mouth. He had a presence about him that commanded a high level of respect. But Raven saw the ugliness simmering beneath the surface. Her mother had died a broken woman because of him.

Hatred fed her strength. She gripped the cell bars so tight, when she released them, the imprints of her fingers would remain.

You could break free if you choose.

That inner demon voice terrified her far more than the man who faced her ever could.

Her stepfather's eyes followed hers to the bars that contained her. "That's it, little demon," he taunted, his words soft. "Show the world what you are. How far do you think you could run then? How safe from the godseekers' assassins would you be?"

That was what stopped her. She didn't want to be hunted—or worse, for Justice to be proven right in anyone's eyes. She had to find another way to escape.

When she did, she would kill him.

"There are some who suspect you for what *you* are," she spat back. "Are you so confident of what I am? If I do burn, more will begin to doubt you. They will watch you." Her glance flickered to the amulet he wore around his throat. "And eventually, when the goddesses fail to return, no matter how many spawn you torture and kill in their name, the people will turn from you."

Justice hooked the wooden jailor's chair with his foot and swung it around, favoring his injured leg, then sat with his arms folded across the chair's spindled back as if he had all the time in the world. He planted his chin on the crook of one elbow and studied her. She had never fully understood the way he watched her until a few short nights ago. Now, she read raw hunger in his expression and thoughts. Her dinner rebelled at the memory of his touch on her bare flesh.

"It seems people have already turned from you," he said.

He, too, spoke the truth. Raven hadn't believed that people she'd known her whole life would agree to his plan. She'd hoped they would see the wrongness of it long before now. Sundown, however, had already passed.

Despair settled in with the night. No one had come to her rescue. Creed, her best hope, was in training at the Temple of Immortal Right, and oblivious to her situation. She had only herself now.

But earning her freedom meant releasing a dark and dangerous presence inside her, one she had never before allowed to be free. There would be no turning back from it once she did.

The ugliness of her stepfather's thoughts decided it for her. She would not burn, and she would not live in fear. She would not be broken by him as he'd broken her mother. She would save herself.

She wore the same dress he'd deemed indecent two nights prior when the nightmare began. Tracing a finger along its prim neckline, she let her eyelids droop to examine him from beneath a dark fringe of thick, curling lashes. Her golden-toned skin gleamed in the lamplight as she pressed against the bars of the cell.

Justice swallowed, then with unsteady fingers, gripped the amulet he wore around his neck. Once, a long time ago, he had been a goddess's favorite. The amulet she'd given him protected him from the seduction of another immortal, and warned him when he was in the presence of a full-blooded demon.

But it did nothing to protect Raven from him.

"Whore," he spat at her.

With that single utterance, she knew she had lost. "Enjoy your final moments of glory," she said, dropping her hand to her side. "Women can't all be whores and spawn, and Faith won't remain silent forever. Not after tonight."

It was a wild guess on her part, based on what she'd read of his ugliest desires and the way the frail, timid Faith was so painfully wary of him, but his face reddened, then paled, warning that her words had struck home. Fear flamed in her chest—not for herself, but for the woman she had named. What had she done?

"Undertaker!" Justice shouted, half turning toward the door. It opened at once, and a tall, gaunt man stuck his head into the room. "It's time."

Her stepfather lifted a heavy black key from a hook on the wall behind the desk, then inserted it in the lock on the cell door. She held her breath, waiting for the right moment to strike. He drew his hand back without unlocking the cell door and regarded her thoughtfully before turning to the battered desk. He rooted around in a drawer, and hauled out a shining pair of handcuffs crafted from a silver metal that had been mined in the nearby mountains and hardened with a special alloy.

"Hold out your hands," he said.

"No." She didn't want to be bound.

"If you don't"—his tone was harsh and deliberate, his eyes hard—"I will burn the jail down around you."

She felt the truth in him. He would do it. Stunned into obedience, she held out her hands. He snapped the cuffs in place. Then, he opened the cell door.

Undertaker reached inside to capture her arm.

"Don't touch her!" Justice snapped, slapping the other man's hand aside. Undertaker turned to him, his bushy black eyebrows raised in silent surprise. "She's a spawn. If you touch her, she can claim you."

The lie came so easily to him.

And yet, it wasn't a whole lie. Raven couldn't claim a man, but she could cloud his thoughts long enough to defend herself. Justice had the knife wound in his leg to prove it.

"Ask him how he knows that," she said to Undertaker, her gaze never leaving her stepfather. "Ask him how he touched me, and for what purpose."

Justice slapped her face with the flat of his palm. Her head snapped back. Pain blossomed as the world darkened.

"You disrespect your mother's memory when you speak like this. Columbine was an innocent, lured by a demon—just as you tried to lure me. She raised you to be better than you were born to be."

Raven refused to shed the angry tears scalding the backs of her eyes. He hadn't married her mother out of love or respect for her innocence. She had been a beautiful woman, a master artisan and an asset for him to own, nothing more, and he had destroyed her.

Raven touched one shackled wrist to the corner of her mouth and wiped away a trickle of blood. It left a dark smear on her skin in the fading light. Undertaker had given her candy when she'd been a child, yet now he'd neither made a move to protect her from Justice's blow nor uttered one word of protest against it. Pity for him displaced any hurt in her heart. He was simple-minded and easily led. She read no malice toward her on his part.

Her chin went up, and she gazed steadily at both men. "There is no need for either of you to touch me. I will walk on my own." She displayed all the dignity she possessed as she crossed the small jailhouse and stepped into the cool embrace of the night.

Inside, she was shaking. She didn't want to die. But saving herself would come at a heavy price she had no wish to pay.

~ **Coming May 2018** ~

The Forgotten

A Wasteland Novel ~ Book 3

Previously published as The Demon Creed

Preview

CHAPTER ONE

Three against one were not good odds for the thin young boy with the dark hair and angry eyes. At first glance it seemed like any other adolescent dispute, with at least one bloody nose or black eye inevitable, so Creed paid it no mind and moved on.

He hadn't come to the very edge of what was once demon territory to intervene in children's squabbles. Rumors of their quiet disappearance from several villages in and around the Godseeker Mountains were what had led him here, to a town called Desert's End, when duty called him elsewhere.

He was hunting a demon spawn named Willow on behalf of the godseekers. While the rest of the mortal world rejoiced over the banishment of demons after more than three hundred years of occupation, Willow had somehow raised one and used it to slay an entire village of innocents. Creed intended to see her brought to justice. Not only was it his duty as a godseeker assassin—trained to enforce the goddesses' will by use of any means necessary—but Willow's actions had nearly killed his half-sister, Raven.

Demons hated spawn. The thought of them working together was troubling, and a possibility that Creed dared not ignore. He'd been informed that Willow was fleeing godseeker territory, and appeared to be headed for the Borderlands, where the world ended. Creed couldn't risk losing her trail. If his curiosity about the missing children wasn't satisfied soon, he'd have to move on.

Children, however, deserved justice too. That meant facing, as well as receiving, it. If they were being abandoned rather than sold, as the stories intimated, then a man had to wonder if there was something unusual about them.

Frightening, even.

He was pushing his way through the throng of people swarming the boardwalk, seeking the local jail and its sheriff, when it struck him that the altercation in the alley he'd just witnessed was not all it seemed. He had passed over it too quickly, as if his attention had been turned from it.

Which meant at least one of the boys had the ability to sway people's actions and thoughts—a talent for demon compulsion that was similar to Creed's own.

He retraced his steps.

A narrow dirt alley separated the stable from the postal station and hotel next door. Inside that alley, out of the sun and away from prying adult eyes, two boys, approximately fourteen years of age, lay gasping for breath on the ground. One held his stomach. The other, his ribs. Neither appeared inclined, or able, to move.

A third boy, heavier set and taller than his companions, possibly a year older, dabbed at the blood trickling from his nose with the blunt of his wrist. He faced the smallest and youngest boy—the one with the angry eyes Creed had first noticed.

So far the combatants hadn't noted his presence, and Creed pressed himself against a wall to watch and listen. He saw nothing wrong with a boy defending himself against bullies. It was how he chose to do so that could lead to problems.

"I warned you. I can take care of myself," the skinny boy said. He might have been thirteen, at the most. He doubled his hands into fists and held them clenched at his sides, ready to use.

The cruelty in the older boy's expression indicated to Creed that he was unlikely to concede defeat to a punier victim. "And I told you that you aren't wanted here, you little freak."

One of the younger boy's fists lashed out in response to the insult. The bully's head rocked backward. The flesh over one cheekbone splotched a deepening red that would purple by morning. Instead of backing off, as he should, he dropped his chin and charged at the younger boy like an incensed bull kyson.

As the younger boy skipped to one side to avoid him, the subtle yet familiar tug of demon compulsion touched the edge of Creed's thoughts. The older boy didn't veer from his original course but plowed on, ramming headfirst into the side of the hotel. He staggered a few steps, reeling. His eyes rolled back to expose the whites. With a soft, almost surprised-sounding sigh hissing from his throat, his knees buckled, and he dropped to the ground, unconscious.

The other two boys, seeing their friend fall, rediscovered their ability to move. They scurried, scorpion-like, from the alley on their hands and knees, ignorant of Creed's presence even as they brushed past him. Out on the street, they got to their feet and ran as if the Demon Lord himself were chasing them.

In the alley, the dark-haired, angry-eyed boy kicked the bully he'd felled, now semi-conscious and drooling in the dirt. The blow was halfhearted and had no real malice behind it.

"Stupid," the boy muttered, his voice low, as if speaking to himself.

"Him or you?"

The boy looked up at Creed, his expressive eyes widening with caution at the discovery he wasn't alone. He glanced behind him in search of an escape route. The alley ended in a huge manure pile at the back of the stable. It would be too soft from the rain and the heat for anyone to safely climb, and there were few worse deaths imaginable than suffocating in dung.

The boy bolted for the street.

Creed peeled himself away from the wall of the hotel. He easily caught the collar of the boy's homespun shirt as he tried to dart past, swinging him off his feet and holding him up so that their noses were inches apart.

"What's the matter, boy?" he asked, keeping his tone conversational, testing him to see how he'd react to discovery. "You think you're the only one in the world who can make others see and do what you want? Or that you're the strongest and fastest spawn who ever lived?"

The boy didn't deny the accusation, but instead struggled in earnest. He kicked a boot at Creed's knee, but Creed, now that he knew for certain what he was dealing with, was prepared for a fight and easily evaded it. He could as easily have compelled the boy into submission, but that wasn't how he wanted to deal with this situation.

He continued to dangle the boy at eye level. "What were you thinking, using your talents like that?" he asked. "No one will believe you bested three boys in a fight—and all of them bigger than you. Questions will be asked."

The boy's face turned sullen. Rebellion displaced the anger in his gray eyes. "I don't care what anyone believes or what they ask. I don't have to hide what I am from mortals anymore. I don't answer to them."

Creed wasn't unsympathetic, but the problem was far greater than this boy and his talent for compulsion. The world had once believed that any offspring produced through demon matings with mortal women were male, and born in a manhunting form. These monsters, whenever discovered, had been killed at birth.

Although still less than a year since demons had been banished from the earth, in that brief time it had become increasingly apparent to the godseekers Creed served that the number of half demons left behind had been underestimated. They weren't all male, and they weren't all born in a monster form. Many had managed to hide what they were, either out of a natural instinct for self-preservation, or because of mothers who protected them despite knowing what they were.

Even more troubling, any powers inherited by demon offspring seemed to be strengthening and developing, and the mortal world was ill prepared to deal with such spawn. Hatred for them ran deep and was almost universal. Already, mortals were taking steps to eradicate them, and the boy would be foolish not to understand the danger he faced. No demon talents he'd inherited would save him in the end.

Creed set the boy on his feet but kept a grip on his arm. "Even so," he said, "the memory of demon rule remains too fresh. There's widespread fear that they might someday return. If you can avoid such confrontations with mortals, why not do so? What if your actions today draw the attention of someone who's more dangerous to you than those three bullies could ever be?"

The boy's lip curled. "I'm not afraid of anyone."

His arrogance didn't surprise Creed, who possessed a fair amount of his own. Half demons, like their full demon fathers, didn't know fear in the same way mortals did. They instinctively suppressed and controlled it, and used it to their advantage. Sometimes that confidence made them stupid and overbold, as this boy's actions proved today.

But half demons weren't always evil and dangerous. Creed and his sister were proof enough of that. Or so he liked to believe.

He wavered, torn between doing his duty and what he believed to be right. He wasn't without sympathy for a child who would have experienced a lifetime of injustices, and he sensed there was little harm in this one—at least not yet. The lessons he'd learn over the next few years would prove crucial in shaping the type of man he became. The boy needed guidance, not persecution.

It made this decision a difficult one.

"You don't need to be afraid," Creed said. "You should, however, exercise more common sense. Do you know who I am?"

"Why should I care?"

His belligerence was a strike against him.

"Because I'm a godseeker assassin, tasked to hunt spawn and bring them to justice. Dead or alive," Creed added, after a significant pause. "What if I were to turn you in?"

The boy flipped a hank of dark hair from his eyes with a toss of his head. "I know what else you are, Assassin. I could turn you in, too."

The threat amused Creed. "Of the two of us, who do you think people would believe? A skinny child who somehow bested three larger and older boys in a mismatched fight, or a trained assassin who serves the godseekers?"

The boy scraped a toe in the dirt. "I can make anyone believe what I want."

"And you want me to believe you did your best to walk away from that fight," Creed said. "But I don't. So now what?"

Guilt flared in the boy's eyes. "They started it."

"I have no doubt. But you could have convinced them to leave you alone instead, if you'd wanted."

A hross kicked a heavy hoof against the wall of the stable next door to the alley. Out on the street, traffic rumbled past.

Again, Creed hesitated. While it was his duty to ensure that any spawn he discovered were brought before the godseekers for judgment, he had no desire to condemn a child. Not without first determining if there might be enough support in his life to bring out the potential Creed sensed in him. True spawn had only demon instincts. They lacked morality. Half demons, on the other hand, tended to be far more complex. More mortal.

At least they could choose to be.

"Where is your mother?" Creed asked. The boy said nothing, his lips pressed in a thin line of rebellion, and Creed lost patience. "I can return you to her, or I can give you to the sheriff to be passed on to the godseekers, who will then determine your fate. Which is your preference?"

"She's selling corn cakes at a stall near the goddess temple." The words dragged unwillingly from the boy's mouth.

Creed tightened his grip. The mother's reaction to having her son presented to her by a godseeker assassin would decide the matter for him. "Come on."

Larger than any other structure in Desert's End, built on higher ground and constructed entirely of colorful stones, the temple wasn't meant to be inconspicuous. It was easy enough for Creed to find. He drew his young prisoner through the crowds.

The land around the town was a farming region, and the noisy market square stank of old kyson droppings and sodden scafhoof wool. While recent spring rains hadn't done the streets any favors with regard to their stench, the wooden buildings surrounding the square had been cleansed and left gleaming in the noonday sun as if freshly painted.

The town had other features to redeem it in Creed's eyes, as well. Sinkholes were rare this close to the mountains, and Desert's End had been built with confidence on the eviscerated ruins of an Old World city. Ancient and hardy gardens remained determined to flourish despite the various indignities the years had wrought. Rose bushes, from a time before demons had razed the earth with fire, bloomed pink and red in unexpected places—to either side of a creosote-blackened boardwalk and from beneath one cornerstone of the town hall.

In front of the temple, a number of tarpaulin-capped wooden stalls had been erected with a variety of goods displayed on long counters.

An older woman with delicate features, golden brown hair and vivid green eyes, and wearing an expression of trepidation mixed with concern, watched their progress toward her, her attention divided between them and a customer. Creed stopped beside her stall, keeping a solid hand on the boy's shoulder, and waited for her to finish with the transaction.

As he did, he quietly observed her. Soft-spoken and displaying a gentle weariness, she reminded him more than a little of his half-sister's mother.

Raven had always considered her mortal mother weak, but Creed, several years older than Raven and more aware of the harshness of the world, had adored Columbine. She'd always been kind to him, even though he wasn't her child.

Columbine was long dead now. He'd not been able to save her from an abusive husband. Raven, however, was safe in the mountains with her lover Blade, a former assassin who didn't need or want Creed's help in protecting her.

That left him without any responsibilities other than to the leaders of the Temple of Immortal Right—and therefore, to the godseekers. Their mandate in this post-demon world was to establish a universal law across the entire land.

Blade hadn't shared the godseekers' faith in their mandate, or their laws. He'd quietly suggested to Creed that if it became necessary to go as far as the Borderlands in his hunt for spawn, then Creed should seek out the Demon Slayer and give him Blade's regards. He'd said the Slayer would understand what that meant.

Creed hoped it wouldn't come to that, because he understood too. The Demon Slayer and his wife, a half demon named Airie, were reputed to be responsible for the banishment of demons from the world. To call on the Slayer meant the godseekers were far out of their depth.

An overladen cart filled with sacks of grain cut through the market, its contents spilling over its sides, its wooden wheels sprawled wide. An enormous black work hross, head bent and back swayed with age, strained at its traces. Feathered fetlocks were caked in fine red dust that puffed in small, dirty clouds with each step the animal took. The cart's load brushed against several stalls, threatening to knock them over, and the vendors shouted their displeasure at the fat driver.

As Creed continued to wait to speak with the boy's mother, he noted there were no signs of a husband or master about. He wondered why not. Women weren't free, and despite her maturity, she retained far too much of the physical perfection that had once captured the interest of a full-blooded demon for her to go unnoticed in a market such as this. Her young son couldn't possibly provide sufficient protection for her here.

Unless, of course, the boy had a demon gift for compulsion, and directed attention away from her.

The woman finished with the customer and turned to her son, as if by ignoring Creed's presence she would somehow avert an unpleasant confrontation. While she pretended not to notice him, Creed was well aware of her sidelong scrutiny. And what she saw.

Most women found the vibrant contrast between his golden skin and unusual, crystalline blue eyes attractive. In the past, he'd shaved his head because his black hair, which had a tendency to curl, had made his physical resemblance to Raven too obvious, and he hadn't wanted others to suspect they shared a father. If they had, they might also have begun to wonder who—or what—that father had been.

After the departure of the demons, however, Creed's scalp had gone naturally smooth. The flaming tattoo that now covered his back and shoulders had also emerged, although he had no idea what its purpose was, or if it held any demonic significance. He had no one to ask.

The woman ran a palm down the front of the tidy apron that covered her simple dress, smoothing imaginary wrinkles from the heavy fabric, an action that betrayed her nervousness at his presence. Women usually loved Creed, and while under other circumstances he wasn't above using that attraction to his advantage, normally he wouldn't be passing judgment on one of their children. Most mothers placed their child's welfare above everything else.

But not all of them did. His own hadn't. And this mother's child was also half demon.

"Where have you been?" she asked the boy. "I expected you here to help me an hour ago." Her tone held reproof and anxiety, as well as an undercurrent of unmistakable affection. Soft green eyes darted from the masculine hand on her son's shoulder to Creed's face. "He's a better salesman than me," she added, with pleading in her eyes as if she already knew without being told what was at stake. "I need him."

The boy's gift for compulsion would indeed benefit her sales and keep them both from starvation. Creed's gut tightened. There was no husband or master. Not that he could discern. Without the boy, this woman's fate would be uncertain and undoubtedly hopeless. Condemning her son would mean a death sentence for them both.

Since Creed sensed nothing but truth in either of them, he saw no pressing reason to remove the boy from his mother. The only fear in her was for her son—and of Creed.

He released his prisoner. "I don't doubt your son is good at sales," he said. "You might want to impress upon him the advantages of walking away from a fight rather than diving in without careful consideration for the consequences. No one willingly draws the attention of the godseekers."

"Thank you," the woman whispered, her green eyes filling with tears of gratitude and relief.

Creed walked away without further comment, confident the implicit warning he had delivered was enough. He threaded his way through a crowd that paid him little attention even though he dwarfed most other men. One of an assassin's greatest attributes was an ability to move about unnoticed, and Creed, thanks to his demon father, was better at it than most.

He finally located the jail on a narrow street backing the temple. It was flanked by green-fingered desert palms and a faded mercantile. He climbed three stone steps and entered the low building. Inside, the high, narrow windows positioned beneath the ceiling beams offered interior lighting while protecting the room from the worst of the dry desert heat.

A tall man, seated in a straight-backed chair, bent forward over a heavy oak desk. He coughed into a crumpled handkerchief, his bony shoulders shaking. His face was as gray as the walls. The rattling cough, combined with the unhealthy pallor to his flesh, suggested the odds were good that he was dying.

Creed waited in silence until the coughing fit subsided.

"I'm looking for the sheriff," he said once it did.

The man mopped at his mouth with the handkerchief. Although reflecting ill health, his gaze was intelligent and thoughtful, as if he hadn't yet given up on living. He tapped the badge on his chest, then extended a hand. "You found him. The name's Fledge."

Creed took the offered hand and introduced himself. "I represent the Temple of Immortal Right and the godseekers. I was told you might have information regarding several children who have gone missing in recent months."

Sheriff Fledge tipped back in his chair. "Why would an assassin be interested in a few missing children?"

"It's not the children who interest me as much as the circumstances in which they're rumored to have disappeared."

Fledge hooked a chair near the desk with the toe of his boot and flipped it around, then gestured for Creed to take a seat. Creed dragged the chair to the far corner of the desk so that his back faced a wall, not the door. A slight grin crossed the sheriff's thin face as he noted the action, but he didn't comment.

"I don't have much hard information," Fledge said. "Besides, there are all kinds of rumors flying these days."

"Such as?"

The good-natured smile faded. "The kind that says those children are spawn. That there's a whore hiding in the Godseeker Mountains who's one of them, too. That maybe the Demon Slayer is to blame for them by taking up with a demon when he should have been protecting people from her kind instead. He's abandoned us, leaving his work half done."

The sheriff had strong opinions. Creed could ignore his use of the term *whore*. It wasn't meant with any disrespect, only as a distinction. Women, owned by men and used as they pleased, were one of three things—wives, daughters, or whores.

But Creed disliked the term *spawn*, especially when used by a mortal. It was a slur against all half demons—and an intentional one. He especially didn't like hearing it associated with Raven, who was the whore on the mountain Fledge mentioned. She and Blade had begun a new settlement in one of the many abandoned mining towns, where they welcomed any half demons who wished to live in peace.

Once he stripped off the prejudice, he sifted through everything Fledge had said to find what was important. The sheriff had heard rumors that those missing children were spawn. The last time Creed had seen Willow, she'd had a misshapen and feral demon child in her company. The memory of that pitiful creature, and how she had used it, haunted him. The thought of her in possession of the missing children made his blood run cold.

"It doesn't sound to me as if the woman in the mountains, or the Demon Slayer, could be held responsible for children who've gone missing in the area around Desert's End."

The sheriff's gray face reflected his agreement before another coughing spasm overtook him. By the time he recovered, his whole body was trembling.

"If you're wanting someone to hold responsible for their disappearance, maybe you should disregard all the rumors and consider slave traders instead. The man to discuss that with lives about three miles out of town on a kyson ranch." The sheriff paused again to catch his breath. The rattling sound in his chest filled the silence of the empty jail. "He sold his whore's son to them about a year ago, and he would have driven a hard bargain. Maybe this season the slavers decided to bypass him and save money."

That was a reasonable assumption, and one worth checking.

Creed got directions to the ranch. As he rose to go, the sheriff stopped him.

"If it turns out slavers aren't responsible, have you asked yourself what else might have happened to them?" The sheriff leaned forward, steadying himself against his desk. "What if they were abandoned, and for good reason?"

So the sheriff, too, thought the children were spawn.

Creed understood people's fear. But half demons weren't entirely to blame for the changes taking place. No longer under the rule of the immortals—goddess or demon—the world had no true law anymore. As far as Creed was concerned, people could choose to make a better place of it or a worse one. What was guaranteed was that it wouldn't be the same. And if mortals and half demons were to coexist, a new path to the future needed to be blazed.

Creed believed he had an obligation to help make that happen. He had a sworn duty to the godseekers, but also an inherent responsibility to others like himself. No matter what the world wished to think, he and his kind were mortals too.

"Whether it was slavers who took them or they were abandoned," Creed said, "what I do know is that those missing children deserve justice, the same as anybody else."

* * *

Visit Paula at www.paulaaltenburg.com[1] where you can check up on her latest releases, follow her on social media, and sign up for her newsletter.

---

1. http://www.paulaaltenburg.com